PRAISE FOR

A SPELL of GOOD THINGS

Booker Prize Nominee • GMA Buzz Pick •
A *New York Times* Editors' Choice

"Adébáyọ̀ established her storytelling prowess in her 2017 debut, *Stay with Me*. . . . In this compelling follow-up, Adébáyọ̀'s hand is just as deft, but her canvas is more expansive. . . . The graceful, stately quality of the sentences evokes restraint. . . . Timely. . . . Adébáyọ̀ humanizes those sucked into the vortex of [power] with a striking compassion."
—*The New York Times Book Review*

"An insightful portrait of an unequal and deeply divided society moving towards a terrible crisis." —Pat Barker, award-winning author of *The Silence of the Girls* and *The Women of Troy*

"As with her lauded debut *Stay with Me*, in Ayọ̀bámi Adébáyọ̀'s second novel domestic strife and the political tensions of modern Nigeria bristle against each other. . . . The compassion Adébáyọ̀ feels for her two protagonists is deep and her social consciousness commendable."
—*The Guardian*

"Adébáyọ̀ is a gifted storyteller, and like her debut novel, *Stay with Me*, her second book does not disappoint. . . . The violence of elections and the empty promises of politicians, the obscene wealth of the connected, the hunger and desperation of the have-nots all intersect in this examination of a community in Nigeria." —Oprah Daily

"Ayọ̀bámi Adébáyọ̀ is a natural storyteller, a spellbinder. Her expansive second novel is Dickensian in scope and execution. It sparkles."
—Helon Habila, author of *Travelers*

"Heartrending. . . . A breeze to read, despite the weightiness of its subject matter. . . . Adébáyọ̀ handles her characters with empathy and nuance, showing their vulnerabilities, yearnings, shame and delusions."

—*Financial Times*

"Adébáyọ̀'s mesmerizing prose is suffused with heart and sharp emotions. Every page of this book was a pleasure to read. Even the hard parts. *A Spell of Good Things* is a triumph of storytelling."

—Chika Unigwe, author of *On Black Sisters Street*

"Ẹniọlá and Wúràọlá come from different classes in Nigeria, and in this dynamic sophomore novel from Adébáyọ̀, we see how socioeconomic stratification, exacerbated by gender inequality, can destroy lives at all levels. Never mind that these layers are all interdependent and innately connected—a paradox that leads here to a shocking, violent act from which there is no turning back."

—*Los Angeles Times*

"All characters matter in Ayọ̀bámi Adébáyọ̀'s intricate, haunting, and timely fictional exploration of classism and sexism set in Nigeria's election season."

—Sefi Atta, author of *Everything Good Will Come*

"Compelling. . . . This immensely readable novel is a blistering indictment of the abuse of power (political and domestic) and the ubiquitous violence that can destroy lives overnight."

—*The Observer* (London)

Ayọbámi Adébáyọ

A SPELL *of* GOOD THINGS

Ayọbámi Adébáyọ was born in Lagos, Nigeria. Her debut
novel, *Stay with Me,* won the 9mobile Prize for Literature and
was shortlisted for the Baileys Prize for Women's Fiction, the
Wellcome Book Prize and the Kwani? Manuscript Prize. It
has been translated into twenty languages, and the French
translation was awarded the Prix Les Afriques. Longlisted for
the International Dylan Thomas Prize and the International
Dublin Literary Award, *Stay with Me* was a *New York Times,*
Guardian, Chicago Tribune, and NPR Best Book of the Year.

ayobamiadebayo.com

ALSO BY AYỌ̀BÁMI ADÉBÁYỌ̀

Stay with Me

A SPELL of
GOOD THINGS

A SPELL of GOOD THINGS

Ayòbámi Adébáyò

VINTAGE BOOKS
A Division of Penguin Random House LLC
New York

FIRST VINTAGE BOOKS EDITION 2024

The Library of Congress has cataloged the Knopf edition as follows:
Name: Adébáyọ̀, Ayọ̀bámi, [date] author.
Title: A spell of good things : a novel / Ayọ̀bámi Adébáyọ̀.
Description: First edition. | New York : Alfred A. Knopf, 2023.
Identifiers: LCCN 2022011733 (print) | LCCN 2022011734 (ebook)
Subjects: LCGFT: Novels.
Classification: LCC PR9387.9.A319 S64 2023 (print) | LCC PR 9387.9.A319 (ebook) |
DDC 823/.92—dc23
LC record available at https://lccn.loc.gov/2022011733
LC ebook record available at https://lccn.loc.gov/2022011734

Vintage Books Trade Paperback ISBN: 978-1-9848-9888-3
eBook ISBN: 978-0-525-65765-1

Book design by Cassandra J. Pappas

vintagebooks.com

Printed in the United States of America
1st Printing

For JọláaJésù. Darling sister,
thank you for the great gift of friendship.

Kinsman

When an elephant walks over a hard-rock outcrop,
We do not see his footprints.
When a buffalo walks over a hard-rock outcrop,
We do not see his footprints.
       —*Kinsman and Foreman* by T. M. Aluko

Caro was angry. After one of her apprentices read the notice of meeting out loud to her, she threw it across the room into a dustbin. Some politician's wife wanted to give a talk to the tailoring association, and their president had agreed to welcome the woman during their next meeting. And, of course, the president thought it meant something to mention that this politician's wife was the daughter of a tailor. Caro was almost sure this was a lie. Those people would claim to be your kinsmen if it would help them get into power. It irritated her that they would waste time listening to this woman campaigning for her husband. This was not why she paid her tailoring association dues.

Caro went to the dustbin in the corner of her tailoring shop. She retrieved the notice, tore it into tiny bits, and walked to her front yard to release the fragments in the air. She would let the association know what she thought at the next meeting. Not that anyone would listen or care. They all knew their president took money from politicians to host them at those gatherings. Closer to the elections, members of the association would get their own share of the sudden generosity of several contestants. Wives or sisters of contestants would come to meetings with bowls of rice, kegs of oil, yards and yards of ankara embossed with the contestants' faces and logos. The men themselves—and the contestants were mostly men—never came in person to answer any questions about what they intended to do in office.

Some of the other tailors accused Caro of arrogance, because she always refused to take the rice and oil or to sew a dress from the useless ankara fabrics. But she did not feel superior to any of them; most if not all had children to feed with the foodstuff. Besides, they knew this was all they could be sure of getting out of the politicians for another four years. So why not gorge on the rice and the oil they brought if that was the only so-called dividend of democracy within reach? Caro understood the reasoning of her peers, but that did not make the whole thing less enraging. How many times had the representatives of those politicians promised that electricity would be fixed if only their candidate got into office? Wasn't everyone in the tailoring association still dependent on generators? Was it not just two weeks ago that one of them had died in her sleep after inhaling generator fumes? The third tailor to die that way in as many years. At the latest news, Caro could not cry. Instead, even though the dead woman was someone whose face she could barely remember, her head had pulsed with rage for days.

Elections were coming up in a year or so. In the next few months, campaign posters would begin to appear, littering every fence and wall in sight with the faces of men whose smiles already showed they should not be trusted. Last time, her wall had been covered from top to bottom with some senator's campaign posters because her front yard faced the street. She must remember to ask someone to paint POST NO BILLS on the wall soon. She'd ask one of her apprentices. Probably Ẹniọlá.

PART I

Everything Good Will Come

Muffled rage stalks like the wind, sudden and invisible. People don't fear the wind until it fells a tree. Then, they say it's too much.

—*Everything Good Will Come* by Sefi Atta

Eniọlá decided to pretend it was just water. A single melting hailstone. Mist or dew. It could also be some good thing: a solitary raindrop fallen from the sky, lone precursor to a deluge. The first rains of the year would mean he could finally eat an àgbálùmọ̀. The fruit seller whose stall was next to his school had had a basket of àgbálùmọ̀ for sale yesterday, but Eniọlá had not bought any from her, and he'd convinced himself this was because his mother often said they caused cramps if eaten before the first rainfall. But if this liquid was rain, then in a few days he could lick an àgbálùmọ̀'s sweet and sticky juice from his fingers, chew the fibrous flesh into gum, crack open the seeds and gift his sister seedlings that she'd halve into stick-on earrings. He tried to pretend it was just rain, but it did not feel like water.

He could sense, though his eyes were downcast, that the dozen or so men who clustered around the newspaper vendor's table were staring at him. They were all quiet, stone-still. Like disobedient children transformed into rocks by an evil wizard in one of those stories his father used to tell.

When he was a child, Eniọlá would shut his eyes whenever he got into trouble, certain that he was not visible to anyone he could not see. Although he knew closing his eyes now and hoping he would vanish was as stupid as believing that people could become stones, he squeezed them shut anyway. And, of course, he did not vanish. He was not that lucky. The newspaper vendor's rickety table was still right in front of him, close enough for his thighs to brush the newspapers that covered its surface. The vendor, whom Eniọlá called Ẹ̀gbọ́n Abbey, was still standing next to him, and the hand he'd pressed into Eniọlá's shoulder just before he cleared his throat and spat in his face was still in place.

Ẹniọlá traced a finger up his nose, inching towards the wet weight of phlegm. Stunned into silence that something so unexpected had rippled through their routine, all the men, even Ẹ̀gbọ́n Abbey, seemed to be holding their breath, waiting for more. Not even one person was taunting Chelsea fans about the way Tottenham crushed their team last night. Nobody was arguing about that open letter the journalist-politician had written about other politicians who bathed in human blood to protect themselves from evil spirits. The men had all gone quiet when the vendor's phlegm struck Ẹniọlá's face. And now these men who gathered here every morning to argue about the headlines were watching to see what Ẹniọlá would do. They wanted him to hit the vendor, yell insults, cry or, better yet, clear his own throat, pool phlegm in his mouth and spit in Ẹ̀gbọ́n Abbey's face. Ẹniọlá's finger travelled all the way to his forehead; he had been too slow. The phlegm had already dribbled down the side of his nose, leaving a damp and sticky trail across his cheek. Flicking the glob away was out of the question now.

Something pushed against his cheek. He flinched, lurching forward into the newspaper stand. Around him, a few people muttered *sorry* as he gripped the table's edge to stop himself from falling. One of the men had been pushing a blue handkerchief against his face.

"Hin ṣé sir," Ẹniọlá said as he took the handkerchief; he *was* grateful, even though the hanky was already streaked with white lines that flaked when he pressed it against his cheek.

Ẹniọlá scanned the small crowd, straightening once he realised there was no one there from his school. The men clustered around the vendor's table were all adults. Some, already dressed for work, pulled at tightly knotted ties and adjusted ill-fitting jackets. Many wore faded sweaters or bomber jackets zipped chin high. Most of the younger ones, whose names he had to prefix with "Brother" or get a knock on the head, were recent graduates from polytechnics or universities. They would loiter around Ẹ̀gbọ́n Abbey's stand all morning, reading and arguing, copying job adverts from the newspapers into notepads or scraps of paper. Now and then they might help the vendor with change, but none of them would buy a newspaper.

Ẹniọlá tried to return the handkerchief, but the man waved him off and began browsing through a copy of *Aláròyé*. At least there was no one here who could tell his schoolmates how the vendor had glared at him for almost a full minute before spitting in his face. The action so sudden he'd moved his head to the side only after he felt wetness begin to spread across his nose, so unexpected it had silenced men whose voices could usually be heard in every house on the street. At least Paul and Hakeem, his classmates who also lived on that street, weren't there to witness that moment. After seeing an old video of Klint da Drunk performing on *Night of a Thousand Laughs,* Paul had decided he wanted to be just like Klint. Since then, whenever a teacher skipped a period, Paul staggered around, bumping into desks and chairs, slurring insults at his classmates.

Ẹniọlá placed a palm against his cheek to press in any wetness and leave his skin unmarked. If there was any trace of saliva on his face when he passed by Paul's house on his way back home, the other boy's hour or so in front of the class this afternoon would be all about him. Paul might say the wetness was there because Ẹniọlá drooled in his sleep, had not taken a bath before putting on his school uniform, came from a family that could not even afford soap. There would be laughter. He laughed too when Paul tortured other people. Most of the jokes were not even funny, but, hoping this would keep Paul's focus on whatever unfortunate boy or girl he'd chosen that afternoon, Ẹniọlá laughed at everything Paul said. When Paul shifted his attention from one person, it would usually turn on a girl who hadn't been laughing at his jokes. Usually. There had been that terrible afternoon when Paul had stopped talking about some other classmate's tattered shoe to say Ẹniọlá's forehead was shaped like the thick end of a mango. Ẹniọlá had been laughing at the girl with tattered shoes and found that as the class erupted into a fresh round of laughter he would hear in his sleep for months after, he could not shut his mouth. He wanted to stop laughing but couldn't. Not when his throat began to hurt with tears or when his classmates became quiet because the chemistry teacher had stumbled in a few minutes before her period was over. He'd gone on laughing until she told him to kneel in one corner of the class with his face to the wall.

Without a mirror, there was no way to tell . . . no. No. He wouldn't ask any of the men around him to confirm if his face still had any streaks. He wouldn't. As his hand slipped away from his cheek, Ẹniọlá squinted at the three-storey building where Paul's family lived on the second floor.

They shared its four rooms with two other families and an old woman who had no known relatives. The woman was standing in front of the house now, scattering grain on the sand while chickens squawked at her feet. No Paul. Maybe he had left for school already. But then, he could also be on the staircase or in the corridor, ready to step out just as Ẹniọlá passed by the house.

Ẹniọlá cupped his forehead, pressing his palm against the point where it jutted forward to hang over the bridge of his nose as though to push it back, all the way back into his skull. Maybe he should just run past that house. This was all his father's fault. Everything. The things Paul might say, the men who eyed his now-clenched fists as though expecting him to punch the newspaper vendor, the vendor's rage. Especially the vendor's rage. It was his father who owed this man thousands of naira, his father who for months had collected Thursday's *The Daily* on credit so he could read all the job placements in the newspaper, his father who had insisted this morning that Ẹniọlá should be the one to go beg the vendor for a copy of the day's paper on credit. That stinking mix of spit and phlegm should be clinging to his father's skin.

He felt a hand on his shoulder and recognised the grip before he turned towards the vendor. The man was close enough for Ẹniọlá to smell his breath. Although, that could still be his own face. While the handkerchief had gotten most of the wetness, the smell stayed on. Ẹgbọ́n Abbey coughed, and Ẹniọlá braced himself. What more could the vendor do? Punch him in the face so that when he got home there would be some unmistakable mark, a bruise or disjointed nose that would announce what had happened here to Ẹniọlá's father?

"You wanted *The Daily,* àbí? Óyá, take." The vendor slapped Ẹniọlá's arm with a rolled-up newspaper. "But if I see you or your father here again, ehn? Tell him. That your father—better tell him—if I see either of you here again, the wonders I will work on your face with my fist? Anyone who sees you will think a trailer ran over you. I'm warning you now, don't choose to be unfortunate."

Ẹniọlá wished he could force the vendor's mouth open and stuff the newspaper down his throat. He wanted to fling the newspaper on the ground and stamp it into the red earth until every page was shredded; he wanted at least to turn his back on Ẹgbọ́n Abbey without taking it from him. This was the kind of nonsense he got from older people all the time, even his parents. He knew there would be no apologies for the vendor's explosive rage; the man would rather drink out of the gutter than admit spitting in his face was wrong. This newspaper was supposed to double as an apology. He imagined an older person, his mother or father, apologising to him for any reason at all and he almost laughed.

"Have you turned into a statue?" the vendor asked, poking Ẹniọlá's chest with *The Daily*.

Someday soon, though, his father would have money again and Ẹniọlá would be sent to buy a newspaper. On that day he would walk all the way to Wesley Guild and buy one from the vendor whose stand was in front of the hospital. On his way back he would pass by this vendor's stand, flipping through the newspaper so that this wicked man could see. But before all that could happen, his father had to find the right job vacancy. And so Ẹniọlá took the newspaper, mumbled something that could be mistaken for a thank-you and began to run. Away from the vendor and his smelling mouth, past Paul's house where the old woman was struggling with a chick as she tied a piece of red fabric to one of its feathers. Faster and faster, downhill towards home.

❀

His father seemed to hold each leaf of *The Daily* with his fingertips as he turned its pages. Or just his nails—Ẹniọlá couldn't tell for sure from where he stood by the door. All this care after he had washed his hands twice and refused to dry them with any fabric, declining even the lace blouse Ẹniọlá's mother had fished out of the special box that held her collection of lace and aṣọ-òkè. Instead, he'd paced the room in every possible direction—wall to bed, bed to mattress on the floor, mattress on the floor to the cupboard that held pots, plates and cups—holding his arms aloft until all the moisture had evaporated from his skin. He'd even tapped each finger against his eyelids before asking Ẹniọlá to hand over *The Daily*. Once they had up to ten copies, the newspapers could be traded for money or food from the women who sold groundnuts, fried yam or boli on this street or the next. He preferred food, especially when it was from that boli seller whose plantains were roasted exactly how he liked them, crunchy on the outside and moist on the inside. But his parents always wanted to exchange the newspapers for money, and the cleaner they were, the more those women were willing to pay for them.

His father was not old enough to have grey hair. Or so his mother said, the first time she plucked hair from Bàami's head, claiming that once she pulled them all from the roots, they would grow back even blacker than before. And yet, last year, every strand on Bàami's head turned grey within a month. The grey had raced from Bàami's temple, claiming every inch of his scalp, so that within weeks Ẹniọlá had to look at one of his father's old photos to remember what he had looked like when his hair was black.

In the creased and flaking photo, Bàami is beside a door, glaring at the camera as though daring the photographer to take a bad picture. His hair is black at the temple and elsewhere. A side parting on the left side reveals a slice of his gleaming scalp. On the door, fitting just within the frame before it is cut off at the edge, a black nameplate says "Vice Principal" in gold cursive letters. Below that, typed out on a rectangular sheet of paper that looked as though it had only just been stuck on that door and would soon be ripped off, is Bàami's name—Mr. Bùsúyì Òní. Bàami stands straight with his shoulder pushed so far back, Ẹniọlá wondered if he wasn't smiling because his shoulder blades had begun to hurt. Over the years since the photo was taken, Bàami had stopped staring directly at cameras or people. Only Ẹniọlá's mother still insisted that he look her in the eye while speaking to her. When he spoke to Ẹniọlá or his sister, Bàami stared at their feet, eyes flitting around as though counting their toes over and over again.

Bàami folded *The Daily* and cleared his throat. "The vegetable that is growing wild in the backyard, what if you sell it? I can help you to harvest . . ."

"No, no, no, there's no way that will sell, Bàbá Ẹniọlá. Face the newspaper, please. Have you checked it from beginning to end?" Ẹniọlá's mother said.

"Have you found something?" Ẹniọlá asked.

His father flipped the newspaper open without responding to either of them. Ẹniọlá wanted to go outside and wash his face, but he felt compelled to stay with his parents. Besides, bathing was done for the day and his mother had stored the soap in one of her countless hiding places. If he asked her for the soap now, she would want to know why he needed it. She would not relent until he explained why he'd asked for it, not even if he changed his mind and told her he didn't need the soap anyway. She would make him reveal what had happened, she always found a way. And he knew that the minute he finished his story, she would rush to the vendor's and spit in his face until her mouth was dry. He did not want that. Yes, he would love to watch the vendor try to dodge his mother's wrath, but that would also mean that more people might hear about how he had been humiliated that morning. He did not really need the soap. Maybe he should just rinse his face and scrub it with a sponge the way he did when they ran out of soap.

He would have gone to rinse his face in the backyard right away, but Bùsọ́lá was not in the room. She could be sweeping the courtyard, washing plates or scrubbing the pot their mother had used to make àmàlà last night. It was best to wait until she came back into the room, since he did not want to leave his father alone with the newspaper. When he could, he stayed with his father and made sure he was not left by himself. His mother was here, but then she was acting strange. She sat at the foot of the bed, folding and unfolding the blouse she had offered Bàami earlier.

"Nobody buys gbúre," she said. "They're all over the backyard now, but nobody buys them. Even dogs and goats have gbúre leaves in their backyard now."

Ẹniọlá leaned against a wall; it would not make a difference if gbúre grew on every inch of the backyard and every surface in this room, sprouting even from his scalp and his parents' foreheads. How much could his mother get for them anyway? Not enough to pay Bùsọ́lá's school fees or his. He knew this from hawking gbúre during the holidays. Though he'd walked all the way past the hospital, crisscrossing through the market beside the palace and past the palace itself, then all the way down until he stopped in front of the Christ Apostolic Church next to the Brewery, he'd still returned home with more than half of what had been piled onto his tray.

Ẹniọlá's father coughed. At first it seemed as though he was clearing his throat, but soon his shoulders quivered with spasms as he struggled to catch his breath. His mother flung her blouse onto the bed and filled a tumbler to the brim, leaving a trail of water in her wake as she went to stand with a hand on Bàami's shoulder. His father drank the water in one long gulp, but the cough persisted until he gripped his knees and sat on the bed.

"You, when are you going to school?" Ẹniọlá's mother asked, rubbing her husband's back as the coughing subsided.

"I . . . I'm waiting to know if Bàami finds anything in the papers."

"Carry your bag and go now, jàre," his mother said.

Bàami pointed a finger in Ẹniọlá's direction. "Don't worry, I already found something promising, it's very promising, Ẹniọlá. I will write the letter today."

"I can help you to post it," Ẹniọlá said.

"That won't be necessary—your mother will take it when she's leaving for the market."

"I thought she wasn't—"

"Why am I still seeing your shadow in this house?" His mother made a sweeping motion with one hand. "Tell your sister to stop whatever she's doing and start going to school. What's the point of looking for money to pay your fees if you're going to be latecomers?"

"Yes ma." Ẹniọlá picked up his schoolbag. "Please, I need some salt."

"Why is this child asking me for salt when he should be in school? Do you want to cook a pot of soup this morning, Ẹniọlá?"

"I—I haven't brushed my teeth yet."

His mother squinted at him as though just noticing that the space where his head should be had all the while been occupied by a large coconut. He held himself still, careful to look in her direction, knowing that if he glanced away, she would suspect he was lying. But he also made sure to look towards her without exactly meeting her eyes. Staring into her eyes would only be taken as evidence of his lack of respect for her, proof that he had grown wings and was now a wild bird prepared to fly into her face unless she stopped him with a well-placed slap. He did not realise he'd been holding his breath until she nodded towards the cupboard that held pots, plates and a small sack of salt.

Ẹniọlá measured a heaped spoonful into his left palm and balled his hand into a fist.

Bùsọlá had just finished washing a pot when Ẹniọlá entered the backyard. She let him have the large bowl of water she had not used so he did not have to fetch from the well that stood in one corner of the yard. Harmattan stung his arms from elbows to fingertips like a million pin-pricks, coating his ankles with a thin layer of dust and cracking his upper lip. He splashed the water onto his face and rubbed salt across his nose until his skin felt raw, ready to peel. He rinsed his face again and again until the bowl was empty. But still he felt that wet weight. He could smell stale onions and eggs gone bad and something else he could not place but would spend the rest of his morning trying to name.

2

Herniorrhaphy—mouth hanging open, his moustache shivering as he snored. Eighteen hours post-op now. No complications. Wúràọlá wrote her recommendation. He should be discharged in the morning. She angled the case note to catch light from the aisle; the bulbs above the patients' beds were always switched off long before midnight.

Appendectomy—septic and sedated. His daughter, frantic after an hour of asking why he was still in the bathroom, had broken the lock to find the septuagenarian almost passed out in the shower. She'd rushed him to A & E immediately despite his protests, which continued even while he was being wheeled into the theatre, that the pain wasn't beyond what he could handle, all he needed was some rest and his pot of herbs. Asked during that morning's post-op review to explain why he'd borne the pain of a perforated appendix for days without telling anyone, he'd crossed his arms and declared to his surgeon, *Bóo ni hin ṣe a mọ̀ wí akọ ni mèrè? Akọ rà i ṣojo.* And Professor Babájídé Coker, general surgeon and current chairman of IEMPU, the Ìjẹ̀sà Elite Men's Progressive Union, had nodded as though he understood what the old man said.

Professor Coker and Wúràọlá's father were good friends. Her family often hosted IEMPU meetings in their home, and she had been serving its members platters of peppered snail and fetching bottles of whiskey to refill their shot glasses since she was a teenager. Born in Lagos exactly five years before independence, Professor Coker let new IEMPU members know within minutes after the meetings began that he had gone straight from Christ Church on Broad Street to King's College when education was still education in this country. Most times, he managed to insert a story about meeting his wife, who was at Queen's College during an interschool debate, before concluding that his training had of course been crowned with his years at the premier university. Where else would such impeccable, foundational understanding of medicine have been possible? Where? If any other doctors were present, he would be cut off with a counterargument about the superiority of Great Ifẹ̀ or Medilag. The men's voices would then rise and overlap until Wúràọlá could not make out what any of them were saying. Her father, who had studied law at University of Lagos, never got involved while the clamour was on, not even when he was asked to speak up for his alma mater by Medilag graduates and other University of Lagos alumni. He would stay quiet until one of the maids whispered in his ear. At that point he usually tapped his fork against his glass until the room was quiet enough for him to announce, mostly for the benefit of new members, that pepper soup would soon be served, and the men needed to tell Wúràọlá and whichever maid was helping out if they wanted goat or catfish pepper soup. Once she got into medical school in Ifẹ̀, Wúràọlá was often drawn into the argument by doctors who had trained there. And though her father still went on to say something laudatory about the University of Lagos just before steaming bowls of pepper soup shut everyone up for a while, it didn't seem to bother him at all if the thrust of her argument was to unravel his and bring his alma mater down. She could tell that he was proud she had become someone who could be co-opted into this standing argument. He hid his smiles by taking sips that did not deplete the contents of his glass.

Ever since Professor Coker took over from Wúràọlá's father as IEMPU's president, her family hosted the meetings only whenever Professor Coker's wife was having one of those allergic reactions that left her indisposed for days.

Professor Babájídé and Professor Cordelia Coker had moved into the town more than two decades ago, when it was still a part of the old Oyo State. Back then, the founding members of IEMPU were lobbying for this town to be the capital city whenever the new state was finally carved out of the old one. There were rumours that, intent on running for governor as soon as what everyone still considered a mere military intermission was over, Professor Coker had hired someone to teach him Ìjẹ̀ṣà the very night Ọ̀ṣun State and its capital were decreed into being. Yet, after all his time here and several rumoured lessons, the man could not understand or speak any Ìjèṣà beyond "hìnlẹ́ àwé," which he deployed with the confidence of a proficient speaker before stuttering his way back to Yorùbá or English once a conversation deepened beyond pleasantries. None of this stopped him from nodding as though he understood the septuagenarian as he repeated, *Akọ i ṣojo àwé, akọ i ṣojo.* Later in the day, while he gave Wúràọlá instructions for monitoring his patients while she was on call, Professor Coker asked her to explain what the old man had meant.

Wúràọlá sighed as she returned the case note. If the patient made it out of this, maybe he would modify his assertion. What he called cowardice would have saved him all this trouble and kept this bed open for one of the men A & E might have to turn away tonight. Her phone vibrated against her thigh as she moved to the next bed.

Rectopexy—stalled as he attempted to turn over, he grimaced as the catheter reminded his body of what was possible and all that would not be for a while.

She took the phone out of her ward coat's pocket and flipped it open. Kúnlé. She flipped the phone shut and slid it into the back pocket of her jeans, where it began to vibrate again as she pulled out the next case file.

Pancreatectomy—knocked out since noon, he might wake up any moment now and spend the rest of the night wide-eyed. But at least—thanks to the small mercies of morphine—he would not be in pain. His was the first pancreatectomy Wúràọlá had scrubbed in for since she started the surgical rotation. On the night before the surgery, she'd fallen asleep shortly before dawn with her head nestled between the pages of *Clinical Pancreatology for Practising Gastroenterologists and Surgeons.* In the end, she wasn't even allowed to touch the surgical tray during the procedure. There had been no electricity in the hospital for over a month, but that in itself was no longer unusual enough to be remarkable. The real problem was a fuel crisis that had lasted for a week because tanker drivers, rig workers, someone or the other was on strike. Wúràọlá was often too tired to go beyond the headlines, but what she could surmise was that some union was on strike, there was a fuel crisis as a result and the hospital's powerhouse was running out of diesel for the generator. A memo announcing yet another power-sharing formula was slid into pigeonholes and stuck with colourful thumbtacks to noticeboards after the strike began. If the intensive care unit and Hurford Ward were to be powered nonstop, other wards and theatres would be powered only when there was a procedure that necessitated the use of electricity. And so, during the surgery, consultants did everything without teaching as they went along. They did not even ask any of the resident doctors to assist. It seemed as though the two surgeons had concluded that losing an extra second to a resident's slower incision or a house officer's inexperienced suturing could rob a neonate of the electricity needed to power its ventilator if the fuel scarcity persisted. When Wúràọlá was assigned to lead nurses as they wheeled the patient through the hospital's darkened corridors after the surgery, she'd burst into giggles as she stepped out of the theatre. Six years of training, and the only skill that had been required of her in a twelve-hour-long surgery was her ability to hold up her phone so its torchlight would guide nurses?

The surgery had gone well. But the medical team already knew that the procedure would not save his life. Extend it? Yes, by a few weeks or months if he was lucky. Was it luck, though, if his final days were spent in pain or an opioid daze? Wúràọlá was not sure.

The patient's brother came in every night to pray for him. He had told Wúràọlá more than once that the surgeons were wrong, the few months they'd predicted would stretch into years and then decades because the patient was destined, after this momentary travail, to enjoy that rare and beautiful miracle: a long *and* happy life. He had spoken with such conviction that Wúràọlá felt cruel when she reminded him of the prognosis and repeated the advisory he'd been given before the surgery. Pancreatectomy was a palliative measure at this stage of the cancer.

The brother was on his knees now beside the patient's bed, forehead pressed against the metal rail, muttering his prayers. As usual, he held a leather-bound book to his chest. The nurses had a running bet about whether it was a Bible or a Quran, since during visiting hours he'd been accompanied on different occasions and in equal measures by women who sat cross-legged by the bed, adjusting their hijabs before counting out prayers on their tasbihs, and women who wore white robes and held wooden crucifixes against the patient's forehead.

Last week, before asking if some of the women could come with him during the night, or even in his place, he'd said to her, *Doctor, you women are closer to God, and we all know, all of us know, that prayers work better after midnight.*

Wúràọlá had told him the hospital's policy did not permit this unless the woman who would spend the night was a patient's wife, daughter or mother. Maybe a cousin if they were to stretch things and the nurses on duty agreed, but whoever was staying had to be a relative. When the man explained that his brother was childless and unmarried, their mother had died years ago and neither of their sisters lived in Nigeria, Wúràọlá almost asked him to lie that one of the praying women was his sister. Even though she found his prayers disruptive and imagined that having two or more of the women there after visiting hours would be worse, she had been tempted to grant his wish. If only to provide him some momentary reprieve. She was almost certain the next histology report would force the praying brother to confront all that would be taken from him sooner than later, despite his unstinting devotion.

The patient had been admitted a month before Wúràọlá started her rotation in surgery. When a nurse informed Wúràọlá that the praying man had spent every single night at the foot of this bed since the patient was admitted, she had been filled with such admiration for him. So far, she had only seen this kind of unflagging consistency in the paediatric wards. There, mothers and the occasional father often slept in the corridor for weeks. Lying on wooden benches or ankara wrappers they spread on the floor, using handbags or their own folded arms as pillows. During that first week in surgery, whenever she was on call, she'd wonder if any of her siblings would keep watch by her if she ever became this sick. At best, Mọ́tárá would check into a hotel that was close enough to the hospital, Láyí would send money and might visit every other week. He hated hospitals even though *he* was the first doctor in the family, the one whose induction photo was the first thing you saw when you stepped into their mother's bedroom. Wúràọlá would rather not have them there anyway; they would only end up bickering and bothering other patients. Her parents would both show up, no doubts there. Though if she had to choose someone to stay with her, Wúràọlá would pick her father. Unlike her mother, whose anxieties would surely spill out in repeated attempts to teach the medical personnel their jobs, he would be unobtrusive. He might play her some I. K. Dairo on his Discman, humming along at a low decibel.

The praying man always promised to keep his voice down, but his mutterings inevitably became groans that were audible across the ward. It did not take a month for Wúràolá's admiration to morph into irritation. And now as her phone began to vibrate again, he let out a sudden reverberating groan that triggered a throbbing in her head.

All those years and endless hours of training, yet no one told her how much actual practice would involve managing relatives and friends. Nothing had prepared Wúràolá for the man who clung to her and blew snot onto her ward coat after his wife's miscarried foetus was evacuated, the enraged woman who had slapped her when it became clear her son's leg would need to be amputated, the man who when told that his friend had already been wheeled to the morgue refused to leave the ward until security guards dragged him out. No one had taught her how to convince a man that his brother really was dying of pancreatic cancer and there was nothing he could do to change that fact.

Although, to be fair, one of her professors had probably talked about all this and she had zoned out because it was happening during the psychiatry or community health posting. Throughout her penultimate and final years of medical school, she'd been consumed with visions of herself as a house officer. Taking delivery, scrubbing in for surgery, clerking a patient and drawing up an impeccable treatment plan. The relentless hours she'd spent getting squashed during lectures in MDL II in her pre-med years were eased by detailed fantasies about clinical postings. How happy she would be to leave that overcrowded laboratory behind and spend her time in the hospital. Striding into wards and theatres, even the morgue. Since she had qualified and started her house job, her focus had shifted to what being a resident doctor would be like. Recently she had begun to suspect that she would always be restless. Maybe she was one of those people for whom satisfaction lay only in the future, forever slightly out of reach.

She touched the praying man's shoulder. He went quiet and slumped against the bedframe. He was gaunt, cadaverous even. Had he always been this way or was it because his eyes were not at this moment framed by his glasses and therefore seemed more sunken than they usually did? She stepped closer to him as he struggled to his feet. Where he'd seemed slim when she first met him, now he looked like someone who could be blown across the room by a strong breeze.

Before she could speak, he launched into the usual apologies. "My dear, I can't leave. I will keep my voice down, ehn. Whisper." He lowered his voice until it was barely audible. "I will whisper now, ehn, you hear?"

He turned away from her and placed his hands on the bed rail, ready to kneel again.

Wúràọlá took a deep breath. "Mr. . . . Mr. . . . you have to leave sir."

The man twisted his upper body towards her, gripping the bed rail as though he might keel over if he let go. "My dear, I can't leave him."

"You have to go sir. Now."

He opened his mouth as though to speak but said nothing. She tried to catch the eye of one of the nurses who were seated behind a desk next to the door. One was fast asleep, and the other was absorbed in a large textbook that was propped open on his knees at an improbable angle that she supposed was meant to keep him awake. If this situation devolved, she could always shout his name or just yell "nurse," since she was too exhausted to remember any name but her own.

"I understand that you're praying," she said. "But your voice gets too loud."

She waited, but the man did not protest. He stood still. He did not say a word or shut his mouth. There was nothing defiant in his stance, and it was clear to her that there would be no arguments, no need for threats about calling security to haul him out. This man was not standing his ground; he simply could not remember what to do with his body when he was not on his knees.

"I've warned you several times."

In a whisper that she strained to hear, the praying man said, "Yèyé mi."

Wúràọlá was not sure if he was appealing to her with this honorific, or if he was indeed calling for his dead mother. Reaching for the comforts she might have given him once, asking her implicitly to save him, his brother or both of them.

"I have to think about the other patients too," Wúràọlá said.

The man nodded, let go of the bed rail and began to walk away. She watched him amble towards the door, noticing for the first time that he favoured his left leg.

Wúràọlá turned to the patient. Pulse—80 bpm. At the point where his wrist, wreathed with wrinkles that blended into his lifelines, was almost indistinguishable from his palm, the man's skin was paper thin, flaking. She reached into her ward coat's pocket—stick of gum, pen, gum, backup pen, notepad, more gum, hair ruffle—yes! She fished out the tiny bottle of hand sanitiser and squeezed some into her palm. As she massaged it into her skin, she noticed the praying man's silver-rimmed spectacles by his brother's feet. He must have taken them off while he was praying. Their lenses refracted light from a nearby bulb towards her. The rays hit her face, sharp like a rebuke. Maybe she should have let him stay. She imagined him wandering through hospital corridors, stumbling into walls, knocking over dustbins, falling into a gutter as he tried to find his way to the car park. She could have let him stay, but she suspected, even as she picked up the glasses and headed towards the door, that he never let his voice rise above a whisper when the doctor on call was a man. He probably would not have referred to any of the guys as "my dear." She was almost sure.

At the nurses' station, the sleeping nurse had woken up and was yawning.

"I am—" Wúràọlá pointed the glasses towards the door. "Call me if—"

The nurses nodded.

The corridor was empty, but dawn was still a couple of hours away, and even with the glasses, he probably would not have been able to leave the hospital yet. Most neighbourhoods, at least the type she imagined the praying man lived in, had self-imposed curfews that began after midnight and ended at dawn. Movement was allowed only in the intervening hours if there was a medical emergency. Several streets would be closed off now, their access points manned by anything from two to half a dozen armed guards. Some had been known to ask curfew breakers to crawl back and forth across the tarmac until dawn. Even the most merciful ones would insist that offenders wait until the curfew ended before continuing to their destination.

At the end of the corridor, she saw him in the distance, already on the tarmac, walking towards the hospital's chapel. She wanted to call to him: *Mister? Mister?* She considered just calling out an "eskiss sir" but could not bring herself to do so. She knew his name, but what was it?

In medical school, she had pursed her lips the first time a house officer told her they needed to check on Chronic Liver Disease in the male medical ward, proud that she could recite the names of all the patients in their care at that moment. But here she was, not even up to a year later, racing after a man she saw almost every day, unable to remember his name or his sick brother's.

She'd barely slept in three days, though. You were not supposed to be on call for three nights in a row, but the hospital could not afford to employ new house officers just yet. And so, two nights ago, she'd been on call in the male surgical ward, last night in A & E and tonight she was back in the male surgical. On her rotation chart, the roster showed only her calls in surgery. A & E calls were supposed to last only until midnight sha, so that was not so bad. But last night, patients had streamed in non-stop, and the guy who was to relieve her at midnight simply did not show or pick up her calls, so she'd stayed till dawn. Yes, she was hungry and tired and could not remember the praying man's name, but she could set a line right at this moment. She had eaten only a pack of biscuits all day, but she knew she could perform a tracheostomy with steady hands if she had to, and maybe that was what really mattered. That she could buy whatever-his-name-was an extra hour or two, keep him alive until the last minute possible before his body, like all bodies were doomed to, inevitably betrayed itself.

The man stopped in front of the church and stood on a patch of grass for a moment, swaying. Then he fell to his knees and Wúràọlá stood still, worried that something private or shameful was about to happen. Perhaps he was about to weep or howl at whatever deity he had been praying to for months now. But all he did was lie on his back in the grass, his face turned towards the moonless sky.

"Mr. . . . Excuse me sir, I'm sorry, but I forgot your name. You left your glasses inside."

The praying man didn't speak or reach up to take the glasses from her.

"Sir?"

Wúràọlá moved closer and knelt by the man, instinctively reaching for his wrist. He began to snore before she touched him, and she exhaled. Beside him, his leather-bound book lay facedown. She placed the silver-rimmed glasses on top of the book, careful not to make a sound. She reached into her jeans pocket for her phone as she walked back to the ward.

Kúnlé had called nine times.

3

It did not make a difference if Ẹniọlá reminded her that their class-rooms were not even in the same building. His mother would still make him wait for Bùsọ́lá before leaving home. She wanted them to walk to and from Glorious Destiny Comprehensive Secondary School together every single day when possible and had even forced Ẹniọlá to promise that he would always follow his younger sister to her desk before going to his classroom.

On most mornings, as they approached the first school building, their white socks already coated with red dust from what was not even a ten-minute walk, Ẹniọlá often thought about the secondary school his father had promised Ẹniọlá would attend. He was sure there was no red dust on the way to that school. It probably had pavements, walkways and grassy lanes leading from its hostels to its laboratories and classrooms.

Ẹniọlá was nine when his father made that promise. He could not imagine then that anything would cause him to end up in this stupid Glorious Destiny school. He had been in primary five at the time, and all his classmates were preparing to write common entrance examinations. Meanwhile, his father insisted that, since the primary school system was designed to go all the way up to primary six, Ẹniọlá must move on to that class instead of secondary school like most of his classmates.

Ẹniọlá had spent weeks thinking about how he could convince his parents that he was ready for secondary school. He was taller than most of the JSS1 students he ran into on his way to and from his primary school, and he always scored higher than at least half of his classmates in tests and exams. He had memorised all the conversions and tables on the back of his Olympic Exercise Book and could recite the times table from one times one, which equalled one, through twelve times twelve, which equalled one hundred and forty-four, all the way to fourteen times fourteen, which was one hundred and ninety-six. During the weeks that led up to his ninth birthday, Ẹniọlá swept the living room before his mother got to it in the mornings, stopped complaining about not being allowed to go outside and play football with their neighbour's children when he was asked to watch Bùsọ́lá, and since he wasn't tall enough to wash the whole car, spent his Saturday mornings scrubbing the tires of his father's blue Volkswagen Beetle. Worried that all his goodness would go unnoticed by his parents, even as he suspected that he might be close to qualifying for sainthood, one Sunday on the way to Mass, Ẹniọlá announced that he wanted to become an altar boy. He was relieved when his mother said she would not allow it because it might distract him from his studies. Throughout that week, he lied often about how much he wanted to be an altar boy, making a good impression on his father, who thought such intense desire showed he was growing up in the fear of the Lord.

Their home at the time was not far from Crystal Nursery and Primary, and on most days Ẹniọlá walked there with some other children in the neighbourhood. On the day he turned nine, his father dropped him off at school. He sulked next to his father while the birthday cake, covered as he'd asked in white, blue and yellow icing, jolted around in the back seat alongside packets of Oxford Cabin Biscuits and a large cooler of iced zobo. Not even his father's careful driving could prevent them from bouncing from one pothole to another. He began to speak when they pulled up in front of the school building but only managed, "I'm the only one who does not have Ugo C. Ugo in my class. Everybody else has the book. Is it fair?" before he burst into tears. "Is it fair?" he whined again and again as his sobs intensified. His father patted him on the back, trying and failing to calm him. Eventually, he'd quietened himself when he realised that some of his schoolmates who passed by the car were staring at him through the rolled-down window.

"This kind of behaviour . . . Look, I can't be late for work. Let's talk about all of this tonight," Ẹniọlá's father said, drumming his fingers against the steering wheel. "Come now, let's take these things inside."

Ẹniọlá stayed in the car while his father got down and began to offload items from the back seat. Some schoolchildren gathered around the car to help, calling out "Happy birthday!" to Ẹníọlá. He did not respond. He could not believe his stupidity. How could he just have wasted all those hours he'd spent in front of the bathroom mirror, getting ready for the moment after that night's dinner when he was supposed to speak calmly to both of his parents? He sat in silence, staring at his Kito sandals and fighting the urge to play with the Velcro strap. Where were all the arguments he had prepared, all those reasonable words he could have spoken instead of whining "Is it fair?" like the small boy his parents still thought he was? Why had they all fled down his throat instead of coming out of his lips like he wanted them to? He began to cry again, quietly this time, sniffling without sobbing.

He did not notice that his father was back in the car until it shuddered and screeched to a start. Ẹníọlá reached for the door.

His father gripped his wrist. "Come on, wipe your cheeks first before you go down. Don't let anyone see you crying."

That evening, Ẹníọlá's father gave him a new copy of Ugo C. Ugo's book of practice questions for common entrance examinations. For a few moments, he thought he'd at last prevailed against his parents, but his happiness lasted only until his father began to speak.

"Look, you can write the exams now if you want, but"—he held up a finger—"but if you wait for a year and complete primary six, which, as I have told you times without number, is an essential part of the six-three-three-four system of education—very essential part of it, I tell you. Even though most schools are just doing things anyhow these days. Anyway, if you do this right and stay on till primary six, you can go to the federal government college in Ìkìrun. The choice is yours."

Ẹníọlá had wanted to attend the Federal Unity school in Ìkìrun since Collins, whose family lived in the flat upstairs, had gone off to secondary school there three years before, returning during every holiday with stories of fun and freedom that Ẹníọlá knew would not be possible if he went to a school that was close to home. Whenever he mentioned the school, his mother had always said she would never allow him to go to that or any boarding school. She often went on and on about how he was too young, his seniors could bully him, he might join a bad gang, and he would surely return home without any manners or sense. Now that his father had somehow managed to convince her to let him attend the Unity school, Ẹniọlá did not have to think twice before agreeing to stay in primary school for one more year.

After his father's promise, it was easier for him to listen as his classmates bragged about secondary school. He could also tell them about how he would attend a Federal Unity school. A year after they all went off to secondary school, yes. But was any of them even going to a boarding school? A Unity school? Ẹniọlá found a way to bring up the Unity school almost every day, retelling the stories Collins had shared with him until he could see that some of his friends had become jealous. Their envy was a comfort as they wrote their common entrance exams and went away to different schools, while he was left behind to complete primary six with two boys who had failed every common entrance exam they wrote. He was going to be like Collins soon. He too would return home thrice a year, and other boys in the neighbourhood would gather around him as he told stories of all he had been up to without his parents monitoring him. He thought about this every day as he walked to and from school alone. The friends he used to make the trip with were no longer his schoolmates, and though he missed them, it did not matter. He was going to be like Collins soon. That would make up for everything; all he had to do was wait.

And then, at the end of his first term in primary six, just a couple of weeks before Christmas, his father and over four thousand teachers in the state were sacked. At first, everything at home went on as usual. His father continued to leave the house at seven in the morning on weekdays, tie knotted, hair shining where globs of Morgan's Pomade had not been combed in thoroughly, side parting still in place. Ẹniọlá went on believing he would still proceed to the Unity school in Ìkìrun as planned. After all, it was only a matter of time before the governor realised that he was destroying public schools and all the teachers would be reinstated with a personal apology from him. At the very least, some teachers had to be reinstated, and Ẹniọlá's father, with his experience and qualifications, would definitely be one of those who would be called back because they were needed. It had to happen soon. How would the school run its syllabus without history? How? Night after night, Ẹniọlá fell asleep next to Bùsọ́lá on the sofa while their parents continued this conversation instead of saying the bedtime prayers.

On the radio, one of the governor's aides explained that most of the teachers who had been retrenched taught subjects—fine arts, Yorùbá, food and nutrition, Islamic and Christian religious studies—that would do nothing for the nation's development.

What will our children do with Yorùbá in this modern age? What? You see, what we need now is technology, science and technology. And how will watercolours be useful to them? Isn't that what the fine arts teachers teach them about? Watercolour.

The man on the radio laughed.

Christmas had come and gone. It was the first day of the new year, and some of his parents' friends, many of whom had also lost their jobs, had come over for dinner. As the man continued to laugh, Ẹniọlá found that although the bowl in front of him was filled with pepper soup, he could no longer feel the sting from the peppers or taste the meat. He felt as though he was drinking water with a spoon. When he returned to school after the holidays, he listed *retrenchment* and *reinstatement* among the new words he had learnt during the Christmas break.

A few months later, his father's blue Beetle sped past him as he returned home from school. It was being driven by a bald man he did not recognise. When he got home, his mother responded to his questions about the car by demanding that he finish his homework before asking foolish questions, sweep the kitchen floor before disturbing her peace, wash the front yard with a broom before frustrating her in this life. It took her a week to tell him that the car had been sold. By then his father had stopped leaving the house at seven in the morning, no longer joined the family for dinner and barely left his room all day. His mother began leading the morning prayers, stumbling over words that Ẹniọlá could pronounce in his sleep while she read to him and Bùsọ́lá from *Devotion to the Most Precious Blood of Our Lord Jesus Christ*.

Soon, they had to move out of the three-bedroom flat that had been home before his father was sacked. When his family moved to the house where they now lived, only a few doors down but nearly a century behind, Ẹniọlá had assumed the move was only temporary. He had believed that after a few months, at most, they would once again live in a house that had indoor bathrooms and at least one water closet. He should have known then, when they left the house that had an indoor kitchen and louvre blades, after the television, bedframes and sofas were sold, before his father tried to sell the VCR and no one would buy it because even video clubs had begun to loan out only Video CDs, he should have known then that his parents would no longer be able to afford the fees for the Unity school in Ìkìrun. But his father taught history. His father taught history, and that laughing man on the radio had not mentioned history on his list of subjects that were useless for the modern age. History still mattered. His father said so.

In the new house, his father seemed frozen in place. He stayed in bed for hours, back to the room, face to the wall, often refusing to eat. When Ẹniọlá asked if it would still be possible for him to attend the Federal Unity school, he gave no sign that he'd heard the boy.

It was Ẹniọlá's mother who sold every piece of jewellery she owned and made just enough money from that to cover the registration form for Glorious Destiny Comprehensive Secondary School and tuition for his first term there. The Federal Unity school was just too expensive, but she was not going to send him to one of the tuition-free state schools now.

"They say it's free education. Free education but half of the teachers are gone," she'd said as she tucked her jewellery box into a bag she was taking to a mallam who would buy the pieces from her. "It's like promising people free lunch and giving them boiled sticks to eat. Just start at Glorious Destiny, we will put you somewhere better when this is over, don't worry."

Glorious Destiny Comprehensive was housed in a crumbling three-storey building that had once been the home of a wealthy trader. On birthdays or during naming ceremonies, it was not unusual for priests or imams to invoke the trader as they prayed: *May your wealth flow from farm to homestead like Adénrelé Àrẹmú Mákinwá.*

It was said that the trader's children, certain their allotments from his will would more than cover their expenses, killed a dozen cows each day to entertain invited and uninvited guests, who ate, danced and drank beneath canopies that blocked half of the street for a whole week. Ẹniọlá had attended one of those parties with his father. He must have been six at the time. His mother was heavily pregnant with Bùṣọlá, and they still lived further up the street in the house that had louvre blades and water closets. When he walked to school now, he sometimes thought of that day a decade ago. How he had walked down the same street with his father to one of those funeral parties, and people had stopped to shake his father's hand without taking offense when he held out his left palm because he was gripping Ẹniọlá with his right hand. How although his mother did not attend the party with them, and there had been enough food at their table to fill one of those black polythene bags she now hid in her purse when she went to parties uninvited, Ẹniọlá and his father had left the party carrying nothing besides plastic hand fans that were embossed with the dead man's face. There was always food at home then, and there was no need to pretend they had not been served so they could get extra plates of jollof rice that his mother poured into a polythene bag and hid in her handbag when no one was looking.

Ẹniọlá liked to think of the funeral, how that day he had skipped down the street with his hand nestled in the palm of a man whom other men stopped to greet. Sometimes, remembering this helped him forget that his father had become a man who now preferred to leave the house after nightfall, because his creditors were less likely to recognise him in the dark.

After Mrs. Suleiman, the retired primary school teacher who owned Glorious Destiny Comprehensive Secondary School, bought the house from Mákinwá's children, a few months before she started the school there with a dozen students, she'd come to Ẹniọlá's home to offer his father a job as school principal. Finishing up his dinner, Ẹniọlá had watched from the dining table as his father leaned back in the armchair he would have to sell a couple of years later and laughed. In the high-pitched tone he often used when rebuking his children, Ẹniọlá's father had told Mrs. Suleiman that her school was only going to end up producing "half-baked graduates," and he would not leave his position in the public school system to be a part of a "mushroom project" that did not even have proper government approval. And so, even after he passed the entrance exams and resumed junior secondary school at Glorious Destiny Comprehensive, Ẹniọlá believed for a while that there was no way he would spend all six of his secondary school years there. Somewhere in his future, the near future, the Unity school in Ìkìrun waited.

Throughout his first term at Glorious Destiny, Ẹniọlá often told his classmates that he would be in a proper school that did not have make-shift classrooms where chairs leaned against wardrobes, by the next school year. There, students did not have to squeal and scream when the family of bush rats that lived in one of those wardrobes decided to attend the social studies class.

During the long vacation at the end of his first year at Glorious Destiny, on one of those rainy days in the middle of August, the three Ghana Must Go bags that had been filled with his father's books when they left their old house disappeared. This time, he did not need to ask about what had happened as he had with the car, the furniture, the television, the radio, the fridge. Yet he asked anyway, and he knew then, as his mother's response disappeared into the sound of thunder and rain, that he would return to the crumbling three-storey in the middle of September to begin his second year. There would be no escape.

After his father's books disappeared, Ẹniọlá tried to forget about the Unity school. His classmates, however, especially the boys whom he'd asked why their parents weren't going to send them to a school where they would not share the cafeteria with rats, lizards and the occasional snake, would not let him forget. At the beginning of every school year, JSS2, JSS3, SS1 and now in SS2, they would ask him why he was back at Glorious Destiny. Had the roads that led to Ìkìrun been closed off? Was the Unity school no longer admitting new students? Had it been shut down? Burnt down? Flooded? At some point before he completed JSS3, several boys in his class took to calling him Unity instead of Ẹniọlá, and by the time he started his senior secondary school years, most of his classmates, even the girls, called him Unity. Someone called that name out now as he approached the school building with Bùsọ́lá. He looked up and grinned as though he liked the nickname. You never let your mates see you cry.

"Go and meet your friend," Bùsọ́lá said. "You don't need to follow me to class."

"He's not my friend."

Last year, the school management had moved all junior classes into a new building in the middle of a dense forest that once marked the end of the street. Since then, a footpath had been forged to where Glorious Destiny's new site stood. The path dipped into a valley and passed over a brook before the terrain ascended again, such that it was an uphill walk to the unpainted block of classrooms that stood in the middle of the clearing, an island surrounded on each side by thickets and towering trees. Ẹniọlá went there every morning even though his own classroom was in the crumbling three-storey building. He would walk with Bùsọ́lá until they were at the edge of the clearing and she was only a few feet from her class. She complained all the way from the house about how she did not need anyone to follow her.

She was old enough to walk to school by herself, didn't he see that?

She would never tell their mother the truth if he let her walk there by herself, just once, just this one time.

Who had walked him to school when he was her age anyway? Hadn't he gone all by himself? Why did someone have to walk her? Was it because she was a girl?

Ẹniọlá had taught himself to ignore her, training himself over time to focus on his own thoughts so he heard her voice as though from a distance, without being able to make out her words. It was his job to walk her to school, and if, as their mother implied, his presence added some extra layer of protection for Bùsọ́lá, nothing she said would make him stop. Not when he had made a promise to their mother.

Bùsọ́lá's voice often rose when they passed by the three-storey building, as though a change in pitch would convince him to take a right turn and head upstairs to his own classroom. Once they got to the brook, Bùsọ́lá seemed to resign herself to his presence.

"Tèmi found a cashew tree behind the school yesterday, and she said the fruits are ripe," she said now, placing her right foot on one of the stones that had been arranged to form a bridge through the shallow brook. "We're going there during break time."

"The same Tèmi you called a liar last week?"

Bùsọ́lá held her arms aloft as she made her way over the stones, tilting them this way and that. Ẹniọlá stayed close to her, angling his body in whichever direction she tilted, ready to catch her if she lost her balance.

Whenever she passed over a body of water, Bùsọ́lá spread her arms out like wings as though she were about to glide or take flight. She had done this since she was a child, even when she was so young she had to be carried.

"Don't follow Tèmi into that bush during break, Bùsọ́lá, there might be snakes behind the school."

"I'm not afraid of anything." She shook out her skirt to shed some of the pollen that had gathered at the hem as they walked through the grass.

"You're no longer afraid of cockroaches, ehn?"

"Come and be going, stop following me. Do you want everyone to think I'm a child?" Bùsọ́lá said, glaring at him as they approached the block of classrooms.

"Unripe cashews will give you stomachache."

"It's sha not your stomach. Be going, jàre. You'll be late for your own assembly."

Ẹniọlá turned away and began walking towards the footpath. At its edge, he glanced backward at the school block to make sure Bùsọ́lá had gone into her classroom and could not see him. Then he ran. He was afraid of many things. He was terrified of bushes and forests, even knee-high grass. Whenever he was in the stretch before and after the brook, covered as they were with blades of elephant grass that fluttered above his head, he could never shake the feeling that the greenery concealed one of the iwins his mother had threatened him with when he was younger. Of course, he knew now that those stories were meant to keep him from playing near bushes, but still. Still, he felt a presence bearing down on him whenever he was alone in a thicket like this one. It would be possible later to think of how this presence was nothing but his own fear, grown beyond what his body could contain, spilling out of him to form a second shadow that stalked him in the grass. For now, every time his feet touched the ground, he imagined a snake, green enough to blend in with foliage, curling itself around his ankle, sinking poisonous fangs into his skin. He ran faster and faster, stopping only when he emerged on the other side, where he stood for a long moment, gripping his knees and panting.

He lifted his gaze towards the balcony of the top floor and could see that lines of students had formed there. The morning assembly was under way. He was late but not late enough to be punished. Or so he hoped as he began to walk towards the building as fast as he could manage with the cramping pain he now had in his left ankle. There was a staircase on the side of the building that had been tacked on after the ground floor became marshy during the rains. He dashed up the staircase, encountering no other student on his way, until he burst onto the third floor's balcony. He tried to join the assembled students without attracting any teacher's gaze and slid into the end of the closest line, not bothering to make sure that he was filing in behind his own classmates.

Mr. Bísádé, the school's only math teacher, who doubled as its principal, was addressing students. He gripped a tasselled trophy with one hand and held a whip in the other. Hakeem, the boy who had outscored everyone in Ẹniọlá's class since they were in JSS1, stood next to the principal. Grinning as he lifted the trophy above his head, the principal droned on and on about how Hakeem had won another trophy for the school in yet another interschool quiz. Hakeem, with his deep-set eyes and a forehead that protruded as though someone had slapped it on as an afterthought, was not just the only student in Ẹniọlá's class to have won a prize in any interschool quiz or debate; he was the only one in the whole school who had ever returned from a competition with any kind of commendation.

"We are very proud of you," Mr. Bísádé said, handing over the trophy to Hakeem.

Hakeem bowed as though to prostrate, but Mr. Bísádé grabbed him by the shoulders and pulled him into a hug.

"Óyá, clap for Hakeem, do I still need to tell you that?" Mr. Bísádé said, cracking his whip. "Louder, louder, louder."

The applause drowned out the principal's voice.

Hakeem took the trophy and made his way towards the back, squeezing himself through the space between lines of students. When he went by, Ẹniọlá reached out for a handshake, but Hakeem was gripping the trophy with both hands and would not let it go for the few seconds it would have taken to shake Ẹniọlá's hand.

Mr. Bísádé stood facing the students, arms akimbo, saying something no one could hear and grinning as though the students were clapping for him. When some boys began to hoot, he cracked his whip, and the clapping ceased.

"Consider today's admonition," Mr. Bísádé said, speaking with the booming voice he reserved for the daily verses he chose from either the Bible or the Quran. "It is taken from the Holy Bible. 'Happy is the one who is always reverent, but one who hardens his heart falls into trouble.' That said, the school management has asked me to inform you that you all have until next Monday to pay your school fees. See how generous, ehn? You've been given a whole week. Now, if you have paid already, bring your teller to me so I can write a receipt for you. If you have not paid your school fees by the beginning of next week, don't bother to come to school at all. All debtors will be?"

"Flogged and sent back home," a few students said.

"Debtors will be?"

"Flogged and sent back home." The chorus was louder this time. Thunderous enough for Ẹniọlá to feel all those voices vibrate in his chest. Or was that his heart, thudding again as though he were still running? He would have to bring this up with his parents soon, maybe tonight. He could barely remember the lyrics as they sang the school anthem, and his right hand trembled as he placed it over his heart to recite the national pledge.

❧

The neighbour's radio was too loud. If he paid attention, Ẹniọlá's father could hear the newscaster's breathing between sentences. He was sure the radio could be heard in the next building too, but he never complained to his neighbour. How could he, when he still owed the woman three thousand naira. More important, though, when he was home alone, Bàbá Ẹniọlá was grateful for any sound that could distract him from the darkness that slithered back and forth with his thoughts.

The darkness had been there for as long as he could remember, nipping at the edges of his mind. He'd grown used to it by the time he was in his late teens. How it came and went like a seasonal cold. He would withdraw while he waited for the despair to lift, ignoring offers to meet up with friends or attend ceremonies, unable to find comfort or pleasure in the things he usually turned to for succour during bouts of sadness. He could tell that it was the darkness when his appetite vanished for days, when he could not be captivated by his favourite books. By adulthood, he understood the pattern, he could always count on it to lift within days or weeks. Until now.

A newscaster signed off on the radio. The one o'clock news was over; Ẹniọlá and Bùsọlá would be home within an hour. Before she left the house, his wife had told him the children were to have gaàrí for lunch. He rose from the bed and went to the food cupboard. If he could not bring himself to leave the room, he could at least set out their lunch for them. He measured out the gaàrí. Just one cup, not even enough to graze the measuring tin's rim. This was all his wife had managed to scrounge together.

She was out again now, probably searching dunghills for used plastics and bottles she could resell. He should be out there with her, offering himself up for day jobs, washing other people's clothes or toilets, looking for bottles on dunghills or carrying cement at a building site. Just a few months ago, he'd been able to do some of those things. Then they were on a dunghill together one day, and he didn't know that he had begun to weep until his wife held him by the waist. He did not realise he was trembling until he tried to follow her as she pulled him away from the dunghill.

What triggered those tears? A realisation that all his education had been for nothing and all his choices must have been wrong if they led him to a moment when his wife was wading through refuse for other people's castaways? The knowledge that if they found an old T-shirt, it would be washed so that Ẹniọlá could have some new clothes to wear?

Ẹniọlá had shot up within a couple of years, and he now towered over his father. It startled Bàbá Ẹniọlá that his son kept growing, advancing into life without many of the things he needed. There were several opportunities he had hoped to make available to his son, but most of them became redundant with each passing year. Time was unforgiving, it didn't stop, not even to give people a chance to scrape themselves off the floor if they'd been shattered. And so his son's limbs kept growing, even though there was no way to provide a wardrobe that kept up with his expanding body. Bàbá Ẹníọlá could not speak with pride about how quickly his son's height had outpaced that of his peers. Not when the hems of the poor boy's trousers kept rising, travelling further and further away from his ashen ankles.

A newscaster announced that it was two o'clock. Time for news on the hour. Bàbá Ẹníọlá held the tin of gaàrí aloft. This quantity would not be enough for both children. He wondered if Bùsọ́lá would once again spend the afternoon stomping around the room and protesting the lack of food. She was not one to bear suffering without reacting. Bàbá Ẹníọlá preferred this to his son's silence. At least he knew what Bùsọ́lá was thinking. He could never tell what lay beneath his Ẹníọlá's silences. Despair? Resentment? Disdain for a father who had failed his family?

The newscaster was reporting that voter registration was now open in the state for the following year's election. Bàbá Ẹníọlá glanced at the scar that cut from his wrist to his elbow. He could not think about elections without remembering his time in Àkúrẹ́ after the ones held in August of eighty-three. He'd been in Àkúrẹ́ to visit a distant relative who was a local politician. Within days of his arrival, thugs descended on Methodist Church Street and surrounded his relative's house. Bàbá Ẹníọlá and the sundry cousins in the house managed to escape over the fence with the man's children. While most of the cousins were unscathed, a thug managed to slash Bàbá Ẹníọlá's arm as he scaled the fence to safety. The politician was not so lucky. He was caught, dragged into the streets and burnt alive by the mob.

Bàbá Ẹníọlá sighed. He filled a large bowl with water and poured the gaàri inside, hoping that it was the type that swelled up really well. The tiny grains mopped up the water in minutes, expanding to fill up the bowl. Bàbá Ẹníọlá sat on the bed, relieved and calmed by a faint sense of accomplishment. Now there would be enough food for both children.

Bùsọ́lá burst into the room first, humming to herself. She brandished a sheet of paper before offering any greeting. "Look, Bàami, I scored ten over ten on the impromptu test today."

Bàbá Ẹníọlá took the sheet from her and examined it. In red ink, her teacher had scrawled *excellent* beneath her scores.

"Good afternoon sir," Ẹniọlá greeted him, as he came into the room.

"Nobody else got above six in the whole class." Bùsọlá grinned. "And me, I got ten over ten."

Bàbá Ẹniọlá examined the test script. Good. The subject was integrated science. This child would not make his own mistakes. She would be a doctor or an engineer. At worst, she might be an accountant. He would not allow her to squander her abilities on anything that did not have a clear path to wealth. She was smarter than he had ever been, why should he let her be a botanist or whatever it was she had said the other day?

He often recognised himself in his daughter. Whenever he saw her sniff a book before opening it, he understood her delight. It hurt that he could not take her to a bookshop and watch her wander around with the kind of rapture he had once known. He saw his naivety in her too. That was where the botanist comment came from. He'd had options at the beginning of his teacher training. He could have gravitated towards some science, something his parents deemed more practical and useful, but no, he had chosen what he loved. History.

Later, when some of his teacher friends branched off into business and began to focus on their stores, to the detriment of their students, Bàbá Ẹniọlá dedicated himself to teaching. He was consumed by the curriculum he wanted to imprint on the brains of his students. What was that nonsense he used to spout at the beginning of the term? An understanding of their past that would equip them for the future or some such rubbish. His dedication had felt like some noble and honourable thing. Look where it got him.

"You're not saying anything," Bùsọlá said.

"What?"

"You're just looking at my paper, you're not congratulating me."

Bàbá Ẹniọlá gave the sheet back to Bùsọlá. He was grateful to her for this; she still made demands of him. She assumed he was capable of more than the reveries he often sank into, able to do more than putter around the house all day. Now and then, her faith was enough to push the darkness away.

"Well done," Bàbá Ẹniọlá said. "Well done."

She grinned and nodded.

"Is there anything to eat?" Ẹniọlá was changing out of his school shirt.

"Yes." Bàbá Ẹniọlá pointed at the bowl of gaàrí.

Bùsọ́lá grabbed a spoon and dug in. "It's too soft now. Why did you put so much water?"

"Stop complaining," Ẹniọlá said.

"Why should it be so soft when there is no sugar or groundnut?"

Ẹniọlá picked up his spoon. "It's so that it will be enough for both of us."

"I was not talking to you." Bùsọ́lá dropped her spoon. "I can't eat this thing. Bàami, have you heard back from any of the jobs you applied for?"

Bùsọ́lá was waiting for an explanation he could not give. Bàbá Ẹniọlá averted his gaze. He feared that if he spoke, he might burst into tears. He lay on the bed and felt the energy drain from him, to be replaced by despair. Even at fixing them lunch, he had failed. Bùsọ́lá repeated questions he could not answer without sinking further into darkness. No one wanted to employ a history teacher. Not even the ramshackle private schools he had once disdained. Those ones did not bother to feature history on their subject lists anymore. If he spoke to Bùsọ́lá about this and began to weep, as he sometimes did without knowing, would the darkness not overpower him?

Bàbá Ẹniọlá turned to face the wall. Bùsọ́lá was asking another question. Ẹniọlá was saying goodbye, explaining that he was headed to Aunty Caro's shop. His children's voices came as faint echoes, not compelling enough for him to lift his head or say goodbye before Ẹniọlá left the room.

❖

There were two signs outside Aunty Caro's bungalow. One was a black knee-high one that said CARO'S SOWING SHOP. It had been there long before Ẹniọlá began his apprenticeship a year ago, and its lettering was almost faded. The other sign, a large one that stood taller than the building itself, had been installed just a few months after he began his training. This sign and a new industrial sewing machine had been Aunty Caro's birthday gift to herself when she turned fifty. Against a white background, its glittering blue letters proclaimed:

TIME WAIT FOR NO 1 INTERNATIONAL FASHION
DESIGNER, TAILOR AND SOWING SHOP.
Contact us for corporate wears, *aṣọ-ebí* and
WEDDING GOWNS.
We are dealing lace, gini brokade, ankara and adire materials.
Women Sowing Only Available. No Men.
A trial will convict you.

Aunty Caro was broomstick thin and taller than most men. She was one of only two people he knew who were taller than him. On most days she wore ankle-length boubous in the same V-neck and A-line style, always embroidered at the hem with gold or silver threads. She was standing outside as he approached, holding an adire fabric aloft with one hand while she snipped it in half with a pair of scissors from the other end.

The front yard was an elevated slab of concrete with three steps leading up to it.

"Hin kúrọ̀lẹ́, Aunty Caro," Ẹniọlá greeted her when he was on the last step.

She looked up and said something he could not hear over the growls of a black-and-yellow generator that stood in one corner of the yard.

Ẹniọlá went to her, held one end of the fabric and then backed away until it was fully stretched out. Brow furrowed, she moved towards him snip by snip until they were standing toe to toe and the fabric had been cut in two. She tapped him on the shoulder twice to say thanks. One tap was a warning, two meant "thank you." Three taps were a little confusing, as they could mean "well done" or "stop that," it all depended on the speed with which they were delivered.

Aunty Caro handed him the fabric and walked to the generator, bending over it and fiddling with a wire. He went with her, feeling somehow that he should be checking whatever it was she was checking and fixing it, even though he knew nothing about generators. His father had been sacked before every other house on their street seemed to have one shuddering in a corridor or front yard. Generators were displayed in front yards during the day and hidden in corridors at night. An order that emerged after one was stolen from a man who spent the rest of that night screaming curses he claimed were spiritual arrows that would pierce the thief to death within three days. Some people swore the man's neighbour had stolen the generator, but though the suspected neighbour did begin to walk with a limp soon after the incident, he was still alive three days and three years later. In fact, no one died on the street for at least another year, not even an old woman who was so ill and aged that her children had already repainted her house twice in preparation for a grand and befitting burial. Soon there were other whispers about the man whose generator had been stolen, that *he* was part of an armed robbery gang and èsan had simply caught up with him when his property was stolen. Regardless, no one left their generator outside at night after that incident. Most of the generators were the blue-and-black or yellow-and-black ones everyone called "I better pass my neighbour." Cheap enough for many on their street to purchase either new or secondhand ones, small enough to be moved inside by a teenager once night fell. If his family had an "I better pass my neighbour," Ẹniọlá knew that his father would have taught him how to pull a rope to switch it on. He would also be in charge of it by now, changing its oil weekly or whatever.

Aunty Caro treated her generator with the same care she gave her newest sewing machine. None of her apprentices was permitted to touch it, not even with the tip of a fingernail. When the generator's growls became louder and its vibrations were so strong it seemed to have started dancing on the spot, Aunty Caro straightened and wiped her hands on her boubou. She took the fabric from Ẹniọlá, flung it over her shoulder and headed towards the door that led into her bungalow. He followed her into the corridor that divided her bungalow into two apartments. Sometimes, when she was talking to an apprentice who was about to leave after being fully trained, Aunty Caro would speak about how she had never lived in another house. This one had been built as a mud house before she was born, and once she inherited it from her parents, she'd had the walls plastered and painted in bright blue. She had done this before Time Wait for No 1, in her twenties, from money she made tailoring as an èjìkánişọọ̀bù, carrying her first Singer on her shoulder as she went from street to street. From Coca-Cola to Ìsàlẹ̀ General, Ìlérí to Àyẹ́sọ̀, patching and mending clothes door-to-door. She'd saved for years and years, spreading the construction out over time, moving forward with next steps as soon as she had enough money to buy a bag of cement here or a bucket of paint there.

Ẹniọlá thought the house looked odd and wondered why she hadn't just pulled this one down and built another. It was small and old, coated with uneven layers of paint that flaked when you touched the walls. But Aunty Caro was proud of what she had done with it and continued to use it as an example of what could be accomplished through tailoring when apprentices were about to leave her.

When her parents were alive, Aunty Caro's family had lived in one apartment while the other one was rented out. Now she lived in one of the apartments and had converted both her corridor and the other apartment into Time Wait for No 1. What had once been a bedroom served as a store with shelves that held yards of ankara and swaths of satin for sale. The former living room housed six sewing machines and two long tables; one was for fabrics that were waiting to be sewn while the other was always laden with finished outfits that needed to be ironed. There were two benches in the corridor for customers, but if a customer was particularly rich or valuable, Aunty Caro took her across the hall into her own living room. Sometimes she let Ẹniọlá sit in there, snug in one of the fat armchairs, his notebook on his lap as he finished his homework. Now and then she would come in and look over his shoulder, squinting at his pen as it moved across the page, hands on her hips even though they both knew she could not read what he was writing.

During the first month of Ẹniọlá's apprenticeship, Aunty Caro taught him how to measure and cut. She assigned him to a sewing machine next to her and showed him how to make stitches. But when the last day of that month arrived and his parents did not pay his apprenticeship fee, she called him aside and explained that she could not continue training him. She understood that his father didn't have a job, but nobody was giving her threads and needles for free either. Did he see what she was saying, ehn? He could keep coming to Time Wait for No 1 after school to learn a thing or two, but she was not going to teach him anything that involved a sewing machine unless his parents paid her.

Aunty Caro had three apprentices who had actually paid their apprenticeship fee. Fúnkẹ́, the oldest and most senior, had been under Aunty Caro's tutelage for two years now and had a year to go before she got her freedom. Accredited by Aunty Caro to be a bona fide tailor, she would be able to join the Union of Tailors and open her own tailoring shop.

Maria and Ṣèyí had started their training just a few months before Ẹníọlá, but because they had actually paid for it, they knew much more than he did. They could now sew skirts, ìró, bùbá and the occasional bou-bou from start to finish without asking Aunty Caro to help with anything. This meant that they got to send him on errands, since whatever he was helping out with could be delayed, whereas they were making something that a client would wear. Sometimes he pretended not to hear them when they asked him to go buy cold drinks and chips. Unlike Aunty Caro and Fúnkẹ́, they never left some of their Coke or Fanta in the bottle for him to enjoy. Ṣèyí and Maria would drink every single drop, then ask him to return their empty bottles and bring back the change that was being held until the bottles were returned. They did this even when they were not actually sewing anything, as if he was their servant. Ṣèyí was not even older than him. She had been his classmate until JSS3 when she became pregnant and was expelled from school because, as Mr. Bísádé told the assembly, her presence would corrupt the school's moral fibre. And though Mr. Bísádé did not mention it, everyone knew that Ṣèyí had been impregnated by Ahmed, another student in the school. Ṣèyí and Ahmed had worn outfits sewn from the same lace fabric during the child's nam-ing ceremony, and it was Ahmed who had read out the infant's names. Ahmed was now in SS3.

Ẹníọlá could sometimes bear it when Maria sent him on an errand, but Ṣèyí? He hated her for the casual ease with which she sent him up and down, as though they were not agemates, for the suddenness with which she removed naira notes from her bra so that he saw the briefest flash of her flesh before she gave him the money. And all the way to the store he would feel the heat of her skin on the naira notes, and always, always that urge to bring the notes to his nostrils, to his lips. Twice, when he had enough money of his own to buy what she wanted, he kept the notes Ṣèyí had given him for days, holding them to his cheeks with his eyes closed, wondering about how they must have felt pressed against her breast. How he might feel.

Ẹníọlá sat opposite Ṣèyí's sewing machine, behind a table laden with yards of lace and old copies of *Ovation* magazine. He enjoyed leafing through the magazine whenever he had a chance, sinking into another world as he flipped through its glossy pages. It gave him the sense that he was preparing for a life that could be his, someday, somehow. Aunty Caro kept a stash of secondhand copies so that her customers could select styles from the endless options provided by any one of the women who had been photographed at some big party in Lagos, London, Abuja, Paris, on some island whose name Ẹniọlá mouthed but did not dare pronounce. He studied the men, prosperous in their aṣọ-òkè agbádás with folds piled high on their shoulders, regal in George wrappers and shirts so white they seemed able to reflect sunlight. He studied their wristwatches, the patterned walls they stood next to, the gilded chairs they sat on, the coral beads that hung from their necks in multi-layered strings or a single one that went all the way to their navels. How they glared or grinned at the camera while their hands rested on the shoulder of a seated wife or on potbellies that testified to their good living.

"Did you come here to read *Ovation*?" Ṣèyí said before he could go beyond the first page. "Oh, some of your relatives are in those pictures, àbí?"

Maria laughed. The sound struck Ẹniọlá like a slap. He did not have relatives who could even buy the magazine.

Ṣèyí held a blue wrapper out to him.

"Can't you fold that by yourself?" he said, returning the copy of *Ovation* to its place on the table.

"Who will sew this boubou then?" Ṣèyí held up her hands then glanced left and right, first at Fúnkẹ́, who was stitching buttons onto a pink jacket, then at Maria, who was marking some outfit with a chalk.

He took the wrapper and turned his back on Ṣèyí so that he was facing the window and could not see her smiling in triumph. Stiff with starch, the wrapper crackled as he folded it. The sky was deepening from blue to indigo, and gusts of wind made the windows' wooden shutters swing on their hinges, while behind him Ṣèyí's foot pedal clattered as she continued working on the boubou.

A red Mercedes M-Class pulled up in front of the shop.

"Yèyé is here," Ẹniọlá announced as he watched a driver come out of the car and open its door for a woman in her late forties. She stared at the gutter that separated the road from Aunty Caro's shop as though ready to turn back instead of walking over the narrow plank that had been placed on it to form a bridge.

"Fúnké, you'll help me to get something for Yèyé to drink," Aunty Caro said. "No, wait, where are you going? You don't know what she wants yet, wait for her to come."

"Yes ma," Fúnké said, drawing out each word as she often did, so that her stutter sounded like a tremor in her voice.

As Yèyé hurried across the plank, the gold threads that bordered the neckline of her floor-length dress glittered each time she moved. Ęniọlá remembered the outfit, Aunty Caro had not allowed anyone else in the shop to even touch the fabric while she worked on it. Once, when Ęniọlá picked up a scrap that had fallen to the floor and added it to the pile of scraps he was planning to make into a patchwork blouse for Bùsọlá someday, Aunty Caro had snapped her fingers at him before saying, "Bring it o, one yard of this lace can buy you and your family, don't bring trouble into my life, please."

The fruity scent of Yèyé's perfume filled Time Wait for No 1 before she stepped into the shop.

"Caro! Caro, torí Ọlọhun, find money and use cement on top of that gutter now. Just make a small bridge. That thing you have there is like a pencil, it will break one day and get you into trouble. What if someone falls inside, Caro? What if *you* fall inside it? I'm warning you, Caro."

"I've heard you ma, I'll do something about it." Aunty Caro reached out to take Yèyé's bags. "Good afternoon, Yèyé, let's go to my sitting room."

"No, no, this place is fine. I'm leaving soon."

Aunty Caro led Yèyé to the only two-seater sofa in the shop, then pushed a mound of fabric that had been piled high onto it to a side, creating just enough room for Yèyé.

"What should we get for you?" Aunty Caro asked as Yèyé sat down. "Coke or Fanta? Àbí zobo?"

"I feel like taking something, but Wúràọlá has said I should stop taking sugary things. Because of my blood sugar kiníkan sha." Yèyé sighed. "In this short life, these doctors don't want us to manage the small enjoyment we can enjoy."

"One bottle won't kill you," Aunty Caro said.

"Àbí? But, you know, I always tell her father o, since we are the ones who sent Wúràọlá to learn, we must suffer from the knowledge she now has. We are enjoying the money we spent."

Aunty Caro chuckled. "How is our young doctor? We've not even seen her shadow here for months."

"Someone that doesn't have time for herself. She's okay, it's even because of her that—" Yèyé stopped midsentence. "Good evening o, what I was saying made me forget to greet you people. Maria? Ṣèyí? Ẹniọlá, àbí? And . . . Fúnkẹ́? Good evening, everybody, gbogbo riín ni mo kí o."

They all replied at once, their voices mingling with hers as she continued speaking to Aunty Caro.

"Ehen, so it's even because of Wúràọlá that I'm here. Can you imagine that this girl has not sewn the lace we picked for my birthday? Since three months ago that we chose this material, you'd think my child would have picked a good style for the day. Ótí o, maybe she's waiting until two days before the ceremony, I don't know. But I've brought." Yèyé leaned over and picked up the golden paper bag she'd dropped beside her on the sofa. One side of the bag bore a large photo of Yèyé smiling, while the other sides had several smaller ones of her seated, standing, mid-dance. Embossed below the largest photo in bold green letters:

CHIEF (MRS.) CHRISTIANAH ÀLÀKẸ́ MÁKINWÁ.

YÈYÉ BỌ́BAJÍRÒ OF ÌJẸ̀SÀLAND @ 50.

Yèyé thrust the bag towards Aunty Caro, who reached into it to bring out a bundle of green lace fabric, before setting it down on the floor beside Yèyé's feet.

"You can keep the bag," Yèyé said. "That's the souvenir we are giving out with the aṣọ-ẹbí. I've wanted to bring one for you since, but I keep forgetting."

"And it's very fine." Aunty Caro picked the bag up and examined it.

"Àbí, Láyí had them made in Àkúrẹ́. Plenty, like one thousand o, and he brought them in time for me to use them to package the aṣọ-ẹbí. Very thoughtful boy. I like the finishing, very beautiful."

"Why won't it be fine, when you're this beautiful?"

"Caro, this my wrinkled face."

"It's your face that makes it beautiful, Yèyé, you look like a sisí still."

Yèyé's plump cheeks creased into a smile.

"Did Doctor send a style for the cloth?"

"Wúràọlá? Style kẹ̀, she said she will call you by tomorrow, but, please, if she doesn't, help me to remind her. You have her number? Good. Make sure she doesn't choose any village style, please, help me to find something current. Sew something that fine girls are wearing nowadays. You know we are pleading with God that we can celebrate her wedding soon. But faith doesn't exclude effort, àbí, Caro? She needs to dress well for that party. Please sew a good style."

"Don't worry, Yèyé. I'll call her tomorrow to remind her about the style."

Yèyé stood. "You still have Wúràolá's measurements, àbí? That's good. She has lost a little weight since she resumed work, but it's not too much. Just sew and bring it first, then we can make adjustments. When will it be ready, Caro?"

"Give me two weeks."

"For what? No o, I want it next week. That way she can try it and make adjustments."

"Yèyé, I already have a lot of work, but I will try to have it ready next Saturday, that's not up to two weeks."

"Saturday?"

"I will bring it to the house myself."

"Caro, don't let's fight again o. Don't disappoint me this time."

"Yèyé, I'm sorry about last month. My generator had a fault ni."

"It's every day that your generator gets spoilt, Caro. Sha, don't disappoint me this time if you don't want God to disappoint you."

"May God not disappoint any of us," Aunty Caro said.

Yèyé picked up her handbag. "Àmín o, let me start going now, I still want to stop in the market before going home."

"What about the clothes you asked me to adjust the last time you came?"

"Ah, you know I forgot about that. Óyá, bring it." Yèyé held out her hand.

"No, let me help you carry it to the car." Aunty Caro disappeared into the other room that served as a store.

"Ótí o, there's no need for that."

Aunty Caro reemerged, carrying a bulging black poly bag. Yèyé reached for it, but Aunty Caro stepped back, leaving the other woman grabbing at air. Both women laughed.

"Caro, okay, let one of your people carry it. Go back to your work. What's the boy's name again?"

"Ẹniọlá. Ẹniọlá, óyá, come."

Ẹniọlá went to them, took the bag from Aunty Caro and followed Yèyé out of the shop.

Her driver was standing by the car door, stretching. When the driver opened the door for her, Yèyé nodded at Ẹniọlá to hand the poly bag over to him.

"Bàbá," she said to the driver, "the change we collected from the filling station? Help me to give this boy two hundred naira out of it."

The man brought a rumpled note out of his breast pocket and gave it to Ẹniọlá.

"Thank you ma. God bless you ma. Thank you ma." Ẹniọlá prostrated to Yèyé, who nodded and said nothing.

She looked up before getting into the car, and Ẹniọlá followed her gaze. The dark clouds were on the move, sailing swiftly elsewhere.

❖

Ẹniọlá left Time Wait for No 1 after dark.

On his way home, he reached into his right pocket again and again to touch the two-hundred-naira note. His two-hundred-naira note.

He could buy new socks, two good pairs that had no holes for any of his stupid schoolmates to laugh at during the morning assembly. No, he should buy a schoolbag. The straps of the one he was using now were both frayed, and once they snapped, he knew his mother would tell him to manage it until the term was over. If he bought okrika, he might even get a bag that had designer symbols embossed on it. Nike, Puma, maybe FUBU. The secondhand sellers always had good things that were even better than new. His mother said that all the time. But would two hundred naira really be enough for a bag? Maybe he should keep the money until he had more and could buy a bag and socks. He didn't know how he would get more money, but Yèyé's generosity felt like a beginning. She had singled him out, from all the other apprentices; maybe he was lucky now and the richer customers would dash him money when they came to the shop. He could save until he had one thousand or two thousand. Maybe he should ask Aunty Caro about how much his apprenticeship fee was; if he learnt enough skills from her, he could put himself through university. She'd told him that when he started the apprenticeship. The only reason she had not gone to university herself was because she did not have the brains to finish one year of secondary school. He on the other hand was in his fifth year already and going to finish. If he worked hard and stayed up to read at night, he might be able to pass the exams next year. He couldn't start staying up to study tonight, though.

There had been no electricity on the street for weeks, but he did not need streetlamps to guide him home. He could walk down the road wearing a blindfold and still be able to tell where each building stood. Maybe he should use the money he saved to buy a rechargeable lamp so he could read at night. Aunty Caro would let him charge it in her shop.

He was going past the now-collapsed clinic where he had been born when he heard someone call his name. He looked left into a side street and saw Hakeem coming towards him.

"You did not come to watch the match this evening," Hakeem said, falling into step beside Ẹniọlá.

"I went to Aunty Caro's place."

"You should have come."

Ẹniọlá shrugged. All Hakeem did, he seemed to do effortlessly. While every time Ẹniọlá approached a football field after school, he could hear his mother saying, *Don't play away your future.* Hakeem played almost every day and still managed to top the class. Maybe he stayed up to read at night. But most likely not; he was one of those people who were just too lucky, people like Yèyé, who were born to have all the good things. Ẹniọlá touched the two-hundred-naira note again; maybe he was one of those people now.

"I scored three goals," Hakeem said.

Of course. In the dark he could see the glint of Hakeem's grin.

"A hat trick, did you hear? I stupefied everyone."

Ẹniọlá grinned and made a sound, something to indicate marvel.

"Astonishing, I know." Hakeem's teeth shone in the darkness as he flashed another grin. Ẹniọlá was familiar with this grin, because he saw it every other day on his sister's face. It was the happy outburst of someone who was used to being adored for coming first in class, winning prizes, doing better than everyone else at almost anything.

"Where are you coming from?" Ẹniọlá said, before Hakeem could begin to describe the hat trick.

Hakeem held up two sticks of white candle. "My mother sent me to buy these. The rechargeable lamp has gone off, and she's terrified of kerosene now because of all those explosions."

A little girl ran towards them, pushing an old bicycle tire along with a stick and screaming with glee. Hakeem turned to watch as she passed by.

A motorcycle appeared in the distance and almost immediately seemed to be inches away from them. Ẹniọlá ran out of its path. Then he looked back and saw Hakeem still staring at the girl, his back to the approaching motorcycle. Without thinking, Ẹniọlá dashed back and pulled Hakeem out of the motorcycle's way as it roared past, close enough for the rider's elbow to jut into Ẹniọlá's side.

"Orí riín dàrú, hin ti fẹ́ kú!" the motorcyclist yelled at them.

"Do you want to die?" Ẹniọlá shoved his trembling hands into his pockets. "What were you looking at?"

"She was wearing only one shoe," Hakeem said. "Didn't you see? Her left foot was bare."

"And so what?" Ẹniọlá began walking away.

Hakeem caught up with him, but neither of them spoke until they got to the fenced building Ẹniọlá's family had lived in when his father still had a job. The one Hakeem's family had moved into right after they had to leave.

"Good night," Hakeem said, and pounded his fist on the gate. Soon it would creak open to admit him into the paradise Ẹniọlá had lost.

Ẹniọlá quickened his steps without replying.

He was almost home when he felt a tap on his shoulder. Startled, he looked behind to see it was Hakeem.

"What?" Ẹniọlá said.

"I forgot to express my heartfelt gratitude," Hakeem said. "You saved my life."

"I don't think so."

"Don't be modest. Thank you, Ẹniọlá," Hakeem said, and turned away.

And as he watched him walk back to the blue house, Ẹniọlá realised that Hakeem was the only boy in his class who still called him by his name. The only one who did not taunt him daily with the memory of a life that could have been if he had been lucky enough to attend the Unity school.

4

Kúnlé was waiting beside her hatchback, wearing that black blazer he liked so much. It was as though he could not feel how thoroughly the sun had banished that morning's harmattan chill.

"Aren't you braising?" Wúràolá said.

"How about, 'Good morning, my love,' or 'It's so nice to see you'? Maybe, 'How sweet of you to have come over,' or better still, 'I was just about to call you back,'" Kúnlé said, counting off each statement on his left hand.

"All of that too, but this jacket, aren't you hot?"

"You were not picking up my calls."

"I wasn't picking up anyone's calls."

"I have become anyone to you now." He paused to make air quotes when he said "anyone," and she watched his hands move in two arcs. Those hands. She thought about them in waking hours, how his long fingers tapered towards the nailbed, how impossibly nimble they were inside her.

"I am just one of the random people who call you, ehn?"

Wúràolá rummaged through her bag for the car keys. "Calm down, please, you know what I meant. Even my mother has been calling about the dress for her birthday and I haven't been able to . . . Where did I put this key, sef? I've not had a minute to myself until now."

"We are taking my car." Kúnlé pointed across the car park to his blue Sentra.

"I want to drop something in my back seat." Wúràolá dangled her keys in Kúnlé's face. "And who told you I'm going somewhere with you."

He laughed and leaned against her car, effectively blocking access to the driver's door.

"Shift, let me open my door," Wúràọlá said.

"You were not picking up my calls."

Most times, Kúnlé seemed to enjoy bickering. He called it sparring and said he found it stimulating. Wúràọlá didn't mind the makeup sex that followed what she thought of as fake fights. She played along, performing a belligerence he could later brag about pleasuring into a pliant state. What bothered her was how tenuous that playful mood was; a so-called sparring session could escalate into combat at some point during the pause between one word and the next.

She held his wrist and tried to pull him out of her way, but he didn't budge or smile. Full combat. Even though she'd put all her strength into that pull, he'd remained unmoved. Maybe he hadn't been bickering at all; sometimes it was hard to tell.

"And you did not even bother to call back or text."

She shut her eyes briefly. Had his voice risen several pitches with each word?

"Are you shouting at me?" she asked.

"You are saying I do not have a right to be upset?"

"I'm actually just asking if you're shouting at me right now."

"What's the implication of that? Doesn't that imply that ignoring my calls does not warrant a reaction from me? Is that the sort of thing we are doing here?"

Wúràọlá glanced around the car park. There were fewer cars and people because it was a Saturday, but that also meant his voice would carry. To her right, some men had stopped putting an empty stretcher into an ambulance so they could stare at them. Yes, it wasn't just that her exhausted brain was amplifying sounds: Kúnlé had been shouting.

"Could you just step aside?" She kept her voice low and even. She wasn't about to start any nonsense in public.

"What do you want to put in your car that's so important, you think it's okay to ignore my questions?"

"Kúnlé, let me just drop this textbook. We can speak when we're on our way. Step aside."

"And if I don't?"

Wúràọlá cocked her head to one side. "Seriously?"

He shrugged and folded his arms across his chest. In those movements she caught a glimpse of what he had been like when they were younger and still attended the same primary school, before they were sent off to different boarding schools for secondary school. Kúnlé would often trail his father to IEMPU meetings, because their parents had assumed he was friends with Láyí. Although the two boys were classmates, two years ahead of Wúràolá, her brother's circle of primary school friends had formed before Kúnlé's family moved into town and never widened to include him. Wúràolá and Láyí used to laugh at him back then, imitating his shrugging and arm folding, motions he made right before going off to rat them out to an adult for teasing him and mimicking his *I will tell my daddy and I will tell your mummy*. He was even pursing his lips now; all that remained was for him to stomp away. Wúràolá almost laughed but managed to suppress her mirth.

She went around the car, opened it up from the passenger's side and flung her *Clinical Neuroanatomy* in the back seat. She had stuffed it into her handbag earlier in the week, hoping—foolishly, in retrospect—that she would at least have some time to skim through. It wouldn't help if her consultants thought she was a spectacular idiot when she started her neuro rotation in a few weeks. Everyone was an idiot when they got to neuro; the goal was to be an average one. She had not gotten around to opening the book all week, but her handbag's strap was frayed from carrying it back and forth. Time for that switch to a laptop bag. She slid into the front passenger seat, then leaned towards the driver's side to switch on the engine.

Wúràolá let the engine roll for about a minute before turning on the air-conditioning. She engaged the central lock and relaxed her chair all the way back. The cold blast of air enveloped her as she smiled at Kúnlé. He glared back. She held her smile in place, certain and pleased that it was infuriating him. For a brief moment, she wondered if he might leave her and go to his car. She would follow him if he did. It didn't make sense to drive that morning. Her hands had been trembling by the time she left the ward minutes ago, and that after she'd made it through the night only with the help of a can of energy drink that another house officer had given her. Kúnlé tapped the glass and motioned for her to open the door. She wound down the glass just enough for him to stick a finger inside the car.

"You need to apologise for shouting," she said.

He grimaced. "Have you said you're sorry for ignoring my calls?"

"I was working when you called."

"You could have texted?"

"Do you really know what doctors do when they're on call?"

"You're so full of yourself."

"Okay. Please, remove your finger, let me wind up well."

"Wúrà, just open this door, abeg."

"Abeg" was not an apology. At least not in that tone, but it would have to do. She was too tired and hungry for drama. If they got over this and set out, she could eat soon. She let him in and braced herself, ready for an extended rant. Kúnlé said nothing before reversing in a swift motion that jolted her.

"I thought we were taking your car." She sat her chair up and fixed the seat belt. "Can we buy food? I'm hungry."

Kúnlé did not respond.

"Can we stop at Captain Cook before going to your place? We could just get meat pie to start with? What do you think? Okay, play dumb. Just don't ever talk to me like that again. I'm warning you now. Why were you shouting in front of everybody, because of what?"

He slowed down as they approached the hospital gate. Somewhere between secondary school and university, whiny, sulky Kúnlé had become the sort of person who now wound down his window to greet the security guards, with such an abundance of *E kú isé, Major,* and *Well done, Officers,* that he was passed through without being asked to open the boot for inspection. His manoeuvre collapsed the gap between aspirations and reality with two words, "Major," "Officers." The men and woman he had greeted had no title beyond security guard. They could not be further away from the military cadres that their beaming responses to Kúnlé's flattery suggested they had once aspired to. Although they were employees of the hospital, there were rumours that their roles would soon be outsourced to private firms. She wasn't sure if Kúnlé's practice of endearing himself to strangers in this way was exploitative or benevolent. Perhaps as with many acts of generosity, it was both. Once they drove out of the hospital, she turned to stare at the stalls and houses that whizzed by until they all blurred into a dream.

It was raining. She was in the middle of a highway, kneeling over a baby whose wails rose above the claps of thunder, listening for his heartbeat. Somewhere a grandfather clock was striking midnight. She could hear the roar of speeding trucks and tankers, the screech of tires on wet tarmac, the screams of a vulture that had perched on her left shoulder. She could not hear the baby's heartbeat. Even when the highway emptied out and the rain stopped as the sun rose, she couldn't hear the heartbeat. When the vulture's cry merged with the baby's into one relentless scream, Wúràọlá tried to drop him but found that her hands were glued to him.

She awoke to the sound of pounding, and that noise was a respite. This time the dream had stopped before another vulture perched on her head. For weeks after he died under her watch, she'd dreamt about the baby almost daily, waking up to wonder if there was anything else she could have done for him. It was better now; these days she only dreamt of him during the snatches of sleep she caught while on call or just after.

Pius: 2.2 kg, vaginal delivery at 29 weeks gestational age. Apgar scores 5 and 6 at 1 and 5 minutes.

Wúràọlá tried to refocus her thoughts on his twin, Priscilla, the one who lived.

"Can you remember your dream?" Kúnlé asked.

"What?"

"You were making this strange sound, like crying. I figured you were dreaming about something."

Wúràọlá thought of Priscilla, how at the precise moment when Pius's breath shuddered to a halt, Priscilla, possessor of a healthier pair of lungs, had woken herself from sleep with a piercing wail that could not be muffled by the walls of her incubator.

"Do you remember?"

"No," Wúràọlá said. She had spoken to Kúnlé about Pius a few days after he died, but she had never told anyone about the dreams.

"We should get down before this batch of pounded yam is finished," Kúnlé said, switching off the engine.

They were at Ọlọ́hunwà, right across from the area where Kúnlé's parents had built their house. People said the Cokers had chosen to build so close to the state capital because Kúnlé's father was still planning to run for governor. When she asked Kúnlé about it, he had told her it was just a useful coincidence. His mother was the one who had inherited those plots of land from her grandmother.

Kúnlé was a newscaster with the Nigerian television authority in the state capital and was working on being transferred to Lagos or Abuja. He was sure the letter would come through any day now and therefore had not bothered to get a flat of his own. Instead, he remodelled his parents' boys' quarters and commuted to work every day.

Wúràọlá yawned. She wanted to crawl into a bed. "Why don't we just buy the food and take it to your place?"

"My parents are still at home," he said, and left her in the car.

Kúnlé's parents seemed to expect her to spend all her time in their living room when she came over, as though she was still the little girl who followed her mother to Mothers' Union meetings when Professor Cordelia Coker hosted them. Whenever the older woman ran into her in their compound, she often gave Wúràọlá a tight-lipped smile that made her wonder if the animal sounds Kúnlé made when he came had somehow carried over the stretch of interlocking tiles between the boys' quarters and the duplex where his parents lived. It was just easier to spend less time there when his parents were home.

She got out of the car and went towards the buka. Outside, men and women pounded yam in wide mortars, the noise muffled, then sharp as pestles hit the white mound before punching through to the mortar's bottom. *Po-ki-po.* Kúnlé was already inside the buka. She sat next to him on a bench and reached for the drink he had ordered.

He laughed. "You're so stubborn."

"You're the one who hasn't apologised for shouting, but I'm stubborn?" She took a long drag of his stout. He put a hand on her shoulder and pulled her close.

"Aren't your parents attending that funeral in the cathedral?" Wúràọlá asked.

Kúnlé glanced at his watch. "Yeah, they should leave in about an hour. We could take the food home if you want to say hello to them."

"Keep making jokes and I'll go spend the day being the girlfriend of their dreams, let's see where that leaves you."

"I've missed you," he said into her hair.

The waitress came then, and they ordered the same thing they always ate here. Pounded yam with ẹ̀fọ́ rírò. Goat meat for her, bush meat for him.

❀

Before that morning, they had not seen each other for two, no, three weeks, and God, she had missed this. Him curving his body around hers after they made love, his breath fanning her temple, the weight of that arm he always flung across her stomach, the comforting heat of his body. Pleasure was the easy part for her. It could be known and understood. Rise euphoric on the wings of adrenaline and dopamine. And now oxytocin for the descent. Love, well, that was too nebulous. As unstable and unknowable to her as Kúnlé's shifting moods. He'd asked her about the phone calls again after they finished eating and lapsed into silence all the way back to his place. But then he was reaching for her breasts right after they got in, and he clung to her now as though all was forgotten if not forgiven. When he began to snore through his mouth, she extricated herself from his grip and went to take a shower.

He did not have any lotion, just a large jar of Vaseline that would probably last him another year. She made do with her hand cream and pulled on one of his shirts before going into the living room. She lay on the sofa, hoping the shower would induce sleep. The sofa was something Kúnlé's parents had used when he was younger, and she remembered sitting on it once, trying to fish out a sweet that had fallen into the space between the cushions. She managed to find it before her mother noticed, but once she popped it back into her mouth, Láyí had shouted, *Dirty girl!* She nearly choked on the sweet when her mother and Professor Cordelia stopped their conversation to stare at her. Láyí tattled on her. The mothers laughed about it and continued their chat. That night, when they were back home, Wúràọlá sat at the dining table with an empty plate in front of her while her family had dinner. According to her parents, she had disgraced the Mákinwá family in public and did not deserve to eat anything for the rest of the day. Later that night, Láyí sneaked into her room with two slices of bread and an apology.

Wúràọlá turned and turned but could not find a comfortable position. The bed would be better, but she did not want to go back there. After rearranging the cushions one more time, Wúràọlá picked up the TV remote and channel surfed. She settled on Channel O because they were playing "African Queen."

Kúnlé had given her the CD when he visited her in Ifẹ for the first time. That copy lived in her bedside CD player for months, unchanged. Later, she bought a second copy and listened to it in her car until the disc was so scratched, it could only play one track. The week before her finals, when her only break from studying came when she drove back to the hostel for a quick shower, "Keep on Rocking" had been the reprieve her mind needed. While her friends yelled at her from the back seat, she would take one hand off the wheel to jab the car's roof when 2Face asked her to touch the ceiling. She released her braids from the ruffle that held them in a doughnut, swinging them back and forth as 2Face crooned. And, of course, getting naughty in the plantation? That called for taking both hands off the wheel so she could punch the air. Grace, the first friend Wúràọlá made in medical school, usually sat next to her during the drive and always managed to sleep through it all. The CD had stopped playing before her finals were over, and she never got around to replacing it.

The second woman to show up in the frame on "African Queen" had always fascinated Wúràọlá. Her hair was cut so low, what was left was barely visible. Sometimes Wúràọlá longed to be free of her tresses, but there were so many things to consider. Her too-big ears might stick out like a rabbit's. She could end up looking like a plucked chicken. Her mother would shoot her I-can't-believe-I-wasted-nine-months-of-my-life-on-you looks for at least one decade or until one of them died. Still, she leaned forward every time the shaven woman came into the frame, studying similarities in their facial structure as a predictor of how successful her own transition might be. People had been known to survive her mother's death stare. Láyí was still breathing two years after abandoning a medical career. She could take her chances too.

Someone knocked, and before she could get up from the sofa, Kúnlé's father stepped into the room. He stared at her for an endless moment, taking in the fact that she was dressed in Kúnlé's shirt. She sat up, knelt to greet him and, having done that, did not quite know what to do with her body, to stand or to sit. She stood, pulling at the shirttail so it was closer to her knees.

Professor Babájídé Coker was tall and potbellied, the sort of man agbádás suited. He'd been bald for as long as she had known him, but his moustache was full and seemed to grow darker as he grew older. Her mother was certain that he dyed it regularly. So far, Wúràolá had restrained herself from asking Kúnlé about this.

"How are you sir?" Wúràolá asked.

"Dr. Mákinwá, good to see you are here," Professor Coker said, staring at her knees, which in spite of all her pulling at the shirt were still exposed.

"African Queen" was gone, and a song she did not know was on television. Four women writhed and crawled across the floor of a warehouse, circling a bare-chested man who was singing into a boom mike. Would it be rude to pick up the remote and switch off the television?

"Where is my son?"

"Kúnlé?" Was it right to leave the television on as the bare-chested man thrust his hips towards the camera?

Professor Coker raised an eyebrow as though to ask her, *Do you know of any other child of mine I'm not aware of?*

"He's in his room sir," Wúràolá said.

"Since you are here," Professor Coker began, in a tone that said she shouldn't be there, "why don't you tell him I'd like to see him?"

"Yes sir," Wúràolá said, happy to leave the living room.

Kúnlé was splayed on his stomach with one hand hanging off the edge of the bed. She gathered his clothing with one hand while she tapped him with another. He might as well be fully dressed when he went out to see his father. Not that it mattered, the man could decipher what had transpired, and it couldn't be the first time he'd found a woman in Kúnlé's living room. When they were teenagers, everyone envied Kúnlé because he was the only one whose parents allowed girls to sleep over. Professor Coker knew his son was sexually active, but the look he'd given her said he did not expect her to be.

Kúnlé finally woke up when she pinched his shoulder.

"Kíni?" he said, sitting up in bed and reaching for her.

She sidestepped him. "Your father is here. He wants to see you."

Kúnlé stretched and glanced at the wall clock. "They're back?"

"They must have skipped the reception. At least I think he did. I don't know if your mum is back yet."

She handed him his clothes piece by piece, giving him a fresh shirt from the wardrobe. When he left the room, she began to put on her own clothes, tucking her rumpled blouse into her skirt as though she was about to head to work. She walked into the living room carrying her shoes and bag, ready to speak with Professor Coker like an adult now that her hair was pulled away from her face the way it had to be on the ward.

"Where is he?" she asked, surveying the room.

Kúnlé shrugged. "He must have gone back to the main house. Let me go and . . . you should come with me."

"Yeah, I should," Wúràolá said, putting on her shoes.

"Did he say anything?"

"He seemed disappointed that I was half naked on your sofa."

Kúnlé laughed. "They like you."

He often spoke of his parents as a single unit, as though he had grown up to see them as fundamentally indivisible.

"You mean they like my parents," she said.

"They think you're from a suitable family."

Her parents thought the same of him. In the first manifestation of any interest in her romantic choices, her father had taken to asking her about Kúnlé's welfare. *He was coughing during that last newscast, is he well? How is he getting on with the job? How far with his transfer?* The conversations ended with her father remarking that Kúnlé was a good man, his parents were good people, he was from good stock. She had learnt through bans on the kinds of girls she could invite to visit when she was in secondary school that her father's view of anyone was refracted through his opinion of their parents. And it was clear that, as far as he was concerned, Kúnlé was the best boyfriend Wúràolá could ever have, one he already deemed eligible to father his grandchildren.

Kúnlé held the door open for her as they left the boys' quarters. He tried to hold her as they approached the main house through a maze of ixoras and hibiscus plants, but she shrugged him off. He seemed to find this amusing. It was impossible for him to understand what she knew and had explained to him every night she had refused to stay over. That his parents would judge her with different standards than the ones they judged him with—hell, her own parents would too. It did not matter that the Cokers thought she was from a good family, whatever that meant; the fact that she acquiesced, no, asked to have sex with Kúnlé was not going to be seen by his parents as a good thing. It had been clear to her since puberty that the extent of her desires would not be judged suitable. Boys were supposed to want sex, and she was to fend them off; that was what good girls did so they would not disgrace their families.

Wúràọlá wished she was the sort of woman who no longer cared about this. If only so she could enjoy what she wanted without guilt and look Professor Coker in the eye as he'd stared her down. But she did care. What he thought of her, and, more important, his wife's opinion, mattered to her.

Wúràọlá had been trying to copy Professor Cordelia Coker's perfectly arched brows since she stole her first eye pencil from her mother's dressing table. Her admiration had veered so close to utter worship during her ophthalmology rotation in medical school that she'd briefly considered going into the same specialty so that Professor Cordelia might be her mentor. The woman had become a consultant before she was thirty, and a professor at forty-six. She spoke in a voice that tinkled and seemed to float through hospital corridors in a cloud of floral perfume. Half of Wúràọlá's class had developed a crush on her. Wúràọlá was glad Professor Cordelia wasn't the one who had walked into Kúnlé's living room. Her husband would probably tell her about what he had observed, but that was better than seeing those perfect brows furrow in disappointment.

They went in through the kitchen, past the maid, who was scrubbing a pot, to the dining room, where Kúnlé's parents sat next to each other, eating a meal of boiled plantain and vegetables.

"How are you, my dear?" Professor Cordelia said, waving Wúràọlá into the chair opposite her.

"I'm very well ma, thank you."

"Would you like some plantain? There should be some left."

"No, thank you ma."

"Are you sure? This is fresh wòròwó, try it with some plantain."

"I'm fine ma."

"We ate after I picked her up." Kúnlé sat beside Wúràolá.

"Oh, you've been around for a while?"

"Yes ma. We, uhm, I was with Kúnlé."

"Oh, I see."

"I didn't see your car when we came back," Kúnlé's father said.

"It's in the hospital sir," Kúnlé said. "You wanted to see me?"

Professor Babájídé glanced back and forth between Kúnlé and Wúràolá.

"You can tell him now, she's his . . . they're together," Kúnlé's mother said.

"Maybe I should excuse myself." Wúràolá stood.

The maid came into the room to clear the plates.

"Bring some juice for Wúrà," Kúnlé said to her.

"Sit down, Wúrà." Kúnlé's mother turned to her husband. "Wúràolá, ni now, why are you acting like this? This is Òtúnba Mákinwá's daughter."

Kúnlé's father leaned back in his chair. "Hmmm. I know your father has high hopes for you, and I do too. You are not a common girl."

Wúràolá willed herself to hold his gaze this time. His intimation was clear: her father's goal for her did not include having sex with her boyfriend and trying to take a nap on his sofa after like a common girl. Professor Coker was telling her this. Professor Coker, whose wedding photos featured Kúnlé as the ringbearer.

"What's this about?" Professor Cordelia asked. "Wúrà, are you struggling in the hospital? House job can be hard, àbí? One day you're a student and the next patients expect you to have all the answers."

"She's doing well, she's actually one of the better ones," Professor Babájídé Coker said.

"I'm glad to hear that, Wúrà, you've always been bright."

The maid returned with a carton of juice. Everyone was quiet until she poured some into a glass and left the room.

"Anyway, Kúnlé, what I wanted to tell you."

"Yes sir."

"The party chair came for the church service, and we had a chance to talk before he left. He thinks the next election could be our chance. Their people are happy to field me, but I need to start preparing now and I want you to be involved."

"Congratulations sir," Kúnlé said.

"Well, let's wait until the nomination is ours—so much can change quickly in politics."

Professor Cordelia squeezed her husband's shoulder. "I have a good feeling about this time."

Professor Babájídé gave Wúràolá a pointed look. "Things change very quickly in politics, that is why we keep conversations about this within the family until it is necessary to share it with outsiders."

"Of course sir." Wúràolá swirled what was left of her juice around in the glass. She would need to finish it, then wait for ten to fifteen minutes before she could make her exit. Her mother had drilled this into her; you waited for a while after being served refreshments so that your hosts did not think you were a hungry person who had come only for their food or drink.

"So, Kúnlé, start coming up with some ideas. The party will give us some media people, but you need to be my point person. I want you fully in charge, and that can only happen if you have better ideas."

"Yes sir. I will work on it. Congrats again sir."

Professor Cordelia rubbed her husband's back. "Allow yourself to enjoy this moment."

Wúràolá drank what was left of her juice, making sure to leave a film at the bottom of the glass, one did not drink every single drop. Her congratulations sat on her tongue, light as a wafer, already melting away. She was not going to congratulate Kúnlé's father, not after the comment about her being an outsider. This was what she had been nervous about when she began to develop feelings for Kúnlé, how the overlaps in their lives could complicate things. His father would not have been so strident with any other person, but because she was his friend's daughter, he felt he could scold her as though he were her father.

"How are your rotations going?" Professor Cordelia's clinical practice was in the Ifè hospital, so Wúràolá would not interface with her throughout her house job.

"They're fine ma."

"It was good for you to come here for training, you'll have more exposure," Professor Cordelia said.

Wúràọlá smiled. "Yes ma, I took three deliveries when I was in O and G."

"That would have been unlikely in Ifẹ̀ with all the resident doctors on ground."

"Yes ma, I'm glad I decided to come back. It's intense, but I'm learning."

"I hope it's not too overwhelming?"

"She's not getting enough sleep," Kúnlé said.

Professor Babájídé Coker grunted as he stood up. "That's what she signed up for, resilience is half the job."

"That doesn't mean she should be too sleep deprived."

"If she has time to spend in Kúnlé's boys' quarters, she's not that sleep deprived." Professor Babájídé left the dining room and went into the living room.

"Don't mind him, Wúrà. He's stressed out about this whole election thing." Professor Cordelia sighed. "Kúnlé, we better buckle up for the next two years."

Wúràọlá stood. "I think I should start going home now ma."

"Back to your house officers' residence?"

"No ma, I go home if I'm not on call during the weekend."

"That's really good of you, my dear."

"I'll go say goodbye to Prof."

She went through the archway that demarcated both spaces.

Professor Coker was seated in an armchair, cracking his knuckles in loud pops while he stared into the distance.

Wúràọlá coughed to announce her presence.

Professor Coker shifted in his seat.

"I'm leaving sir." She forced a smile.

"All right. Give my regards to Ọ̀túnba and Yèyé."

"Yes sir, I'll tell them."

"Wait, Wúràọlá. Come here."

Wúràọlá went closer to him.

"Look, if you and Kúnlé plan to get married, and I assume you do, you need to make sure you don't get pregnant before the ceremony. The cathedral will not conduct your wedding if you're pregnant, the new vicar is strict about those things. You understand me?"

Wúràolá nodded, fixing her gaze on the spot where light from the chandelier pooled on Professor Coker's bald head, making it gleam.

❀

Kúnlé's mother insisted that Wúràolá should not drive until she had gotten some rest.

"Sebì, Kúnlé will have to pick his car up from the hospital anyway? Let him do that after getting you home safe."

"He plans to do that on Monday ma. He'll come with Prof to the hospital and then leave for work from there."

"How many minutes would it take him to get you home?" She turned towards the house. "Lakúnlé! It's right next to my glasses."

They were standing by Wúràolá's car, waiting for Kúnlé to bring a Mothers' Union souvenir bag his mother wanted to pass on to hers.

He emerged with the cloth bag, holding it aloft until his mother nodded to indicate he had gotten the right one.

"You'll take her home, àbí? Do you have any other plans for the evening?"

"Well, Wúrà likes to play superwoman and sometimes I let her," Kúnlé said.

"Óyá, give him the keys, you can even take a nap while he drives."

Kúnlé began talking about the campaign once they got into the car.

"We can't let it look like a campaign yet, we'll have to continue the community projects for a while and make sure his name is more prominent on them."

"Projects? Isn't there just one borehole?"

"We can easily drill like six more, distribute them across the state. Then some skills acquisition thing for young people. We can put his photos on the poster for those."

"What skills?"

Kúnlé frowned. "As in?"

"What skills are you going to focus on? For the skills acquisition thing?"

"Anything—what are women learning these days? Beadmaking or what?"

Wúràolá shook her head. "How would I know?"

"You're a woman?"

"That doesn't make me an expert on what skill all women are learning at this point in time. At best, I can give you anecdotal information, but you should probably try a feasibility study?"

"It could be baking or whatever. And something just for the young guys too."

"What's your plan, really?"

"I'm explaining it to you."

"I mean your father's platform, what will it be? You can refract everything you do through that. It could be your organising principle."

"Better healthcare, good roads, good education. We can't put those on the skills acquisition project yet. We should find a way to use his initials, that can go on everything as soon as we roll out, so it'll be consistent with what we'll use for the campaign proper. What do you think?"

"Everyone calls him Prof B in the hospital, to differentiate him from your mom, I guess."

" 'Prof B' is too weak. Babájídé Coker. We could use Professor BJ."

Wúràolá stifled a chuckle. " 'BJ' might be unfortunate."

It took a moment for him to get it.

"PJC then, Professor Jídé Coker. We need to keep the 'Professor' in somehow, it's more impressive."

"I was asking you about the measurable metrics. Better healthcare, what does that mean? More primary health centres? How many? Is he improving pay for state doctors? Post-qualification training? Working conditions? Isn't that what you're going to build his media campaign around? Even this skills acquisition thing, you're sounding like it's really about getting his photos on posters, not the youth."

"You don't understand politics."

"That's condescending."

"It's a fact." His hands tightened around the steering wheel. "You don't fucking know everything."

"Lakúnlé Coker." Sometimes this was enough, calling him a fuller version of his name could reset his senses.

"I'm sorry, but the point I was trying to make is, that's not how politics works in this country, okay. We need simpler messaging, something that can fit on a bag of rice or salt. You know that will be the main campaign material, right? Rice, salt, yards of Ankara. You can't print a comprehensive plan on those. Maybe a seven-point thing."

Wúràọlá thought of Pius's slack mouth and toothless gums. How he'd died with his eyes squeezed shut as though he had realised, even as he fought to breathe, that this world was a terrible thing to behold. She turned away from Kúnlé. She should have insisted on driving herself. If she'd kept the window down, the wind and noise would have kept her awake until she got home.

They drove past the Obòkun statue and headed towards the central mosque.

"Stop," she said when they were in front of the mosque.

Across the road, traders had set up tables to display everything from fruits to shoes, VCDs, and clothes. She leaned over to wind down Kúnlé's window, then signalled a vendor.

He ran towards the car.

"You get *Face 2 Face*?"

"You say wetin?"

"*Face 2 Face*. 2Face album, you get am?"

"That one, yes na. Na everybody get am. Wait small, I dey come."

"I would think your dad has a plan for healthcare, at least. I mean, he just has to. Talk to him about that before you settle on a campaign strategy. You'd be amazed by how much that would connect with people. People are dying unnecessarily, Kúnlé. You don't even want to know."

The vendor returned with the CD, and Kúnlé paid before she could open her wallet. He honked at a taxi before pulling ahead of it into traffic.

"He had right of way." She took the CD out of its paper jacket.

"That doesn't mean he should be slow."

After she slid the disc into the player and skipped all the way to "Odi Ya," Wúràọlá shut her eyes and let the song silence Pius's final gasps. She surrendered to the percussion, 2Face's voice multi-layered—thrice? Four times? And the unexpected delight of that transition to acapella towards the end.

"I don't like the way you talk to me."

"How? I was just trying . . . What did I . . . ? I'm too tired, Kúnlé. Can we discuss this later?"

"You're always too tired."

"As a matter of fact, yes, and you're not helping. You are also stressing me out. Can we just drop this?"

"You've not even acknowledged my apology."

"Saying 'I'm sorry but—' doesn't count as an apology, not that it matters. I said let's forget this. Can't I just listen to music in peace?"

"I just meant that people want something different in this country, okay? All those things you're saying don't win elections here, okay?"

"Dear God. Okay, whatever."

"I feel you don't even care enough to fight for us."

"Fight for what? Kúnlé, I like you a lot, you know that. Just. Please."

"You know I love you." He placed a hand on her knee and squeezed. "Even though you're so fucking stubborn."

Wúràọlá did not say anything. At some point after they started dating, he had convinced himself that she was obstinate, and when he brought it up, it could be in anger, as an insult, or because he was somehow turned on by the idea or saw her refusal to yield on a certain point as a challenge.

He moved his hand up her thigh. Turned on, then. Always better than when he thought she was challenging him.

They had turned into the street her parents had named after themselves because they were the first to move there. Her parents' home was the second on the end, and only its roof was visible behind barbed-wire-topped walls.

The gate was opened after Kúnlé honked twice, and Wúràọlá waved at the guard as they drove in. He responded with a mock salute. The house itself was set back from the gate, leaving room for a lawn wide enough to host novelty football matches and an artificial waterfall that was turned on only when her father had special guests. They drove up the gravelled driveway that led past the front door to a concrete-floored rectangle where cars were usually parked beside a cluster of masquerade trees.

Kúnlé put an arm around her shoulder as they cut across the lawn to the house.

Wúràọlá rang the bell twice, then reached into her bag for her keys.

The door burst open before she could slip the key into the lock, and Mọ́tárá nearly walked into her as she stormed out of the house, wearing shorts and a tube top that their mother would never have allowed Wúràọlá to wear in the house when she was a teenager.

"You, you've forgotten how to greet your elders?" Wúràọlá said.

Mọ́tárá kept stomping her way towards the cluster of masquerade trees.

"Sorry about that," Wúràọlá said to Kúnlé. "That girl is something else when she's in a mood."

Kúnlé shrugged. "She's a brat."

It was something she had said many times to Kúnlé, her parents, Láyí and Mọ́tárá herself, but it irritated her to hear Kúnlé repeat it. She shook his arm off her shoulder as they stepped into the house.

There was no one in the living room, but the television was on upstairs. Wúràọlá could make out Bukky Wright's voice. Her mother was watching *Ṣaworoidẹ* again.

Kúnlé reached for her hand as they went up the stairs, but she pretended not to notice this and went ahead, taking the steps two at a time. The landing spilled into the family room. It was closed off to most visitors except those who, like Kúnlé and his parents, were practically family. Family friends, as her parents called them.

Wúràọlá's mother was reclining on one of the long sofas with her feet propped on two pillows. Her face brightened when she looked away from the television and saw Kúnlé.

"Lakúnlé, Lakúnlé! Wúràọlá didn't tell me you were coming."

Kúnlé was prostrate on the floor, chin touching the edge of a throw rug. "Good afternoon ma."

"Pẹ̀lẹ́, mummy ńkọ́? Àti Professor?"

"They are both fine ma. They send their regards."

Wúràọlá hugged her mother from behind. "Yèyé o. The one and only Yèyé Bọ́bajírò of everywhere, any other one is a counterfeit."

"Wúràọlá omo Yèyé, you finally remembered your mother today, ehn?"

"Just confess that you've missed your favourite child."

"Get up, Lakúnlé, get up. Omo dada, sit down, please." Yèyé glanced at Wúràolá. "Such a well-behaved young man. You don't get so many of them nowadays."

Kúnlé was always welcome here, and most times, Wúràolá was happy that his presence animated her mother. Once in a while, though, her mother's warmth towards him annoyed her. She could feel that anger now, incipient and bitter, flooding her throat with something like bile.

This same woman had walked past Nonso without responding when he prostrated, chin to the floor, in the same spot Kúnlé had been just now. Poor Nonso. He had stayed that way after Yèyé left the family room, rising to his feet only when a door was slammed shut down the corridor. She had met him at a freshers' welcome party when she was in her first year of medical school and he was in his third. They did not become friends until her second year, while they worked together on the health week committee. By the end of her third year, they had become friends who spoke on the phone until their batteries ran out. Friends who hung out together on Valentine's Day and fell asleep in each other's arms. Friends who sometimes kissed and felt each other up. Sometimes they saw other people but stayed friends, catching up and sharing horror stories, touching each other only in the gaps between exes. She'd always trusted more in the permanence of friendship than in romance anyway, or so she said, until he asked to come visit her during the break when she was home with her parents, and everything between them became tremulous with promise.

Nonso sat on the edge of his seat throughout the rest of his visit, too nervous to touch the bottle of Coke she'd served him, glancing at the corridor as though worried her mother might return brandishing a machete. And she did return. Nonso prostrated again, but Yèyé focused her gaze on Wúràolá. *Don't you dare bring any strange boy into my house ever again.* Nonso hurried out of the room before she continued, *Wòó, if I see that Igbo boy in this house again, ehn, God will surely receive someone's soul into heaven on that day. You even brought him upstairs! Kíló fa effrontery kè?*

Throughout, their thing—fling, love affair? Whatever you could call that year they never defined—Nonso had been worried about how his own parents might react if he introduced a Yorùbá person to them as his girlfriend. She'd never imagined that his ethnicity could be an issue for her family. Not with her mother who went on for days about how blessed she was whenever Mr. Okorafor led Bible study during midweek meetings at the cathedral.

They had decided over text that it would not be worth the upheaval to try for more, their friendship was enough. And though the sex stopped, they stayed in touch even after he graduated and moved to Nsukka, their lengthy conversations lapsing into silences that sizzled with possibilities. It did not feel like a breakup until he got married.

Wúràọlá was invited to the wedding but did not attend. All their mutual friends flooded Facebook with photos from the event, and she spent the day feeling raw and broken, as if she had watched him exchange vows with another woman. The wife was taller than Nonso, and her wedding dress accentuated the tiniest waist Wúràọlá had ever seen on an adult. As she scrolled through the photos, Wúràọlá wondered if this was what he had wanted all along. Some light-skinned woman who could have stepped off the cover of a magazine. It was easier to think of his wife in those terms and not consider that she had graduated at the top of her class in Ìbàdàn with distinction in surgery and paediatrics. Dr. Rukayat Quadri. Not just a Yorùbá woman, a Yorùbá *Muslim*. Someone worth every possible upheaval.

"Can't you hear me? I said you should get Kúnlé something to eat."

Wúràọlá removed her arms from Yèyé's shoulders. "I need to change."

"Get him the drink first."

"Has Rachel gone to the market?"

"What is my maid's business with your guest?"

"Kúnlé, you can wait, right? You're not starving to death?"

He could end all of this by telling Yèyé he didn't want anything, but no, he just smiled and said nothing.

"Wúràọlá, how many minutes would it take you to bring something up from the kitchen?"

"Mummy, I'm coming, let me change."

Wúràọlá turned away and went down the corridor to her room. She was kicking off her shoes when her mother walked in.

"When did all this disrespect start, Wúràọlá? I was asking you to do something and you were telling me you needed to change. And in front of a guest. Is your blouse made of scorpions and soldier ants?"

Wúràọlá unzipped her skirt. "If you care so much, why don't you get him something by yourself?"

"I should go and do it by myself?"

Wúràọlá folded the skirt, careful not to look up at her mother's face.

"Me? Wúràọlá? I'm now too small to send you on an errand?"

"You could just tell the maid."

"You want to start sending me on errands in my own house now, àbí? You have grown so big you are now my elder."

"I didn't mean it that way ma."

"When did you become Láyí or Mọ́tárá? I expect them to behave like this, not you, Wúràọlá, no, not you."

"Can I at least put on some clothes or you want me to go out there in my chemise?"

"Don't bother. I will take care of your guest myself, but just know that this is unbecoming. It doesn't matter if you saw him eat a mountain earlier, you offer him something. Especially when it's lunchtime, that's just what you do."

When the door slammed shut behind her mother, Wúràọlá sank into a chair and took off her blouse. This, this constant opining about her behaviour, was why she preferred to spend her weekends in the dingy rooms the hospital assigned to house officers. She wouldn't have come home if she could trust Láyí or Mọ́tárá to help their mother plan her birthday party. At best, Láyí would send money and Mọ́tárá would manage not to get in the way. The details were always up to Wúràọlá. She was the one her mother planned and worried with, and this birthday was important to her. While she was not sorry and did not see why she needed to serve Kúnlé before doing anything else, she would apologise to her mother when he was gone; it was the only way to keep the peace.

❖

One knock and a pause, two knocks and a pause, three knocks and a pause. Ọtúnba smiled. His first daughter was at the door. He liked to think this was their code, that Wúràọlá knocked this way only when she was standing outside his study. Four knocks and a pause. He glanced at his watch. Almost eight p.m. Maybe dinner was ready, and she'd come to ask if he wanted the food brought up to him. It was the first time in weeks that Wúràọlá had been home for the night; he would rather go downstairs so he could spend some time with her while the family ate. Five knocks and a pause.

Ọtúnba shut the book he was reading and leaned back in his chair. "I didn't lock it this time. Come on in."

Wúràọlá walked in.

"You finally decided to come make sure your old people are still alive."

"Ahn ahn. But I still came home a few weeks ago. Good evening sir."

"You lost my number between then and now?"

"I've just been so busy." Wúràọlá winked. "I'm trying to be rich like you."

Ọtúnba laughed and nodded at one of the chairs on the other side of his desk.

"Professor Coker is here to see you."

"Oh, and here I was thinking you came to spend some time with me."

"Yèyé has plenty things for me to do. I've already annoyed her today, so I'm just going to be a good girl and please her this evening."

"You could always buy her a gold necklace, that solves everything."

"My peace offering can't be that expensive," Wúràọlá said. "Prof is in the family room, should I tell him you'll join him soon?"

"No, no. You can bring him here."

"All right sir."

Ọtúnba left his desk as Wúràọlá shut the door behind herself. He settled into one of the easy chairs beside the bookshelves to wait for his friend. This time there was no knocking before the door was opened.

"I should have called ahead, but I just happened to be in the neighbourhood and decided to stop by for a quick visit," Professor Coker boomed after he entered the study.

"You're never a visitor here." Ọtúnba waved Professor Coker into the chair beside him. "What are you going to drink?"

"Yèyé has given me something already."

"How's Cordelia?" Ọtúnba asked.

"She's all right."

"No complaints?"

When the Cokers had just moved into town, Cordelia was in and out of the hospital almost every month. If she didn't have a fall, it was some home accident. Then there were those allergic reactions she had so often. They left sections of her face swollen for days or weeks. It had bothered Ọ̀túnba for a while, and he'd pressed his friend to make sure there was no mould in the house they lived in at the time. As the years passed, though, he came to accept this as part of Cordelia's constitution. She still showed up at gatherings with some part of her face swollen because of an allergy, but she no longer seemed to end up in the hospital as much as before.

Professor Coker shrugged. "She's fine, sends her regards."

"And Kúnlé?"

"Didn't you see him this afternoon? He came to drop your daughter off."

"I told my wife not to disturb me," Ọ̀túnba said. "I wanted to finish proofreading our proposal for that Ministry of Labour contract. I can't always trust those boys at the office, I have to make sure I look at everything well before they submit."

"Oh, so I'm interrupting."

"It's okay, I needed a break from it anyway."

"Okay, let me make this quick, then." Professor Coker cleared his throat. "I wanted to tell you in person that I've decided to run for governor."

"Finally?"

"I've picked up the nomination form."

"Fantastic." Ọ̀túnba clapped his friend on the back. "This is wonderful news. We should toast this!"

Professor Coker shook his head. "We'll toast when I win."

"Coker, enjoy life small now. I have some champagne in the fridge here. Let's celebrate."

"There will be time for that. What I need from you now is more important."

"And what is that?"

"Your support."

"Of course, you have it. Why do you even have to ask?"

"I mean your money. I need you to invest your money and your name in this campaign. Your name is very important."

Ọ̀túnba sighed.

"You know what I mean, your father is still legendary in this town. So I'm thinking campaign posters that say, *Courtesy Ọ̀túnba Adémọ́lá Mákinwá* or better still *Ọ̀túnba Adémọ́lá Àrẹmú Mákinwá.*" Professor Coker leaned forward. "Include your middle name, since that was also your father's name. People still pray with his name, you know, so they can have that kind of money."

"I'm going to need that drink." Ọ̀túnba went to the mini fridge that sat next to his desk. He took his time fishing out a bottle of beer. He wasn't surprised that Coker had come to him. Everyone talked about how much money Ọ̀túnba's father had in his lifetime, but few considered how diminished the assets were once they were split thirty-something ways. Not that Ọ̀túnba was destitute. He had inherited enough cash to last him decades of no work, and on top of that, he had worked hard. Switching from legal practise within two years of being called to the bar, he'd set up a company to import sundry supplies for government offices. The military was still in power when he started the company, and his brother had connected him to all the right people who could approve his proposals. Business slowed for a while when the military left power. He even ran the company in the red for over a year before understanding how the new power brokers in Abuja operated.

"Think of it as an investment," Professor Coker said as Ọ̀túnba returned to his seat.

"Is Fẹ̀sọ̀jaiyé not running for this same governorship seat?"

"Look, I have the party chairman's backing. He told me this personally, that's why I went to pick up the form. This is my moment, and I'm not going to miss it or back down because of Fẹ̀sọ̀jaiyé. These are just rumours anyway, it's not as if he has declared publicly that he's running. I promise you, it will be a good investment."

Ọ̀túnba gulped some beer. Investment. That was what Fẹ̀sọ̀jaiyé's people had called it too. Invest in the campaign, reap returns in contract allocations. A phone call, a signed note or a text from Fẹ̀sọ̀jaiyé would more often than not smooth Ọ̀túnba's path to approval whenever he was bidding for a contract in the ministries that Fẹ̀sọ̀jaiyé's committee had supervision over. His monthly contributions towards Fẹ̀sọ̀jaiyé's next campaign weren't bribes. They were investments.

"And for all we know, Fẹ̀sọ̀jaiyé might want to retain his seat in the House of Representatives."

"The thing is that I've also invested in Fẹ̀sọ̀jaiyé. His people approached me during the last elections, and I donated to the campaign. I've also been donating monthly to a future campaign since then, so I'm almost sure the man is planning to run for governor."

"Oh, oh, I see." Professor Coker drummed his fingers against his knee. "This is how your business picked up?"

"Fẹ̀sọ̀jaiyé has been helpful, yes."

Ọ̀túnba took another gulp while Professor Coker stood and began pacing the floor.

"Your support would really be valuable to us, Démọ́lá."

"It's two things. One, this is a business decision, okay. I have to consider what is most viable. The other thing is, I've only been in the same room with Fẹ̀sọ̀jaiyé maybe twice. I don't even have his number, but once I reach out to his personal assistant, I get what I need within days. He's held up his end. And you must know he has a reputation for being vengeful." Ọ̀túnba paused to finish the beer.

"I've heard stories."

"I must think of what it would mean for me and the business if I switch camps now. It's one thing for me to pull back from contributing to Fẹ̀sọ̀jaiyé's funds, it's another thing to be visibly in support of another candidate. That man could decide to block anything my company wants to do in Abuja. All the plum ministry contracts could be gone just like that. You see, there's a lot for me to consider."

"Ọ̀túnba, there's one thing you've missed out."

"And that is?"

"We could be in-laws very soon. Your investment in my ambition is not just about business. It's an investment in Wúràọlá's future too."

"You think these kids are that serious?"

Professor Coker nodded. "I know my son is."

"Hmmm. Okay, I'll factor that in." Ọ̀túnba leaned forward. "Sit down and let's talk numbers. How much are you looking at initially?"

Wúràọlá's peace offering to her mother was a visit to Aunty Caro's. They left the house late and arrived there after dark, so she had to light their way with her phone's torchlight when they were about to cross the gutter. She held her mother's hand as they walked across the rickety plank.

"Why doesn't she fix this thing?"

"You know, I still told her the last time I came here? And I've been warning her since. It's probably money."

"She just needs to find better wood and nail it down. I'm sure she has enough money for that."

"Thank you." Yèyé let Wúràọlá's hand go as they stepped into Aunty Caro's front yard. "You shouldn't think you know everything about how other people live their lives."

Wúràọlá laughed. "You're always certain about how I should live mine."

"That's different, you're a part of me."

Aunty Caro opened the door before they knocked. She was holding a kerosene lantern. "Yèyé, good evening. Dr. Wúrà, I called and called about your style."

"That's why we are here, Caro. She will choose something now."

"I'm sorry, Aunty Caro. I wanted to call you back, but I kept forgetting."

Aunty Caro led the way into her living room, then went across the corridor to get some magazines, taking the kerosene lantern with her.

On the centre table, a candle flickered, pooling even more wax onto a wax-encrusted milk tin. Shadows slid across the room as its flame wavered. Unable to dispel darkness, the candle had settled for rearranging it.

Aunty Caro soon returned with a stack of magazines that she thrust into Wúràọlá's arms.

"Thank you for accommodating us at every hour, Caro," Yèyé said.

Aunty Caro smiled and set the kerosene lantern down on a stool beside Wúràọlá.

The magazines were mostly old copies of *Ovation;* the most recent was at least two years old. There was nothing Wúràọlá particularly liked, and when she finally pointed out a floor-length long-sleeved dress, her mother shook her head.

"No way, this one would look like you're coming from a convent."

"I think it will be nice."

"You're a sisí, there is no reason to dress like an old woman. Look good o, there will be many eligible bachelors at that party, Láyí is inviting many of his friends from Lagos. Show your legs or your shoulders, this thing would cover your whole body."

"What about Kúnlé? Your good boy from a good family? You don't like him again?" Wúràolá asked.

"I like him," Yèyé said, "but this one, that after one year, you people are still doing boyfriend and girlfriend, maybe he is not your destined husband."

"Seriously? Destined?" Wúràolá laughed. "Àfi destined husband, Yèyé o."

"Boyfriend and girlfriend when you people are not fifteen. I like him o, but he has not married you yet, he has not even engaged you, so we must keep our options open. Àbí, he has spoken to you about marriage, ni? Let me know quickly o, so I can plan."

Wúràolá picked up another magazine and angled it towards the kerosene lantern. Kúnlé had talked about marriage a few times, but she was not about to tell her mother that just yet. She could do without the swarm of advice that would come first in person, then via text messages and phone calls that would wake her up at dawn. When she'd turned twenty-three and was, thanks to various university strikes, still in her third year of medical school, her mother had gone from telling her to face her books and not follow any foolish boys to being interested in every detail of her romantic life. It was one of the reasons she'd felt confident about allowing Nonso to come over.

Wúràolá was twenty-eight now, and though her mother had so far not talked to her about how thirty was looming, her aunties exercised no such restraint. Some of them had made it clear that Wúràolá was already doing overtime as a single woman, twenty-five was the prime marriageable age, and after that she was past her sell-by date, might end up with a widower or worse a divorcé or, nightmare of all nightmares, alone. She had stopped picking up their calls more than a year ago, but most were undeterred and would often call her from an unknown number. It was disconcerting. To feel that she was already failing at something she did not even know until recently mattered so much to anyone. She had thought she knew what was required of her. Get good grades and become a doctor. But the closer she had gotten to earning a medical degree, the more it seemed to pale into nothingness in their estimation, since she didn't have a man waiting to marry her when she was done. At her induction party, she had felt bewildered when her mother's sisters told her to wait in the house until Kúnlé arrived so they could emerge to greet guests together. Two aunts had scrutinised the dress she wore for that party and found it wanting; she was sure they would have strong opinions about whatever she chose for her mother's birthday.

"Aunty Caro," Wúràọlá said, "this is the style I want. I like the classic cut."

Aunty Caro glanced at the page and then at Wúràọlá's mother.

"You don't want to hear word, Wúràọlá, this style is too old-school, you will look like a grandmother," Yèyé said. "See the woman that is wearing it here, sef, she looks like someone that has sixteen children and forty-eight grandchildren. At my birthday, is that how you want to look?"

"But that's what I like."

"Ha, Caro, help me talk sense into this girl now. When she's not SU, it's only nuns that should be dressing like this when they are not married, and those ones have kúkú married Jesus now."

"Yèyé, I think this style will look good on Dr. Wúrà o."

"Caro, ìyen nípé, you are a Judas. Let's join our voices and talk sense into this girl."

Aunty Caro laughed. "She should wear what she likes."

"Thank you, Aunty Caro," Wúràọlá said.

"This is not about what she likes, it's about the thing that she wants, ehn, and what that thing likes."

"And what do I want?"

"Husband now."

"Aunty Caro, please, when will the dress be ready? Can you send someone to bring it to me at work?"

"Wúràọlá, you are going to take the advice of a woman who has never had a husband in this crucial matter?"

"Mummy!"

"Caro knows I'm joking. Àbí?"

"Dr. Wúrà, stand up and let me take new measurements," Aunty Caro said. "You have lost weight since the last time."

5

The Biro kept slipping from Ẹniọlá's hand. His palms were slick with sweat. His face felt damp, his armpits sticky. He capped the Biro and placed it in the middle of his geography notebook. It was impossible to follow what the teacher was writing on the board, and he could copy it from Hakeem later. His notes were always better anyway; he underlined titles and subtitles with a green felt pen and wrote definitions with a red Biro.

It was Monday but there had been no mention of school fees during the morning assembly. In previous years, the names of students who were still owing the school would be read after prayers and those who, like Ẹniọlá, still showed up in spite of Mr. Bísádé's warnings would then be punished before being sent back home. But that morning, the assembly had ended without any punishments, and Mr. Bísádé had disappeared before it was even over.

Ẹniọlá rubbed his palms against his arms until his fingers felt dry. He was always the last person to pay school fees in his class, so he was used to the punishments. It was this delay that he found unbearable. He had planned to go to Aunty Caro's shop once he was told to leave the school. He wished he were there already, folding wrappers and forgetting about the laughter of schoolmates whose parents had paid their school fees on time.

When Mr. Bísádé showed up in his class just before the first period ended, Ẹniọlá was almost happy. Whatever would happen was going to happen now, and his hands could finally stop shaking.

The class rose as Mr. Bísádé entered the room. "Good morning sir, we are happy to see you sir. May God bless you sir."

"Sit down, sit down," Mr. Bísádé said. He was carrying his three-pronged whip.

"Should I—" the geography teacher began.

Mr. Bísádé glanced at his watch. "Five minutes, no, don't wait, you can go."

The geography teacher gathered his notebooks from a desk in the corner and left.

"I'm coming from a special meeting with the proprietress, and I am happy to announce to you that our school management has decided to be merciful to those of you that are still owing us school fees." Mr. Bísádé cleared his throat. "Instead of sending you home today if you have not paid all of your fees, we will extend a grace period. So, if you have paid half of the fees, you will not be sent home until after the midterm tests."

Someone began clapping and stopped. Ẹniọlá heard some of his classmates sigh with relief, but he could not join them. His parents had not paid one naira out of the total of five thousand naira that was due. He chewed his nails as his classmates began to speak to each other. Who knew if they could even pay two thousand five hundred naira anytime soon? He thought of the two-hundred-naira note Yèyé had given him; he had refolded it this morning and slipped it into his breast pocket. What percentage of two thousand five hundred was two hundred?

"Silence!" Mr. Bísádé shouted. "Better. So, this is how we will be doing things from now on. If you have paid half of your school fees, you have nothing to worry about until after midterm. Now let me move on to the perpetual debtors who have refused to pay anything."

Paul laughed.

"We will have mercy on you too. You will not be sent home this week, in fact you will have a grace period that will last for two whole weeks, but, every morning, I will serve you breakfast. And when you get home, you will remember to tell your parents that they should pay your school fees so that your teachers will not go hungry. What did I say? They should pay your school fees so that . . . ?"

"Our teachers will not go hungry," the class chorused.

"Louder."

"Our teachers will not go hungry."

"Good. We will allow you to attend all your classes, but first of all we will serve you breakfast every day, and if you don't want the breakfast, you can stay in your father's house. Do you want to know what the breakfast is?"

"Yes," Paul shouted.

"I say, do you want to know what the breakfast is?"

The whole class mumbled a yes.

"You will be served six strokes of this." He cracked the whip. "Every morning throughout the period of grace and mercy. After the two-week grace period is over, you will be sent home. Is that clear? Good. If you have two heads, ehn, come to this school after this grace period without paying at least fifty percent of your fees. When I finish flogging you, you will forget your name. Now, the people who will enjoy this morning's breakfast." He reached into his pocket, pulled out a foolscap sheet and unfolded it.

Ẹniọlá clasped his hands to keep them still.

"Just two in this class, that's good. Óyá, clap for yourselves. Sandra Oche and Ẹniọlá Òní, you people are clapping too? Eyin chronic debtors. What are you clapping for? Come out here and eat your breakfast, jàre."

Ẹniọlá and Sandra went to the front of the class.

"Óyá, Sandra, ladies first. Where do you want it?"

Girls could choose to receive their strokes on their left hand or on their backs. The boys had no options, Mr. Bísádé always lashed them across their backs.

Sandra was already crying so hard she could not answer. She stretched out her left hand and the punishment began. The poor girl retracted her hand after each stroke and held her wrist, jumping on the spot several times before stretching her hand out again. Her sobs were overshadowed by outbursts of laughter from some of their classmates.

As Sandra sobbed her way back to her seat, Ẹniọlá stepped forward, turned his back to Mr. Bísádé and stiffened his body for the first stroke. He was ready. He had worn three singlets under his uniform that morning. The first five strokes fell on his lower back, and the singlets cushioned the impact. But Mr. Bísádé aimed higher with the final one, and the whip coiled itself around Ẹniọlá's neck. Still, he stopped himself from crying out and instead bit his tongue until he tasted blood. He spread his lips in what he hoped looked like a smile as he walked back to his seat. No one was laughing at him. He had managed to stay still this time.

When Mr. Bísádé left, Sandra's friends gathered around her to say they were sorry, but their attention only caused her sobs to intensify. Ẹniọlá wanted to scream at her to shut up. He wished the next teacher would come in on time so the girls who had gathered around Sandra would stop glancing towards him with pity in their eyes. At least in previous years he could leave the school right after he was flogged and nurse his shame in private. Now he had to sit here and be pitied by his mates. If this was mercy, he did not want it.

❈

The landlord had never bothered to paint the two-storey building where Ẹniọlá's family rented a room on the ground floor. Like most houses on their end of the street, its walls were an accidental mix of concrete grey and mould.

On his way home from Aunty Caro's shop, Ẹniọlá saw that his father was crouched beside one of those walls, holding a kerosene lamp. At first, Ẹniọlá thought he was trying to scrape off some of the mould, but as he got closer, he saw that the ground was covered with gaàrí.

"Good evening sir," Ẹniọlá said.

His father nodded without looking away from the ground.

The wasted gaàrí was enough for at least three meals, and he did not need to crouch to see that there was no way to separate it from the sand. If it had been in a heap, they could have scooped the top off and might still have been able to get a meal out of it.

"What happened?" Ẹniọlá asked.

"Bùsọ́lá." Ẹniọlá's father stood. "She fell and scattered everything. Let's go, there's nothing we can do."

Inside, Bùsọ́lá was sitting on the bed, and their mother had knelt beside her.

"It's painful," Bùsọ́lá cried as their mother wiped her scraped knee with a piece of cloth that had been dipped in kerosene.

"You have to stop shouting," Ẹniọlá's mother said. "I've told you to be more careful. See what has happened? Thank God it wasn't your head that hit the ground."

"Do we have more?" Ẹniọlá's father asked.

Ẹniọlá's mother shook her head. "I used all the money I had to buy that gaàrí."

"I will go and see my former principal tomorrow," Ẹniọlá's father said. "Maybe he can lend us . . . Last year, he promised me that, if I needed something small."

"People promise all the time, but when you get to their house nobody opens the door when you knock." She patted Bùsọlá's leg. "What are we going to eat tonight?"

Ẹniọlá leaned against a wall. He reached into his left pocket, slid his fingers over the two-hundred-naira note. The money could buy some gaàrí and some palm oil.

"That man is different," Ẹniọlá's father said.

Ẹniọlá's mother reached out to her husband; he gave her the lamp. She held it close to Bùsọlá's knee and nodded in satisfaction. "Lie down," she said. "You'll be fine in the morning."

She gave the lamp back to her husband. "What do we do tonight?"

"Do you have any money?" he said.

"If I have money anywhere on this earth, would I let my children starve?"

Ẹniọlá wrapped his fingers around the note. His mother opened her mouth to say something, then closed it. She folded her arms and stared at the wall opposite her. When she spoke, her voice was hoarse. "Will we sleep without food again?"

"I have some money," Ẹniọlá said.

His parents turned to him, their eyes wide with surprise, as though he had just told them he was pregnant with twins. Even Bùsọlá sat up in the bed.

He brought out the two-hundred-naira note. Both parents reached for the money at the same time, and their hands bumped over Ẹniọlá's. He gave the money to his father.

Ẹniọlá's father examined the note as though it might be fake.

"Where did you get this money?" his mother asked. She was standing over him, hands on her hips, a lecture about honesty brimming in her eyes.

"One of Aunty Caro's customers gave me."

His mother pressed her thin lips together.

"You can ask Aunty Caro," Ẹniọlá said. "I am telling you the truth."

His mother drew him into her arms. He winced when she pressed her fingers into the tender spot where Mr. Bísádé's whip had bruised his neck that morning.

"Thank you, my Ẹniọlá," she said. "May you have children who will care for you."

6

Wúràọlá's aunties descended on Wednesday. They came bearing complaints and coolers brimming with fried meat, live goats and exclamations, jars of Aboniki Balm, rebukes and bags of rice.

Complaints and coolers of fried meat—nítorí Ọlọ́run, how could Yèyé hold a party like this in her compound? When it was not Wúràọlá's tenth birthday or Mọ́tárá's naming ceremony. This was her fiftieth birthday, kẹ̀! How many people lived long enough to turn fifty? Their mother—may she continue to be pampered in the afterlife—did not see the sun rise beyond her fortieth birthday. And this after their father had bid the world farewell before he turned forty-nine. Wasn't that enough reason for fiftieth birthdays to be celebrated by all their offspring as a victory? A great victory called for a beautiful and big celebration. And thanksgiving. Yes, of course, and thanksgiving. Were there no event centres in this town? Yèyé should have come to Lagos, Ìbàdàn, Abuja to have this party. Was money a problem? They could all have contributed more towards the celebration. If they had done so for every sister when she turned fifty, why wouldn't they be eager, happy, excited to do it for the youngest? If Yèyé did not have money to throw a party, couldn't she have confided in her older sisters? Was Yèyé too proud to ask for help? Had the sibling cord that bound them all together weakened with time and distance? No? Why then was this important party being held on Yèyé's *lawn*? If only they had known about this before they arrived, something could have been done. It was on the invite? Why would they read that when they spoke to Yèyé every week? Why didn't Yèyé use her mouth to tell them this was where the party would be held? Invite kọ́, insight ni. Anyway, this must not be allowed to repeat itself when Yèyé turned sixty. No way, not when they would all be alive and well to make sure it did not. By the special grace of God. No one would be missing, in the mighty name of Jesus. No one would be on a sick bed, by the mercies of the Almighty.

Now, who would carry the coolers inside so that Mótárá could count the meat?

There were five coolers, one from each sister. Two hundred pieces of turkey from Aunty Bíọlá, who should not have bothered to bring anything. Not after all she had done for Yèyé and her sisters since their parents died. Only God could reward that woman o, only God. Four hundred pieces of chicken from Aunty Àbẹ̀ní. That one, she had always been so generous. Did Wúràọlá know that when they were all children, Aunty Àbẹ̀ní would divide her fish into two so that Yèyé could have more? And if Yèyé asked, she would even give her the whole fish. One wasn't supposed to pick favourites among siblings, but Aunty Àbẹ̀ní's heart had always been so good. Aunty Sùnmbọ still managed to give one hundred pieces of ram in spite of all she was going through with that her stupid husband. She was so brave, ehn. Two hundred pieces of pork from Aunty Mosún. Yes, from that pig farm she just started. And would Wúràọlá believe that Aunty Jùmọ̀kẹ́ had brought two hundred pieces of beef? Beef? Why would anyone bring beef? They all knew two cows would be killed on Thursday, they'd even contributed money to buy one of them. One should not speak ill of one's elders, but Aunty Jùmọ̀kẹ́ should really be more thoughtful.

Live goats and exclamations—Mótárá was all grown. Mótárá was rude now, her mouth big enough to swallow a house. See her tiny shorts and her low-cut top? Was that a tattoo? No? But why would she even draw one with a felt pen while she was still living at home? How could she be so bold? What would she do when she went off to university? Yèyé had to do something about this Mótárá before she became a real disgrace. Better put her in a private university, a Christian one. Yèyé had made arrangements for someone to smoke and stew the two goats they had brought, right? No?

Rebukes and bags of rice—Yèyé was sure she had prepared well for this party? Really? One of the pairs of shoes Yèyé planned to wear were too high for her age. Didn't she remember how Jùmọ̀kẹ́ fell on the dance floor at her own fiftieth birthday party? Those shoes were too low, did she not remember how good the photos Jùmọ̀kẹ́ took on her fiftieth birthday looked? The shoes were not the right shade for her outfit, though. Yes, yes, yes, yes and yes. And they could have brought something for her from Lagos, Ìbàdàn, Abuja. Yèyé needed to stop behaving as if she did not have sisters. They wanted to help, why wouldn't she let them help? Was there space in her store for the bags of rice she had said they should not bother to bring? Why were they sisters if they could not give her rice for her birthday? Rice o, ordinary rice. And Yèyé kept telling them there was more than enough. What did Yèyé know? They had all celebrated their fiftieth, they knew better. There was no such thing as too much rice at a party. It was always better to have leftovers.

"You can give that rice away after the party, when they've all left," Wúràọlá said when her mother paused to take a breath.

"Do you want to speak with them?"

"I don't really have much time ma. I stepped out of the ward to take this call, and I need to go back in very soon."

"I can put you on speaker, they've all been asking after you."

"I spoke with Aunty Jùmọ̀kẹ́ before she left Lagos this morning."

"What about Aunty Àbẹ̀ní?"

"I spoke with her son last week."

"You should be calling her more."

For many years now, Aunty Àbẹ̀ní had been convinced she was dying of something that her doctors had not diagnosed. Whenever Wúràọlá allowed herself to be pushed and prodded into calling the healthy (as any blood test or CT scan could see) sexagenarian, the discussion quickly turned to some new silent killer Àbẹ̀ní was sure had invaded her body.

"I will see her when I come home."

"And when is that?" Yèyé asked.

"It's still Friday."

"You can't leave tomorrow?"

"There's no way for me to do that."

"No way? You're sure? You could just come home after work tomorrow, spend the night and go to work from here on Friday morning."

"I can't, I'm on call tomorrow." She'd managed to switch her weekend call with a colleague, but there were no takers for Thursday night.

"Even Láyí will get here before you."

"I'll be home before four-thirty."

Yèyé sighed. "Aunty Jùmòké keeps rubbing Aboniki on my knees and ankles every five minutes. She still thinks it will cure my limp. These people want to kill me with their wahala."

"Why don't you put all of them in a hotel?"

"My sisters? Hotel? Hotel, what is that? We are talking about my sisters here. What is wrong with you?"

"Okay, sorry. I was just trying to be helpful."

"Helpful how? Is it because you have to share a room with your own sister because they are around? They are right, I've spoilt you children. Me and my sisters shared a room when our parents were still alive. Six of us o, in a single room. Now you want me to put them in a hotel because you can't share a bed with Mótárá? Anyway, I have to go, Aunty Mosún is making ègbo, I think it's ready and I don't want them to finish it before I get downstairs. Better come home, she's cooking èwè tonight so we can have múké èlèwè tomorrow morning. You know me, I don't have time to spend twelve hours cooking beans, come and enjoy it now that she's around."

❀

When Wúràolá got home on Friday, several men were setting up canopies on the lawn while others were offloading plastic chairs and tables from the back of their rental company's truck. The aunties watched the men, calling out intermittent instructions. They sat on plastic chairs arranged around a plastic table that was laden with several plates of meat. Each woman was nursing a soft drink except for Aunty Àbèní, who only drank water.

Wúràolá knelt before them in greeting and rested her chin on the table while they responded to her pleasantries. Most businesses were doing well, some children still refused to hear word, would Wúràolá talk to them? She was such a good example. One or two husbands were still useless, but all in all, glory be to God for life. She stood up and hugged each person, then took a chicken drumstick from one of the plates on their table.

"Ehen, Wúrà, before you go in, what kind of beer do you people have in this house? Not the one we are using for the party tomorrow. Just what you have in the fridge."

"Aunty Mosún, should you still be drinking?" Aunty Jùmọ̀kẹ́ asked before Wúràọlá could respond.

Aunty Mosún shifted in her seat. "Is that how you should talk to your elder?"

"I'm just advising you." Aunty Jùmọ̀kẹ́ slapped the back of one hand into the palm of the other.

"Advise yourself, Jùmọ̀kẹ́. The person that is a doctor is not saying anything, it's you that wants to be adviser general. I kúkú don't know which university gave you a medical degree so that you can be distributing advice." Aunty Mosún squeezed Wúràọlá's hand. "My dear, when you get inside, ask someone to bring me a bottle of stout. Any cold one. You know what I mean? Send me a bottle that has done serious jail time in the fridge."

At least a dozen plastic chairs had been brought into the living room to supplement the furniture there, and every single one was occupied. Yèyé bustled from one end of the room to the other, directing Rachel and Mọ́tárá as they served her well-wishers. As Wúràọlá made her way towards the staircase, she recognised women from Yèyé's market association, leaders of the diocesan Mothers' Union and several wives of IEMPU members. She greeted everyone in her path then dashed upstairs, sure that if she loitered long enough in the living room, Yèyé would assign some urgent task to her.

She was surprised to meet her friends Tifẹ́ and Grace in the family room. They had been invited to the party, but she was not expecting them to show up until the next morning.

"Babes, you didn't say you would arrive today."

Grace moved in for a hug while Tifẹ́ stayed seated, sipping a glass of wine.

"I hope we are welcome," Tifẹ́ said.

"Of course, why would you not be welcome here?" Wúràọlá sat beside Tifẹ́ and squeezed her shoulder. "Thank you so much, babes. How have you been? How is Ifẹ́? You were both able to get away? Neither of you is on call tonight, àbí?"

"Which question do you want answered first, madam?" Grace asked.

"Where are you going to sleep tonight? This house is so full I have to share my room with Mótárá, my aunties have taken almost every room. Maybe we can find a hotel?"

Grace grinned. "Kúnlé already took care of us."

"My Kúnlé?"

"He made all the arrangements, booked the hotel, paid for everything. Such a sweetheart."

"Ehen? We spoke just before I left the hospital, and he didn't tell me about this."

"I'm changing my opinion about that boy o." Tifè swirled her wine.

"And which opinion did you have before?" Wúràolá asked.

"Say na fuckboy now," Tifè said.

Grace scoffed. "You think every guy is a fuckboy."

"And when have I been wrong?" Tifè asked.

"Abeg, abeg, don't start this one now," Grace said.

Tifè set her wineglass on a stool. "The truth is bitter, babes."

"Have you been given something to eat?"

"Kúnlé took us out once we arrived. We went to that pepper soup place around Akewusola. I'm not ashamed to say I had three plates," Tifè said.

"You've seen him? He didn't mention this at all when we spoke."

"That would have ruined the surprise," Grace said.

"So you don't need anything? Kúnlé has already taken care of you?"

Tifè rubbed her belly. "Good care, sef. That guy, he might be one of the better fuckboys. You know, fuckboy lite. Mo wà impressed, sha, just a little bit."

❧

Kúnlé and his parents joined them for dinner that night. Six plastic tables were set up outside to make a long dining table that had Wúràolá's father at the head at one end. Yèyé, Kúnlé's parents and Láyí sat next to him while Grace, Tifè and Kúnlé flanked Wúràolá at the other end of the table. The aunties sat in the middle with Láyí's pregnant wife, Odúnayò, telling her all about the ever-dwindling proceeds from the palm oil trees they had inherited from their grandfather. For some reason, Mótárá had decided to set her chair closer to the canopies, far away from everyone else.

Grace was barely touching her food. She wanted to write her primaries before the national youth service but couldn't decide between internal medicine and paediatrics.

"It's not as if you can start working when you pass," Tifẹ́ said, spilling grains of rice from her mouth as she spoke. "You still have to serve Nigeria first, so calm down and think it through before you decide."

"It'll most likely be internal medicine. I just have to decide soon, I'm going to register for the exam next week."

"Why the rush?" Tifẹ́ asked.

Grace shrugged. "When are you going to write yours, Wúràọlá?"

"Not now."

"See? That's the sensible thing to do, give yourself time to think, you don't want to be stuck in a residency program that you hate." Tifẹ́ stabbed a piece of meat with her fork.

"Tifẹ́, Grace has been thinking about this since we were in part five. She's ahead of us and—"

"Wúràọlá, could you get me some cold water?" Kúnlé asked.

As she stood up, Wúràọlá stifled the urge to ask why he'd asked for room-temperature water earlier. In the kitchen, Rachel was supervising two hired cooks as they fried fish. Wúràọlá grabbed a bottle of water from the fridge and sipped some of it.

When she stepped outside, everyone was standing, and, next to the porch, Kúnlé was down on one knee, holding up a ring box.

She did not hear what he said.

All her aunties were clapping, and Aunty Mosún was tapping her feet, ready to break into a dance. Grace was already dancing to some unheard beat. Even Tifẹ́ was grinning. Her parents were leaning against each other, and her father's face was creased into a rare grin. Professor Cordelia's hand was pressed against her chest as if to hold her heart in, and her husband had already lifted his wineglass for a toast. A flash blinded Wúràọlá as Láyí took a photo.

"Say yes, say yes!" Ọdúnayọ̀ screamed.

Wúràọlá held out her left hand.

PART II

On Black Sisters Street

The world was exactly as it should be. No more and, definitely, no less. She had the love of a good man. A house. And her own money—still new and fresh and the healthiest shade of green—the thought of it buoyed her and gave her a rush that made her hum.

—*On Black Sisters Street* by Chika Unigwe

· 7 ·

Eniọlá could not bring himself to remind his parents about his school fees. In all the terms and years since his secondary school education began, he'd had to tell them several times that he would be sent away from school if they did not pay up within a month, two weeks, a day. Each term, his lips grew heavier and heavier whenever he wanted to discuss his school fees with his parents, and sometimes it would take days of thinking through when and how to speak before he could open his mouth to talk, only to—in many instances—shut it again for another hour or day. When he did manage to speak, tripping over his words in his hurry to be done with the conversation, he was often saddened by his parents' response. How his father stared at the floor or the ceiling, eyes trained on a single spot. The way his mother's chin sank into her chest while she wiped her face with her palm as though to catch invisible tears. Whenever he asked them for something that involved money—a copy of *New General Mathematics,* school trousers that didn't stop above his ankles or dig into his balls, a shirt that wouldn't chafe his armpit—he felt so sorry for them, he wished he was one of those students who could complete assignments without referring to multiple examples in a textbook.

Meanwhile, Bùsọlá seemed unbothered by their parents' discomfort. She complained about the beatings she received in school throughout the first week of grace and mercy that Glorious Destiny had extended to its students. As the week went on, she lifted her blouse daily so their parents could see welts multiply and climb over one another like worms across her back. She asked them when they would pay the fees, raising her voice, bursting into tears, refusing to wash clothes or plates until she received a response. And although he understood her anger, it astonished Ẹniọlá that she could not bear it in silence as he had learnt to do. He was grateful for her voice, though; it had pushed their parents to beg every relative and friend within reach for money. For most of the week, their mother had also gone to several refuse heaps to fish out plastic bottles and used tins that she sold to a groundnut seller for much less than she'd expected to make.

On Saturday morning, Bùsọ́lá woke everyone up as she stacked the plates and pots she had refused to wash the previous night, slamming the items on top of each other so the noise she made became louder each time she moved an item. Ẹniọlá sat up on his mattress as she began throwing spoons into a pot. On the bed, their parents yawned and turned, clinging to sleep until Bùsọ́lá dropped a frying pan. As Bùsọ́lá picked up the frying pan and threw it back into the cupboard that held kitchen utensils, Ẹniọlá wondered why she had brought it out in the first place. The thing was not even dirty. No one had fried anything in months.

When their parents sat up in bed, Bùsọ́lá knelt to greet them, but before they could even respond, she began complaining about the school fees.

"Bùsọ́lá." Their mother swung her legs off the bed. "The sun is not even up yet, let the day dawn before we start talking about all of this this morning."

Bùsọ́lá pointed at the window. "It's dawning already, the day is dawning. Is it not me they will flog in school on Monday? I will not take it o, I can't take another week of flogging. If you're not going to pay, let me just stay at home as from Monday. They will kúkú start sending me back home the Monday after this one if you have not paid yet, let me just be staying at home."

"Not in this house. If you've started paying rent elsewhere, you can go and stay there, but you are not staying in this house. We are trying, Bùsọ́lá, we are trying."

"How much do you have now? Can you pay half?"

"Why are you looking for trouble this morning? I've told you we are looking for this money. You were in this house when I came back from the market yesterday, you were here when your father went—"

"Why won't you say how much you have, ehn? Why? Just say how much you have and—"

"You still have one week of school before we have to pay, why can't you be patient?"

"But it's not you they are beating, it's not you." Bùṣọ́lá's voice was rising. She was almost shouting at their mother. Their mother, whose voice shook and got smaller as she spoke, chin sinking into her chest. Ẹniọlá caught his sister's eye, frowned at her and shook his head. She should know better than this by now. What was all this shouting going to achieve?

"Why are you like this? Are they not beating your brother too, Bùṣọ́lá? Have you seen Ẹniọlá talk to me or your father like this? Why are you behaving as if it's more than this?"

"Because of you my back is swelling everywhere. Every day, beating. The people in my class will be laughing at me. You're the one that caused all of these things." Bùṣọ́lá pointed at their parents as she spoke, stabbing her forefingers in their direction.

"But did you die?" Ẹniọlá jumped up from the mattress, unable to bear the quiver in his mother's voice anymore. "Why are you shouting as if something is happening to you that has not happened to anybody? Why are you being so rude? Are you the only one in this house that they are beating in school?"

Bùṣọ́lá rolled her eyes. "Maybe you, you like to suffer, I don't know. But me, I'm saying my own. Me, I don't want any stupid teacher to beat me again this week. Suffer your own suffering as you like. Me, I'm not going to suffer in silence o."

"Who told you I'm suffering in silence? Did I tell you I'm—"

"The two of you, shut up, just shut up your mouths, please. Do you want to give me and my husband headaches this morning?"

Their mother's voice was barely above a whisper, but it was enough. Ẹniọlá kept quiet, and even Bùṣọ́lá stopped speaking. Although, since it was Bùṣọ́lá, she still mumbled under her breath.

8

As soon as her daughter stopped complaining and took the dirty plates out into the backyard, Ìyá Ẹniọlá brought out the money she had been putting in an old purse since her children resumed school for the term. She always counted the notes four times daily, before going to bed and after she woke up. On that wonderful day in January when she had been able to add a five-hundred-naira note to the slim bundle, and on the many days when she could not add even a five-naira note, Ìyá Ẹniọlá counted the money. Twice in the morning and twice at night.

Once upon a lifetime, when the only name anyone called her was Abọ́sẹ̀dé, before she met the husband who now lay on the bed and turned his back to her, she had enjoyed doing arithmetic. Everything else in school had confused her, right from the day she held a chalk and copied her first "A" from the blackboard onto her wooden slate. But numbers always seemed real and useful to her, somehow; they stayed in place while alphabets and words swam across the board. When she stopped going to school after repeating so many classes, she was both the tallest person in her class and the only girl who already wore a bra; the only thing she missed for a while were the sums. A few days after she overheard one teacher tell another that she was a brainless dullard, Abọ́sẹ̀dé told her parents she wanted to stop going to school and would like to move in with her grandmother. Neither parent objected. The grandmother lived in the same compound, and all Abọ́sẹ̀dé had to do was walk across the courtyard into her new home.

Abọ́sẹ̀dé's grandmother was the only person who sold àkàrà in their neighbourhood. Everyone, including all her six children, called her Ìyá Alákàrà, and depending on which great war she really was born after, Ìyá Alákàrà was eighty or ninety years old when Abọ́sẹ̀dé dropped out of school. Ìyá Alákàrà soaked and peeled the beans she used to make the àkàrà all by herself, refusing any help from her children and grandchildren. When she began living with her grandmother, Abọ́sẹ̀dé's relatives—stepmothers, married uncles, divorced aunts and cousins who lived in the five houses that made up their family compound—thanked her for deciding to take over their oldest relative's daily chores. Meanwhile, Ìyá Alákàrà continued to wake up before anyone in the compound to fry the àkàrà she sold every morning, threatening to send Abọ́sẹ̀dé back to her parents' home if she dared touch any of her utensils or ingredients.

Abọ́sẹ̀dé found another way to get involved in her grandmother's business. She started writing down the sales figures in one of her old notebooks and tallying up how much had been made at the end of a month. When she announced the total amount to her grandmother, the woman laughed until she began to cough so hard Abọ́sẹ̀dé had to get her some water. "Thank you o, but have you subtracted how much I spent to make the àkàrà from this amount you say I made? The money for firewood? Palm oil? Beans? What about onions and salt? Pepper? This is good, but you should ask me about how much I'm spending on all these things next month, ehn. I've been doing this business before your father was conceived, Abọ́sẹ̀dé, I know how to calculate my profit. Even if I didn't study in school, I have studied the wisdom within me. I just don't know how to write the amounts down, so it's good that you have started doing this. I thank you, thank you for trying to help." Ìyá Alákàrà had paused for a while and covered her mouth with one hand. "I will say it, Abọ́sẹ̀dé, I didn't want to talk because I am not your mother. But the truth is that I am also your mother, so open your ears wide and listen. In this world we now live in, you must study both the wisdom they give you in school and the one God has put inside you. As the world turns, we must track the direction it has turned towards and follow it. And from what I can see today, this world has turned towards the wisdom they teach in schools. I've been watching your father's children as they've been leaving school one after the other. At first, I thought you would stay, but now you too, you've joined them. I'm afraid for your future, Abọ́sẹ̀dé, why did you stop going to school? Kòìtiírí? Why?"

Abọ́sẹ̀dé could not bring herself to speak about how letters seemed to dance across the page whenever she tried to read. She'd done this once, and the teacher she'd explained things to had concluded that she *was* a brainless dullard. "I'm just tired of going to school every day. But don't worry, I will marry someone who has a degree. Nothing less than Grade II teacher training. I promise."

"Abọ́sẹ̀dé. Abọ́sẹ̀dé. Hmmmm. Abọ́sẹ̀dé! How many times did I call you?"

"Three times ma."

"How many ears do you have?"

"Two ma."

"What do you do with your ears?"

"Hear ma."

"Now hear me well—what is not yours is not yours o, even if you marry the person that has that thing. If it is not yours, it is not yours o. Don't be lazy, Abọ́sẹ̀dé, I'm warning you, don't be lazy."

Ìyá Alákàrà's concerns about what would become of her granddaughter did not change, and she returned to the conversation about school again and again. Until her last day on earth, a decade later, Ìyá Alákàrà remained convinced that Abọ́sẹ̀dé should go back and complete her education, even if it meant that, at twenty-five, she would be older than some of her teachers.

Abọ́sẹ̀dé's parents were not worried about her future. They assumed that Ìyá Alákàrà was showing Abọ́sẹ̀dé how she made her àkàrà so crisp on the outside and soft on the inside, people came from the other end of town to buy from her. Àkàrà so peppery and tasty, one of the Ọwá's wives sent a messenger to buy a dozen every other day. And though it was impossible to tell if the queen bought the àkàrà for herself or served them to the Ọwá, everyone in the family bragged about how the àkàrà from their compound made it into the palace every week. Abọ́sẹ̀dé's parents expected that when the old woman died—no one thought she would live for another decade or outlive two of her children—Abọ́sẹ̀dé would inherit her large frying pan and become the family's new and legendary Ìyá Alákàrà.

When Ìyá Alákàrà died two days before Abọ́sẹ̀dé's wedding, the large frying pan was added to the pile of things she was to take with her to the flat her husband had rented. She held on to the pan but never managed to make àkàrà as perfect as the ones her grandmother had made when she was alive. Throughout the first month of her marriage, she tried and failed daily. She soaked the beans for too long and the skins became hard to peel off, she heated the oil too much and ended up with àkàrà that was blackened on the outside before the insides were properly cooked, her dollops of paste scattered into fragments upon hitting the oil instead of becoming nice and round. Bursting into tears as she tasted the results of her labour, Abọ́sẹ̀dé longed for Ìyá Alákàrà's hand on her shoulder, her hoarse all-knowing voice. That voice would have told her what to do with her failing àkàrà business, about the shouting matches she and her husband got into every day, with her life.

It took about a year for Abọ́sẹ̀dé to accept that she was never going to become an Ìyá Alákàrà. She packed away the frying pan, but once she had her son and became Ìyá Ẹniọlá, she made sure her family had àkàrà for breakfast every Saturday morning. Often, while they ate, she would tell stories about her grandmother until her husband and son began to nod in that way they did when they were no longer listening. And now, even though the money she was counting came to only ₦2,370—not even enough to pay half of one child's school fees—she peeled off a fifty-naira note and asked Ẹniọlá to go buy as much àkàrà as the money would cover. Yes, there was some gaàrí in the cupboard that held pots and food-stuff. Yes, sometimes the children were not hungry in the morning or pretended not to be. Yes, her husband now seemed able to live on just air and water. But she had fed her family àkàrà every Saturday morning for fifteen years, and no, nothing was going to change that now. She was still, no matter what else had become of her, the granddaughter of Ìyá Alákàrà, and every Saturday morning, she ate àkàrà. That was that. Spending fifty naira out of the school-fees stash was not what would keep her children out of school.

Having Ẹniọlá had been good for her marriage. That, as a baby, he would wake up screaming if someone dropped a pin in the next room meant she and her husband had to disagree without shouting. And after a few months of not screaming at each other, she began to remember why she had chosen him and not any of the suitors she'd wondered about since she got married. She started her ice lolly business after Ẹniọlá began crawling, and so many young children in the neighbourhood loved her mix of Tasty Time, sugar and water, she was soon able to buy a small fridge that was used only to freeze the lollies. Her life had spread out before her, bright and open as her son's smile. For her son, she created a menu that she hoped he would remember with some longing once he left home. Sunday nights were for fried rice, and every first Saturday, to celebrate the start of a new month, she made pounded yam and two different soups. Egusi for the normal people in her home, and okro for her husband, who would not eat pounded yam with anything else. Now all Ìyá Ẹniọlá could do was cook whatever was available. But on Saturday mornings, she could pretend she was still in a version of her life where menus were possible.

Throughout that week, as her children came home from school, backs bruised red, faces creased with pain and anger, bodies testifying to all the ways she had failed them, before Bùsọlá even opened her mouth to speak, her mind had returned to Ìyá Alákàrà's opinions about schooling. It did so again as she pushed the money back into her purse, resisting the urge to count a third time, reminding herself that money could not multiply no matter how much she wished it would.

She squeezed her husband's shoulder. "Bàbá Ẹniọlá, you should get up. Sadness won't pay these school fees, it will only sap your strength. I know you're awake, Bàbá Ẹniọlá. Bàbá Ẹniọlá?"

Ìyá Ẹniọlá stood and began to tidy the room. Believing it would have been unfair to worsen her children's chances by marrying someone who, like her, struggled to read and had given up on writing, she had resolved to marry a man with some academic qualification. When she met her husband at an Easter cantata, he was already studying at the Baptist college in Ìwó. The Grade II teacher training degree he was working towards had been good enough to earn him her family's P.O. box number. He travelled back to Ìwó shortly after their first meeting and from there wrote several letters to her.

My beloved Abọsẹdé,

  I hope this missive of mine meets you in a state of merriment, if so, doxology.

He filled pages of foolscap sheets with declarations of love and news about his life—he went to bed with the photo she had given him tucked beneath his pillow, he was reading Achebe's new novel, *Anthills of the Savannah,* he dreamt of her every night and would travel to see her soon. Assisted by a neighbour who took dictation and composed her love letter for a fee, she wrote back only once, to let him know she loved him too. She had hoped that he would write to her less often after she declared her own love, but after that he began to write every week. She did not tell him that it took hours, furrowed brows and a headache for her to go from *My beloved Abọ̀ṣẹ̀dé* to his usual farewell.

As I return my pen to the golden basket of love, I think of your beautiful neck.

Your admirer forever, Bùsúyì.

Her neighbour offered to read the letters to her. For a fee, of course. But she had preferred to struggle through them, worried about what the woman might tell other neighbours if she read the parts of Bùsúyì's letter where he wrote things like:

My paragon of beauty, when we are reunited, I shall hug you very tightly to me again, so your body can be close to all the places where I want you to touch me.

He gave her books when he came visiting, and she received them with smiles. She read out loud from the book covers, pretending to admire the designs before she was certain enough to say out loud: *One Man, One Wife* by T. M. Aluko, *Àjà ló lẹrù láti ọwọ́ Ọládẹ̀jọ Òkédìjí, Silas Marner* by George Eliot. She loved him for the gift of books she could not read. For the letters that made her head ache, because to celebrate their engagement, he took her to Ìbàdàn so they could buy books from Odùṣọtẹ̀ Bookstore and because when a month into their marriage she told him how hard it was for her to read, he did not look at her as if she was stupid but began to read poems to her before bed. Even when they had just screamed at each other and she listened with her back turned to him, he read to her.

Despite all the nonsense her brothers now said about him, she knew her husband was not a lazy man. For years she'd wondered if her teacher had been right after all, and her struggles in school meant she was a dullard. Then her husband's steady faith in her ideas—about where they should live, what they should do with their money, when they should have children—began to convince her otherwise. If despair was stopping his body from obeying his heart right now, she was not going to agree with her brothers that he had become a lazy man since he lost his job. And she knew, she knew and was sure that, in his heart, this man who had wept into her shoulder the night they decided to sell all his books did not want their children to stop going to school. If he could, he would get up and help her with getting money for these fees. Sometimes her brothers spoke as though the past were a dream to be forgotten and today was all that mattered. And so, what if she was the one who also had to find money to pay some of their long overdue rent? Had he not taken care of that for the first decade of their marriage? While she bought foodstuff with the money from her ice lolly business, he had paid school fees and rent, fuelled their car and sent a monthly allowance to her parents until they died. If her brothers chose to forget all of that when they spoke about her marriage, that was their problem.

Done with folding the clothes her children had flung all over the room, Ìyá Ẹníọlá went to her husband. The springs creaked as she sat by him on the bed and put a hand on his shoulder. She gripped his flesh when he tried to shrug her off.

"I didn't want to say this yesterday because of the children," she began. "It's bad enough that they have to worry about their school fees—I didn't want them to overhear and worry about this too. You understand? Bàbá Landlord says he wants to see you this morning. Maybe you can go upstairs and talk to him after we've eaten? Ẹníọlá should be back with the àkàrà soon, and we still have some gaàrí."

His skin felt thin and did not seem to have anything beneath it besides bones. He was staring at the unpainted wall beside the bed. Did he still remember how he had spent days deciding between three shades of yellow when they decided to repaint their former bedroom after Ẹníọlá was born? Was that one of the things he thought about in all the hours he spent staring into space these days? She wanted to lean down and trace his jaw with her tongue, snap him out of this morning's wall-watching session, but restrained herself. One of the children could walk in.

"I asked the landlord if he would talk to me about what he wants to discuss with you, but he said you were the one who rented this house from him, not me. You know I would go and talk to him in your place if he would allow it. Will you go after we've eaten?"

She traced his flaking lips, hoping he would part them and let her fingers slip in. He didn't.

"What could he want to discuss with you besides the rent? I'm sure that's it. You just need to beg him well, prostrate and everything. Ask him to give us more time. Maybe you can tell him about the children's school fees. Yes, tell him we've been focused on that. The mountain right in front of us prevented us from seeing the one in the distance, something like that. You remember how he likes proverbs? Once we are able to pay the school fees, we'll have to think about the rent, but the school fees are the most important thing right now. No, no. Don't say the school fees are the most important thing. You can just tell him we'll pay soon. Bàbá Ẹniọlá? Please talk to me, we need to think about this together. I've tried everything, and I don't want to go and beg my brother for school fees again."

Worried that her children would struggle with reading like she had, during each pregnancy, Ìyá Ẹniọlá prayed that they would have their father's ability to go from the beginning of a page to its end with an ease that still seemed magical to her. She was also anxious about how they would learn to write. What might become of them if this was as difficult for them as it had been for her? Was there a world in which they could be allowed to answer exam questions with their voices and not in writing? A world where they would not be labelled stupid and taunted when they needed more time than their classmates to respond to a question that involved reading something from the blackboard, a textbook, their own notebooks? There were moments when she wondered if she should have had children.

For the first few years of Ẹniọlá's education, she made her husband read his schoolwork to him every day, sure that whether her prayers had been answered or not, her son would understand what was read to him. Most of the things her own teachers said when she was a student had been easy enough to understand and remember. Even when his report cards showed that he was getting average scores on his tests and exams, she did not believe her son was not struggling until he spent a Saturday reading *The Queen Primer* out loud from cover to cover. Only when her husband nodded in approval after Ẹ̀niọlá shut the book did she believe that he had been spared.

She was more relaxed with Bùsọ́lá. That one knew her ABCs by heart before she started nursery school and from her first term managed always to be among the top three in her class. In primary two, she had won prizes in social studies, mathematics and English. It used to make Ìyá Ẹ̀niọlá smile in the middle of her chores, this gift of children who learnt without pain and would not suffer the humiliation she had experienced from her teachers and peers. That joy was long gone now. A decade before she even conceived them, she had been making decisions to protect her children from pain. And yet they still suffered. She had been whipped for her low scores. They were being whipped for her failure to pay their school fees. Her brothers insisted that this was all her husband's failure, and she should tell him so as often as she could.

She swung her legs off the bed and spoke with her back to her husband. "Bàbá Ẹ̀niọlá, I want to visit my eldest brother this afternoon. I think we should ask him to lend us some money."

Two years ago, the same suggestion had resulted in an argument that lasted a whole week. Now she waited for the bedsprings to creak as he sat up, for his voice to rise or tremble. She wanted him to be angry, hurt. Something.

She stood and grabbed a broom. She would talk to him again once she was done sweeping, drag him out of bed if that was what it took for him to answer her questions. Maybe it was time to try the methods her brothers had suggested? She had just stood up her children's mattresses so she could sweep beneath them when Ẹ̀niọlá came in and the room became fragrant with the smell of àkàrà.

Her husband sat up in bed as Ẹ̀niọlá took the broom from her.

"Should I bring you àkàrà?" she asked her husband.

He shook his head.

At least he was responding. He had gotten out of bed and might stand up soon. He was suffering from something she could not fully understand; she would be patient with him.

A few hours later, Ìyá Ẹniọlá stood in the courtyard of the compound she'd grown up in, watching two girls draw lines in the sand. Dressed in knee-length gowns cut from the same floral fabric, the girls could have been mistaken for twins if one was not much taller than the other. Ìyá Ẹniọlá did not know either girl. They were probably the children of some new tenant who had moved in since the last time she was here. The girls did not notice her as they dragged short sticks across the sand, pausing only to dig out the stones that made their lines crooked. First, they drew a rectangle; then they traced a line in the middle to divide that in two. When they began to draw an arc at one end of the rectangle, Ìyá Ẹniọlá decided they must be preparing for a game of suwe and continued towards her brother's house.

Before she had asked him to cut off her legs if she ever returned to their family compound, Ìyá Ẹniọlá had visited Alàgbà, her eldest brother, often. They were the only two who had not moved elsewhere, chasing dreams that led to Lagos, Lokoja and Port Harcourt, as their other siblings had done. She had found comfort in those visits, staying on until the sun vanished from the sky and Alàgbà asked her to head home to her husband before it was too dark. When her children were younger, she went with them, because he knew how to soothe and trick them with sweets. She took bottles of vegetable oil and bowls of rice to him at Christmas when her husband still had a job, adding cans of tinned tomato when her iced lollies began to sell so well. After her husband was retrenched, Alàgbà never let her leave his house empty-handed. He would give her smoked grasscutters from his hunts and press naira notes into her palm as she said goodbye. Of all her three brothers, he was the one she could rely on to always give her money whenever she begged him for some. This was probably because he did not have to worry about his wife and children like the others did. Though fifteen years her elder, Alàgbà was not married and had no known children.

Alàgbà was also the only one of her brothers who still called the family compound home. He lived in a house that had been built by a long-dead great uncle, refusing to rent out any of its extra rooms even though two out of five remained empty. He used one room as a living room and slept in another. When he'd finally bought a kerosene stove, she had helped him set it up in a former bedroom so he would share only the outdoor latrine with tenants in the compound. One house in the compound had been rented out, but others were in various stages of collapse. Ìyá Alákàrà's home had been burnt to ashes when there was a power surge some years ago, while the house their father had built lost its roof to a storm a few months after their mother's death. Now the walls had caved in, and grass grew tall and lush in the corridors of their childhood.

The last time she was here, all her brothers had been in town for Easter, and there had been some talk, over plates of pounded yam and egusi soup, of all the children contributing to rebuild the house. Alàgbà had stressed what an important duty it was for them to make sure their father's house did not come to ruin. Someone, she can't remember who, had said he wished the family compound was located next to a major road, so that one of those new banks could buy it off their hands. Alàgbà had been enraged by the idea, and for an hour her brothers had argued about whether banks were really paying families millions of naira to build banking halls in their homestead, on the land where parents and ancestors had been buried. When Alàgbà fell silent, too disgusted to even discuss the possibility, the other brothers argued about how they would have shared the money if banks had been interested. Split into four, according to the number of wives their father had, or into twenty-six, so all the children could have an equal share? Or better still, into five, since they were the ones who had the idea and none of their half-siblings had even stepped into the family compound since their father died. Ìyá Ẹniọlá had chewed the dry fish in her egusi and waited for them to stop shouting so she could speak. Although her brothers' wives kept glancing at her with eyes that pleaded with her to intervene, she knew that all they had to do was wait. She was used to her brothers' raised voices and the veins that became visible in their temples as they shouted arguments that went nowhere.

After the meal was finished and licked-clean fingers had been dipped into shallow bowls of soapy water, her brothers yawned, stretched their legs and wondered if their wives had bought any toothpicks. Their children took the dirty plates into the courtyard and their wives left for the makeshift kitchen to start preparing dinner, while the men, getting no definite answer about the toothpicks and assuming it was not their job to find them, began stabbing at their gums with overgrown nails. Finally alone with her siblings, Ìyá Ẹniọlá brought up her idea.

She had gone to her family compound that day without even discussing the idea with her husband. If she had, maybe his response would have prepared her for the way her brothers reacted to her suggestion. She might have been ready to see their eyes bulge, to watch their mouths fall open and stay open until she feared they might drool. As though she had suggested they exhume Ìyá Alákàrà and incinerate her skull in the marketplace. As though the first patch of earth her feet had touched in this lifetime was not the soil of this same compound, as though she had no portion or inheritance here.

It seemed so simple to her. The retrenchment had forced her to begin sharing a room, one room, with her husband and children, in a house no better than the ones in her family compound. After a couple of years there, the landlord was insisting that they pay two years' rent in advance, something she knew they could not afford. It had made sense to her that she might as well move back to her family compound and live in the house that was being rented out to strangers. But that Easter Monday, her brothers had insisted that it was unseemly for her to move back home with her husband and children. When Alàgbà suggested that the only way she could return was as a divorced woman, she had thought he was joking until he went on to call her husband a useless, lazy fool.

She should have picked up her handbag and walked away then. Instead, she had lacerated her eldest brother with words that would keep her awake in the years that followed. She left only after she swore never to return to the family compound, daring her brothers to chop off her legs if she ever did. Well, here she was again in front of Alàgbà's house.

She knocked twice, and when no one answered, she put her ear to the door and considered dropping a message with one of the tenants. It did not feel right that after over three years of not speaking to him, she should reenter Alàgbà's life through a message from someone she did not know. She knocked again, and this time heard feet shuffling towards her. She pulled away from the door, glanced down at her dress and adjusted the matching scarf.

The door opened, and he was there, leaner and more stooped than she remembered, squinting still. He stood in the doorway without step-ping back to let her in.

"Good afternoon sir." She knelt before him.

"You've remembered your family." He swung the door open and reached down to pull her up.

They went into his living room. She was happy to see that the cushion covers were different. The years must have been kinder to him. Kind enough for him to replace the brown cotton covers he'd been using for decades with brown suede ones. Not kind enough for him to change the sofa, though, but still. He did not seem worse off than the last time she saw him; he should be able to spare a few thousand if she asked right.

They sat on opposite ends of the room, legs pressing against a large centre table that took up most of the space. She pushed back her chair to make some room.

"If you shift that chair too much, the door won't open well."

She nodded and stopped herself from asking why he still needed the table. One leg was unstable, and Formica was peeling from its surface in all directions.

"How is Ẹniọlá?" Alàgbà asked.

"He's fine sir. He sends his greetings."

"Hmmm. Would I still recognise him if I see him? He must be grown now."

"He's taller than his father."

"Hmmm. And Bùsọ́lá?"

"She's now in secondary school."

"Still doing well?"

"Very well sir."

"That's good. We thank God, who has caused us to reunite in joy."

She chewed the insides of her mouth through a moment of silence, wishing he would ask about her husband. He did not.

"And how are you too sir?"

"Well, you can see that I'm right where you left me, but we thank God." He paused and glared at her. "Human weaknesses and human wickedness cannot stop the work of God."

Ìyá Ẹniọlá pushed back the chair and went onto her knees.

"I'm sorry, Alàgbà. E ni mo mí bínú lúgbẹẹ. I'm so sorry." She rested her elbows on the table and leaned forward towards her brother.

"Get up, Abọ́sẹ̀dé."

She did not get up, and he continued to glare at her, blinking only when his eyes filmed over. It hurt that she had brought him to tears again, although much less than the fact that he had chosen to call her Abọ́sẹ̀dé. She let her gaze fall from his dampening cheeks to the centre table's cracked Formica. Even though he was older and owed her no such regard, Alàgbà had taken to calling her Ìyá Ẹniọlá after she had her son. He'd reverted to Abọ́sẹ̀dé the last time she saw him, and she knew he was using her first name deliberately now. Taking away what he had bestowed, to remind her that something had shifted in their relationship.

"Please, I beg you, forgive me. The things I said were terrible, blasphemy. I don't know what possessed me."

"What is that thing they say?" Alàgbà asked. "Blasphemy and the truth were conceived by the same mother. So, why are you sorry? Everything you said was true."

But she had said many things that were not true, repeating insults overheard from cousins and neighbours over the years, things she did not even believe about her brother. She had stopped speaking to some of their cousins because they used the same words she hurled at her brother while she raged on that Easter Monday. When Alàgbà said her husband was a useless, lazy fool, she had responded by calling him an idiot and a failure, a ne'er-do-well who could not even move beyond the compound where he had been born, a firstborn unworthy of his position, one who took from his younger brothers instead of giving to them, a disappointment to their parents and then to all the women who had refused his offer of marriage. A terrible driver. She had even paused to imitate his limp as she mocked him.

"Please forgive me, I did not mean those things at all. I only spoke in anger."

"Anger is good, it reveals. When people speak in anger, I listen to them, because that's when their real thoughts about you come out, all they have kept hidden."

"That is not true. I don't believe those things about you."

"What is not true? Abósèdé? What is not true? Did I have a wife? Did I have any children?"

Ìyá Ẹniọlá placed her forehead against the table, not caring that a dislodged bit of Formica dug into her skin. She deserved this. Her siblings had tried to calm her down. They had pulled at her dress, pinched her arm, pushed her down into her seat only for her to spring back to her feet to continue shouting. Advancing on Alàgbà until she was standing directly before him when she asked where his wife and children were since he wanted to advise other people about their marriages. The room fell silent then, her siblings stopped imploring her to shut up and just stared at her. Her immediate elder brother, Bàbá Ṣùpọ̀, had gone to sit by Alàgbà, to hold him as he wept. And after her tirade, when she suddenly felt so drained she wondered if she might collapse into a silence interrupted only by the rustling of a curtain as the wind blew past it into the room, Alàgbà had said, *Abósèdé*.

Before he could continue speaking, she had stomped out of the room, pushing past her sisters-in-law, who had clustered in the corridor to eavesdrop, swearing never to return to the wretched family compound.

"Alàgbà," she said now, unable to lift her head from the table. "Please forgive me."

He had been married once. He had been a taxi driver, saving up money to move his pregnant wife out of the family compound before their child was born. But one day while he was driving his wife home from a friend's wedding, a trailer had rammed into his taxi. By the time he woke up in the hospital, his wife was in the morgue. After that, he seemed uninterested in moving out of the family compound. Their parents had spoken to him repeatedly about this before they died, insisting that women turned him down because he still lived there.

"I'm so sorry for all I said, for shouting at you. Shame has kept me from coming back since, all these days. I didn't know how to even start apologising. What can I do to erase what I said? I wasn't even sure you would open the door for me today. Of all our brothers, only Bàbá Ṣùpọ̀ still talks to me. Since the ones I did not insult are so angry with me about what I said, I didn't know what to expect from you. I've been afraid to come here. Please, Alàgbà."

"Hmmm. That's why it's taken you more than three years?"

"I've been too ashamed of myself." She lifted her head from the table and looked up at him. His eyes were pink, as though rubbed raw, but his cheeks were dry. "Alàgbà, please believe me."

"Okay, I've heard. Sit down."

"Alàgbà, please, I'm begging you."

"Ìyá Ẹniọlá, I say I have heard you. Why would I be afraid to tell you the truth? If I was still angry, I would say it."

"Thank you, thank you so much sir." She pressed her hands onto the table as she stood, wincing as its surface scratched her palms.

Shame had stopped her from coming back here, but she had also been overwhelmed by her own life. At the beginning of each year, she would resolve to make amends with Alàgbà, but before the end of January, fees, bills and the many minor disasters of living without certainty about where the next meal might come from would have dampened her fervour. She really had hoped that she would not have to beg him for help the first time she showed up after all these years. That way he would not think that she was only apologising because she needed his help, that way he would know that he was wrong about her husband. She had been ashamed, but she had also been waiting for something to change in her fortunes that would cause her to return not on foot but in a car, and from a house that had taps and sinks.

"Would you like some water?" Alàgbà asked, leaning forward in his seat as though about to stand.

"Let me get it myself."

The cups were still where they had always been, arranged on a stool beside the large clay pot Ìyá Alákàrà had given Alàgbà's wife when he got married. Ìyá Ẹniọlá had always suspected that he never bought a fridge because he wanted his daily life to depend in some way on an object that reminded him of the wife he had lost. Not because he could not afford even a secondhand fridge, as he usually claimed when she complained about the pot. She lifted the pot's cover and took a plastic jug from the stool. The water level was low, and her hand went in all the way to the elbow before the jug touched any water.

"I hope you are not the one who still fetches water from the well?" Ìyá Ẹniọlá asked as she filled a cup. "Are there children in the neighbourhood that can help you?"

"God has not abandoned me. He sends me helpers."

She set the cup down in front of him. "I didn't abandon you, Alàgbà. I'm sorry."

"Did I mention your name?"

She filled her own cup and returned to her seat, trying to decide when it might be right to speak up about the money she wanted from him. It was wrong to make a request on the same day she came to apologise, but she had no choice.

"How have the years treated you?" she asked.

"God has not repaid my good deeds with evil, so I am grateful." He reached for his cup and examined the contents before drinking from it. "What about you? How are things now?"

"The children are fine. We've all been in good health."

"Well, thank God for his mercies."

"My husband is still looking for a job. He does some odd jobs from time to time, he's tried bricklaying, but you know how people build houses."

Her brother stared at her as though he had never heard of houses or bricks.

"The bricklaying, it's not every time that he has work. Once a house is complete, that job is over until there is another one. And they don't pay well. So, we are still hoping he will get an office job."

"Hmmm. Office job."

"Yes sir, the kind of person he is, that's what he is really suited for. But it's not laziness o, it's not laziness at all. For now, he does whatever he can find. He's even wanted to be a porter in the market, I'm the one who said he must not try it."

"Why?"

"They carry very heavy things, and he's so skinny now. I'm just afraid that he will collapse under the weight of a bag of rice and end up dead."

Her brother smiled for the first time since she came in. "Work doesn't kill people."

"He's not afraid of work, it's only that—he's looking, he's searching very hard for something."

"And he's been searching for how many years now?"

Ìyá Ẹ̀níọlá sighed and glanced around. The walls were bare except for a Christ Apostolic Church almanac. On its top half, four smiling faces orbited Apostle Joseph Ayọ̀ Babalọlá's portrait, while below them, a calendar displayed dates in January, weeks after it should have been turned to February.

"You are still young enough to leave this man and marry a better one. Even if you squeeze your face as if you are squeezing an orange, Abọ́sẹ̀dé, I must still tell you the truth."

"Abọ́sẹ̀dé" again. Anger was stinging its way up her throat, sharp and acrid. She took a sip of water to push it down. Why had she hoped that apologising would stop him from undermining her marriage yet again?

"Let's say Bàbá Ẹ̀niọlá is even as lazy as you say, can't I make something of myself? Why must the solution to my problems be another marriage? Shouldn't I be able to take care of my children by myself? Am I not the one who brought them into this world?"

"Two people had those children. Why should you shoulder the responsibility alone when he's alive and well? Why? When there are better men out there who can help you, Abọ́sẹ̀dé. If you don't care about yourself, do it for your children."

"Why do you think I am here, Alàgbà? They are all I think about."

Her brother cocked his head.

"I'm so sorry for shouting. I didn't, I . . . I . . ."

"It's okay, it's okay." Alàgbà sighed. "You've been coping well with the children's welfare?"

"I came to discuss their school fees with you."

"I knew it."

"That's not the only reason why I came here."

He rested his chin on a fist and stared at her.

"It's why I came, but it's not why I apologised. I swear I've wanted to do that long before now, I just . . . I swear on my mother's gravestone."

"Leave our mother's grave out of this. Let her rest in peace, please."

"I meant . . . I don't know how . . ." Close to tears, she stared at her clasped hands. The bitten-down fingernails and reddened nailbeds still startled her. A nail dangled off one thumb, chewed halfway through. Had she bitten that off after she got to her family compound or before? She'd developed this habit when she was still a student, always seeing the evidence after the fact but never remembering when she had raised her hands to her lips and attacked one finger after the other. A few years after she dropped out, her nails had grown out, long and sloping, more beautiful than any of the artificial ones that were becoming popular. She'd begun to coat them with polish when she got married. Reaching into a bag bulging with bottled colours and wonder became a pocket of joy and rest when the children arrived. She never let them watch; it was her time alone. Locked in the bathroom for the half hour it took to coat her nails, she did not worry about her husband's shifting moods, or fret over Bùsọlá's loose tooth or Ẹniọlá's bruised knee. All that mattered for that quiet half hour was getting the layering right. Blue, green, gold and silver had been her favourite shades, applied every Saturday so the coatings would be fresh on Sunday morning when she wore her open-toed shoes to church. And now she had gone back to biting her nails, attacking them with a force that reddened her flesh.

"Go on," her brother said.

"We can't take care of their school fees. I have tried—I mean, we have tried. My husband and I have done all we can to gather enough money to pay the fees. To tell you how much I have tried, Alàgbà, one day—was it last week?—I gave Bùsọlá some money to buy gaàrí for dinner. On her way from the place where they were selling the thing, that's how this child fell and the gaàrí poured away. There was nothing else for us to eat in the house on that night, but I did not even touch the money I was keeping for their school fees. I was happy for us to go to bed hungry that day, Alàgbà. To me, that was better than taking more than what I had planned to spend on food out of the savings. But all my efforts—all our efforts have come to nothing. I wouldn't have come to beg you for money, but we now need to raise more than the ten thousand naira. Our landlord is asking for his rent . . . No, Alàgbà, no, I'm not suggesting we move here."

"Even if you suggest it, it is still not possible." Alàgbà shook his head. "It's just not done, láyé láyé."

"Okay sir."

"Ehen. So, how much are the school fees?"

"The money is ten thousand naira for both of them, but we've only managed to raise two thousand plus. By last week, they had started flogging them in school every day. As from this week we'll take hold of tomorrow, the teachers will double the number of strokes." She swallowed and pressed a palm against her throat, hoping this might still her trembling voice. "After that, I think they will be asked to stay home. Bọdá mi, I want to beg you. If there is anything at all you can give to help, no amount is too small sir. You're the only one I have left. Last week, I called Bàbá Ṣùpọ̀, and he couldn't send any money. I'm not angry or anything o, I understand, everybody has their own bukata. He also has children, and he's paying school fees right now. So, please sir. Anything."

"Hmmm. You need . . . let's just say eight thousand."

"Yes sir. They're already in the cheapest school we could find. The other option is for us to send them to public school."

"And what will they learn in public schools?"

"Àbí? That is why we are struggling, so they can attend a private school, even if it's the cheapest one, at least they would have a better chance at leaving with some knowledge."

"Well done, that's what a good parent does."

"Yes sir."

"Ìyá Ẹniọlá, I want to help, but I can only spare one thousand naira."

"Alàgbà, please, don't remember how I have offended you. If you can make it two thousand, please. I will do what I can to find the remaining one thousand. That way we can at least pay half and beg the teachers for more time."

"Ìyá Ẹniọlá, if we offend God and he forgives us, why would I, a mortal, not forgive? This is not about the past. If I am angry with you, would I then take it out on your children? Even though you've hidden them from me these past years, I still think of them like my own. If good comes to them, it is for my own good. The Bible that I read every day says that I should not withhold good from those to whom it is due, when it is in my power. Why would I allow you to be the reason I offend my God? And anyway, let's say God forgives me for withholding this money from you, will alajobi forgive me? Won't the ancestral spirits that roam this compound haunt me until the day I die for being so mean to you? If I had the power, Ìyá Ẹniọlá—look at my face, ehen—if I had the power to help you, I would."

"Please, I want . . . I want these children to go to school. It's their only chance in life. I don't have any property I'm going to leave them. I have nothing else to give them that can—"

"You think I am happy to see you suffer like this? Why do you think I am angry with your husband? God has not blessed this family with wealth, but were you ever hungry? Look at the wells in your neck. If he knew he could not take care of you, why did he marry you? You too look at what you are wearing—were you not better dressed when you lived here?"

Ìyá Ẹniọlá looked down at her washed-out ankara dress. The hem had come apart, and if you stared long enough, you could see that it had been patched at the hip.

"Let me stop talking about your husband before this becomes another fight."

"Okay sir."

"But, Ìyá Ẹniọlá, I can't afford to give you more than one thousand five hundred naira. Me too, I just finished paying school fees last week. My purse is still recovering from that."

Ìyá Ẹniọlá leaned forward. Surely she'd misheard. "You just finished paying what?"

"School fees, I said school fees."

"For?"

"My children."

"Children? It's okay, Alàgbà, you don't want to give me the money. No problem."

"Well, our God did not abandon me where you left me." He gestured towards the door. "You might have seen them outside when you were coming in, my wife has two children from her first marriage."

"Wife?"

"Yes, because the sun never sets on God's mercies, I got married last year. My wife's first husband died after the last child was born, and since then, she was shouldering the responsibilities of those children alone. That is until last year when we got married. Now they are my responsibility too."

This was joyful news, but Ìyá Ẹniọlá could not even force herself to smile. She let her chin sink into her chest. Alàgbà was the only person she could always turn to at the last minute, certain that he would give her the last cup of gaàrí in his house. There were times when he'd assured her that he would rather starve than allow Bùsọ́lá and Ẹniọlá to go without food. And now she realised that, somewhere in her mind, she had always assumed there would never be anyone in his life whose welfare would come before hers. Who would she turn to now? How would she pay her children's school fees? And the rent? Would he have told her about his marriage if she hadn't asked him about the school fees? She studied his face and realised, from the way he held her gaze, as though it was normal for her to learn he was married a year after the event, that he would have kept the information to himself, safe from her. How had she let the years pass without coming to see him? Why had her pride mattered more than her brother? And how, how had she become a woman she did not recognise, someone for whom the happiness of others inspired only despair?

"Congratulations sir."

"I wish Ìyá Favour was home now."

"Who?"

"Ìyá Favour, my wife. She has gone to Sabo to buy onions. She sells pepper and such in front of the house."

"No one told me about the marriage. Nobody. I would have attended, I would—"

"I asked our siblings to make sure they did not tell you about it."

"Alàgbà, I know I offended you but why—"

"That's in the past, let's face the issue of your children's fees. You must think about it very well, because you can't keep doing this every year. Remember what I advised you to do the last time we saw each other?"

"That I should leave my husband?"

"Not that. About the children."

"You said I should ask them to learn a trade?"

Alàgbà nodded.

"Ẹniọlá is doing that. You know the tailor in our neighbourhood?"

"Caro?"

"He's now her apprentice. The only problem is that we haven't been able to pay her either. We need to pay these school fees and our rent first, then we'll find a way to pay her."

"Which of your children is doing better in school?"

"It's Bùsólá."

"Then gather money to pay Bùsólá's school fees. You can do that one. When I add my own, you will have more than half of her school fees already. Just pay her fees. And this is the one you may not want to hear: Let Ẹniọlá drop out and—"

"God forbid bad thing." Ìyá Ẹniọlá snapped her fingers.

"Ah, I see, you don't need my counsel."

"I didn't mean to shout. Please continue."

"Let him drop out and concentrate on tailoring. He already has more education than any of us did. If he combines that with tailoring, he can do something with his life. Then you will focus on Bùsólá, and she can get the best out of that school. That's better than if both of them spend half of the term at home because you can't pay school fees, and then they both get patch-patch education. Think about what I said."

She had considered this before. How her life would be much easier if she did not have to worry about school fees, new uniforms, socks and sandals, notebooks that finished too quickly because her children wrote in arcs that took up more space than they should, the textbooks they sometimes threw across the room so she had no choice but to yell at them. Did they think she had a money tree under her bed? She had thought about taking her children out of school and been ashamed about the thrill she felt when she realised there would be much more money for food, rent and possibly a bottle of nail polish. If they dropped out, when she had goods to hawk, she could also place a tray on their heads on weekdays instead of just during the weekends. Her sales would almost triple, her nails might grow out, she might even sleep through the nights again. But her children.

"I can't do that, Alàgbà. It's my duty. I must give them the chance to have a life that is better than the one I have."

"All I ask is that you think about it. Think well." He stood and shuffled away from his seat, past the clay pot, to the door that led to his bedroom.

When he shut the door behind him, she twisted around in her seat, seeking some sign of this wife's presence in his life. There were no new curtains, no wedding photos on the wall or on the ankara-covered table where a large Bible sat beside a handheld bell. The only thing that seemed to have changed in the room was the chair cover, which, now that she could touch it, was too scratchy to be velvet.

The bedroom door squeaked open, and her brother returned, holding out folded bills to her.

"Thank you so much sir." She took the money and knelt. "You will not fetch water into baskets or save in ripped purses. Your purse will never be empty, and there will be no waste in your life."

"Sit down, Ìyá Ẹniọlá, all glory must be to God. I said you should sit down. Ehen, better." He sighed. "I wish I could do more. But think about all I said. Invest your money in Bùsọ́lá, she has the best chances. If a miracle happens and you can sponsor both of them, that's good, but if you have just one in school and you can provide her with everything she needs to focus and come out as the best, me, I think that is better than if the two of them get patch-patch education that can't take them anywhere. The world has changed, it was in the olden days that people could make a career out of school cert and Grade II. Now? Even the ones that go to university are struggling to get jobs. Better pick the one that can go all the way and do very well and invest in that one."

"I will think about it."

"And as for Ẹniọlá, he will be fine. If he learns tailoring, he can take care of himself very well. He won't need to beg anyone for a job."

After she tucked the notes into the deepest recesses of her handbag, they spoke about his wife and he insisted that she would not be back until much later, so there was no reason for Ìyá Ẹniọlá to wait.

"Maybe there is somewhere else you want to get to?" he asked. "Someone you can ask for more money?"

"Yes sir, let me be going. Help me to greet Ìyá Favour when she returns. I will come visiting again soon, so I can meet her."

"Hìnlẹ̀ àwé," he said as she stood.

She paused for a moment, waiting for a bámi kí'kọ̀ rẹ that did not come. It was hard to accept that his farewells were now stripped of that extension of courtesy to her husband. Harder still was how he did not rise to walk with her to the junction as he used to before.

Outside, Favour and her sister were done drawing lines in the sand and had started their game. A pebble hit the sand with a thud as Ìyá Ẹniọlá approached. It missed its mark and skittered out of the rectangle.

The younger child hissed and stamped a foot in defeat. It was suwe. Ìyá Ẹniọlá studied the girls, wondering if they had inherited their bulging eyes and dimpled chins from the woman who was now her brother's wife.

❁

Ìyá Ẹniọlá negotiated one side road after the other until she burst onto the tarred road that led to Roundabout. She wove her way around hawkers, okadas and street vendors, clutching her handbag tighter when she entered the press of bodies pushing towards the central mosque. Every jab of an elbow, each pull at her dress, felt like a bag-snatching attempt, and she worried about the money Alàgbà gave her. It would take just a moment to reach into her blouse, cup a breast and slip the notes into her bra. She could have done this when she stepped out of her brother's house. Instead, she had waited until she was on one of the busiest streets in town to worry about keeping the money safe.

She turned into a petrol station, planning to cut through it to the point where she could cross to the other side of the road. Three little girls surrounded her as she approached the first fuel pump. They linked hands, arranged themselves around her in a semicircle and implored her with pale eyes that seemed almost transparent, leaning back so their silky hair swung past their waist. Whatever they were saying was drowned out by the chatter of customers haggling with vendors who lined every side of the street, sharp honks from passing vehicles, the occasional ring of laughter. Their hair and pale skin announced that the girls were from elsewhere. Most people said they came from a neighbouring country. It baffled Ìyá Ẹniọlá that anyone would leave another country for this one, but maybe she just did not know enough about all the pain there was in the world. She shook her head at the girls, lifting her gaze when one seemed close to tears. There were other beggars in the petrol station, clustering around cars and passersby, holding out plates and bowls. An old woman crawled from car door to car door. A jeans-clad man clutched the shoulder of a young boy, stumbling after him from window to window. A woman stooped by a fuel pump, stroking her goitre with one hand while counting the money in her begging bowl with the other.

The little girls who stood before Ìyá Ẹniọlá were the only beggars with no visible ailment. She tried to go around them, but they backed away and swung to the side, allowing her to go forward only a few steps before they were in her way again. They would disperse if she scolded or threatened them, but she did not do this. She had nowhere to be in a hurry and could give them some kindness if she did not have money to spare. So she darted this way and that, allowing the girls to swing with her, going forward a few steps each time. One of the girls began to giggle as they moved, and the other two grinned. Ìyá Ẹniọlá smiled at them, surprised by a thrill in her heart that felt like joy. And then one of the girls backed into the jeans-clad beggar's guide and fell, pulling the other two with her. The girls knocked over the beggar and his guide and sent their bowl of money flying. Ìyá Ẹniọlá reached for the girls, but before she could touch any of them, they had scrambled up and were running away from the filling station and the attendants who had started yelling at them.

"Hope you're not injured?" Ìyá Ẹniọlá called after the girls as they darted out of the petrol station into the street.

Since the girls seemed fine enough to run, Ìyá Ẹniọlá turned her attention to the jeans-clad beggar and his guide. The beggar sat on the ground while his guide picked up the scattered naira notes.

"Ah, sorry o, sorry," Ìyá Ẹniọlá said to the beggar. "Can I help you?"

He turned towards her, his eyes unfocused and unblinking. "No. Let my guide come back."

Ìyá Ẹniọlá glanced around. They were not in the path of vehicles that sped into the station to refuel, but who knew what crazy driver might decide to veer towards them.

"Should I help you to get up? Your guide is still busy, we can wait for him together. Should I help you?"

"What if there is someone behind you? Somebody that you have planned with to kidnap me. I can't even see to know if that is happening. Leave me alone, woman. My guide will come and help me."

Ìyá Ẹniọlá decided to wait with him until his guide returned from following the trail of scattered notes. A car revved past, lifting one of the twenty-naira notes that had fallen near Ìyá Ẹniọlá's feet. She bent to help the beggar pick it up before it fluttered away. But as her hand went towards the money, the beggar snatched it out of the way.

He glared at her as he stuffed the note into a breast pocket. His eyes were clear and focused.

"Ehn!" she said. "You're not blind."

He put a forefinger against his lip. A plea.

No, a warning. Swift as a snake striking, he brought out a small bit of wood from his pocket and, flicking it with his thumb, revealed its serrated blade.

Ìyá Ẹniọlá stumbled back and walked away, resisting the urge to glance back at the man when she was out in the street. She crossed the road immediately, darting between taxis and ignoring the angry drivers who yelled curses at her.

9

Wúràọlá decided to get up when Mọ́tárá kicked her shin again. She had been awake for about an hour. Drowsy but unable to drift back into sleep, even after she had counted four hundred sheep. Meanwhile, Mọ́tárá thrashed around on the bed, evidently still the restless sleeper she had been when she was a toddler who rolled off the bed with such consistency that her mattress had been placed on the floor.

When the clock on her bedside table blinked 4:17 in red, angular digits, Wúràọlá sat up and tapped the floor with one foot until she found her bathroom slippers. It was going to be a long day of shuffling between guests to make sure the endless stream that was expected left satisfied with: their starters and souvenirs, the size and type of meat they were served, the exact temperature of the drinks that weighed down their tables. She still did not understand why those details mattered so much, but she knew that many people cared about such things. An older cousin on her father's side of the family had refused to speak to Wúràọlá for two years because she had been supervising caterers at another cousin's wedding when they served him fish instead of chicken.

Wúràọlá was sure that by six-thirty a.m. her mother would barge into the room and demand that she help with one of the million things that needed to be done before the party began at noon. Yèyé thought being in bed after dawn was a sign of laziness and did not seem to understand the concept of sleeping in on Saturdays or during the holidays. On occasion, Wúràọlá wondered if the reason her parents no longer shared a room was Yèyé's insistence that everyone rise with the sun.

Wúràọlá pulled apart the curtains so that she could make her way around by the refracted glow of the outdoor lamps. She moved from the window to the dressing table, trailed by the muffled voices of the caterers who were working in the backyard. The previous night, after they celebrated Wúràọlá's engagement with exclamations, two bottles of champagne and suffocating hugs, Yèyé's sisters had drawn up a timetable of women who would supervise the hired caterers through the night. Wúràọlá was asked to take the time slot between midnight and one a.m. When she declined, Aunty Bíọlá had eyed her with a disappointment that went unspoken because Kúnlé was present. Wúràọlá heard all Aunty Bíọlá was saying without moving her lips. Aunty Bíọlá, whose expectations and admonitions bent unerringly towards marriage, was asking as she had done ever since Wúràọlá was old enough to walk, *Is this how you will behave in your husband's house?* Wúràọlá and her cousins often joked about how Aunty Bíọlá managed to make everything—their hair and skin tone, their grades and the courses they chose to study, the number of times they went to church, whether they wore weaves or lipstick—about their future as wives. Recently, their laughter had begun to shrink into a mix of coughs and sniffles, fraying stopgaps for the tears some of them were holding back.

She could be the woman Aunty Bíọlá wanted and race downstairs to relieve whichever aunt was monitoring food preparation now. She just did not care if the caterers stole some pieces of meat while they cooked. Wúràọlá searched the dressing table for Patricia Cornwell's *All That Remains,* then looked under the bed and behind the curtains. There was still time to read a chapter or two before her attention was demanded by someone. Eventually, she found the book beneath a pile of underwear in her wardrobe.

When she was a teenager, Wúràọlá's parents had punished her every time they caught her reading the Regency romances she loved. Yet scrubbing carpets with a toothbrush, climbing the stairs on her knees and the occasional smack of a slipper against her palm had not deterred her; she simply figured out how to hide the books. She had since gravitated towards thrillers and whodunits, but her instinct for hiding novels remained intact. Even though the book covers were no longer steamy, and Yèyé had stopped poking through her things in search of evidence that she was drinking, smoking, having sex or doing any of the things that Yèyé warned would lead to Wúràọlá's death, penury and arrival in old age as a spinster. Clutching her mobile and *All That Remains,* Wúràolá stepped into the hallway and shut her bedroom door. She held out her left hand and admired her engagement ring as she walked down the corridor. She had fallen asleep with it on her finger, too enthralled by its gleam to take it off. The band was rose gold, its stone pear-shaped and luminous. Well, she was not going to be a spinster in old age.

She went through the quiet corridor, stopped for a moment in the family room, then decided against sitting in one of the chairs. A passing aunt could easily hijack her there. Out on the adjoining balcony, she settled into a cushioned wicker chair. She tried to read, but her mind refused to settle into Dr. Scarpetta's world. Kúnlé had left about an hour after he proposed, and they'd spent another hour on the phone once he got home, discussing how he had planned the proposal, reviewing their life together so far, revisiting the moments when each had realised they were in love with the other. By the time Wúràolá drifted off to sleep, the proposal felt like a culmination, the point to which the arc of their lives had been bending, a convergence as inevitable as fate. She set down the novel and sent Kúnlé a text.

Awake?

Her phone did not vibrate in response. She leaned back in her chair and stared at the inky sky. Kúnlé's alarm usually went off at five a.m., and he always dragged himself out of bed for a run around the compound without ever hitting the snooze button. Maybe he was out running. He could also be ignoring her call because he was still upset with her. They had argued before getting off the phone last night. He wanted them to get married within six months, but she wanted to wait for at least one year. She was supposed to start her national service year right after her house job and could be posted to any state in Nigeria. If they got married before the service year started, Wúràolá would be allowed to serve wherever her husband was domiciled. His argument made sense, but she was unwilling to budge. She was looking forward to living elsewhere during the service year, far from the two cities where she had spent most of her life. Marriage could come after that year of freedom from the close-knit circles that had orbited her from childhood through university, where she always seemed to be in a room with someone her parents knew. Her phone vibrated.

"Hello, baby," Wúràọlá said, holding the phone to her ear.

"Hello," Kúnlé said.

"Have you been running?"

"No."

"Is it raining in your area?"

"I wasn't in the mood to run."

She knew he was trying hard to keep his tone light, but the tremor in his voice betrayed him and reminded her of the first time she had noticed a wobble in his voice while he faked a smile. Kúnlé had graduated from secondary school and Wúràọlá was home from her boarding school on a midterm break when her father sent her to the Cokers with a sealed envelope. She knew from eavesdropping on her parents that the white envelope contained dollar notes for Kúnlé's father, who was preparing to leave for a sabbatical in Saudi Arabia. Kúnlé's family still lived in the General Hospital's staff quarters, and though the row of identical bungalows confused Wúràọlá, her father's driver had driven straight to the Cokers' doorstep. Kúnlé had been standing on the lawn when she stepped out of the car, his back to the house, where his parents were fighting about his results. Láyí, who had aced all his exams, had already told Wúràọlá about Kúnlé's terrible results. Kúnlé had failed biology and chemistry, key requirements for admission into any medical school in the country. Kúnlé's father wanted him to write the exams again. Meanwhile, his mother thought he should take on other subjects and forget about a future in medicine. Kúnlé's bloodshot eyes announced that he had been crying or was about to, but he smiled as Wúràọlá approached him. He held the smile in place while she stood before him, unsure about what to say after she thrust the envelope into his hand. He kept asking her about school, reeling out questions at a rising pitch that did nothing to obscure the fact that his parents were fighting in the house. It was impossible to ignore the cursing, the screaming, the sharp sound of something crashing to the terrazzo floor. Overwhelmed by a sudden surge of tenderness towards a boy she had barely noticed before then, Wúràọlá had stepped forward to hug Kúnlé before running back to the waiting car. She felt that surge again as she imagined him splayed on his bed, still deflated by last night's argument.

"I'll think about the wedding," she said.

"That's all I was asking for last night before you shouted me down."

"I didn't do that."

"I just want our lives to start as soon as possible. I wish I were already waking up next to you every morning. Wúrà, don't you understand that you're such a comfort to me?"

"Don't worry about it, we'll figure out a compromise. Can we talk about something else?"

"Yeah . . . What are you wearing?"

She tugged at the hem of her nightgown. "Nothing."

His breath stuttered while she watched the ascendant sun streak the clouds with a flamelike glow.

10

B efore she showered or even brushed her teeth that Saturday, Yèyé Christianah Àlàkẹ́ Mákinwá sat at her dressing table and polished her gold jewellery. She nestled each piece in her palm and recalled how many grams it weighed. For necklaces and rings, she did this without consulting the grey notebook in which she recorded major purchases. Every other week, Yèyé asked Alhaja Ruka, a former neighbour who traded secondhand gold jewellery, about her buying price per gram. That way, she could estimate how much she would get for hers if, heavens forbid, her husband was duped of all his money, she lost her stores in a fire and some disaster or the other befell her sisters so that she sank down a hole of misfortune with no hope of rescue from impoverishment. If that ever happened, these pieces of jewellery would be her saviours.

Yèyé wrapped all the eighteen-carat items—necklaces and earrings, rings and bracelets, the few never-worn anklets—in anti-tarnish tissue before placing them in a wooden jewellery box. The box was not new, but it had never been used. Bought and reserved since Wúràọlá turned twenty-five, the age Yèyé had hoped her first daughter would marry or at least get engaged, it had been waiting in the left corner of the dressing table for this day.

Done arranging all the eighteen-carat items in the plush belly of the jewellery box, Yèyé snapped it shut and clasped her hands above it. She felt like skipping to the bathroom as she used to when she was a child, singing while her mother scooped water from a steel bathing bucket, gyrating with arms flung out as water was splashed on her body. Yèyé often toned her dancing down to squirms once her mother gripped her shoulder with one hand to scrub her back with the other, but she always sang until soapsuds had been rinsed off her skin and a towel slung over her shoulder. If her mother was in a hurry, Yèyé's restlessness earned her a slap on her buttocks, but most times, her mother just begged her to stop moving. Yèyé still danced her way to the bathroom on most mornings, but these days she stayed still while she showered. Now that there was no hand to grip her shoulder, it would be so easy to slip with no one there to catch her if she fell. Today, all her gyrations would happen on the dance floor. She could wait until then.

She tucked the wooden jewellery box into a drawer and turned her attention to the lesser pieces that lay before her on the dressing table. Fourteen carats and ten carats, Italian and Brazilian, somewhere in the pile, the gold-plated earring-and-pendant set Aunty Bíọlá had given her before she got married. It had been the only jewellery she had owned for the first two years of her marriage, that time before she became the wife whose husband joked about how he spent more money on her jewellery than he did on their children's school fees. This line had only been true when the children were in primary school, but he held on to the joke through the decades, shaking his head as he wrote cheques for her to buy "those baubles." Yèyé did not mind his mockery, so long as the cheques were signed and handed over to her.

As it turned out, Aunty Bíọlá had been right about everything. That Adémọ́lá, Colonel J. D. Mákinwá's bespectacled younger brother, was attracted to Yèyé, that Adémọ́lá was not the type to deny paternity as Aunty Jùmọ̀kẹ́'s husband had done initially, and even if he was, the colonel would make sure that his younger brother did the right thing.

Yèyé was nineteen when Aunty Bíọlá introduced her to Adémọ́lá Mákinwá at a New Year's party in the seventies. The military had been in power for nearly a decade, Aunty Bíọlá had been the third and favourite wife of a brigadier general for three years, and their mother had been dead for four. So what if the brigadier was married to other women already? Aunty Bíọlá had one of his duplexes to herself in Bodija, and he took care of her younger sisters as if they were his own children. He opened Yèyé's first bank account for her and paid her a monthly allowance until she married Adémọ́lá Mákinwá.

During her reign as the brigadier's favourite wife, Aunty Bíọlá dedicated herself to making sure that her sisters met and married suitable men. The men Aunty Bíọlá considered suitable were university educated, moneyed and single. She told her sisters often that though there was nothing she could do about them ending up in polygamous marriages, she wanted to make sure they could at least be first wives, because any position after that was worthless. She said this even when the brigadier was in the room, which made Yèyé's face hot but did not seem to bother the man.

Most of the officers Aunty Bíọ́lá knew were already married, but they had cousins and brothers whose proximity to power made them suitable. Adémọ́lá was one of those suitable men. From their meeting on New Year's Day until they got married, Yèyé's side of the relationship was directed by her eldest sister. She sat at Adémọ́lá's table during the New Year's party, positioning herself across from him as instructed by Aunty Bíọ́lá, in his line of vision but just out of reach. He stared at her all night. Once, he bent over the table to speak to her, but the music was too loud, and she did not lean towards him. They talked when the party ended at dawn, yawning between sentences. He invited her to two birthday parties later that month. She gave him a hand job after one of those celebrations, grinning as she startled him into open-mouthed silence in the back seat of his car. Even her body obeyed Aunty Bíọ́lá's counsel, and she conceived Láyí within a month after she met Adémọ́lá. And just as her sister had planned, Yèyé ended the year with a son and a wedding band. Eighteen carats of Italian gold, no less. Aunty Bíọ́lá made sure.

Yèyé stopped following Aunty Bíọ́lá's advice after the wedding, but that did not prevent the older woman from telling her how to live during the few calls that NITEL allowed through to the blue dial-up phone. Frustrated by the crackling phone lines, Aunty Bíọ́lá even came down from Ìbàdàn at one point to spend hours cajoling, instructing and, finally, commanding Yèyé to get money from her husband—steal it if necessary—to make sure she bought gold.

To Mrs. Christianah Àlàkẹ́ Mákinwá, beloved wife of Adémọ́lá and doting mother of Ọláyíwọlá, Aunty Bíọ́lá's words seemed increasingly bitter and jaded. Unsurprising counsel from a woman who had come to the end of her reign as favourite wife and could not make peace with that fact. But for a woman whose husband adored her? Stupid advice to follow. Aunty Bíọ́lá did not know how Adémọ́lá looked at Yèyé when they were alone, had not heard the promises he continued to make to her before she drifted off to sleep. Unlike her sisters' husbands, who barely noticed their children until those kids could walk or talk, Adémólá helped with Láyí from the day they brought him home from the hospital. He fit a cot into his study so the baby could spend Saturdays there with him while Yèyé slept in for as long as she needed. When she got up during the night to nurse or croon Láyí back to sleep, Adémólá got up too. Occasionally, he would tie the boy to his back with an old wrapper and dance around the bedroom. This did not stop Láyí's wailing, but it made Yèyé laugh.

For a brief and wondrous period, Yèyé believed that the bond she shared with her husband was incomprehensible to anyone but the two of them. Their marriage was like no other. Their love—and she did come to love him around the time Láyí turned one—could not be understood by any of her older sisters, who by then were pooling together money to buy a swath of land their husbands knew nothing about. Yèyé would not be part of their scheme, would not lie to her husband to get the money she needed to have four plots allocated to her, refused to stash away gold as protection against future misfortune. Two as one, she and Adémólá would sink or rise together. Instead, Yèyé had saved up parts of her housekeeping allowance during the first two years of marriage until she had almost enough money to buy a plot of land in Òkè Omirú. When she told her beloved husband about this land, he had asked her what she needed it for, when he had inherited two hectares in Ìdó Ìjèṣà and everything he owned belonged to her even if her name was not on the deed. The next month, Yèyé told him she no longer wanted to wear gold-plated jewellery. What would people think of him if they knew his wife wore cheap pánda?

While speaking to her husband about her intention to buy a plot of land had been followed by a family meeting where her in-laws accused Yèyé of plotting to kill their son, Adémólá never argued when she asked for money to buy a new necklace. Sometimes he spoke about how vain she was in an almost admiring tone, and Yèyé responded by insisting she could not wear outdated jewellery. And as Aunty Bíólá had instructed, she never said a word about the resale value of each item.

Yèyé could no longer consider her eighteen-carat pieces as part of her emergency fund now that Wúràolá was engaged, but if this fiftieth birthday party was followed by a series of unexpected misfortunes of the variety Aunty Bíọlá always worried about—fire, robbery, Adémọ́lá losing vital contracts, Adémọ́lá losing his life, divorce—she could raise four to five million naira from the sale of fourteen-carat items alone. Done polishing and storing all the gold items, Yèyé put on the gold-plated earrings Aunty Bíọlá had given her when she turned eighteen. She studied her face in the mirror. The earrings grazed her shoulders, inappropriate for the celebrant at a fiftieth birthday party. Today, she would wear something more subtle, clip-ons that covered her earlobes but did not dangle. She caressed the spots where the earrings' tendrils touched her skin. If she could not wear Aunty Bíọlá's decades-old gift, it would be nice to see the earrings on one of her daughters during the party. They were both young enough to pull off the look, but it was best to offer the pair to Wúràọlá. Wúràọlá might agree to wear them, and since she would be married soon, it might be an opening to discuss how she dressed. Yèyé was sure her oldest daughter was probably planning to wear nearly invisible studs today. Should she have said something earlier about Wúràọlá's endless rotation of black, grey and brown outfits? Maybe brighter colours would have secured a fiancé for her daughter earlier instead of now when she was veering dangerously towards thirty. Yèyé laughed. Probably not, but for God's sake the girl dressed as if she was in mourning.

Yèyé clasped her hands in prayer and shut her eyes. Her Wúràọlá was getting married. At last. Olúwáṣeun. Glory be to God in the highest, and on the earth, peace.

When Láyí screamed his way into her life just before Christmas all those years ago, Yèyé had assumed that the fear she felt was transient. One more consequence of how close she had been to death during those twenty-three hours of labour. But the fear did not dissipate as expected. It was with her while she nursed first Láyí, then Wúràọlá and finally Mọ́tárá. While she packed lunches and helped with homework, pronounced punishments and studied report cards, fear was a perpetual companion, closer and more constant than her shadow. It lapped at the edges of her mind while she slept, so that she called out the name of one child or the other even when her nightmares had nothing to do with them. And then something strange and wonderful had happened when Láyí got married. Where her fears about him had congealed into utter terror after that foolish decision to stop practicing medicine and "chase his dreams," they dissolved into only the mildest agitation as soon as he said his vows.

During the week that followed Láyí's wedding, Yèyé had waited in vain for her agitation to intensify. Instead, she felt unburdened, like someone who had finished a class and received a final passing grade. Eventually, her mild agitation gave way to something like peace. So what if Láyí had decided to throw away a career in medicine? At least he still had that MBBS, and whatever he decided to do with it was really his wife's problem. This new feeling of freedom was accompanied by a trace of guilt, the suggestion that by worrying less she had become a bad mother.

Guilt was fickle and easy to ignore. So was the thought that Láyí might be upset by her diminished interest in the details of his life. Yèyé had long made her peace with the idea that she would be found wanting in some way by her children. If they believed what everyone claimed—that mothers were peerless gods forged out of precious gold—how could she not fall short of their expectations? It was the destiny of gods to be toppled. Yèyé never worried that her children might think she was not a good mother; that was inevitable. What terrified her above all was the possibility that they might come to harm under her watch. Now that Láyí was married and belonged to his wife in a way that, though it would never equal his connection to her, managed to be as overarching, Yèyé no longer called out her son's name while she slept. In a year or less, she would stop calling out Wúràọlá's name too.

Yèyé rose to her feet, invigorated. One week ago, she had been worried that this Kúnlé boy was wasting her Wúràọlá's time. Now she had a wedding to plan.

❖

"The photographer is here. He's waiting for you downstairs. Should he come up to the family room?"

Yèyé held the ends of her gèlè against her ears and glanced towards the doorway. Mọ́tárá stood there, holding a piece of fried meat.

"Why didn't you knock? How many times have I warned you?"

"I can't even count the number of times you've just barged into my room." Mọ́tárá took a bite of the meat. "This month alone, countless."

"Ehen, and so, therefore? Are you saying I need your permission to enter any room in this house? Warn yourself, ehn, don't annoy me this morning o."

"Okay, okay." Mótárá shrugged. "I actually knocked."

"Omótárá Mákinwá."

"It's true now. I knocked before coming in." Mótárá pointed at Yèyé's gèlè. "You were tying that, and it was making noise like the one I helped you with last Christmas. That's why you didn't hear me. Mama the mama. You are looking really nice. Your shoes are fine, sha, and the clutch and your lace. Operation Blind Them with the Sequins."

Yèyé glared at Mótárá. A teenaged Wúràolá would confess the truth within seconds whenever Yèyé glared at her without blinking. Láyí could hold out for longer, but he would glance around the room, scratch his head or repeat what he had said as though that would make it true. But this Mótárá. She stared right back and continued chewing the fried meat. Unfazed. Wúràolá would never have lied about something so trivial, she would just have apologised for walking in unannounced. But Mótárá lied all the time, to get something she wanted, to avoid being punished, because she was bored.

Yèyé rested her elbows on the dressing table's surface, careful to maintain her grip on the gèlè. This gèlè was not noisy. It was àlàárì, woven cotton threaded through with soft silk. Unlike the crackling damask from last year, it barely whispered. Yèyé glanced at her watch. She did not have time to say this and catch Mótárá in the lie. They had just over an hour for portraits before the party began.

"Come here," Yèyé said. "Come and help me with this."

"But my hands are greasy."

"Go and wash them in my bathroom."

"What about the bones?"

"Bones?"

"From the meat. What should I do with them?"

"Let me see, hmmm. You could always put them on my head, àbí?"

Mótárá stalked off to the bathroom, muttering and rolling her eyes. Yèyé was relieved that no one else was there to witness the exchange. Already, everyone in the family thought she did not discipline Mótárá enough. At that age, Láyí and Wúràolá would have been punished for mumbling after she spoke to them. Wúràọlá would have pointed this out if she were in the room, pursing her lips and tapping her forehead. Her diction had improved, but her body still spoke of disappointment in the same way it had when she first tottered off to report Yèyé to her father. Yèyé no longer justified the way she was raising Mọ́tárá. She had tried to do this for a few years, but her older children only interpreted anything she said as confirmation of their suspicion: that she had become a mother who chatted into the early hours of the morning with her teenager instead of making sure she was studying because she finally had a child she liked.

What was it Láyí had said the last time they discussed the so-called dreams he was chasing instead of putting his certificate to good use? *I know you love me, but I don't think you've ever liked me.* This was the charge he brought. That Mọ́tárá, who overslept and lied and hardly helped around the house, who had average grades because she could not be bothered to study, was the only child Yèyé liked. Where had Láyí learnt to make such distinctions? If he were busy completing a residency training, he would not have time to come up with theories about who liked him and who did not smile widely enough when he showed up unannounced. Of course she liked him.

The truth had always been simpler than Láyí thought it was. Mọ́tárá was the only child who had not become a sullen and silent version of herself when she hit puberty. Where Mọ́tárá had crept into Yèyé's bed every night during her first period, Wúràọlá had been menstruating for a full school term before Yèyé even knew about it. She had been going through the shopping list Wúràọlá gave her during an Easter break when she found "sanitary pads" nestled between "Nixoderm" and "Venus body lotion." Yèyé had always known there was a chance that Wúràọlá's first period would come while she was away in school. She had imagined Wúràọlá whispering to her about it while they drove out of the school compound at the beginning of a vacation, her voice tinged with a mix of fear and excitement she could not hold in any longer. When they got home, Yèyé would take Wúràọlá to her room, where they would sit side by side on the bed. Then she would drape an arm across her daughter's shoulders before telling her about the first time she got her period. They would laugh together at how silly it was that, longing to be like her older sisters, Yèyé had lied twice about getting her period before it actually came in the middle of a math class. Trickling through her underwear and skirt to pool beneath her while the teacher explained Pythagoras's theorem. Staring at the piece of paper Wúràọlá had torn off a school note, Yèyé knew she could not allow that moment, their moment, to be flattened into two words on a shopping list. She had gone to Wúràọlá's room, ready to talk about what it had been like. For Wúràọlá, for her, for her elder sisters, who had traded stories in the room they'd all shared when they were young.

"I hope it wasn't too painful the first time. It wasn't when you were in class, àbí?"

"What?" Wúràọlá said.

Yèyé sat at the foot of Wúràọlá's bed. "Your first period."

"Okay ma."

"How was it?"

"Fine ma."

"Tell me how it happened."

"Why?"

"All right, come closer and let me tell you about—"

"It's happened since January, and my housemistress has already told me everything I need to know about it."

"January? Wúràọlá? January, lọ́hùún lọ́hùún? Why didn't you tell me when I came for your open day? Or during your midterm?"

"Please don't shout at me. Just buy the pads ma."

Maybe the problem was that Láyí and Wúràọlá had been students in a boarding school. It was a detail they sometimes pointed to as yet another piece of evidence that Mọ́tárá was the favourite. Forgetting, until Yèyé reminded them, that they had wanted to go away. Láyí had begged to leave with his friends. Wúràọlá had discussed school choices with her father long before Yèyé got to know what had been decided. They got what they wanted and then came home at the end of each term coiled tighter and tighter into themselves, until they were hidden from her, unknowable and impossible to unravel.

Mọ́tárá was not unknowable. She usually said whatever was on her mind. Maybe too much of what was on her mind, but most times, Yèyé liked this about her. Take this lie about the crackling gèlè; in a week or two, while they were talking about something else, Mọ́tárá might confess that she had been lying and shrug it off. If she was in a good mood, they might even laugh about it. It was not favouritism. No, she just knew her last child better than she knew the others when they were this age.

When Mọtárá returned from the bathroom, she took the gèlè's ends from Yèyé and immediately began to spread it out.

"You should tie a knot before doing that," Yèyé said.

"Ṣé, you will just let the makeup person do this for you? She's kúkú tying gèlè for one of your sisters in my room. Should I go and call her?"

"I prefer to tie my gèlè by myself."

"But you are not tying this one, I'm the one that—"

"Just finish it." Yèyé picked up her clutch and double-checked the contents. Phone, an envelope of new naira notes, two pens, a small notebook.

"Turn your head to the left," Mọtárá said. "Okay, good. Like that."

Yèyé snapped the clutch shut.

Mọtárá sighed.

"Are you all right?"

"I have a major problem."

"What is the matter? Mọtárá, what?" Yèyé tried to read Mọtárá's expression in the mirror, but her face was obscured by the folds of the gèlè.

"Sit still, you're scattering what I'm doing now."

"You said you have a problem."

"Yes, a big one. My perfume is almost finished, and I don't have any other bottle. I have like five sprays left."

Yèyé took a deep, steadying breath. "That's your problem?"

"And you can solve it."

This was Mọtárá's idea of a problem? Láyí's seemed to be whether his parents liked him as much as they loved him. Shielded by the lineage she had chosen for him when she married his father and equipped with the education he could afford to ignore because her choices guaranteed he would not starve while he chased silly dreams, Láyí complained that she did not like him enough to believe in those dreams. And Wúràọlá? She did not have any problems Yèyé could see. Not now that she was engaged and would be married before she was thirty.

Yèyé smiled and adjusted her coral bracelet. Her children had the life she once wanted but could not have. One in which, even if they experienced sudden disaster, as long as it did not kill them, it would be cushioned by their surname and the bank balance of the man she had chosen to be their father. A wealthy uncle or aunt or cousin would rescue them if their parents could not. If all else failed, there was a stash of gold waiting for her daughters, tucked away now in that fireproof safe. And for all three of them, her share of the swaths of land she and her sisters had acquired together after she had wasted those first two years of marriage believing a man's love was some limitless thing.

"Is your father ready for the photos?" Yèyé asked.

"Yes, he's waiting in the family room with Kúnlé's dad and your sisters."

"Professor Coker is here?"

"Yes, he came in just as I was leaving the family room."

"Ehen. Did he come with his wife?"

"Nope." Mótárá took a pin from the dressing table and stabbed the gèlè. "Kúnlé was not with him either."

"He must have something to discuss with your father. Be careful o, don't injure me. Squeeze your face anyhow you like, just don't stab me to death."

"With a safety pin?"

"Mótárá, now that Kúnlé is going to marry your sister, you need to stop using just his name. Stop calling it anyhow, add something, put some respect."

" 'Brother' or 'Uncle'?"

"Yes, use 'Uncle,' that one has more respect in it."

Mótárá laughed. "Maybe I should start calling him 'Daddy'? That one is top-tier respect, level ten."

"All right, put 'Brother' in front of his name if 'Uncle' is too much for you."

"Me, I'm not doing that thing. He can't be expecting me to call him Uncle Kúnlé when I don't even call my own brother Uncle Láyí or Brother Láyí. I'm sure he doesn't even care about all that."

Mótárá had refused to prefix either of her sibling's names with any of the options—Brother, Uncle, Sister or Aunty—Yèyé presented once her speech became clear enough to be understood by strangers. Unlike Wúràọlá, who, aged five, had switched to Brother Láyí when he was present and stuck to Láyí when he was not, Mótárá defied threats, ignored entreaties and continued to use her older siblings' unadorned names at all times. Members of the extended family found Yèyé wanting when Mótárá called the names of older cousins just like that, as though they were mates. That Mótárá responded without a trace of shame or remorse when they complained, giving that one-shoulder shrug that meant she was too uninterested to argue about a subject but planned to carry on with whatever it was she had been told to stop doing, was taken as a clear indication that Yèyé was spoiling her youngest child. When Mótárá began to prefix her siblings' names with Doctor after Láyí began clinical rotations in medical school, the relatives did not accept this as an improvement, only as proof that this was a child Yèyé allowed to do as she pleased.

"How do you know Kúnlé doesn't care?" Yèyé asked.

"Don't worry about this, I've been calling him Kúnlé since I was small, he doesn't mind."

"He was not your sister's fiancé when you were small, Mótárá. Things should be different now that they are getting married."

"Okay." Mótárá raised one shoulder in a shrug. "I'm done with your gèlè o. Do you like it?"

"It's perfect."

"You're welcome." Mótárá began walking towards the door.

"Come. Come back," Yèyé said. "Come and help me get up."

"How's your knee?"

Yèyé gripped Mótárá's hand. Her knees were just fine. She could have gotten up by herself, but she wanted to stand close to Mótárá and spend a moment looking into those eyes that never really met hers. The left one stared directly at her, while the right seemed trained on the dressing table. When the family doctor suggested corrective bifocals years ago, Yèyé had been pleased that Mótárá refused to wear them.

Mótárá squeezed Yèyé's hand. "Óyá, let's go."

Yèyé could hear strumming once they stepped into the corridor. She recognised the first riff in King Sunny Adé's "Congratulations" and began to sway. Someone had put on *Seven Degrees North*. When Yèyé got to the family room, Aunty Bíólá was dancing beside the centre table.

"Come, my dear. Come." Aunty Bíólá held her arms open.

Yèyé let her daughter's hand go and began to dance too. Swaying to the music as it swelled, she moved towards Aunty Bíọlá, while around her, her other siblings clapped and sang and whooped. They were all on their feet by the time Yèyé stepped into her eldest sister's embrace. Aunty Bíọlá leaned back and swept her gaze over Yèyé. Satisfied with what she saw, her face creasing into a wide smile, she sang with KSA, *Congratulations on your birthday today, celebrant, we wish you happy birthday!*

"Fifty!" Aunty Bíọlá's voice shook as she gripped Yèyé's shoulders and pulled her close. "The baby of the house is fifty."

"Hin șé, Aunty mi. Hin șé gbogbo ùgbà, gbogbo ọjọ́," Yèyé whispered. She could spend the whole day repeating *hin șé, hin șé, hin șé,* and it would not be enough. She owed her sister gratitude beyond words. About three and a half decades ago, Aunty Bíọlá had squeezed her forearm as she told Yèyé that, yes, their mother had died in the car accident Yèyé survived. And while Yèyé—legs encased in plaster of paris and propped up towards the hospital ward's ceiling—tried to remember how to breathe, Aunty Bíọlá had leaned over her bed and whispered a vow she would sacrifice all she had ever wanted for: *I will take care of you, don't worry, I will take care of you.*

"I've told you to stop thanking me for doing my duty." Aunty Bíọlá pulled away and clapped her hands. "The photos you need to take. Kà rí photographer, hin pè? Where is he? Oh, gentleman, you are the one? Șe kíá àwé, start doing your work."

The photographer, a man whose upper lip disappeared into a thick moustache, pointed to an armchair. "We can start with some shots of her sitting in that."

"No, no," Aunty Bíọlá said. "You can't use that background, no, the wall is too plain. Láyí? Come here and join this man. Help him to carry that chair. You people should put it in front of a curtain. Let's see how that looks."

While Aunty Bíọlá ordered Láyí and the photographer around, Yèyé moved through the crowded room, stooping to greet her brothers-in-law, who had all arrived that morning. She began with Aunty Bíọlá's second husband and worked her way from sofa to sofa until she had thanked Aunty Jùmọkẹ́'s husband for the keyholder souvenirs he had brought for the party. The armchair had been positioned to Aunty Bíọlá's satisfaction by the time Yèyé was done acknowledging all their gifts and souvenirs. She walked to the chair, knowing from the worried frown on Aunty Bíọlá's face that her limp was more pronounced than usual. Only a little dancing and already she felt that dull ache in her left knee.

"Where is your father?" Yèyé asked Wúràọlá as she sank into the armchair with a sigh.

"He's in his study," Wúràọlá said without looking up from her phone. "He's speaking with Kúnlé, Professor Coker and Honourable Fèṣọjaiyé."

"Ehen, Honourable is here?" Fèṣọjaiyé, whom Yèyé knew of but had not yet met, was their constituency's representative in the national assembly.

"He had gone to see Kúnlé's father at home, but that one was already here. So Kúnlé brought him over."

Aunty Sùnmbọ nodded towards Wúràọlá. "That Kúnlé, he is a marvellous boy, and I can see he's also from a suitable family. Congratulations, my dear, you brought a good one home."

"Very suitable," Aunty Bíọlá said. "Well done, Wúràọlá."

Wúràọlá squinted at something on her phone. "Okay . . . thank you ma."

Yèyé smiled for the camera. God forbid she ever say it out loud, but Kúnlé was a much better catch than she expected for Wúràọlá. The longer Wúràọlá had remained single, flitting from one unserious boyfriend to another, the more Yèyé had worried that, when she did decide to commit to one of them, closer to thirty than twenty, she would be left with a pool of expiring men who were unmarried because no one wanted them. On her worst days, she had imagined Wúràọlá ending up with some barely educated drunkard whose parents lived in a house with no indoor plumbing. And how would that have improved on her daughter's fortunes in this life?

Look at God, though. Look at Lákúnlé Coker. Any woman, at twenty-one or twenty-eight, would be lucky to marry him. Yes, there had been that debacle about his grades when he was leaving secondary school. Mrs. Àjàdí from the Mothers' Union once said his first WAEC result had left his mother in tears. Five F9s out of nine subjects. Truly terrible. He had worked harder once his parents stopped insisting he study medicine, graduating with a second-class upper in some other course. Public administration or business administration. It could have been public relations. Whichever it was, he had done well at it. Sharing her testimony at a Mothers' Union prayer meeting after his graduation ceremony, Kúnlé's mother let everyone know he had missed a first-class grade by just a few points.

In any case, his family was well connected. Yèyé knew from his mother that Kúnlé had had multiple job offers of the best kind, the types he did not need to apply for to have. An uncle in Abuja who wanted Kúnlé to head his company's marketing department. An aunt in NNPC who had a slot she wanted to give him. And now Wúràọlá said he'd stopped trying to get a transfer to Lagos or Abuja, because his father wanted him close by for the campaign. Such a sensible boy and a good son. What was a shot at reading the news at nine to the whole country if he could help his father become state governor? Yes, he would have been perfect if he was a doctor. Just imagine, Wúràọlá as the second half of a Dr. & Dr. (Mrs.) unit. Perfection. But whatever Kúnlé had lost by not studying medicine, he had in family connections that would nudge him up any ladder he chose to climb and cushion any falls before propelling him upward again and again. Yèyé had lived long enough to realise that Aunty Bíọ́lá had always been right: real wealth was intergenerational, and the way Nigeria was set up, your parentage would often matter more than your qualifications.

The photographer asked Yèyé to stand in front of a blank wall with her children clustered around her.

"I should be next to you," Mọ́tárá said to Yèyé.

"That's not the order," Láyí said. "I'll stand to her right, Wúràọlá will stand to her left, and you will stand beside Wúràọlá."

"Why? Dr. Wúrà is the shortest. Shouldn't she be here at the edge?"

Yèyé felt Wúràọlá's body stiffen next to her. Even in heels, Wúràọlá was shorter than her sister. When Wúràọlá was a teenager, Yèyé had hoped she would add a few more inches. Good thing Kúnlé was much taller. His genes would at least give their children a fighting chance. Yèyé adjusted her bùbá. Yes, Kúnlé was almost perfect.

"Mọ́tárá, there's no need to insult your sister because of a photo." Yèyé squeezed Wúràọlá's shoulder.

"But I wasn't—"

"Just stay where your brother told you to stand." Yèyé adjusted her necklace. "Óyá, smile. Is everyone smiling?"

The photographer nodded. A click. A flash. Another position, Yèyé seated with her children fanned out behind the chair.

"Okay, now the in-laws." Aunty Sùnmbò stood and gestured to her husband.

Aunty Bíólá waved them back into their seats. "Láyí, where is your wife? Your wife should join the photo."

"Maybe Kúnlé should join them too?" Aunty Jùmòké asked, twisting in her chair to glance towards the corridor.

Aunty Bíólá shook her head. "They can do that later. He is still in the study, and we need to finish taking the photos soon. I want to see if those decorators have finished adjusting that podium. Láyí, where is Odúnayò? Wasn't she just here?"

"I don't know," Láyí said. "I saw her go downstairs."

Although he was standing behind her, Yèyé could tell that he was scratching the back of his head and glancing around the room, already bored with the photo session, ready to move on to the next thing.

Wúràolá flopped into a chair. "The Honourable who came to see Kúnlé's father brought some young men with him. So I asked her to go downstairs and help us make sure they are being given something to eat. Fried rice should be fine, right?"

Aunty Sùnmbò stood up. "Aunty Bíólá, let's just move on to taking photos with our husbands."

"Yes. Yes." Láyí hugged Yèyé from behind and was gone, adjusting his agbádá as he dashed down the stairs. He'd been in a hurry to get somewhere as soon as he could walk, and sometimes she wondered if he would ever arrive.

Yèyé leaned back in her chair. "Let's wait for a few minutes, maybe my husband can join us soon."

Aunty Sùnmbò cleared her throat. "My husband can't wait much longer. He has a meeting."

Of course that useless man had to leave. Which new wife was he off to see today? Who married six wives in this time and age? Especially when Aunty Sùnmbò never stopped him from having all the girlfriends he wanted. No, he had to marry them all. Even the brigadier had stopped at wife number four.

Yèyé smiled at Aunty Sùnmbọ̀'s husband. "All right, Engineer, please come. Ọ̀gá Photographer, you heard her, let's be quick about this."

While Yèyé's sisters argued about which background was best for the photo, Wúràọlá and Mọ́tárá went downstairs, slinging matching bags over their shoulders and pulling up the hems of their flowing dresses. Yèyé's sisters decided to pose in front of the sliding door that opened to the balcony, and then another argument began about whether to pull the heavy curtains over the glass door or not.

"Let's just take both, for goodness' sake." Aunty Sùnmbọ̀'s strained voice cracked through the bickering.

The men left for the canopy after a few photos were taken. Aunty Sùnmbọ̀'s husband was leaving for his so-called meeting, but she did not go with him to his car and they did not say goodbye to each other. Aunty Àbẹ̀ní gave the other husbands instructions about how to locate the tables that had been assigned to them under the canopy.

"They can just look for Wúràọlá or Ọdúnayọ̀ when they get downstairs," Yèyé said.

"Well, they can't get lost." Aunty Bíọ́lá rummaged through a large handbag.

Yèyé turned away from her sisters, pushed the curtain aside just a little and looked out through the glass door. Cars already lined both sides of the street outside the gate. Guests were streaming in in twos and threes, pausing to hug people they recognised before disappearing beneath the large white canopy.

The band should start playing music soon.

Yèyé's mother had wanted a party for her fiftieth birthday. Even before, there was no way she could have afforded one as big as what Yèyé was having today. Regardless, Yèyé was sure her mother would have had a live band because of how much she loved to dance. Discussions about this dream party had happened during the few years before. Before Yèyé's father fell ill. Before all his businesses and assets were sold to pay his hospital bills. Before Yèyé's mother sold her gold. Before Aunty Bíọ́lá and Aunty Àbẹ̀ní had to drop out of university. Before the only valuable thing the family had left was the house their father had built. Before he was buried in the backyard of that house three years after the first tumour was removed from his brain. Before the end of all that could have been.

Yèyé's father had been the first in his family to go to school, the only one of his siblings to earn a university degree, the first and only one to build his own house. Although he had only just clawed his way up from poverty, her father had been convinced that he was already a rich man. Half of his money had gone to cousins and nieces and nephews. That endless stream of relatives who came to her parents for money and favours until her father fell ill. The same people who then pretended they were not in when Yèyé and her mother went to knock on the doors of their rented homes. What could they have done if they had answered the door? Sold a house that was not theirs to pay for yet another operation? A rich man amid ten wretched men was not really rich; he just had not discovered yet that he was poor.

"Àlàkẹ́? Àlàkẹ́?"

Yèyé turned away from the balcony, thinking for a moment that her father was standing behind her, calling her name. But it was only Aunty Bíọ́lá reverting to Àlàkẹ́ after calling Yèyé for a while. No one called her Àlàkẹ́ anymore, not since she and her husband received their chieftaincy titles the year Wúràọlá was born.

"Ṣéèsí" Aunty Bíọ́lá asked.

"I'm all right."

"Kóìtiírí kí o mí wò sìì."

"Aunty Bíọ́lá, don't worry. Àní, I'm all right. Óyá, let's take the photo." Yèyé moved away from the glass door and settled into a chair.

Aunty Bíọ́lá handed her a framed photograph, and Yèyé set it on her knee without glancing at it. It was a photo of their mother. From before. Had she even taken any pictures after that diagnosis? Yèyé and her sisters used the same photo at every wedding and major birthday. Their Mother. Seated on a chair in the yà mí tùkatùka pose. Hands on her knees, one gripping a clutch, the other splayed to show the gold rings on every other finger, both wrists decked with beads. Her ìró tied above her waist. Two layers of coral beads nestled against her bùbá. The aṣọ-òkè ìró and gèlè were probably red, but there was no way to tell for sure, since the photo was black-and-white. She was smiling. One eye gazed directly at the camera while the other, the right one, glanced at something outside the frame. Yèyé thought of them often, those eyes that never really met hers.

"Óyá, smile." Aunty Bíọlá hovered, as though waiting to grab the frame if it slipped from Yèyé's hands. "And hold the photo a little higher, a little more. Ehen, good."

"You smile like her," Aunty Jùmọkẹ́ said.

"No," Aunty Àbẹ́ní said. "It's that Mọ́tárá that really smiles like her."

They had done this for the first time on the morning of Aunty Bíọlá's wedding. Hers was the only wedding that they held in the front yard of their father's house, as though he were alive to receive his new in-laws. Much had changed in that house, but the living room's yolk-yellow walls were still adorned with several photos of their parents. Aunty Bíọlá had pointed to this picture of their mother when her photographer arrived. It was Yèyé who climbed a stool to dislodge it from the wall. When Yèyé reached for their father's photograph too, Aunty Bíọlá asked her to stop. At first, Yèyé had mistaken the stricken look on her sister's face for grief refreshed. Then Aunty Bíọlá spoke, voice strident with rage: *I don't want that man in my wedding photos, let his precious son take photos with him.* Later that day, after the sisters had clustered around Aunty Bíọlá while she held their mother's photo on her knee, the precious son would sit in their father's place at the wedding ceremony. He would not be invited to any of the other weddings. At those, all held in the brigadier's house in Ìbàdàn, Aunty Bíọlá sat in their mother's place and left the chairs meant for their father empty.

Aunty Bíọlá claimed that she did not want a relationship with the precious son because, although he was their brother, he was not their mother's son, and one could never truly trust a sibling who had not suckled from the same breast. Behind her back, though, Aunty Àbẹ́ní and Aunty Sùnmbọ̀ told another story. Aunty Bíọlá and the precious son, who was named Festus, after their father, were born in the same month. He was born to their father's mistress while she was born to their mother, whom their father had been married to for two years at that point. Aunty Bíọlá and Festus Jr. were classmates from their first day of school, but their father had always paid his son's school fees first. When it was time for both to leave for the university, their father had just opened his second electronic store and did not have enough cash to sponsor both children in their first year. Aunty Bíọlá had to spend two years at home—working as an unpaid cashier in the brand-new branch of Festus Akínyẹmí and Sons Electronics—before resuming her first year alongside Aunty Àbẹ̀ní when Festus Jr. was already in his third year. According to Aunty Àbẹ̀ní and Aunty Sùnmbọ, this was why Aunty Bíọlá acted as if their father had never existed. Maybe they all allowed her to erase him from their lives because on his sick bed he had willed all he had left, which by then came to a few wristwatches and the house he had built, to Festus Jr. The sisters never discussed how they had become unwelcome visitors in their own home once Festus Jr. took possession of the house after their father's death. Rehashing it all was unnecessary, because they had survived it. Aunty Bíọlá's marriage to the brigadier had saved them from being homeless. They had survived. All of them.

Now Yèyé gripped Aunty Bíọlá's hand as her sisters gathered round for a group photo with their mother. This was how they did it every time. First, the celebrant with their mother—who, trapped in time, was now the youngest in the photos—then all of them together with her. And always, Aunty Bíọlá called each sister's name softly to make sure they were all there.

"Aren't you coming?" Aunty Sùnmbọ asked.

Yèyé's sisters had all picked up their clutches and were walking or ambling towards the landing.

"I've not taken any photos with my husband."

Aunty Bíọlá glanced at the doorway that opened to the corridor. "Can't you take the photos later?"

"I should wait for him." Yèyé wanted her husband by her side when she made her entrance into the party. Yes, she was the one who sometimes danced into her bathroom, but Adémọ́lá was a much better dancer. He held her hands whenever they danced together. Pulling her into his body so she leaned on him and put less strain on her knees.

"Call me when you're about to come in so we can wait at the entrance and dance in front of you. Ṣebí, that's how we are going to do it?"

"Aunty Bíọlá, thank you so much for everything."

"I said you should stop thanking me. When will you listen?" Aunty Bíọ́lá began to descend the stairs. The other sisters followed, heels clacking against the marble tiles.

Yèyé leaned back in her chair and trained her gaze on the centre table. She stared at one spot until she tuned out all the sounds clamouring for her attention. The relentless percussion accompanying Yinka Ayefele while he sang "Beru Ba Monuro" beneath the canopy, chatter filtering up from the ground floor, clinks and thuds as the photographer searched through his knapsack. Yèyé had learnt to do this when Wúràọlá was a toddler who trailed her around the house and chattered nonstop until she feared that she might sew her daughter's mouth shut just to have some peace. Sometimes she wished she had paid more attention then. Perhaps there was some key in those babbles that could have unlocked the tight-lipped teenager Wúràọlá became. She never let those thoughts settle, chasing them off with memories of a teenage Wúràọlá, legs drawn to her chest and chin on her knee, chatting into the night with Adémọ́lá in this same family room. Adémọ́lá, who shut himself in his study when the children were toddlers, safe from all the babbling.

No one expected the birthday party to start at noon anyway, but what were those men talking about? Yèyé glanced at her watch. She could spend another thirty minutes waiting for Adémọ́lá. Making her entrance forty minutes late was not too bad. Besides, he would be hurt if she left without him, and she would have to spend the next month proving she cared about him. Just him. Not the cheques he had signed to throw the party or all the dignitaries and chiefs, even the Léjọ̀kà, who would attend because she was Adémọ́lá's wife. His need for reassurance often made her irritable. So what if she chose him because of his name and his wealth and his family in which no one was wretched? How could she not care about him when she was so grateful for him? When she always supervised his meal and served him herself, slipped into his room once a week so they could make love and never turned him away if he came into hers and tugged the drawstring on her nightgown during the night. But he had always wanted more from her, dismissing the things she enumerated as her duty. As if duty could not be some form of devotion, of love. She did not sulk for days hoping he would prove that he cared. After over three decades of marriage? Why would she need that? He let her lean into him when they danced so her knees would not suffer. That was enough proof for her.

A door was slammed shut down the corridor, and Yèyé sensed there was trouble. Adémọ́lá never slammed doors. Not when he was in a hurry or running late. Not even when he was so angry that the whites of his eyes turned red, as though he might weep with rage. His movements were always measured. Teacups set in saucers without a clink, back turned on her in a fluid motion that barely disturbed the mattress, doors shut in her face with a firm click. If Adémọ́lá had slammed a door, something must have gone wrong in that study. It had to be him; none of the men he was meeting with would be so rude. Yèyé craned her neck.

The men were spilling out of the study into the corridor. Honourable Fẹ̀sọ̀jaiyé led the way, belly straining against his green bùbá. He was flanked by two men who, as they got closer, turned out to be boys. Both boys were seventeen at most. They were tall and muscular, sporting scraggly beards that reminded Yèyé of when Láyí tried to grow one by rubbing methylated spirit on his chin every night. A few paces behind them, Kúnlé and his father walked side by side. And then came her husband, Ọ̀túnba Adémọ́lá Mákinwá. Towering over them all, adjusting his agbádá as he advanced with the confidence of a man who had known all his life that others would wait for him. The frown on his face confirmed what she had thought when she heard the door slam, that this had not been a pleasant meeting.

"Good uhm." The Honourable glanced at his watch. "Good afternoon, Yèyé."

Yèyé rose to her feet. "Good afternoon sir."

"We've never been introduced, but I've seen you at parties before. Happy birthday ma."

"Thank you so much."

"And congratulations on your daughter's engagement." He glanced towards the corridor. There Kúnlé and his father had paused to speak with Adémọ́lá in whispers. "The lucky man himself told me on our way here."

"We are so happy about it. Maybe you will come when we are celebrating the wedding?" Yèyé smiled.

"May God preserve all our lives until then and beyond. If I get an invitation, I will be there. I have spoken to the men, and they have been doing strong head. Yèyé ria, let me talk to you, so that you can help me to speak to them." The Honourable gripped Yèyé's shoulders and squeezed. "Ask your husband to warn his friend not to be unfortunate. Yèyé, I am the next governor of this state. Professor should not let anybody deceive him. When we were inside, I kept begging him to be my commissioner for health when I become governor, but he refused. That offer is now off the table. It is time for him to be warned. If he does not heed that warning? Yèyé, none of us will weep over our child's dead body o."

The Honourable was gone before Adémọ́lá's fist could connect with the back of his head. His boys followed, walking backwards until they reached the landing.

"The effrontery!" Professor Coker shouted, rushing into the family room on Adémọ́lá's heels. "The effrontery of that man. Do I resemble someone who can be threatened?"

Adémọ́lá put his arm around Yèyé, and she held his waist, digging her fingers into the folds of his agbádá to keep them from trembling.

"They are empty threats," Kúnlé said. "That's how they do, intimidation and threats, there is nothing to it."

"I'm so sorry you had to face that embarrassment," Professor Coker said. "Yèyé, I'm really very sorry."

"Kò sí problem." Yèyé swallowed. "Could you join the party now and give us a moment?"

"Of course, of course. Again, I'm so sorry." Professor Coker and his son left the room.

"You too," Yèyé said to the photographer.

"But the photos with your husband ma."

"Capture that during the party."

She waited until all the footfalls had faded into silence before she began to pace.

"Are you okay?" he asked.

"No." Yèyé sighed. "What that man said—"

"Don't mind him."

"Our daughter is marrying Kúnlé o."

"And so?"

"What if something happens?"

"Like what?"

"Assassination."

Adémólá laughed. "Don't worry. Assassination lóhùún lóhùún, that can't happen. Fèsòjaiyé would not dare. Coker has the party chairman's support. Will this small rat go against the chairman? When he's not stupid."

Yèyé came to a halt in front of her husband. "Why is it so funny? What happened to Williams is not up to five years yet."

"Williams?"

"Fúnsó Williams, didn't they kill him in his own house over governorship?"

"This is not Lagos, my dear. Ìwọ don't worry. Nothing will go wrong, it's just politics."

"Why did you take the meeting in your study?"

"Why not?"

"Once you knew there was going to be trouble, you should have told Professor to meet them in the car or something."

"Coker and I are in this together now. I'm funding half of his campaign."

"You are what? Adémólá, kílódé? Why didn't you tell me? Isn't that risky?"

He adjusted the folds of his agbádá. "Don't worry about this, it's a good investment."

She studied his face. The bushy brows he refused to let her trim, the laugh lines that branched out from his nostrils to kiss the edges of his full lips, the chin that could have been chiselled out of stone. She searched for a sign that he was troubled too and was only trying to reassure her. She found nothing. He stared back at her, unconcerned. She had always marvelled at his calm assurance that everything good in his life would either remain the same or get better. He took good fortune for granted. As though it were impossible that it would abide only for a spell. She had never been able to shake the sense that life was war, a series of battles with the occasional spell of good things.

"Are you ready?" he asked, holding out a hand to her.

Yèyé slipped her hand into his and let him lead her down the staircase.

B y afternoon, Ẹniọlá felt trapped in the house. Though it was a Saturday, he could not go to Aunty Caro's shop because she was taking the day off to attend her customer's birthday party. Everyone in the shop had been surprised and thrilled when the invitation arrived via Yèyé's driver. Aunty Caro made Ẹniọlá read the invitation's contents to her, as though still unsure that she had really been invited. The next day, she had brought out all her lace dresses for the apprentices to see, asking again and again, *Does this look like something a rich madam would wear?* Ẹniọlá had pointed at a gold dress with silver chiffon trimmings after Ṣèyí and Maria chose it too. Although he was certain, from hours spent poring over *Ovation,* that the dress did not look like something any rich madam would wear, he liked the safety of agreeing with Ṣèyí and Maria. Later, if Aunty Caro became unhappy with her decision to wear the dress, her blame would be split three ways and his share of it would be a manageable size.

Hoots, whoops and the loud thwacks of a ball being kicked back and forth filtered into the house from the front yard, torturing Ẹniọlá as he lay on the mattress. He could be out there now, playing with the other boys. Yet here he was, stuck inside because the landlord often sat on his balcony to watch when boys in the neighbourhood played football in front of the house. Ẹniọlá worried that if he went outside to enjoy that afternoon's game, the landlord would ask him why his father had not come upstairs to meet with him. Maybe the landlord would even ask him about the rent, yelling about it for all the other boys to hear. Paul might be there with his big mouth and long legs, dribbling and scoring, ready to memorise all the things the landlord might shout down at Ẹniọlá. Come

Monday, Paul would definitely dramatise everything in front of all their classmates while everyone laughed.

Ẹniọlá turned so he lay on his back. His mother was not home yet, and his father was an immobile, crumpled mass on the bed. He'd gotten up once since Ẹniọlá's mother left, to urinate. At least, that is what Ẹniọlá assumed when he dashed back in a few minutes after he stepped out. Ẹniọlá had hoped he was planning to go upstairs and chat with the landlord, but no, the man was going to wait for Ẹniọlá's mother to remind him of his responsibility. Ẹniọlá swallowed the anger flaming up inside him, quenching it with a memory still so vivid, he could almost smell garlic when it came back to him.

A few months after the state government sacked hundreds of teachers in one day, Ẹniọlá's family had gone to visit Mr. Ọlábọ̀dé, one of his father's friends who had also been sacked. The door was slightly ajar when they arrived at the house, and after two knocks, Ẹniọlá's father nudged it open. When they stepped into Mr. Ọlábọ̀dé's sitting room, it took them a few moments to register what they saw. Mr. Ọlábọ̀dé hanging from the ceiling fan by a thick rope, dressed up as though he was leaving for work, belt and shoes matching his brown tie. They all stared up at the body in stunned silence for a while. Then Ẹniọlá glanced at his father's face and saw that he was gazing up at Mr. Ọlábọ̀dé with envy and admiration. He'd been so terrified by the look on his father's face that he gasped, breaking the trancelike moment. Ẹniọlá's mother had covered his face with her hands, pressing her fingers against his eyes and nose so he could not escape the smell of the garlic she'd chopped before they left home.

On the funeral notice that was printed a few days later, Mr. Ọlábọ̀dé was said to have died of a brief illness. Several sacked teachers died from brief illnesses in the next couple of years, and always, when Ẹniọlá heard about their deaths, he remembered the look he'd seen on his father's face before his mother covered his eyes. Now, years later, whenever he wanted to stand over his father and scream at him to get up and do something, Ẹniọlá would remember how the man had once longed to be dead. His anger often dissipated then; sometimes it was replaced by fear.

The air was hot and stale. Ẹniọlá had already taken off his T-shirt and singlet. He wished he could take off his shorts, but Bùsọ́lá lay on her stomach beside him, reading a book.

"What's it about?" Ẹniọlá asked, fanning his face with his hands.

Bùsọ́lá did not speak for a while, and he wondered if she'd heard him; then she said, "It's for my friend's sister, the eldest one. They read it for WAEC in their set. What is your own set reading?"

He had seen his contemporaries in the art class clutching copies of *Hamlet* and *The Joys of Motherhood*. "I said, what is it about?"

"Chichidodo."

"What?"

"Chichidodo," Bùsọ́lá said. "It's a bird, but I don't know if it's real."

"The book is about birds?"

"No, it's not. But the Chichidodo is . . . You will understand if you read the book. I can give it to you when I'm done. I've almost finished."

He was not interested in reading a book. He wanted to be outside, running free on the red sand, feeling the breeze on his back as he scored a goal. Not stuck in this room hearing about some bird while the bedsheet clung to his sweaty back.

The door yawned open as he rolled over to his side.

His mother walked in, removing her scarf as she entered the room. "Today's heat can fry an egg from start to finish."

"Hin káàbọ ma," Ẹniọlá said, sitting up.

Bùsọ́lá shut the book she was reading. "Did you get the school fees?"

Ẹniọlá's mother sat by her husband on the bed and placed a hand on his shoulder.

"Did you get the money?" Bùsọ́lá asked.

"Have you lost all your manners? Offer me a cup of water, no. Welcome me home like your brother just did, no. Instead, you are there asking me about school fees like someone with no home training."

Bùsọ́lá took the deep breath that often preceded one of her complaints, but someone knocked on the door, saving Ẹniọlá from hearing her whine.

"Who is it?" Ẹniọlá said.

"The owner of the door." The booming voice was unmistakable—it was the landlord.

Prone for most of the day until then, Ẹniọlá's father sat up and glanced around the room as though hoping a wall might split open so he could step into it.

"You're the one he wants to talk to, Bàbá Ẹniọlá," Ẹniọlá's mother said.

Ẹniọlá's father stood up. "Please," he said to Ẹniọlá's mother, rubbing his palms together in supplication before sliding under the bed in one swift movement.

"Do I need to break down this door?" the landlord shouted.

"It's open sir, but let me come and—" Ẹniọlá's mother rushed towards the door, then fell to her knees as the landlord barged into the room. "Good afternoon sir."

"Don't bribe me with empty greetings, Ìyá Ẹniọlá," he yelled, hitting the floor with his carved walking stick. "I'm here to see your husband. Where is he?"

"He has gone out," Ẹniọlá's mother said. "Erm, he has gone on a travel . . . on a journey. He had to travel some hours ago. Erm, his brother's uncle called him and said there was an emergency he needs to attend to in—"

The landlord scanned the room. "I heard a man's voice when I was standing outside the door."

"Yes, yes, it was my son." She pointed towards Ẹniọlá. "His voice is becoming a man's voice and he now sounds like his father. Óyá, Ẹniọlá, speak up, greet Bàbá Landlord."

"Good afternoon sir," Ẹniọlá said.

The landlord moved through the room, past the wooden cabinet that held clothes, pots and schoolbooks, past the closed window and the raggedy curtain that was drawn across it. When Bàbá landlord stopped at the foot of the bed, Ẹniọlá held his breath as the man stood still with his head cocked to the side, listening for something.

"Ìyá Ẹniọlá, tell your husband, wherever he may be, that I want my money next week. If you don't pay me my money by the end of next week, you are leaving my house."

Ẹniọlá's mother nodded. "Okay sir, yes sir, yes sir. I will tell him."

The landlord turned around and walked towards the door. "I've only been pitying you people because of your children, but I can't pity you anymore. Remember when I told you people not to pay electricity bills for two months?"

"Yes sir, I remember sir, thank you sir." Ẹniọlá's mother bent towards the floor, almost touching her head to the ground. "We are grateful."

"You can't say I've not been kind. This time, whether your husband is here or not, I will chase you out." The landlord hit his stick against the door. "Do you understand my words?"

"Very well sir," Ẹniọlá's mother said. "Thank you sir."

The room was quiet after the landlord left.

Ẹniọlá's mother stood up, shut the door and stayed there with her hand on the doorknob. "We are going begging tomorrow morning."

"What did you say?" Bùsọlá asked.

Without turning around, their mother repeated, "We are going begging tomorrow morning."

12

"Tell me, how does it feel to be engaged? Different, ehn?" Grace asked. Wúràọlá was supervising tables one to twelve and had stopped by table six to make sure her girlfriends had been served grilled fish.

Tifẹ́ rolled her eyes as she speared a piece of catfish. "Who told you there's a special feeling? She did not acquire a new finger. She's just wearing a ring on one of her old fingers."

Wúràọlá had not expected it to feel so different. It hadn't at first. Not so much after the proposal or even this morning. But now, three hours or so since the party began, she felt being engaged as something real and tangible. It was a distinct category from the one she had belonged to at this time yesterday. When she stopped to check on a table, women patted her on the back or abandoned their food and stood up to hug her. The men shook her hand so vigorously, she worried they might dislocate her shoulder. The aunties smiled at her whenever they caught her eye. Even Aunty Bíọ́lá, whom Wúràọlá had expected to hold a grudge over the disagreement about supervising the cooks during the night.

The difference was there in the way her parents had danced in when they finally decided to show up, ecstatic beyond what a fiftieth birthday party called for, revelling already in all the ceremonies that would lead to Wúràọlá's wedding. It was in how she overheard Yèyé whispering about the engagement to everyone who greeted her, *Thank you, thank you. You know you'll be back soon to celebrate with us again, our first daughter is getting married*. It was her father introducing Wúràọlá and Kúnlé to his friends as *the intending couple*. As though they had both been reborn and needed to be reintroduced to the family friends who had known them since they were little.

Wúràọlá was surprised at how pleased she was with all the attention. She had assumed it would only feel like a different kind of pressure, the flipside of being asked when she would get married at gatherings that preceded this one. Instead, her father was grinning the way he had at her first prize-giving day in secondary school when she'd won all the prizes available in her class. Tacking Most Punctual and Best-Behaved awards to prizes for mathematics and integrated science. She would never repeat the feat again, even though she continued to win prizes every year. And she would never forget the pleasure she'd felt from her parents' pride, like light trapped beneath her skin, radiating outward and bathing everyone else in joy. What she felt now at her mother's fiftieth birthday party was even more intense. The smiles that greeted her spread wider than they had for anything else she'd ever accomplished. The hugs lasted longer, pats on the back transitioned into rubs as though no one wanted to let go of her. *The whole Mákinwá family is proud of you*, her father's brother, the retired colonel, had said to her when he arrived. *You have not let your brains prevent you from being homey, we are so proud.*

What did it feel like to be engaged? At this party, it was like being a celebrity. Everyone wanted to touch her or talk to her. Wúràọlá did not have time to explain all of this to Grace and Tifẹ. She would have had to shout over the music, and her voice was already getting hoarse. She'd decided to speak in whispers or via the Post-it notes she carried in her clutch for the rest of the day. It would be silly to arrive at the hospital on Monday unable to communicate with her patients. She smiled and moved to another table. This one was occupied by three of her father's siblings. Before she'd finished scribbling her question on a Post-it, the colonel asked her to get another round of drinks for the table. She zigzagged her way towards the exit, dodging servers who were ferrying trays laden with plates of food to the guests.

When Wúràọlá opened the canopy's flaps and emerged into a much smaller one that was not air-conditioned or covered at the sides, she almost bumped into Aunty Jùmọkẹ. Her aunt did not notice. She was busy shouting at a caterer about how quickly they'd run out of peppered turkey. Wúràọlá sidestepped the women and kept her gaze averted. She could not afford to get dragged into the fray. Or worse, be badgered by her aunt into confessing where Yèyé and Aunty Bíọlá had hidden fifty pieces of every type of meat. At these parties, *meat is finished* only meant you weren't one of the select few for whom we'd been asked to open the secret vault of meat. Aunty Jùmọ̀kẹ́ knew this too, which was why she was screaming, *No way, I don't want chicken, my guests won't eat chicken. Do you know who I am at all?* Unfazed by Aunty Jùmọ̀kẹ́'s speech about how she had changed the celebrant's nappy many times, the caterer stood arms akimbo as she shouted back, *Madam, the turkey is finished, and I can't turn myself into peppered turkey.*

Wúràọlá quickened her pace, slowing down only when she was safely out of the food zone. The servers who worked in the drinks section wore black shirts that bore a company logo. Most were busy, arranging wines in a fridge, reaching into drums brimming with ice for bottles of water, filling coolers with soft drinks. Wúràọlá grabbed a server by the elbow.

"Take two bottles of Dom Pérignon to table five," she whispered to him. "Don't stop anywhere. Come closer, let me tell you something. If they ask you for another one, tell them you're bringing it right away, but don't take anything to that table for another two hours. You hear me? You heard me, right? Ehen, okay. Tell your people. No drinks for table five after these ones. Not for two hours. Just water, you can send them water, okay? Now give me one Coke."

While he fetched the Coke, she scanned the space for an unoccupied chair. Who knew how many miles she had traversed beneath that canopy, dashing between tables to make sure everyone was satisfied with what they had been given. It helped that she had traded those pointy heels for a pair of flats, but, kai, she would be so much more comfortable in shorts right now. Wúràọlá laughed as she took the Coke from the server. Yèyé would faint with shame if she came back to the party in shorts. Wúràọlá took a swig and shut her eyes. Maybe she should go back to the food zone and get something to eat. All day, the only thing she had eaten was the spring roll she'd picked off Kúnlé's plate when she stopped by his family's table. No, she didn't have time to eat yet. They would need to share souvenirs soon, and none of her siblings had brought out the customised notebooks they'd embossed with *Courtesy: Celebrant's Loving Children.*

Wúràọlá dug into her bag for her phone and texted her siblings. *Meet me by the drinks stand. We need to get souvenirs.*

She felt a firm tap on her shoulder, followed by, "Hey, golden babe."

Only one person called her that: Kingsley. She was grinning by the time she stood up. It was Kingsley, gap-toothed, bespectacled Kingsley. The first of a string of classmates she had gone out with after Nonso's disastrous meeting with her mother. By Tifẹ́'s reckoning, she'd dated one person each month during their fourth year in medical school. Wúràọlá had never bothered to do a headcount.

"You remembered? Oh, Kingsley, that's so kind of you." Wúràọlá had mentioned the party only in passing the last time she saw him. That must have been a couple of months ago.

Kingsley shrugged, as though it wasn't any trouble to give up a free Saturday. "You look incredible."

"Thanks. Did you just get here?"

"No, I've been around for like an hour. I was calling your name while you were under the canopy, but that noise, ehn."

"Have you seen Grace and Tifẹ́? No? They'll be so happy to see you." Wúràọlá pointed towards the larger canopy. "Come, let me take you to their table."

Kingsley did not move. Instead, he stared at her left finger, squinting at her engagement ring. He took off his glasses and put them on again. "Is that . . . ?"

"Yes, only just yesterday."

"Wow, congratulations, golden babe." He shoved his hands in his pockets. "Don't worry, I'm sure you have a zillion things to do right now. I'll find Grace and Tifẹ́ by myself."

He brushed past Wúràọlá before she could say anything else.

She glanced round; neither of her siblings had shown up, so she texted Kúnlé. He was with her in minutes.

They walked towards the house together, stopping to greet guests who had come out to the lawn to smoke or chat.

"Am I the only child? The two of them always leave me to sort out these things. I chose the design and picked it up from the printer, am I now supposed to carry five hundred notebooks by myself? They know Yèyé cares about these things, but they won't lift a finger, especially that Mọ́tárá."

Kúnlé cleared his throat. "Did you invite Kingsley? I think I saw him as I was coming to you."

"Yes, I wasn't even expecting him to come, you know. I know just how busy he is, and he's giving up a Saturday for this. But that's Kingsley, sha, he's always thoughtful."

A man in green was holding court with three other men, who formed a semicircle around him. He waved at Kúnlé as they passed by them, but Kúnlé looked away. Wúràọlá smiled and bent her knees; the man grinned back.

"Isn't that one of those politicians? He's a senator or something, right?"

"Honourable Fẹ̀sọ̀jaiyé. He's in the House of Reps."

"Why did you snub him?"

"Don't worry about it."

Of course, Mọ́tárá was lazing about in the living room. She was surrounded by six girls, who giggled while she told a story. Wúràọlá recognised just two of them, Aunty Jùmọ̀kẹ́'s twins. Wúràọlá wanted to ignore Mọ́tárá and focus on what she had come to do, but their eyes met as she started up the stairs, so she beckoned to her.

"Didn't you see my text?" Wúràọlá asked.

"What?" Mọ́tárá sighed. "Hello, Kúnlé."

Wúràọlá leaned over the banister. "Did you get my text? You should come with me."

"Why are you talking like that? My friends are here, I can't just leave them." Mọ́tárá lifted the hem of her dress and wiggled her toes. "Anyway, I can't find my shoes."

"Get your friends a table under the canopy, why do they have to be inside?"

"Didn't you hear me? I took off my shoes after we danced in with Yèyé, and I can't find them anywhere."

"And so? You are not making yourself useful at all, Mọ́tárá. Come on, let's carry those souvenirs together."

"Ahn ahn, why do I need to do that? Kúnlé is going to help you now. And you can always ask one of the servers to carry them. My hands are hurting o—me, I can't carry anything. Everybody is just stressing me out, Aunty Bíọ́lá them, they are all stressing me. And now you too. Please,

I need to rest first before carrying anything." Mótárá returned to her friends without waiting for a response.

Wúràọlá shook her head and continued upstairs; she did not have the time to berate her sister. That could happen later.

"Your parents have really spoilt that girl," Kúnlé said when they got to the landing. "See how she spoke to me."

"She wasn't speaking to you."

"Why are you always defending her? She was rude to you too."

"I'm just saying, I don't get the point you are making. She wasn't addressing you."

"She spoke about me. I don't like how she uses my name just like that, as if we are mates."

"Well, she doesn't call our elder brother Brother Láyí and she doesn't call me Aunty or Sister either. You've noticed that, right?"

"Why are you siding with her?"

They were standing in front of Wúràọlá's bedroom, but the door was locked. The other thing about being engaged? Kúnlé was now allowed—no, welcomed—beyond the family room. Was it not Aunty Bíọlá who had encouraged him to stop by in Mótárá's room and greet Wúràọlá when he arrived this morning? Same Aunty Bíọlá of the *Entertain any boy downstairs until he proposes, why should he get to come into your family room?* counsel. Wúràọlá rummaged through her bag for keys, trying to remember if one of the aunts who stayed in the room last night had collected them from her since the party began.

Kúnlé glared at her. "Why are you taking sides with Mótárá?"

"I just want to be sure you understand the context."

"She doesn't just call you Wúràọlá." He frowned. "She calls you Dr. Wúrà."

"Well, that's who I am." Wúràọlá zipped up her bag. "You should have gotten a medical degree if you wanted someone to call you Dr. Kúnlé."

He slapped her cheek with his palm wide open, so his forefinger poked her eye. Then he followed that with a backhand as he brought his arm back to his side.

Wúràọlá staggered backward. He stood with his arms folded across his chest, lips pursed into an angry line, watching her press a finger against the eye he had poked. The eye she could not bear to open because it hurt so much.

At first, Wúràọlá thought she was the one who kept yelping, but once she could open both eyes, she saw it was Mọ́tárá, standing at the end of the corridor, holding her chin as if to keep her jaw in place.

PART III

Waiting for an Angel

As I turned and surveyed the gate and the fences beside it, I saw the fences suddenly transform into thick walls, standing tall, top-tufted with barbed wire and broken bottles, arms widespread to restrain and contain and limit. I wanted no more limits; only those I set for myself.

—*Waiting for an Angel* by Helon Habila

13

Eniọlá did not want to do it, but according to his mother, there were no alternatives. Every relative within reach had been begged to contribute the little they had. And now, as his mother counted the money that had been gathered so far, Eniọlá wished it would all add up and somehow be enough. For school fees, for food that week, for what was left of rent. He would even settle for just rent and school fees. He'd gone for days without food before and would gladly do so this week to avoid begging in the streets again.

"Three thousand two hundred and ninety," Eniọlá's mother said. "We made 3,290 naira yesterday."

It had been almost nine p.m. by the time they all got home the previous evening, and Eniọlá's mother had refused to count money in the dark. They'd been on the street twice since Eniọlá's mother suggested it. Last Sunday and yesterday. Today would be the third day.

"Today will be better than yesterday," Eniọlá's mother said, folding the bills she'd just counted. "People are more generous on Sundays. Remember last Sunday? Six thousand o, almost six thousand in total."

His mother also believed people were more generous on Fridays. That, fresh from Jummat, most people were eager to do good deeds. After their first outing last Sunday, she had suggested they all go and beg in front of the central mosque that Friday, but Eniọlá's father found his voice and insisted that the children should be in school instead. When his mother did not argue, Eniọlá had wondered if she was simply too surprised by his father sounding as if he cared about something for the first time in a while. Eniọlá assumed that she went to the mosque while he was at school but did not ask her about it. He'd noticed crayfish in the soup that night and tried to enjoy it without thinking about how wasteful it was for them to eat like that, since the landlord's rent was not completely paid off and not a naira of his or Bùsọ́lá's school fees had been paid.

"So, 10,000 naira deposit to keep us in school, and 25,000 balance for the landlord. That's 35,000 naira. Minus this 3,290, you have 31,710 naira. We have 31,710 naira to go," Bùsọ́lá said, flipping a page and scribbling in her notebook. She was intent on completing all her homework before leaving the house that morning.

"It's not that much." Ẹniọlá's mother gave the money she just counted to his father. "We paid the landlord five thousand naira on Friday."

Although Ẹniọlá's father never went begging with the rest of his family, all the money they got was always handed over to him. He took the notes to their landlord upstairs, paying in instalments and pleading for an extension on the ultimatum the man had given them. None had been granted yet, but since today was just over a week since the landlord's angry visit, the family assumed that the partial payments had appeased him somewhat. Yesterday, Bùsọ́lá had complained that nothing was being set aside for their school fees.

"So, 26,710," Bùsọ́lá said.

"Okay." Ẹniọlá's mother spread out a scarf on the bed and flattened the wrinkles with her palm.

Bùsọ́lá chewed her Biro. "Or 36,710 naira."

"What?" Ẹniọlá's mother said.

"Thirty-six thousand seven hundred and ten naira if you want to pay our school fees in full." Bùsọ́lá shut her notebook. "Nobody is going to be that generous."

"We're not paying school fees in full. Who pays school fees in full all at once?"

"Many people. Nonye's parents, Tinúọlá's parents, Rẹ̀mí's father—"

"Did I ask you any question?" Ẹniọlá's mother picked up the scarf and shook it out with more force than was necessary.

Bùsọ́lá stood up from the mattress and tucked her notebook into her schoolbag. "But you said—"

"If you don't keep shut there."

"It's okay," Ẹniọlá's father said, tucking the money into his breast pocket. "Please don't shout at Bùsọ́lá."

"We will take this step by step. Pay the fifty percent they asked for first and then . . ." Ẹniọlá's mother slung the scarf over her shoulder. "Óyá, Ẹniọlá, come here."

Ẹniọlá sat beside his father on the bed and let his arms rest by his side. Every time they had gone out to beg, his mother insisted on getting him ready to play his part. The signs they used were prepared by their father, who wrote why they should be pitied and followed that with details Ẹniọlá thought were unnecessary. Wasn't it enough for people to think Ẹniọlá was deaf? Did they need to think he had lost both parents in a fire too? Ẹniọlá never complained about the signs. Apart from the application letters he sent to schools and companies that never responded, the signs were the only things his father had written in at least a year. And though Ẹniọlá's mother said they could keep using the first signs he'd made last Sunday, he'd gone ahead and written new ones ahead of yesterday. Now he spread liquid starch on the flipside of the ones he'd gotten up to make early that morning and passed them on to Ẹniọlá's mother. She stuck them to Ẹniọlá's T-shirt. One in front, another in the back.

Ẹniọlá wanted to say something to his mother as she prepared him. Anything that could make her stop breathing as though she were drowning and gasping for breath. He searched but could not find the right words. She stained his trousers with dirt and rubbed some ash into his forearms until his skin looked dry and flaky.

"Are you sure you're ready?" she asked.

"Yes ma. I am," he said, although he knew the question had nothing to do with his feelings. It was really about how she needed to feel about making them do this. So he told her what she needed to hear. Bùsọ́lá would speak the truth bluntly enough for both of them.

"Please. I beg you in God's name. Make sure you don't talk. You hear me?"

"Yes ma."

He sat still while she covered his torso with the scarf she'd slung over her shoulder. She twisted it around his body twice and tied the edges into a knot under his chin.

"What did I tell you?"

"I know." He stood up. "I won't say anything." He smiled at her, because he thought it would remove her frown. "I'm deaf and dumb, I can't say anything."

She did not stop frowning. "Don't make jokes. Look how tall you are, if people catch you, they won't have mercy on you. You can be accused of being a thief or ritualist. Anything can happen."

He knew he was supposed to leave as soon as his signs were covered with the scarf, but after he picked up a white plastic bowl from the bed, he stood by the door and watched his mother and Bùsọlá get ready to start their day as a blind woman and her daughter.

"You, this boy," Ẹniọlá's mother said, smearing liquid starch all over her closed left eye. "Are you going to wait until the sun sets before you leave?"

He walked briskly uphill, hitting the plastic bowl against his thigh. His steps slowed when he got to the first turn out of the street.

At that junction, there was a wooden stall to his left where a woman with all grey hair was frying àkàrà. He walked towards the stall, drawn by the smell of onions frying in hot palm oil. He could tell that it was the woman's first batch for the day because her large metal sieve was still empty. He watched her scoop the mix from a plastic bowl into the hot oil with a long iron spoon. Ẹniọlá held one of the stall's pillars, slid his fingers across the grainy wood and breathed in through his open mouth. He could almost taste the finished product, the moist mix of beans, pepper and onions.

"Ehen?" the woman said. "Are you here to buy?"

He looked up from the sizzling balls. The woman's eyes were hard, as though she already knew from the way his mouth was open that he did not have any money in his pocket.

"Óyá," she said, swinging her long spoon in his direction. "Disappear. It is too early to sell on credit. Disappear right now. Don't bring me bad luck."

Ẹniọlá shut his mouth and took a deep breath. He filled his lungs with the sweet smell rising from the frying pan before walking on. After the feast of ẹ̀bà and okro soup with crayfish on Friday, there had been no food the previous night, just two unripe bananas and water. By this morning, the bananas were all gone. He tried to keep his mind focused on something else as he turned onto another street. He began counting the cars and buses that drove past him, but he kept losing count because his stomach would not stop growling. When he got to Ijofi, a motorcycle accident had brought traffic in front of the hospital to a standstill. For a few moments, he forgot his hunger as he watched a woman, her yellow head tie about two feet high, get down from her jeep to yell at the traffic warden, who stood in his little metal kiosk drinking from a sachet of water.

Ẹniọlá held his plastic bowl over his belly and wove through the space left between the static cars. He was careful to avoid the motorcycles that whizzed by, carrying men in suits and women who held on with both hands to towering headgear that flapped in the wind like birds eager to fly away. Further up the road, a woman fanned firewood beneath a large pot of corn. Beside Jostade Pharmacy, a pregnant woman sat beside a tray of fruits, peeling the skin off an orange with a blade. On her tray, slices of cellophane-wrapped pineapple and pawpaw had been arranged to form several pyramids. At the next turning, a girl spooned rice into a leaf cone and topped it with fried pepper stew. As he passed by her, he could see the pieces of fish and meat in the pot of stew. By the time he got to Ìfòfín, he felt as though there was food waiting on every corner to taunt him.

More than once, he wanted to take off the scarf and try his luck with the women, but he remembered his mother's instruction; he was not to let the signs show until he got to the church. And even though his stomach growled, and he began to feel as if there were ants in there trying to claw their way out, he kept walking. Past a freshly painted local government building and the tall billboard from which the local government chairman, exalted above the two-storey structure, smiled down at him.

By the time he turned into Ìlọrọ̀, the ground under his feet had gone from warm to hot, and he felt as if he was walking barefoot on smouldering firewood. The street was different from all the other ones he had passed through. Gone were the mud houses nestling next to shopping complexes; gone were the ditches and potholes in the middle of the road. As far as his eye could see, the road was fully tarred. Most of the buildings he walked past were fenced; some of the fences were so high that he could see only the roofs of the houses that stood behind them.

St. Paul's Cathedral was about halfway down the street. Grey with green windows and topped off with two steeples. Its fence was lower than most he had seen earlier, and he could count three levels of the cathedral rising above it.

Strains of organ music grew louder as he approached the cathedral. Though the melody sounded familiar, he could not recognise it. Maybe it was a Protestant one. When he was about three buildings away from the church, he tried to untie the knot his mother had made under his chin, but she'd made it so tight, it was impossible to untie the thing with one hand. He put the plastic bowl between his knees so he could use both hands.

As he moved closer to the church, Ẹniọlá saw a woman where he would have liked to sit. She was seated on a low stool with her back to him, braided hair hanging halfway down her back. Last Sunday, he'd gone to Holy Trinity because his mother said big men worshipped in cathedrals. He had been the youngest of three beggars at the entrance. The other two had been grown men. Now here was this woman. Would she worsen his chances? He hoped she was not carrying a baby on her knee.

When he was beside her, he noticed the large metal bowl at the woman's feet, printed with flowers and fruits; its matching cover doubled as a tray that sat on the woman's lap. She scooped roasted groundnut from the bowl onto the tray, rubbed the nuts between her hands to remove the peel, then threw the nuts up so the dark peel floated away while nuts clattered back onto the tray. Ẹniọlá sighed. She wasn't his competition, but now he had to sit close to her as she peeled and wrapped groundnuts in old newspapers. Meanwhile, the ants gnawing at his stomach had multiplied.

Ẹniọlá stood before the groundnut seller and held out his begging bowl to her. He made sounds in the back of his throat until the woman looked up and smiled at him. Encouraged, he stretched his bowl towards her, hoping she would throw some groundnut in the bowl instead of giving him money.

"I just got here." She shook her head. "I have not made any money yet."

He put the begging bowl between his knee, then rubbed his stomach with one hand and pointed at his mouth with the other.

The woman tilted her head to one side and studied his motions. When she spoke again her brows were drawn together in a frown. "So you're here to mock the people God actually created this way? What kind of wickedness is this?"

Ẹniọlá made as many gestures as he could come up with, desperate to convince her that he was not pretending.

"You can't fool me, child. Of all people? No, not me." She swept her gaze over him and hissed. "You better wait for the church people that you have come for. I know your type. Better stop begging me for anything if you don't want trouble. Rádaràda òṣì, as if I don't have my own children to feed."

Although he felt ashamed, Ẹniọlá did not stop his wild gesturing immediately; he waited till she returned to her work and was no longer paying attention to him. Then he went as close as he could get to the gates of the church. There, he folded his mother's scarf into a square, placed it on the ground and sat on it.

While he waited for the church service to be over, he rubbed his palms against the floor repeatedly and smeared his face with whatever came off it. His mother had told him that the dirtier he looked, the more pity he could get out of people. Pity meant money. He tried not to think about what the groundnut seller had said. Was this wrong?

It was a temporary solution. His mother had said that in the beginning. Once they had enough money for rent and could relax without worrying about sleeping on the streets, they would stop this.

He watched the groundnut seller throw up another batch of groundnuts. Now and then one groundnut would fly out with the chaff and land on the ground. Did she think anyone would do this if they had other options? Did she know if she would be doing this in a year? His own mother had sold groundnuts once. His mother had sold everything she could until she ran out of options. Ẹniọlá scanned the ground, careful to angle his head away from the woman. He didn't want her trouble. He counted fourteen groundnuts, maybe ten. The last four could just have been pebbles.

Ẹniọlá inched closer to the groundnuts, dragging his mother's scarf across the ground as he went. When he picked up the first one, he wanted to throw it into his mouth right away, but he decided that a mouthful might ease his hunger better than one nut after the other. He could chew a mouthful for longer before it lost all taste and slid down his throat or blended with his saliva. He sat in his new position, further from the gate and closer to the groundnut seller. He picked up one nut after the other, pausing between each pick to make sure the woman did not notice his movements.

The last groundnut—it was his lucky day, there were fourteen—was near the woman's feet. He considered letting it go and waiting until one more fell to the ground, closer to where he sat. But he was feeling light-headed, he needed something in his stomach, anything, as many nuts as possible. He moved closer to the woman, reaching for the last nut with the same hand that clutched what he had collected so far.

"You, this boy," the woman said. "What are you doing?"

He made nonsensical sounds and hid his nut-filled hand behind his back.

"You better don't touch my goods, this boy. You better don't."

He stood up and went back to his former position. This time, he sat on the floor and placed the scarf on his lap. He hid the nuts in the scarf and rubbed them against the material to get any sand out. When he was satisfied that each one was clean, he gathered them in his palm and threw them into his mouth. He swirled the nuts around in his mouth, soaked them in saliva, pressed his tongue down on them and sucked them. When he could not think of anything else he could do to prolong the pleasure of having food in his mouth, he began to chew, proud of himself because his teeth did not encounter a single grain of sand.

When churchgoers began to spill out of the cathedral's smaller gate, Ẹniọlá went to stand at the point where he imagined cars would pause before pulling into the street. The first car to come out of the church was a white limousine that had three windows on each side. All were tinted black. He approached the front window and held his bowl against it for a moment before moving to the second one. When he got to the third window, he pointed to the sign on his chest and tapped the glass with his bowl. He'd learnt last week that this enraged most car owners into winding down so they could yell insults. *Has your father ever owned any-thing like this? This window could buy your whole family.* He'd also learnt that their anger could dissolve into shame if they were convinced by the sign on his chest. And that shame often moved them into opening their purses. The window did not go down, and though he stared hard at it, he could not see inside the car. Without eye contact with the occupants, there was no way to know if he'd even moved them at all. The white car swung out into the street and sped off. He stood there, watching it go. What if many of the big men who worshipped here came to church in cars that had tinted windows?

The next car to come out of the church was identical to the first, but the driver's window was rolled all the way down. When it slowed to a stop, Ẹniọlá stuck his bowl inside the window and pointed at the sign on his chest. The driver, who wore a plain white T-shirt, scoffed before hunching over the steering wheel to look past Ẹniọlá at the lane to his left. Ẹniọlá bent down to bring his face closer to the window. The driver glanced right and left again before honking at pedestrians who were coming out of the church compound into the street.

"Samson," a woman's voice said from somewhere in the car.

"Yes ma!" The driver sat up straight.

"Read that boy's sign to me."

"Madam, this one I'm looking at is not a boy-o, he's taller than me, sef. Small time now, he will be growing beard."

"Samson!"

"Okay ma." The driver glared at Ẹniọlá before squinting at the sign. " 'Please help me. I'm a deaf and dumb orphan.' "

Ẹniọlá grunted and pushed his face closer to Samson's, hoping that whoever was in the back seat would see him.

"Give him that change from this morning," the voice from the back said.

"Yes ma." Samson reached into his trouser pocket and dropped a crumpled two-hundred-naira note in Ẹniọlá's bowl.

Ẹniọlá bowed his head in thanks and waved at the car as it drove off.

The road was clear when the next few cars came out. Ẹniọlá's mouth went dry as he watched them speed away, leaving him with a nearly empty bowl.

Fees paid or not, Ẹniọlá knew his parents would insist that he go to school the next day. Just in case, his mother would say, just in case the school decides to write off some fees, just in case the principal forgets about the debtors, just in case you're allowed to take a few classes before being sent away. All of this would seem possible to him until the moment came when Mr. Bísádé shouted his name. It might be during the morning assembly or before the end of first period, but always, always, it was in front of his peers.

Although a light breeze fanned his face, sweat trickled down Ẹniọlá's back as cars zoomed past him. If all the car-owning parishioners left before he made enough money, he would be stuck with people who could not even afford to bring a car to church. How much would those ones drop in his bowl? Tattered, dirty, sellotaped five-naira notes? Those coins that had just been reintroduced but were useless, because not even bàbá dúdú was sold for fifty kobo or one naira anymore? Was one naira actually money if you could not even buy sweets with it? Twelve one-naira coins had been thrown in his bowl yesterday, but no trader accepted them from his mother when she tried to buy salt with ten. Ẹniọlá gripped his begging bowl. He had a short window to make enough money, or he would end up wandering the streets like he had the day before. And look what had come out of that, useless coins and tattered notes.

Ẹniọlá crossed over to the groundnut seller's corner to stand in the shadow cast by a church gate. After watching her for a while, he realised that pedestrians were not the only ones buying from the woman; some cars also stopped beside her. Now and then, drivers got out to negotiate prices, but most times, the woman stood up and went to the cars with a tray. Ẹniọlá noticed that when she did not attend to her customers quickly, a small queue of two to three cars would form by the groundnut seller's corner.

This mini holdup was an answer to Ẹniọlá's unspoken prayers. He moved closer to the groundnut seller, and whenever a car stopped, he assessed the situation for an opening to approach its passengers. If the driver got out, Ẹniọlá rushed to the vehicle, grunting and pointing at his sign until a window went down and someone dropped a note in his bowl. If whoever was driving stayed in the car, he usually had more time to go through his routine while the groundnut seller struggled to balance her attention between pedestrian customers and those in cars. Once, he had enough time to go all the way from pointing through grunting until he got to the part of his routine where he acted as if he were about to faint.

Ẹniọlá never let his bowl fill up. As soon as he had up to five notes, he would stuff three of them into his pocket. His mother had told him that emptier bowls attracted bigger notes, and though he suspected she was wrong, he continued to obey her instructions.

A red Mercedes pulled up. While its driver dashed towards the groundnut seller, Ẹniọlá studied the couple in the car's back seat. The woman was seated behind the driver's chair. Her head was lowered, and most of her face was hidden behind a wide-brimmed purple hat. The man, whom Ẹniọlá assumed was her husband, angled his head this way and that as he pulled at a bow tie that matched the woman's hat. Ẹniọlá decided to focus on getting the man's attention, since the woman seemed too focused on whatever she was staring at on her phone. He ran to the man's window and almost smiled when it slid open after just two raps.

". . . and this is how you know you can't buy pedigree, with all the money he's stolen in Abuja, he thinks it's appropriate to bring this up again in church? In church?!" The man reached into his pocket and pulled out a wallet. "What rubbish."

"Let me finish . . ." the woman mumbled, "sending this text."

The man opened his wallet. "I think he's even right behind us. Honourable? Honourable, my ass."

"We're still in church." The woman glared at her husband for a moment. Her voice was clear and sharp.

"Do you have change?" the man asked.

"Rárá, I don't think so." She returned her gaze to the phone, slid a thumb across its surface and squeezed her mouth into a tight circle.

Taking in a vertical scar that cut through the man's greying left brow to graze his eyelid, Ẹniọlá tried in vain to catch his eye. The man folded his wallet and placed it beside him. When he pressed a button, Ẹniọlá leaned against the car and placed a palm on top of the glass as it whirred its way back up. He grunted and pointed at his chest. But the man merely shrugged and kept his finger on the button until Ẹniọlá rolled his head towards his shoulder.

The man tapped his wife. "Are you sure you don't have any change?"

The woman lifted her face, and Ẹniọlá felt as though he might faint while she blinked at him. When their eyes met, he saw the spark of recognition in hers. He swallowed hard and clutched his bowl to his chest. It was Yèyé.

"Let's ask . . ." She pointed at the driver, who was now sliding back into his chair.

The man in the back seat rubbed his scarred brow. "I don't understand why you can't eat bottled groundnuts like a normal person."

"Ọ̀gá, this one is better," the driver said as he stacked the groundnut cones in the seat beside him.

"Did you get any change?" Yèyé asked the driver without looking away from Ẹniọlá's face.

Ẹniọlá could feel his insides quivering. He was finished. Dead. He wanted to run. Why were his legs not working?

The driver craned his neck to look at Ẹniọlá and burst out laughing. "Is it this boy that you want to give the money? This one? This one is just pretending."

Sweat poured down Ẹniọlá's back. The driver would soon shout his name and tell everyone he was a faker. Or Yèyé would do so first. Anyway, there was no point running now. They would always catch him, if not here in the middle of the street, then at Aunty Caro's shop.

"And how would you know this?" Yèyé's husband asked.

"I know him very well. Yèyé, don't you remember this—"

"I said, do you have change?" Yèyé snapped her fingers. "Did I ask you for any story?"

"Sorry ma. Yes ma." The driver passed two fifty-naira notes to the back seat.

Yèyé took the notes, leaned over her husband and dropped them in Ẹniọlá's bowl. Then she removed her hat and stared at Ẹniọlá until the window went back up and the car pulled away.

14

Àrò meta. Gold, frankincense and myrrh. Cinderella's three wishes . . . Bùṣọ́lá could go on. So what if Tèmi rolled her eyes? Bùṣọ́lá knew what she knew. Number three always meant something. Always. She was sure of it.

When Bùṣọ́lá was in primary school, her mother and Ẹniọlá had laughed at her because she refused to leave their room for a whole day after she ran into three chicks in the corridor. *Who told you this nonsense?* her father had asked, his lips curved upwards in a smile as rare as the laughter in his voice. After that incident, Bùṣọ́lá began pretending that she was no longer paying attention to the number three.

"But why? You should be the third. Sunday will read it after you," Tèmi said, adjusting a button on her pinafore.

Bùṣọ́lá shook her head and glanced at Sunday, who stood beside her and was drumming his fingers on Tèmi's school desk.

Tèmi leaned forward in her chair. "But you got here before Sunday."

"Let him read it first." Two was just coincidence. But three? Thrice? Even though Bùṣọ́lá was never sure if it was good or bad, she knew it was always an omen.

Tèmi shrugged and laid her head on the desk. "I want to sleep before short break."

Bùṣọ́lá walked to the back of the class where her own desk stood next to Zainab's.

"Tèmi didn't even keep the book for me." Bùṣọ́lá turned toward Zainab as she slid into her chair. "She gave it to Kànmí. Can you believe it? Am I not the one that is her friend, ehn?"

"Maybe Kànmí asked before today?" Zainab asked.

"He didn't, jàre. But even if he did, even if, is it good like that? When

I'm Tèmi's friend, shouldn't I be the first to read the book? She knows I'm fast. Normally, am I not always the first to read the books? Tèmi is saying that if I'm not around for one minute she can't keep a book for me, ehn?"

Zainab put an arm around Bùsọlá and squeezed her shoulder. "Why don't you tell her how you feel?"

"Just because I was . . . because I wasn't . . . because—" Bùsọlá shut her eyes against the tears that had been threatening all morning and took a deep breath. She could not cry in class, especially during a free period, when someone might call her a crybaby and the name would stick forever and ever. She would draw. That always calmed her. She shrugged off Zainab's hand and fished out her jotter from the pile of notebooks on her school desk.

Hian. The travesty. Fourth in line. Not first as usual or even second. Fourth o, fourth. Hian. She flipped through her jotter until she got to the section where she wrote new words she had recently come across. She dragged a finger across the page and stopped at "travesty." There was a colon after the word, but it was not followed by a meaning yet. She needed a dictionary. *Oxford Advanced Learner's* or *Longman*. It was the first item on the list of books she'd given her father after passing the common entrance exam, but her parents did not buy even an ordinary pocket dictionary, and she was almost halfway through her second term in secondary school now. She turned a page in the jotter. Even if she could not remember exactly what the word meant, it was, sha, still a travesty that she would be the fourth to read *Death Is a Woman*. After Kànmí, Mojeed and now Sunday. And all because she hadn't paid her school fees and had decided to hide in the forest until Mr. Bísádé left for the senior school.

Bùsọlá and Tèmi had been classmates since they were in primary school and were even seatmates from primary three to five. They should have been best friends by now, but when Zainab asked Tèmi who her bestie was while they walked back to their class from morning assembly last week, Tèmi had glared at Bùsọlá before saying, *Jesus*. Tèmi was a liar and a cheat who sometimes elbowed Bùsọlá for no reason at all, but none of that mattered, because Tèmi's father sold secondhand books to students at the College of Education and she owned a lot of storybooks and novels as a result. You name it, Ladybird books, Enid Blytons, Pacesetters series, abridged Dickens, African writers' series. Tèmi even claimed there was a stash of Mills & Boon she had read but would only start bringing to school once they were in senior secondary, but that was probably a lie. Bùsọ́lá knew that Tèmi did not enjoy books. She was the one who had read Ladybird Tales out loud to Tèmi so she would be able to narrate the stories to her parents and prove she was indeed reading the books her father kept giving her.

Ever since they were in primary school, Tèmi showed up with a new secondhand book every other Monday. Right after morning assembly, she would wave it in the air while interested classmates rushed to her desk. Congregants answering a call to worship. Bùsọ́lá was always the first to pick a reading slot. She usually walked back from morning assembly with Tèmi and would wait by her friend's desk while she opened her schoolbag to bring out the book.

A good friend would have reserved Bùsọ́lá's slot even though she skipped morning assembly today. A good friend would have held on to *Death Is a Woman* until Bùsọ́lá sneaked back into class. Especially since it was a Pacesetter book that everyone would want to read. No one had been so interested in *The Beautyful Ones Are Not Yet Born* two weeks ago, or in *Great Expectations* last term. But bring a Pacesetter and suddenly they were all readers. Now that stupid Kànmí who sometimes laughed at Tèmi because of her bowlegs was enjoying the book, while Bùsọ́lá had nothing to read for the next few days except her own jotter. It was that or *Sugar Girl,* the only book she owned that was not a textbook.

Bùsọ́lá had read *Sugar Girl* so many times, she was sure she could recognise Ralia the sugar girl in a crowd if she ever stepped out of the pages. She knew for instance that Ralia would be a good friend if they were classmates. Ralia with all her travails would have understood that today of all days, after hiding for hours so she would not be sent back home with other debtors, Bùsọ́lá did not just want to read something, she *needed* to have a book in her hands.

Travails. Bùsọ́lá looked through her jotter until she found the word. She had written a meaning in front of it two weeks ago. Yes, like Ralia, she too was travailing, or she had travails. Which was correct? She should ask Hakeem if she saw him on the way home. Sometimes he walked home with Bùsọ́lá and Ẹniọlá. Hakeem was always happy to give her his dictionary so she could look up words. He never complained about how long he had to wait in front of Bùṣọ́lá's home while she copied out meanings. He would understand why she was so upset about the book. Her own brother would just tell her to wait for her turn like a normal person, as if wanting something to read right away was strange. But Hakeem? Hakeem understood her and usually knew all the words she was just learning. She showed him her jotter from time to time so he could confirm that the examples she made up for herself were the correct usages of the new words she had learnt. Yet, even though she was almost sure he would not laugh at her drawings, she showed him only the words section of her jotter. She showed no one the plant or animal sections.

Bùṣọ́lá's mother had given her two jotters at the beginning of the term. While she used the first one as her mother had instructed, to make notes whenever she was studying, she kept the other as a personal jotter. She drew a skull on the cover and wrote FOR BÙṢỌ́LÁ'S EYES ONLY DO NOT OPEN beneath it. Its first section was devoted to the shrubs, trees and fruits that she found in the forest beside the school. Bùṣọ́lá knew that her parents thought that going to a school surrounded by thick bushes would scare her, but she did not mind. If only they would listen to her and stop telling Ẹniọlá to follow her all the way there and then have to go back to the senior school alone. He never said anything, but she could tell from how he moved so fast his feet barely touched the ground that Ẹniọlá was scared of passing through even that small thicket that separated the senior school from the new site.

Some of her classmates were afraid too, but many of them, like Tèmi and Zainab, liked exploring the bushes to discover fruits. So far, they had discovered an orange tree, several mango trees, a guava tree and most recently two àgbálùmọ̀ trees. Bùṣọ́lá wrote about all of them in her jotter. She described the height of the trees, following that with the shape of their leaves, before settling in on the taste of the first fruits she plucked from them. She visited the trees even when they had no fruits and studied them, writing her observations by the light that filtered through their branches. While her friends were always careful to note landmarks—trees with odd depressions in their sides, patches of earth covered with rotting fruit and buzzing flies—before going too far from the clearing that marked where their school began, Bùṣọ́lá wanted to wander endlessly in the forest. Its unknown depths did not terrify her; instead it called to her. All she had already seen, the constant chirping and rustling, the mix of wetness, ripeness, rot and greenery that she breathed in when she was surrounded by trees, promised even more wonder to be discovered.

That morning, when her mother had insisted that she show up in school even though not one naira of her school fees had been paid, Bùsọ́lá had headed straight into the bushes after telling Tèmi and Zainab where she would be. For what must have been the first time, she did not wander. Instead, she had sat on the exposed roots of a tree she could not name and waited while hours crawled by, each as long as a decade.

Maybe she would have felt better if the yellow-tinged snake passed by. She had hoped it would, although she knew she would probably never see that particular one again. The yellow-tinged snake was special to her; it had made her decide last term that she wanted to become someone who spent her life wandering through forests and making notes about what she saw.

Later, Hakeem had said all she needed to do was study forestry in the university and the rest should be easy. He had helped her to give a name to what she wanted when she told him about it, but that desire had begun with the snake. On the day Bùsọ́lá saw the yellow-tinged snake, Tèmi had said something during the short break that made Bùsọ́lá want to cry. She had run off into the forest. Away from the playground, where Tèmi and other girls were playing ten-ten, past the boys who were peeing against the grass at the forest's edge, and then further in until the foliage overhead only allowed sunlight to filter through in thin threads. Bùsọ́lá was approaching a mango tree when she saw the snake wrapped around another tree. She stood still and breathed as quietly as she could, watching as it made its way up the trunk and disappeared into the branches. She counted the colours of its shimmering skin. Green, black and that brilliant shade of yellow she had never seen anywhere else.

After school, she'd asked Hakeem what someone who studied forests was called, and when she got home, she'd told her father she wanted to study forestry. It was one of the few times she heard her father's voice swell into a shout. He had stood over her and screamed that she was going to be a doctor or an engineer, declaring that she would not waste her life like he'd wasted his. While her mother pleaded with him, Bùsọ́lá left the room. She went to sit in front of the house, wishing she could visit Hakeem but sure she would not be allowed to because he was a boy. She already had breasts even though she was just about to turn thirteen. Pebble-like but breasts still. Visible through her blouses and painful when she ran into something. Her mother had started the "stop playing with boys" campaign when she noticed them. Hakeem would have been able to answer the question her father had yelled at her. He would have given her the response to *Who will employ you?*

Her father was wrong. She was not sure about what he had studied, but it was definitely not forestry. So what did he know about that? How could anyone with eyes think being in the forest would be a waste of her life? The very ground she walked on there was different, constantly in motion. Alive with wriggling worms, twisted roots as thick as yams, and tendrils pushing through the earth towards the light. Her father was a strange and quiet man. Her mother and Ẹniọlá claimed he had once been very different, but more and more Bùṣọlá found it hard to believe them.

Of course, the snake did not show up that morning while Bùṣọlá waited for assembly and the first two periods to be over, but she did see a squirrel that made her laugh. She opened her jotter to the middle, where her drawings were squeezed together so she did not run out of space too soon. After chewing on her pencil's eraser for a while, she began to draw the squirrel she had seen while hiding in the bushes that morning. They had locked eyes for barely a moment before it disappeared behind a shrub, but Bùṣọlá could remember how a bit of grass clung to its chin, dropping off like a goatee. That was what had made her burst out in laughter, announcing her presence and startling the squirrel. When Zainab had come to get her after the first two lessons were over, she'd found Bùṣọlá nestled against the tree trunk, jotter on her knee, trying to re-create the squirrel's tail on the page.

Zainab had laughed all the way back to the classroom when she realised that Bùṣọlá had been trying to draw a squirrel's tail. Bùṣọlá's drawings were terrible. Her chickens looked like mosquitoes, her squirrels like rats. This did not stop her from sketching daily. It calmed her and kept her thoughts from things that upset her. So what if Zainab laughed whenever she caught a glimpse of this page in her jotter? Right now, if she could focus on that squirrel she saw in the morning and make strokes on paper that reminded her of its grass goatee, she would be fine. Only she could not focus. Tèmi had always been a little mean, but she had been acting as if they were not really friends for about two weeks now. Zainab had asked that best-friend question a day after the first time Bùṣọlá led her mother around while she pretended to be blind. They had gone to Roundabout and stood close to the Union Bank there. Maybe Tèmi had seen them somehow? Maybe she had recognised Bùṣọlá despite the makeshift head covering her mother had forced her to wear?

Bùṣọlá slammed her jotter shut and stood. Kànmí sat two rows ahead of her, and because he was so short and held books up while he read, she could see how far he had gone if she craned her neck. He was on page nine. Page nine! Bùṣọlá sank into her seat. Since morning, just page nine.

Tèmi said she'd given him the book right after morning assembly. That was before first period; now they were halfway through the fourth period, which on Mondays was a free one, and he had not gotten past page nine. She would have been on page twenty-five before the second period was over. She had long perfected the art of reading novels during lessons without getting caught. If only her parents had paid her school fees and she did not need to hide from the teachers who taught during the first two periods.

Bùṣọlá felt someone pull on her shirt.

"I said, isn't that your mother?" Zainab was pointing towards the doorway.

Bùṣọlá glanced towards the door, sure Zainab was mistaken. It was her mother, standing on the threshold, peeping into the class, still searching for Bùṣọlá.

For a wild moment, Bùṣọlá thought her father had died. Her father often seemed slightly surprised and disappointed to have woken up. More than once, she'd wondered if he spent so much time in bed because he was hoping to sleep his way out of this world. She shut her eyes and tried to see the room her family called home as it had been that morning. Where was her father when she left for school? Had he been awake? She tried but could not see him in the room, asleep or awake. An image of her parents' empty bed swirled round and round in her mind until she remembered that when Mojeed's father died last year, it was his eldest sister who had suddenly appeared in the classroom to interrupt their math lesson so she could inform him and take him home. Bùsọ́lá hid her jotter beneath other notebooks and walked towards the doorway.

Bùsọ́lá's mother was standing with one foot in the class and the other outside. She had not been back here since she came with Bùsọ́lá on her first day of secondary school. Then too she had stayed on the threshold, hovering as she studied the classroom, saying nothing after she asked a teacher when doors and windows would be installed. Soon, the teacher had said, very soon.

"They haven't fixed you people's doors and windows." Bùsọ́lá's mother put an arm around her and pulled her close, drawing her into the corridor that ran from one end of the classroom block to another.

Bùsọ́lá shrugged. "Is everything okay at home?"

"I hope you always check inside your desks before you sit down in the morning?"

"Yes ma. Bàami ńkọ́?"

"You check it after all your breaks?"

"Yes ma. I check all the time. Bàami ńkọ́? Is he okay?"

"Your father is fine. His back is paining him so he can't go out today, but he's fine. Why did you ask?"

"Why are you here?"

"I came to—" Bùsọ́lá's mother slid her handbag down her arm and dug into it. She fished out a folded piece of paper and gave it to Bùsọ́lá. "I came to give you your teller."

Bùsọ́lá stretched out the piece of paper, pressing out the creases with her index finger. Seven thousand naira paid. More than enough for her to stay in school right now. She threw her arms around her mother and hugged her tight. Only three thousand naira left for the term's fees to be completed.

"Thank you, Mọ̀ọmi, thank you so much."

"No need to cry. Wipe your eyes."

Bùsọ́lá touched her cheeks and found they were wet. She had not known she was crying.

"Óyá, where is the accountant's office?"

Mrs. Rufai, who taught business studies and doubled as the school's accountant, did not have her own office. Instead, she shared a staff room with ten other teachers at the other end of the classroom block. The staff room was the only space in the new school site that had doors and wooden shutters. Both were always wide open, the door held in place with a broken-off concrete block so it would not swing shut.

Bùsọ́lá's mother said hin káàsán to all the teachers they passed by on their way to Mrs. Rufai's desk. Some answered with words, or grunts, but most of their replies were drowned out by the sound of nearly a dozen hand fans flapping away in vain attempts to drive the heat out of the narrow room.

Mrs. Rufai was fanning herself with the ripped-up back cover of a notebook when Bùsọ́lá and her mother stopped in front of her desk.

"Good afternoon ma," Bùsọ́lá said, holding out the bank teller.

Mrs. Rufai took the teller and squinted at it for a moment before glancing at Bùsọ́lá's mother with a slight smile. "This is not the full payment."

"Good afternoon ma. So it's only three thousand left for Bùsọ́lá?"

"Yes." Mrs. Rufai grabbed a higher education notebook from the edge of her desk and opened it to a tabulated page.

"Her father said I should ask about when we need to pay that?"

"Uhm." Mrs. Rufai wrote Bùsọ́lá's name in the notebook and scribbled 7,000 beside it in brackets. She looked up when she was done and furrowed her brows as though surprised to see they were still there.

"My mother said—"

"Oh, okay, yes. Let her be coming until the exams start. But if you people have not completed the payment then, she won't write exams o."

"Okay, thank you ma," Bùsọ́lá's mother said, and turned to leave.

"Wait, wait o." Mrs. Rufai tapped the table with her pen. "Isn't there another one in senior school?"

Bùsọ́lá's mother did not stop walking.

"You've not paid anything for that one? Should I divide the money into two?" Mrs. Rufai called.

Bùsọ́lá's mother quickened her pace and did not stop walking until she had put two classroom doors between her and the staff room.

"She was asking you about Ẹ̀niọlá's fees," Bùsọ́lá said when her mother stopped.

"I want to get to the market, but I should have returned home by the time you come back from school. If I'm not back, just check the cupboard for gaàrí."

"Are you going there to . . ." Bùsólá could not bring herself to say "beg" out loud. Even when her mother raised a greying brow, Bùsólá waited in silence until her mother's eyes lit up in realization.

"Oh, no, not today."

"You already gave Ẹniọlá his own teller, àbí?" Bùsólá asked.

"Where would I get that kind of money? I've paid your own fees for now. I will take care of Ẹniọlá's own later."

Bùsólá watched her mother pick invisible lint from her dress and knew something was wrong. Her mother looked people in the eye when she was speaking; she only looked away when she was upset or lying. "But why don't you divide the money in two? You can still tell Mrs. Rufai, she was asking if you wanted her to do that when—"

"If I do that, it won't be enough to keep both of you in school."

"That doesn't make sense, we had—"

"What? Me, I'm not making sense, ehn? Thank you o, Bùsólá. You know I did not think about this your suggestion at all, at all. I've been scraping this money together since so I could pay your fees and Ẹniọlá's own. But no, it did not occur to me that the money could be divided in two, ehn. I was waiting for you to tell me this. Thank you so much. What would I do without your wisdom?"

Bùsólá scratched her head. "I'm sorry ma. I was just asking because, since we had like nine thousand naira yesterday, maybe you could have waited a little before paying, so the money would be enough as half and half. I thought that was the plan?"

"We already gave the landlord two thousand, so."

"There's nothing left for Ẹniọlá?"

"Keep your voice down, jàre. Where would we have slept this night if we didn't give the landlord more money this morning?" She pointed towards Bùsólá's classroom. "On the floor of this uncompleted building?"

"But it's not fair to pay just my own fees."

Bùsólá's mother sighed. "Wo, we had to give the landlord something. Don't worry, we'll take care of Ẹniọlá's fees soon."

"Are you saying I'm going to stay in school while he gets sent home?"

"Go back to your class and stop querying me." She waved Bùsọ́lá towards the classroom. "As if you have money to give me for your brother's school fees."

Bùsọ́lá folded her arms and stood in her mother's way. If she said it out loud her mother would accuse her of disrespect, but the truth was that they had all begged and scraped money together. Shouldn't they all have a say in how it would be spent? Ẹniọlá had been alone while they went begging the previous day. Singlehandedly, he had come back with almost two thousand naira that Sunday. Now their parents were not going to direct any of the money towards his school fees? Ẹniọlá, who had suggested she hide this morning so she could take some classes in the afternoon before leaving school. Her tall, lumbering brother who almost no one called Ẹniọlá in school. He was either Unity on a good day or agùnmáníyè when his peers wanted to laugh extra hard. She had thought about the second nickname a lot after she overheard it. Ẹniọlá could not do anything about being the tallest boy in his class. And why, why wouldn't he seem brainless to his mates when he usually spent anything from two weeks to a month at home during a term because their parents could not pay his school fees until after midterm?

"It's not fair."

"I said we will pay it soon."

"Soon is never, tell me the time. Next week? Tomorrow? This weekend? Are you people going to wait until after midterm again? We would have done the first test by then."

"I don't know, Olubùsọ́lá, let me pass, I have other things to do today."

"You know they beat him more than they beat me for his school fees? Senior school students get more strokes. Mr. Bísádé told us himself. They would have beaten him again this morning, you know, he doesn't have anywhere to hide there, and you people made him go to school today."

"We'll pay his fees soon."

"When? When are you going to pay? Mr. Bísádé has only flogged me like this for two terms and I'm tired. Ẹniọlá has been facing this for years. Years, and you don't want to do anything about it." Bùsọ́lá wagged a finger in her mother's face. "Did you see his back last week? You want them to do that to him again, àbí? You people will make him come here again tomorrow—"

"Okay, he's not coming to this school again, you hear me? Nobody is going to force him to come here. He is going somewhere else. Public schools are free, we won't have to worry about school fees. Are you happy now?"

With that, Bùṣọ́lá's mother pushed past her and walked away.

15

Eniọlá heard sharp cries from the class next to his and considered leaving. In spite of what his mother had said, there was no reason for him to stay in his seat like a fool, waiting for Mr. Bísádé to come into his class and beat him too. He had endured punishment during the previous weeks knowing he would still be allowed to continue taking classes. Today, the flogging would be followed by a barked command to leave the school promises. If he did not move quickly enough for the principal, the man would chase him around the class, hitting him whenever he got close enough for his cane or whip to make contact. They would go round and round until Eniọlá finally managed to gather his things and find the exit. Doing either of those things was always complicated by the fact that his hands were busy rubbing his broken and bleeding skin. Also, his inability to predict where the next stroke would land on his body made it harder to keep from crying. Even walls look like doorways when your vision is blurred with tears. One term he had run out without his bag after dropping it twice while zigzagging away from Mr. Bísádé's whip.

Halfway through his first term at Glorious Destiny, Eniọlá had refused to go to school on the Monday Mr. Bísádé threatened to start flogging people. His father had been away in Ìbàdàn for some job interview that morning, but when he returned a few days later, he'd knelt before Eniọlá and pleaded with him to go back to school and stay in class until the minute he was asked to leave. *Every drop of knowledge counts,* he'd said, pressing his forehead against Eniọlá's while he spoke. *The scars will fade, but what you learn is yours for life. Nobody can take your certificates from you.*

This morning, his father had not left the bed when Eniọlá set out for school with Bùsọ́lá. Did he still believe what he had said back then when he still spoke in sentences instead of grunts and monosyllables? What if he no longer did and Ẹniọlá's suffering meant nothing to the man he was hoping to please and make happy? Ẹniọlá capped his Biro, shut his geography notebook and put both in his bag. His class had just one exit and it was next to the blackboard. There was no way to leave without distracting Mrs. Isong from the note she was copying out on the board.

For all nine terms of his junior secondary school years, he'd repeated his father's words under his breath while Mr. Bísádé, always that wicked Mr. Bísádé, slapped a whip, cane or belt against his body before commanding him to get out of the class and leave the school premises. By his first term in senior secondary, he had replaced the sound of his father's voice with a scene from his future. In this future he is an engineer, doctor or politician who can afford to drive a new Mercedes-Benz. Not second-hand new, but brand-new, tear-rubber new. Most important, he is married to a woman who could be Fúnkẹ́ Akíndélé's twin. One day, with his wife beside him and their two children in the back seat, while it's raining so much people are wondering if the sky might collapse under the weight of water, he drives past Mr. Bísádé without stopping to offer him a ride. He speeds past him even though their eyes meet and Mr. Bísádé is waving him down, begging for his help. On days like this, he usually held that image of Mr. Bísádé begging him in his mind as he waited for the man to come into his class, the hope of revenge making the terror of anticipation a little more bearable. But it was not working right now. Not with the yelps from the next class blooming into howls. It probably would not work when he was actually being flogged by the principal either. A Fúnkẹ́ Akíndélé look-alike? What woman as beautiful as Fúnkẹ́ would want to be with someone who had once begged on the streets? Ẹniọlá picked up his bag and made for the door. Mrs. Isong called his name as he walked out of the class, but he ignored her and broke into a run once he was in the corridor.

He had two options. Go home or go to Aunty Caro's shop. All night he'd wondered how he would explain his encounter with Yèyé to Aunty Caro if the woman decided to report him to her. Yèyé had recognised him. He was sure of it. Her driver had too, and who knew if they would report him to Aunty Caro so she would know he was a deceiver? They would probably tell her while Ṣèyí was there. Ṣèyí would tell Ahmed he was a beggar. If Ahmed got to know, then his whole class would know, the whole school, sef. If Aunty Caro confronted him this afternoon, he did not know what he would say to save face. He headed home.

Ẹniọlá's father was lying in bed when he got home. Ẹniọlá took off his school sandals and sat on the bed. He cleared his throat, hoping his father would turn away from the wall he was focused on and speak to him.

"I didn't wait for the principal to get to my class before I left," Ẹniọlá said.

Ẹniọlá hoped this would provoke some reaction, even an "okay" would have been enough, but all his father did was grunt. The sound hit Ẹniọlá like a slap in the face, and he felt as though he might explode with rage. Here he was, home long before noon, and his father had not said a single word. No apology for the fact that the school fees remained unpaid. No question about how many lessons he'd been able to sit in on before leaving school. No reaction to his decision to leave before being sent away.

If she were home, his mother would have spent the last few minutes talking to him about how things would get better soon. Ẹniọlá wanted his father to sit by him and promise that everything was going to be fine, the fees would be paid, and he would be back in school soon. Bùsọ́lá was going to hide in the bushes for most of the morning. His mother was probably somewhere doing everything she could to get some more money for his school fees. Meanwhile, his father stayed in bed while everyone around him suffered and floundered. Ẹniọlá pressed a clenched fist into the mattress and thought of Mr. Ọlábọ̀dé, hanging from that ceiling, dressed up as though he was leaving for work, belt and shoes matching his brown tie. After a few minutes, he felt his anger sink beneath the fear of losing his father.

"I'm going out sir," Ẹniọlá said.

Another sigh followed by something that sounded like "all right."

Ẹniọlá took off his school shirt and two of the T-shirts he'd worn underneath it to cushion Mr. Bísádé's strokes. His mother would have asked about where he was going. She would never let him leave home without a clear sense of his destination. Ẹniọlá did not bother with saying goodbye as he left the room, but he did slam the door shut. On his way to Time Wait for No 1, he practiced and discarded responses to questions about his encounter with Yèyé, but none of the lies he came up with sounded right when he whispered them to himself.

Aunty Caro was showing Ṣèyí how to sew a pleated skirt when Ẹniọlá stepped into the shop. Maria sat bent over another sewing machine, pedalling away.

"Ehen, you, I've been waiting for you," Aunty Caro said when she looked up and saw Ẹniọlá.

"Good afternoon ma," Ẹniọlá said.

Aunty Caro nodded. "You remember this madam that comes here, Yèyé?"

Ẹniọlá walked past Maria's sewing machine to a table laden with finished clothes that needed to be ironed.

Aunty Caro stuck a pin in the check fabric. "She said that she saw you yesterday."

Ẹniọlá gripped the table with both hands. He looked straight at Aunty Caro and shook his head from side to side; her question had revealed the only answer that could get him out of this mess. If he acted as though he did not even know who Yèyé was, he could claim whatever she said about him was not true without saying one of Aunty Caro's favourite clients was lying. He would say she must have been mistaken.

"You know her, now," Ṣèyí said, putting one hand on her hip.

"How do you know that? Are you in my head?" Ẹniọlá picked up a blouse and began folding.

"You need to iron that blouse first," Maria said without looking up from the bùbá she was sewing.

"And it's not long since she left o," Aunty Caro said. "Anyway, you must find a way to thank her. Maybe you will do that the next time she's here. You know she just came this morning and said she wanted to pay your apprenticeship fee."

Ẹniọlá leaned against the table. "What?"

"Àbí?" Maria said, slapping the back of one hand into the other palm. "It's as if she dreamt about you, we had not even finished sweeping the shop before she came."

"She asked me about your parents and so on, and I explained that they've not been able to pay your fees here and she gave me the money."

"Just like that, cash." Maria grinned at Ẹniọlá. "You are lucky o."

Ṣèyí scoffed. "That woman is just a cash madam. This Ẹniọlá is not lucky anything. When we were classmates—"

"Ṣèyí, if I hear your voice again, you will go back home today, since you know how to sew a pleated skirt," said Aunty Caro. "As for you, Ẹniọlá. You will have your own machine as from today. We'll decide on which one once I'm done with this."

Ẹniọlá arranged his face into what he hoped resembled a smile. So Yèyé had not mentioned anything about the previous day. Maybe she was not upset and only felt sorry for him. He turned away from the women and dug through the pile of clothes for Aunty Caro's ancient iron. He pulled it out and switched it on.

He knew everyone expected him to be happy and grateful. This was a good thing. He now had the opportunity to truly learn tailoring instead of being an errand boy around the shop. Who knew, before the year ended, he might be able to sew dresses, jackets and agbádás from scratch. He touched the iron with a finger; it was still cold. The thing took forever to heat up. A smile or something like one stayed on his face, yet he felt no joy. He had to keep smiling. For Aunty Caro, who seemed so pleased for him, and Maria, who would not stop beaming in his direction. But he might as well still be in his classroom, jumping at every sound as he waited for Mr. Bísádé to show up. All he really cared about, even now, was how long it would take for his parents to gather his fees so he could go back to school. He liked Aunty Caro well enough, and he knew the skills he learnt here would be useful, but what he wanted was the chance to study in a university or at least a polytechnic. Definitely not a college of education like his father. He would rather spend the rest of his life begging than become a teacher. God forbid, God forbid bad thing. He thought of the scraps of leftover fabric he'd been putting aside for months. Maybe he would be able to make the patchwork blouse for Bùsọlá soon. It would make her happy.

"Come, come," Aunty Caro said. "Take this bùbá from Maria and start ironing it."

"Yes ma." Ẹniọlá went to Maria's sewing machine.

Aunty Caro looked up and frowned. "Wait, where did she see you?"

"Who?" Ẹniọlá grabbed the bùbá and dashed to the ironing table.

"Yèyé. She didn't tell me, and I've been wondering where you two would meet."

Ẹniọlá pushed the pile of clothes to one side and spread the bùbá out carefully, so his fingers did not snag the lace fabric.

"Ẹniọlá?"

"It was in church ma."

"Oh," Aunty Caro said. "I didn't know you people go to the same church."

Ẹniọlá said nothing.

"Quick, quick. Iron that bùbá."

"Yes ma."

He held a finger against the iron to test it and yelped when it seared his skin.

❋

Bùsọlá was pacing the corridor when he returned home after nightfall. She ran to him while he was still standing in the doorway.

"Did you see any three on your way back home?" Bùsọlá asked. "Did you count?"

"What are you talking about?" He could not see her face clearly. There was power, but the current was so low, the single bulb in the corridor was no better than a candle.

"I saw three eggs in the bush behind the school—"

"Not this again, Bùsọlá."

She grabbed his arm. "Wait, wait, don't go inside. Mọọmi came to my school to give me my teller, then I went there during short break after she left, because she told me she had not paid your own fees yet and I was not happy. That's when I—"

"She paid yours but didn't pay mine?"

"And she said you're not going to Glorious Destiny again."

"You don't know what you're saying."

"Look, she told me—"

He shook her hand off. "You're wrong."

Ẹniọlá knew she was not wrong when his parents smiled at him as he stepped into the room. They were seated side by side on their bed, and while his mother gripped his father's knee, he realised that he could not remember the last time he had seen his father smile.

"Welcome, Ẹniọlá," his father said. "How are you?"

Ẹniọlá took a step back and bumped into Bùsọlá.

His mother stood. "Are you ready to eat?"

"What is going on?" Ẹniọlá asked. "Why are you people acting strange?"

His mother went to the food cupboard and opened a pot, releasing the wonderful aroma of the stone-ground pepper and crayfish that gave her concoction rice dishes life. The last time she made the concoction was during a Christmas so long ago he could not remember which one it was. Now she was offering him a steaming plate of his favourite meal before he'd even taken off his shoes. Just how he liked it, topped with a big ọfọ̀ọ̀rọ̀. Ọfọ̀ọ̀rọ̀? When was the last time they'd had any type of fish? And why would he be getting a whole ọfọ̀ọ̀rọ̀ to himself?

Ẹniọlá went past his mother to his father. "Bùsọlá said I'm not going to Glorious Destiny again."

"Ẹniọlá, I'm the one who told Bùsọlá that. Don't shout, leave your father and let him—"

"I'm not talking to you. He's the one I'm asking a question."

"Please, just keep your voice down. You know how we've been struggling with everything. School fees, rent, everything. We just think we should lessen the pressure on everybody. Look at me, Ẹniọlá, please, look here. They keep beating you, you don't even have time to attend all the lessons. Before we will be able to pay your fees now, another month might pass and by then your classmates would have written tests."

He had raised his voice twice, but his mother had not shut him up. Instead, she was still holding the plate out to him, speaking as if she had no intention of telling him how he must never shout at his father again. Her calm alarmed him. "What are you saying?"

"Your father has a friend in United, one of his former colleagues. He went there to speak to her this morning, and they say you can start next week."

Ẹniọlá moved closer to his father. "Start what? Where?"

"The school now, United Grammar School," his mother said.

"Stop speaking for him. Let him talk, let him open his mouth and say something. He lost his job, not his tongue."

"Please, take it easy with your father."

"Which father? Is this one a father?" Ẹniọlá felt his mother's grip on his shoulder, but he did not turn towards her. He pushed his face into his father's and yelled as loud as he could, "Speak now, speak!"

"You won't even need to write an entrance exam," his father said.

Ẹniọlá grabbed his father by the collar. A throbbing began in his forefinger, right where he'd pressed it against Aunty Caro's iron. At first, he felt only pain, as though he'd just touched the iron again. As though the disappointment from all the promises his father had broken—about the Unity school and Glorious Destiny—was pushing against the skin of that one finger before radiating through his body. Then he felt anger, pulsing beneath his skin, pounding in his head. United was the closest public school to them, the word an abbreviation of a longer name he did not care to remember. His father did not appear shocked by the hand gripping his collar; his lips were slightly down, but he seemed almost relieved. Had he been expecting this day to come?

"Ẹniọlá, please stop, let him go," Bùsọ́lá said.

Ẹniọlá summoned the image of Mr. Ọlábọ̀dé's suicide but felt no rush of pity for his father, no fear that he might return tomorrow to find his body hanging from a ceiling. There were no fans in this wretched room. If his father wanted to leave this world, he would have to use poison or something else. And wouldn't that be better for everyone? His mother would be free of one mouth she had to feed all by herself. Maybe she would even marry another man. A better man. Someone who did not stay home while his family had to beg on the street to survive.

"Ẹniọlá, please, please," Bùsọ́lá screamed. "Mọ̀ọmi, say something now."

He let go, terrified by how quickly the thoughts unspooled in his mind. He punched a fist into his palm and turned away from his father. His mother was standing in his way, still holding out the plate of rice. He took it from her and flung it across the room, spraying rice on everything and everyone. The plate clattered against a wall and landed beside Bùsọ́lá, who was sitting on the mattress, head in hands, sobbing.

His mother stepped out of his way, and he felt a burst of fear that disappeared as he looked down on her. What could she do, really? He was taller and stronger than her and had been for years. Why had he even let her continue telling him what to do? He had always listened to her. Since he realised how useless his father had become, he had done everything he could to make her life easier, and now that it came to it, she had chosen Bùsọ́lá over him. Ẹniọlá felt breathless, as if he'd been punched in the neck.

"Ẹniọlá, sit down. Let us talk about this," his mother said.

Ẹniọlá shook his head. He wanted to speak but was worried that sobs would emerge if he opened his mouth. The two bulbs in the room began to flicker as though a full current was about to be restored.

"I'm not angry at all, just sit. Let's talk."

What right did she have to be angry at him when she had used the money he'd laboured for to care for only his sister? Ẹniọlá walked to the door. She would not tell him what to do. Not again. The lights flickered out as he stepped into the corridor.

"Where did you put the lantern last night? Ẹniọlá?"

He shut the door behind him and stood still for a moment, so his eyes could adjust to the darkness. A long bench had been nailed into the ground in front of the house before his family moved in. He felt his way to it and sat down. Soon he heard footsteps in the corridor but did not look up even when he felt his mother settle in beside him on the bench.

She placed a hand on his nape and began to drum out a beat. Ẹniọlá glanced at her face, expecting it to be creased in anger, but her cheeks were wet. Well, let her cry. He would not feel sorry. She had made this decision. Even though she liked to say "your father and I" did this or that, pretending to everyone that she still had a husband who was interested in his family, Ẹniọlá knew she made most of the decisions alone now. And she had chosen Bùsọ́lá over him. Even though Bùsọ́lá still had five classes to go before she finished secondary school and he had just one.

"Why?" Ẹniọlá said. "Why?"

His mother sighed. "Ẹniọlá, you know."

But he did not know, not for sure. Was it because Bùsọ́lá had always been brighter? Had come top of her class in her first-term exam while he had muddled his way through junior secondary, never rising above the thirty-first position in a class of fifty-five? Was it because his parents thought he was stupid and the money they had spent so far had been a waste? Was it because they loved Bùsólá more or did not love him at all? He did not know why. All he was sure of was that his parents had decided he was not worth the effort it would take to give him whatever little chance he could get from writing his final exams at the cheapest private school they could find. Instead, because it was tuition free, they were dumping him in the public school he'd heard both of them describe as useless over the years.

"I'm just tired," his mother said. "Why can't something good happen for us? If only for a day. Even for just a little while. I will take it, anything, just for a while."

Ęniọlá looked away from his mother to watch a man cycle down the street, headlamp brightening sections of the road as he forged a twisting path to avoid gullies. He couldn't help feeling sorry for her. At least she'd tried, right?

He began to tell her that someone had paid his apprenticeship fees, but electricity came on, and his voice was drowned out by that of several children screaming the words he'd learnt to chant before he knew they celebrated the restoration of power to the street. *Up nepa, up nepa, wón ti mú iná dé o.*

16

D r. Fidelis, a consultant neurologist, ran an outpatient clinic every Thursday from noon until three p.m. Several resident doctors had warned Wúràọlá to be well prepared before showing up to assist during Dr. Fidelis's clinic and yet she had forgotten to replenish her glove supply ahead of time. Wúràọlá and Dr. Ali, the only senior registrar in neurology, were seated beside Dr. Fidelis. She considered texting him about the gloves but decided against it; she had heard that using a phone during Dr. Fidelis's clinic was prohibited.

Wúràọlá took a deep breath and pointed to the pack of gloves in front of Dr. Ali. "Could I have some gloves sir?"

Dr. Fidelis peered at Wúràọlá. "Did you just start your house job today?"

"Um." Wúràọlá swallowed. "No ma."

"That was a rhetorical question." Dr. Fidelis spoke slowly, as if she were talking to a kindergartener. "Do you understand me?"

"I'm sorry ma. I forgot that I'd run out of them." Wúràọlá stood up. "Please, I'll go to the ward and ask the matron if they have some."

Dr. Fidelis had already turned away from her.

The matron was not at her station, and the nurse who was in her seat rolled her eyes when Wúràọlá asked for gloves.

"Why didn't you bring your own?"

"Ordinarily, the hospital is supposed to provide us with these things."

"Doctor, do I look like the CMD? Please go to his office to ask for gloves, or better still go to Abuja and ask Yar'Adua."

She was running towards the pharmacy when she bumped into Kingsley. He gripped her arms to keep her from falling.

"Slow down, golden babe." Kingsley nudged his Coke-bottle glasses up his nose.

"Hey, Kingsley. Thanks for coming to my mum's party, I'm sorry I didn't return your call the other day." Although they'd started their house job together, their schedule was such that they would never be in the same department at the same time. They only worked together when they overlapped on the call roster for A & E, but Kingsley called her every other week to check in or offer her something or the other. A ride into town for pepper soup, a motivational frame he thought she would like, a tin of Altoids. She'd stopped picking up his calls after three tins of Altoids.

"Yeah, I just wanted to offer you a ride to Tífẹ́'s birthday party this weekend. I know you don't really like to drive for long so." Kingsley shrugged.

"Oh, yes, yes, thank you. I have to run, I'm in Dr. Fidelis's clinic and I—"

"And you are here?" Kingsley glanced at his watch. "You're late now, that woman doesn't take any nonsense. She showed me pepper during my neuro rotation, my life was hell men. I've heard she refuses to sign people's logbooks at the end of house job if she wasn't satisfied with how they behaved in her clinic."

"I've run out of gloves so I'm—"

"I was on call last night, so my pack should still be in the call room. Start heading back to the clinic, ehn. Just wait outside for me, I'll bring it to you."

He was breathless by the time he brought the gloves to her. She tried to extract a few from the pack, but he shook his head, told her to keep everything and dashed off before she could say thanks.

Wúràọlá held up one of the gloves as she slid back into her seat. "I got some ma."

"You've kept patients waiting, Dr. Mákinwá." Dr Fidelis stared at Wúràọlá as though she were a cockroach that had shown up in her food. "I advise you to get to work and prove you actually have an education."

"Yes ma."

Another thing no one told Wúràọlá about her first year as a doctor? How angry and irritable many of her superiors would be. She supposed they were also tired. Perhaps even more so than she was. For a woman like Dr. Fidelis, one of only two neurologists in a tertiary-care system with four hospital units, Wúràolá could imagine how tiredness had morphed into an exhaustion that reached beyond her muscles into her marrow. Who wouldn't be irritable after decades of running on little sleep and bad pay, working with obsolete equipment, buying their own gloves and masks because patients would all be dead and long buried before the hospital could get PPE to them?

Wúràolá's first patient was a man who had not noticed any significant improvement after a regimen of corticosteroids had been prescribed for his spondylosis. And though Dr. Ali supervised her as she worked, she wondered about what she might have missed when Dr. Fidelis beckoned the man once he stood up from her table. Four patients later, it was clear that Dr. Fidelis intended to provide a second consult to all the people Wúràolá attended to that day.

"You seem like the forgetful type," Dr Fidelis said after asking Wúràolá's sixth patient to come to her table.

"She's actually quite efficient," Dr. Ali said, pulling at his green tie.

Dr. Fidelis scribbled something in the case note before her. "Which must be why she forgot her gloves."

Three hours in and Wúràolá was second-guessing everything she was saying to her patients. She lowered her voice, worried that Dr. Fidelis would find even more fault with her. Dr. Fidelis, so brilliant and always put together in her pastel suits and kitten heels, was the kind of woman she liked to impress. It rankled that she seemed to have decided that Wúràolá was disorganised.

Her wristwatch's dial hit three p.m. and sailed on. She was hungry, but since neither Dr. Ali nor Dr. Fidelis stopped to eat, she drank more water and kept going, gripping her pen to stop her fingers from trembling.

Finally, around five, two hours after the clinic was supposed to have ended, Dr. Fidelis capped her pen and turned to Dr. Ali. "Whoever is still out there must have arrived terribly late. Let them come next week. I can't, I can't do anymore today, Ali."

"Okay ma," Dr Ali said.

Dr. Fidelis slid her handbag over her shoulder and stood up.

"Have a lovely night ma," Wúràolá said.

Dr. Fidelis pursed her lips and left the room.

"Don't worry about her," Dr. Ali said after Dr. Fidelis's footsteps faded away.

"I can't believe I forgot."

"It's not you, it's something else that is worrying her today. Two of her residents in Ifẹ̀ passed their exams, and she was pushing for them to be retained as consultants. Last last, sha, it is not going to happen, because there's no allocation for that from Abuja or something. The usual nonsense. She's really mad about it." Dr. Ali opened his laptop bag and brought out a pack of Beloxxi crackers. "Do you want? Oh, you ate well in the morning? Then take it now, chop something before you faint."

"Thank you."

"And you know what is going to happen? Both of those residents are my guys. One has an offer from like four private hospitals in Lagos. By next week, he should decide on which offer he'll take."

"Good for him."

They began walking towards the corridor, matching each other's pace.

"Yeah, but terrible for us here. You know how many consultant neurologists we have in this country?"

Wúràọlá shook her head and bit into another cracker.

"Not up to one hundred in the whole fucking country. We're well over a hundred million people now, that's one neurologist to over one million people." Dr. Ali laughed. "And we're not even retaining the ones in training. You know my other guy who just passed his exams? He has written USMLE already. Small time now, he will leave this country. If we're not careful, ehn, all these public hospitals will become glorified hospices. Give it ten to fifteen years."

Wúràọlá unzipped her bag and pulled out her phone.

"And there are people like your brother who just say fuck it to the whole thing."

"Oh, you know Láyí? Did you finish from Ifẹ̀ too?" She checked her notifications. Four messages from Mọ́tárá, two missed calls from Kúnlé, five from her mother. She switched the settings from silent mode to vibrate only.

"We were classmates."

"I'm never leaving medicine."

"Just leave Nigeria, that's what you need to do."

Her phone began vibrating as they stepped into the corridor. Kúnlé.

"I'll see you tomorrow, sha, take care." Dr. Ali waved as he headed towards the car park.

"Thank you so much sir." Wúràọlá held up the pack of crackers before continuing down the corridor.

She finished another cracker before dialling Kúnlé's number. He picked up immediately. "Sorry, I've been in the consulting room since noon. My day has been one kind."

"I know. I'm behind you."

She stopped walking and turned around. There he was, dressed in jeans and a polo shirt, leaning against an iron pole with his legs crossed at the ankles. She stuffed the pack of crackers into her bag as he began walking towards her. He had been surprising her every other day since her mother's birthday. He showed up on her doorstep in the evenings, or in corridors in the middle of the day without calling ahead. She turned her head and suddenly he was there behind her. Sometimes he came bearing snacks. Packs of digestives, Pringles, half-melted ice cream. He slept over once on the Monday after he slapped her in front of Mọ́tárá, but on other nights since then, he left just before midnight. He could not bear the squalor of her lidless water closet and all the missing tiles in the bathroom that were clogged with soap and dirt. She had felt that way at first but barely noticed it anymore. Her showers had become shorter and shorter except for when she went home to spend the weekend and could luxuriate in a bathtub.

"How long have you been waiting?"

Kúnlé stood behind her and began kneading her shoulders. "Maybe an hour."

"Don't touch my ward coat, please." Wúràọlá stepped out of his reach. "I've been seeing patients all day. Who knows what germs I've picked up."

"Come on, I was just trying to help. You seemed tense."

"It's fine." She glanced at the car park. "Where did you park, abeg? I'm so tired."

"I parked near your hostel, so we have to walk. Let me help you with your bag."

"Thank you." She gave the bag to him, and they started out. "It's not a hostel. It's a residence, house officers' residence."

"It's worse than some hostels." He reached for her hand. "Move in with me. Come on, let's do this."

"Your place is too far from the hospital."

"I'll drop you off and pick you up at any time."

Wúràọlá laughed.

"Or you stay here whenever you're on call so you can change or whatever."

"And what would your mother say?"

"She says it's fine after the introduction."

"You already spoke to her about this?"

"I spoke to your mum too. She says there is no problem as long as we do the introduction first." He pulled off her scrunchie and ran his hand through her twists. "Look, I really want you to move in with me."

"My mother said that?"

"Just think about it, and let's talk after the ceremony."

"Okay." She had six weeks before their introduction. It was the first step before the actual wedding ceremonies would happen, and they'd reached a compromise about it the day after her mother's birthday party.

Kúnlé wanted the introduction within two months of their engagement, the wedding within six. Whereas Wúràọlá wanted at least a year between their engagement and the wedding. Kúnlé had agreed to wait a year before the wedding if they could have the early introduction he wanted. Their parents were ecstatic. His parents were pleased that the introduction would happen a full month before the party primaries. Hers were glad she would get married before turning thirty. Yèyé checked in every day to tell her what she was planning for the introduction. It had become clear in the couple of weeks since the dates were fixed that Wúràọlá's decision making would be limited to what she wanted to wear for the ceremony; her mother was taking charge of everything else.

Mọ́tárá was the only relative who was not excited about the upcoming ceremony. In person, over the phone and via more text messages than she had ever sent to anyone, Wúràọlá told Mọ́tárá that Kúnlé had never slapped her before. *Ever. Never ever. Not even once.* She whispered the words right after the incident, while Mọ́tárá swung her beaded bag at

Kúnlé as he dashed away. She shouted them that night when Mótárá brought it up as Wúràolá tried to slip into sleep, legs aching and almost numb from doing a million circuits beneath the canopy to make sure everyone was happy. And then again and again over the phone and by text in the weeks since then, she stuck to her story no matter what Mótárá said. *Ever. Never ever. Not even once. It was the first time this happened, he has promised it will never happen again and I believe him.*

She stopped picking up Mótárá's calls after a week, but she occasionally responded to her texts. Her persistence was no longer cute or touching. It was just insulting that a teenager was sure she knew, from observing a few minutes of interaction, what her relationship was like. Oshisco. The thrust of Mótárá's messages—*you're lying to protect him, he is abusing you, you just don't see it, don't marry a wife beater*—annoyed Wúràolá. She was not some helpless victim who needed to be saved by Mótárá of all people. She knew what she was doing.

Of course, it was not the first time Kúnlé had hit her, it was the third. Three times in two years and so much in between that was not visible to Mótárá. Twenty-four months. Seven hundred and thirty days. How many minutes and seconds? Three slaps that barely lasted a minute, and this was what Mótárá wanted her to base her judgement of the whole relationship on? It was emotional and dramatic, just like Mótárá, who had urged her to go under the canopy, take the mike from whoever was speaking and accuse her fiancé in front of everyone. She had laughed at the suggestion, because she thought it was a joke. Then she saw that her sister was staring at her, face serious and earnest.

Láyí was right about Mótárá. Their parents had spoilt the girl rotten and now she was incapable of considering the impact of her actions on other people. How could she think it was justifiable to disrupt their mother's birthday by making a scene? Ruining a birthday party that for Yèyé represented how far she had travelled, all she had accomplished and survived in her life. How could Mótárá not recognise that this was probably the most important moment in their mother's life? This orphaned child telling her world, *Look at me now.* Mótárá existed in a bubble where she did whatever she wanted without consequence. Of course she could not begin to fathom what it would mean for everyone if Wúràolá left Kúnlé.

As they walked through the hospital corridors together, Wúràọlá and Kúnlé ran into several people who knew one of their parents or all four of them. Only one man, a professor who had just returned from a sabbatical in Saudi Arabia, did not already know about their engagement. Kúnlé immediately introduced her to the man as his wife-to-be.

"Why don't you just say fiancée?" Wúràọlá put her key in the lock.

Kúnlé shrugged as they entered her tiny flat. "I'm just so excited."

She walked straight into the bedroom. The exhaustion she'd been staving off since noon had begun to set in. Wúràọlá longed to collapse on the bed as soon as she stepped into the room, but she forced herself to take off her clothes. She was in her underwear when Kúnlé brought her a glass of water.

"Thank you." She gave him the empty cup then flopped into her bed. "Could you help me to switch on the fan?"

"Of course."

Yes. Of course. No problem. Kúnlé had become so yielding and solicitous since her mother's birthday. After he switched on the standing fan, he lay beside her and placed a hand on her stomach. He had also become clingy. His hand sought out her body at every opportunity. He caressed her and ran his fingers across her skin, his touch so featherlight, it was almost imperceptible. They had not made love since that day. Though his eyes brimmed with longing, he held himself back, paying penance. She sensed that he was waiting for her to give him permission by initiating lovemaking, but Wúràọlá felt no desire. Had felt none since he slapped her. It was like this each time he'd struck her. Any yearning for him would disappear for days before returning with a force that surprised her. She traced his moustache with a finger. It was so thin it looked like something drawn in with a pencil.

"Do you want me to massage your shoulders?" he asked.

She rolled over onto her stomach and shut her eyes.

He began kneading her flesh. "Do you have some stew?"

"No. Why?"

"I could boil rice for you or make ẹ̀bà."

He did not want to lose her. Their love gave his life meaning. What they had was special. Neither of them could re-create it with anyone else. He had said all this every day after the incident until she made him stop because hearing him grovel made her sick. Now he had replaced those words with offers to cook for her or bring her food.

"Let's go to Captain Cook and get their asaro again," Kúnlé said.

"I'm not going anywhere, abeg."

She wanted to stay in this moment. Tickled by the whisper of his breath against her skin as he bent to press his lips against her shoulder blade, unsullied by what had happened before or all that might come after. No man had ever made her feel like this, not even Nonso. Ensconced in his attentiveness, she was the splendorous sun around which his life revolved.

"Have you spoken to your mum today?"

"I need to call her back." Wúràolá yawned. "I don't have the energy yet."

"I saw her just before coming here."

"How?"

"I went to her shop." He rubbed her forearm. "It sounds as if your mother has been planning this introduction since you were born."

Wúràolá laughed. "You people are best friends now, ehn?"

"She has the colour coordination on lockdown, the menu, guest list. You won't have to do a thing, just attend."

"I think we might even end up fighting if I try to do anything beyond choosing my own clothes."

"And I spoke to her about Mótárá."

"For goodness sake, Kúnlé."

"We are practically family, Wúrà, I should be able to speak to your mum directly about these things. I just explained that I wanted Mótárá to stop calling me by name, and she agreed immediately. Everything is okay, darling. She had even been thinking about how it would be best for Mótárá to call me Brother Kúnlé. I've sorted that out." Kúnlé let out a slow breath. "That is what I should have done instead of confronting you about it. I should have gone directly to your parents all along. That's the mature way to handle things."

He was gone when Wúràolá woke up around midnight. She stumbled into the living room to check the door and found that he had locked the door from the outside and slipped the key under the door. Kúnlé had also left a nylon bag on one of the ratty armchairs that had come with the

216 · *Ayòbámi Adébáyò*

apartment. It contained a bowl of asaro and foil-wrapped chicken lap. She sat in one of the chairs and ate the meal, crunching the chicken bones so she could suck out the marrow.

❋

Kingsley picked Wúràolá up before noon on Saturday. His car smelled as though the seats had been soaked in perfume overnight. It took a while before Wúràolá adjusted to the musky scent and could notice that Kingsley was humming.

"Can we just play some music?"

"Let me sing for you instead." Kingsley moved his shoulders to some internal rhythm. "Óyá, special request. You know you want it."

Wúràolá chuckled and began fiddling with the radio. As Kingsley launched into Styl Plus's "Call My Name," she was reminded of the calming weeks they'd spent exchanging handwritten notes and giving each other novels as gifts. They enjoyed the same kind of books and would spend hours chatting about a plot twist. He sang to her when they were alone and sometimes rocked her to sleep while humming a lullaby. He'd been just what she needed after the possibility of something permanent with Nonso had flamed out. The only thing that rankled during that month with Kingsley was how he always signed his notes to her with *Love, Kingsley.*

Now Wúràolá cleared her throat when he switched from "Call My Name" to "Imagine That."

Kingsley laughed. "Relax, golden babe, it's just a song."

When Kingsley sat her down at Banwill to say he was not sure they could ever be in love with each other, she'd been so relieved she sputtered rice all over the tablecloth in a rush to agree with him. Tifé was the one who months later had pointed out that the conversation Wúràolá understood as a breakup had been designed to wrangle a greater commitment from her.

"I know you're engaged, and I'm happy for you." Kingsley's voice was thin and faint. "So happy."

Wúràolá looked out the window and watched a petrol tanker overtake them. They were on the expressway, speeding then coming to abrupt stops just before they hit potholes. In their final year, Tifẹ́ and Grace labelled Kingsley her assistant boyfriend for how willing he was to run errands for her. Grace was amused, but Tifẹ́ had asked Wúràọlá to stop stringing him along in the name of friendship.

Wúràọlá had spent her undergraduate years trying to become like Tifẹ́. Astute and often prescient, Tifẹ́ seemed unencumbered by anyone's expectations and, perhaps as a result, possessed a boundless capacity to enjoy herself. Throughout medical school, Tifẹ́ took breaks every month to climb a mountain, visit a beach or wander alone through a garden. Sometimes she travelled out of town but would settle for the university parks and garden if that was not possible. She celebrated every birthday with a party. Even in their third year when her birthday fell on the day before the anatomy OSCE, Tifẹ́ had partied with her roommates until midnight.

Their house job year was the longest Wúràọlá and Tifẹ́ had been apart since they met. Wúràọlá missed seeing her friends every day and was surprised that they didn't speak or text as often as she had assumed they would. Weeks often went by before Tifẹ́ returned a text or a phone call.

"I have *Expressions* in the dashboard," Kingsley said. "You can play that."

"What?"

"The Styl Plus album."

"Oh, it's fine."

"Are you okay?"

"I'm fine."

"You seem somehow. Mellow."

"No, I'm all right. I just have stuff on my mind." Wúràọlá was almost certain that Tifẹ́ would ask her to end her engagement immediately if she knew Kúnlé had hit her even once. "Have you ever slapped a woman? Any woman?"

Kingsley frowned. "Maybe my younger sister when we were kids."

"A girlfriend?"

"Never. Why?"

"Nothing."

"Wait, is . . . is he hitting you?"

"Keep your eyes on the road, please."

"Wúràọlá."

He'd always pronounced her name wrong, getting "gold" right in the first half but switching "wealth" in the second half with "tomorrow." She could not remember the last time he'd called her Wúràọlá; he'd settled for "golden babe" long ago.

"You're not saying anything."

"About what?" She opened the dashboard and riffled through for the Styl Plus CD.

"Is he—"

"Oh no." Wúràọlá laughed. "Why would I be with someone like that?"

Kingsley gave her a look.

"Don't kill us o, Kingsley, abeg, face front." Wúràọlá removed the CD from its jacket. "I've been meaning to ask you, have you decided on a specialty?"

"It's not easy at all. The thing is, it feels like such a big decision, you know?"

Kingsley had earned a degree in biochemistry before applying to study medicine. He'd already done his national service after the first degree and unlike Wúràọlá could begin residency right after his house job. Relieved that Kingsley was not probing any further about Kúnlé, she nodded as he continued weighing his options. Dermatology, community health or psychiatry. He kept talking until they drove into the teaching hospital.

Tifẹ́'s party was happening in Springhill, a space in the university's New Buka that was used for everything from birthday raves to prayer meetings. Kingsley reached for Wúràọlá's hand after he parked the car. She flinched at the unexpected touch.

"Wúràọlá."

"It's nothing. I didn't know you would . . . We don't hold hands."

"The thing is, I don't know if you're telling me the truth. A part of me hopes you are because, yes, why should you be with someone like that?" Kingsley reached for an errant twist that had slipped from her loose bun. "But if I'm honest with myself, a part of me also wishes you were lying. That he has been hitting you and does not deserve you. Because maybe then I could still have the slimmest chance with you."

"Kingsley, you're a nice friend but I've never—"

"You don't have to say it. I know." Kingsley sighed. "The thing is, you need to leave him if he's slapping you. You know that. Right?"

"But to be clear, he's not."

Wúràọlá did not want to leave Kúnlé. It was not just a question of the embarrassment of a broken engagement or how disappointed and ashamed her parents would be. In the week after her mother's birthday, she'd been surprised at how bereft she felt whenever she thought about ending things. It was clear to her then that she wanted to be married to Kúnlé and only wanted him to stop hitting her when he was upset. There had been no escalation beyond slapping. He was working on himself. She knew what she was doing. There was nothing to worry about yet, no reason to cough up details to Tifẹ́ and watch judgement seep into her gaze. *Why didn't you leave him after the first time?*

Lágbájá was playing on the sound system when they got to Springhill. The party had not started yet, but Tifẹ́ was dancing konko below while the dozen or so people in the room cheered her on.

Kingsley joined the chant. "Go, go, go, Tifẹ́."

Tifẹ́ turned to them, threw her arms open. "Kingsley! Wúrà!"

"Where is Grace?" Wúràọlá asked as they hugged.

"Have you lost weight?" Tifẹ́ pulled back and poked at Wúràọlá's collarbones. "You've lost weight. Hope you're not starving yourself to fit in a stupid dress?"

"You're the only one gaining weight during house job, Tifẹ́. I don't even understand." Grace came in bearing a birthday cake. She was followed by other people who carried varying sizes of coolers and covered dishes.

"Man dey hunger, please," Kingsley said. He was going round the room, shaking hands with everyone he recognised. "Grace, abeg, can I have something to step down?"

Grace opened one of the coolers, wrapped something in a serviette and held it out to Kingsley. "Meat pie?"

"God go bless you." Kingsley bit into the pie. "Do you people remember Success?"

Wúràọlá nodded. "My God, nobody does meat pie like that one they sold."

Before they were all burnt to the ground in a fire outbreak, a strip of stores opposite the university sports centre had been a destination for undergraduates. Wúràọlá had gone there often. For the occasional perm at Megacall, to browse through motivational titles at Bádéjòkó before buying pens and the colour-coded five-in-one notebooks she loved. Whatever it was that took her there, Success was always her first point of call, its spread of pastries a constant pull.

Wúràọlá asked Grace for a meat pie.

"Kúnlé didn't come with you," Grace said. She was arranging all the coolers and dishes along a wall.

"He's running around for his dad's campaign thing." Wúràọlá swallowed. The pie's crust was too dry, its filling made up of more potatoes than was necessary in a meat pie. "The primaries are in just over two months."

"That's really close."

"They're very hopeful that he'll win."

"Isn't—what's the name of that guy in the House of Representatives?"

"Fèsòjaiyé?"

"Yes." Grace stabbed a finger in the air. "I think I read somewhere that he's running?"

"See, ehn, it's a bit messy because Kúnlé's dad already had a promise from the party—"

"No, no, no." Tifẹ́ pressed a finger against Wúràọlá's lips. "This is my day. You people are only allowed to talk about how wonderful I am or ask about my ten-year plan to take over the world."

"Óyá, tell us the ten-year plan." Wúràọlá grabbed a La Casera and sat in one of the plastic chairs that lined the wall.

Tifẹ́ launched into a plan Wúràọlá had heard before. Residency in the United States followed by a return to Nigeria to set up her own hospital in Abuja. Along the way, Tifẹ́ was going to learn how to play five instruments, visit all the continents except Antarctica and start a real estate company. Wúràọlá's ambitions always paled in the light of her friend's. She wanted to finish a residency, get a teaching position with a university and become a professor. Unlike Tifẹ́, Wúràọlá could not imagine any paths for herself outside of medicine.

"When are you going to get married?" Bíódún, who had been their class representative in medical school, asked when Tifé was done.

"You should be asking me if I plan to get married at all."

There was an uproar. Laughter and a dozen *aaahhhs* sprinkled through with snickers. Springhill had been filling up with guests since Wúràọlá and Kingsley arrived, and it was now packed.

Tifé raised up her arms as though to stop traffic. "You people need to calm down. I'm just trying to decide if marriage is what I want or what I'm supposed to want. It's so easy to confuse the two."

"Are we starting this party with prayers or—?" Grace asked.

Tifé shrugged. "Sister Grace, pray for us if you want now. I don't mind."

Grace pulled out a handkerchief from her handbag and covered her hair with it. "Let's all bow our heads, please. Bíódún, take off that face cap."

Wúràọlá shut her eyes but did not hear Grace's words. There was no point discussing her concerns about Kúnlé with Tifé. Not when Tifé had such clarity about her life, could slice neatly between her desires and what was being imposed on her, and would want Wúràọlá to do the same. She did not have the words to explain how such distinctions had never been a primary consideration for her. She could not explain how much she still wanted Kúnlé. Why, even though she worried that he might never stop slapping her, she could no longer imagine a future without him in it. Maybe it was because she did love him, could not remember being enamoured with anyone the way she was with him. Could no longer imagine the possibility of someone like that in her future. Didn't options thin out the older one got? Kúnlé loved her, needed her, even. And hearing him reiterate how much he needed her always felt so good. Besides, it would be an utter disgrace to her family to turn back now, her mother would not be able to show her face in the Mothers' Union for months. But perhaps this was not only about that. Maybe she did want to get married before turning thirty, did not want to be like her cousin who married at thirty-five and had, for the last five years of her spinsterhood, been the subject of extended family gossip, wild speculations and mountain-top prayers. Whichever way her mind swung, Wúràọlá found explanations that Tifé would surely disdain. No, there was no way to talk about what was going on without Tifẹ́ becoming disappointed in her.

❈

Wúràọlá slipped the key into the lock, but her door swung open before she turned the key.

Kúnlé was on the other side of the door.

"How did you get in?"

"With my key."

"What do you mean?"

Kúnlé shut the door behind her. There was a key in the lock. He turned it. "I made a copy a while ago. One of those Saturdays I spent here while you just slept."

"But I didn't give you my key."

"Why wouldn't you want me to have it? You have mine and we're getting married so." He had turned away from her and gone to the desk that doubled as a dining table.

"You should have asked me, Kúnlé."

He set a plate of rice on the table. "How was Tifẹ́'s party?"

"She is fine, she liked her gift and says to thank you."

"Yeah, she already texted me."

"And how was your meeting?" Wúràọlá kicked off her shoes and sat in the chair while he moved around in the kitchenette.

"That Fẹ̀sọ̀jaiyé guy is not letting go. My dad was supposed to run unopposed. That's what the chairman promised would happen, but now there's this idiot who thinks he can stop us."

"I'm sorry about that." She went into the room to change, then joined him at the table.

She could tell that he was upset. He was so intent on his father's dream, any disappointment on that front often spoilt the rest of his day. By morning, he would be in a better mood, full of new ideas and more optimistic about their chances. Wúràọlá tried to rub his shoulder, but he shook off her hand.

"What's the matter?"

"How did you travel?"

"What?"

"Your car was here all day. How did you go to Ifẹ̀?"

"Oh, Kingsley was going too, so he gave me a ride."

"Kingsley."

"Yes." Wúràọlá kept her gaze on Kúnlé, watching every movement he made.

"You wore a yellow dress." Kúnlé drank some water. "Wasn't he the one who told you that yellow was made for your skin to glow or some shit?"

Wúràọlá stifled a laugh.

He grabbed her wrist. "It's funny to you?"

"That you still remember that, yes."

His grip tightened around her wrist. She balled her hand into a fist and tried to pull her hand free.

"You and Kingsley, alone in his car for thirty minutes? Forty-five. One hour. You've fucked him in that car before, àbí?"

"Let go of me, Lákúnlé."

"Just the two of you driving back and forth so you could reminiscence, àbí?"

"Let me go." She was becoming nervous.

"Why didn't you take your car? Why did you go with your ex?"

"Lákúnlé, stop this nonsense."

His grip tightened. He pressed his thumb against her radial artery, and she was suddenly aware of his strength, the brutal capacity of the biceps she'd long admired. Her fingers began to go numb.

"Why did you go with your ex?"

Wúràọlá took a deep breath, then shouted as loud as she could, "Let me go!"

She did not see him move until she felt his hands close around her throat. He pushed her back in her seat, pressing his face against hers. Her eyes watered. The chair stood on its back legs, ready to topple. She stared up at him, scratched his arms, flailed at his face until she could not breathe and was gagging and sputtering, struggling for air. He finally let go, and she fell across the table, drooling and coughing.

Kúnlé brought her a cup of water. She took a gulp too quickly and began choking on it. He patted Wúràọlá on the back, took the cup from her and held it up to her lips. She pushed his hand away and stumbled towards the door, unable to see well through the film of tears. He was blocking the door when she finally made it there.

"Don't leave." He fell to his knees. "I deserve it, but please don't. Wúràolá Àbèké, please."

"Go away." Wúràolá backed away from him. She wanted to scream, but her voice came out as a hoarse whisper. Her tongue was a towel stuffed against her throat.

"No, please, Wúràolá. Àbèké mi, I'm sorry. I just wanted to stop you from shouting, that was all. That's all, baby, that's all. I didn't mean to hurt you." He crawled around the room, following Wúràolá as she paced. "I swear, on my life. Àbèké. On my mother's life. I swear. I'm so sorry. Wúràolá. Please."

When he reached for her leg, Wúràolá ran into the bathroom and bolted the door behind her. She switched on the tap to drown out his blubbering. There was a small mirror above the sink. She leaned forward and studied her reflection. There were no visible bruises on her neck. Her eyes were bloodshot, but her lipstick was not smudged, her hair was still held in the loose bun. The only thing out of place was the errant twist Kingsley had touched in the afternoon.

17

Yèyé burst into the room like she always did, without knocking first. Mótárá sat up in bed. "You didn't knock."

"And so?"

"You should respect my privacy."

Yèyé picked some chocolate wrappers from the floor and threw them at Mótárá. "Look around you, this house is my husband's house. It is my own home. When you are in your husband's house, ehn, and I come there to visit you, talk to me about privacy."

"Why can't it be my own house?" Forty-seven. On Sunday morning, when her father asked if she planned to keep her husband waiting as she'd done to him before they left for church together, Mótárá had decided to spend the week keeping a count of how many times anyone in her family would speak about how she planned to behave when she was married. Or living in her husband's house. Her husband's house was the destination everyone had been referring to since she was old enough to understand what they meant. If all she had noted that week alone was any indication, the husband's house was the destination of all good girls when they became women, just as heaven was the destination of all good people when they died. So far, between her parents and the aunts she'd spoken to on the phone that week, she'd counted forty-seven references to how she would behave in her marriage, in her husband's house, towards her in-laws.

Yèyé pulled the duvet away from Mótárá's body. "Wo, go and bring in the clothes on the line, I think it might rain soon."

"But why can't Rachel do it?"

"You, what have you been doing since morning? You have not even cleaned up your room. What are you doing right now that is stopping you from bringing in the clothes? Ehn? What?"

Mọtárá had spent most of the day in bed reading and rereading texts from Wúràọlá, veering between fear and anger until her head ached. Since Yèyé's birthday, she had been dreaming about Wúràọlá. In some of the dreams, her sister was dead or in mortal danger. Hit by a car, burnt in a fire, attacked by a mob. The scenarios changed, but one thing remained the same—the instigator was always that Kúnlé. Last night, she had woken up bathed in sweat, nightdress stuck to her skin. Once, she'd crept into Yèyé's bed, and her mother had spent almost an hour prodding her about what dream had driven her out of her room. That was her chance to tell Yèyé what that coconut-head Kúnlé had done. Instead, she had pretended to fall asleep so Yèyé would not worry about her.

"I don't understand why you can't get up from the bed and throw these things in the dustbin. You better receive sense and start cleaning up after yourself. Is this how you will behave in your husband's house, ehn?" Yèyé pointed at the carton of juice Mọtárá had left on the floor the night before.

"And forty-eight," Mọtárá said, standing up.

"What?"

"Nothing."

"Wúràọlá's room was never like this."

For as long as she could remember, Mọtárá's parents had been asking her to be more like her sister. They wanted her to earn the kind of grades Wúràọlá had in secondary school, be as quiet and agreeable as Wúràọlá was with them, help around the house, become a doctor. She had mostly disappointed them on all counts. Crowning it all by failing, of all things, biology in A levels. Now she was supposed to be studying to retake her A level papers, but her textbook had remained unopened since she came back home from boarding school the year before. A second failure would mean they had to give up on their dreams and listen to hers. At least she hoped so. She could not waste another year because her parents wanted her to become Saint Wúràọlá the Impeccable. Mọtárá picked up the carton and binned it.

"Sort out the clothes and fold them before distributing to each person's room. Don't just dump clothes on my bed or wait for Rachel to come and help you fold."

"But—"

"Don't 'but' me, just do what I say, you hear."

Mótárá left the room. There was no arguing with Yèyé when she was upset, and she'd come back from her shop yesterday in a bad mood.

The thud of pestle against mortar was audible from the landing. It got louder as Mótárá moved closer to the kitchen. Rachel stopped pounding when she saw Mótárá.

"You shouldn't pound things in the middle of the kitchen." Mótárá wrinkled her nose. The kitchen smelled like blood. Something must have been gutted and cleaned just before she came into the room.

Rachel squatted and braced her body against the wooden mortar, grunting as she pushed it across the floor. It made a scraping sound until it stopped beside the back door.

"I'm hungry, do we have chin-chin?"

"Yèyé bought some yesterday," Rachel said before continuing with her pounding.

All four burners on the gas cooker were on, and the room was hot. Occasionally, a gust of wind blew in through the open windows, pregnant with the possibility of rain, lifting the disgusting smell of blood just a little bit each time.

Mótárá searched the countertop for the bowl of chin-chin. It was crowded with several bundles of ugu and gbúre, each tied together at the stalk with a blade of elephant grass. Most of the leaves were fresh and green. A few were turning yellow, but their descent into decay was still at a beautiful, consumable stage; no leaf was brown or dry just yet. She pushed the vegetables to one side, yet there was no bowl of chin-chin in sight. Just tiny jars of curry, pepper and thyme.

"Where is the chin-chin?"

Rachel kept pounding, her chest heaving with each movement of the pestle high into the air. The noise drowned out Mótárá's voice. She picked a pair of kitchen shears from the assortment of dirty pans and cutlery in the sink. Its serrated blades were bloody and smelled like fish. Something oily, probably Titus fish. She banged the knife against the insides of the sink until the screech of metal against metal drew Rachel's attention.

Rachel balanced the pestle against a wall, making a whistling sound as she breathed through her mouth.

"Where is the chin-chin?"

Rachel scratched her head then wiped her hands against her brown dress.

"Did Yèyé hide it?"

"She's keeping it for tomorrow. Aunty Wúrà's husband is coming here after church service."

"He's not her husband! They've not even done their introduction."

Rachel shrugged and began scooping the pounded yam from the mortar.

Mọ́tárá went to the gas cooker. She opened all the pots until she found the one with fish in it. It was Titus. She pierced one through with a fork before turning off the burner. Yèyé must have forgotten that it was so close to being done. Mọ́tárá spooned a piece into a saucer, divided it along the bone line and cut off a small piece.

It started drizzling outside as she took a bite. She stepped closer to an open window to watch. Yèyé had mentioned that she had invited Kúnlé to dinner, but Mọ́tárá could not remember if Wúràọlá was coming with him. If that happened, they could talk again, and, hopefully, Wúràọlá would come to her senses before the introduction ceremony. Sometimes families discussed and picked wedding dates during the introduction. Once that ceremony was done, Wúràọlá would be as good as married. Wouldn't all that was left, the bringing of yams and signing of government registers, be mere formality?

Mọ́tárá sighed, dug into her pocket for her phone and read the last message she got from Wúràọlá again.

> You need to drop this, Mọ́tárá, you're just being rude now. I don't know what you think you saw but the last thing I'll say about this is that your perspective was and is all wrong.

It clicked as she read all the previous messages. Nothing in Wúràọlá's messages affirmed what Mọ́tárá had witnessed. She couldn't show this to anyone as proof.

"Ọmọ́tárá, what is wrong with you? You've not packed those clothes. You're just here eating food and pressing phone. What's all this nonsense now?"

Mótárá looked up at her mother, who was standing on the kitchen's threshold.

"I'm so sorry, I—"

Yèyé hissed and swept past Mótárá to the back door.

Mótárá dropped the saucer onto the countertop and touched her hair. The weave had been installed less than a week ago. She couldn't go into the rain without a shower cap.

When Yèyé came back into the kitchen, her relaxed hair was plastered to her skull, greying and short. She stood in front of Mótárá, dripping rainwater onto the floor.

"All the clothes are absolutely wet. I couldn't even salvage any."

"I'm sorry ma."

"Sorry for yourself, be sorry for yourself. The people who are saying I've spoilt you are not wrong." Yèyé turned to Rachel. "Switch off all the burners and excuse us, please."

"I just felt like eating something before going to bring them in, then I forgot all about it."

When Rachel left the room, Yèyé continued speaking. "You know, Kúnlé came to my shop yesterday and said the same thing."

"Kúnlé said I'm spoilt?"

"He's too cultured to say it like that, but I got his message."

"What do you mean you got his message?" Mótárá took a deep breath to keep her voice from rising or trembling. "Kúnlé was bad-mouthing me to you, and you just sat there and believed him?"

"Who are you shouting at? Me? It's me you are raising your voice at, ehn? Is it your fault? No, it's not your fault. I'm the one that allowed this rubbish. This is what everybody has been telling me about you, but no, I did not listen. Now open your ears and hear me, today is the day you stop calling Kúnlé by name. He's Uncle Kúnlé to you from now on."

"What are you saying? He's not my brother or my uncle."

"He will soon marry your sister."

"God forbid bad thing."

"What? Mótárá, are you okay at all?" Yèyé advanced on Mótárá, arms akimbo, face crumpled in rage. "You are saying that about your sister's marriage?"

Mótárá folded her arms and stared down at her feet. She felt sorry about forgetting the clothes but could not see how her mother had made a leap from that to a conversation about Kúnlé. Days had become weeks as she thought about if, how and when to tell anyone what she had seen during Yèyé's birthday. No moment seemed right. Maybe there was no perfect moment to make sure someone else knew Wúràọlá was in danger.

"Is something wrong with your ears? Explain yourself. Why on earth would you say that?"

Mọ́tárá took a deep breath and stepped closer to her mother. "Kúnlé slapped Wúràọlá, I saw him do it."

Yèyé frowned, then burst into a laugh. "Which kind of lie is this?"

"No, no. I'm not lying this time, I'm not lying. I saw him, it was during your birthday. He slapped her. They can't go ahead with the introduction. You have to stop them. So yes, God forbid bad thing."

"Shut up there. What rubbish are you saying? Me, I will not be put to shame. It is not me that will fix the introduction for my daughter and cancel. My joy will never turn to embarrassment."

"Kúnlé slapped Wúràọlá, are you even hearing what I'm saying?"

Yèyé wagged a finger in Mọ́tárá's face. "You're lying."

"But what if I'm not?"

"The same Kúnlé that I've known since he was tiny?" Yèyé shook her head. "No. I know you, Mọ́tárá, you lie for fun."

"Not this time."

"Stop this nonsense right now." Yèyé glanced at her wristwatch. "It's almost seven. Serve your father's food. Me, I need to change. Don't let me hear any complaints from your father o. I'm warning you now."

Mọ́tárá felt stupid about how the conversation had gone. Why didn't she wait until Yèyé was in a good mood? She should have been smart enough to realise that talking about this right after she'd upset her mother was terrible timing. Given that Wúràọlá's safety was at stake, she should have been more thoughtful about how to bring this up in a convincing way.

There were sets of porcelain bowls in one of the many cabinets in the kitchen. All five sets were dedicated to serving her father's food. Mọ́tárá chose a set of three and placed them on a tray. There would be no room to revisit the conversation with Yèyé if she did not get this right.

She dished the egusi into a midsized bowl, then selected four wraps of pounded yam from the brown cooler Rachel had stored them in and put those in the largest bowl. Before covering the dishes, she arranged an assortment of snails, fish and chicken in the other midsized dish.

Mótárá walked slowly to the dining table so the soup would not slosh around in the bowl and streak the sides with palm oil. Her father would not like that. After she arranged the bowls on the table, she removed the cover to inspect the soup bowl. Seeing there were no tracks on the insides gave her a burst of satisfaction as she continued setting the table.

Her father wore cloth slippers when he was indoors and moved like a hunter, coming suddenly upon Mótárá when she thought she was alone. She never stopped trying to preempt his approach, because she preferred to avoid him. Particularly now that she'd come back home from secondary school as the only child who had ever failed a paper in her final exams; she avoided him as much as she could. His disappointment in her was unrelenting and unmetered by the kind of affection Yèyé often expressed towards her. He was a man who took pride in his children's achievements and expected them to reward his investments in them with spectacular grades. Mótárá's grades had only ever been just above average, and now she'd actually failed an exam. He came into the living room just before seven, startling Mótárá even though she had been listening for his footfalls.

She went on her knees as he sat down, inclined her head a little as he drummed his fingers on the table. "Good evening sir."

"Where is your mother?"

"She needed to change."

"Hmmmm. Okay, get up."

She stood and uncovered the dishes, placing the covers face up in a row on the white tablecloth.

She transferred the wraps of pounded yam onto a flat plate.

"Put that back," he said. "Two wraps are enough."

She spooned egusi from the porcelain bowl into a smaller bowl, careful not to make a splash or drip oil onto the tablecloth. She stabbed the snails with a fork and had transferred four into the bowl of soup before he raised a hand to indicate that it was enough for now.

Mótárá stood with her hands clasped behind her back as he ate his first few bites. He coughed and took a sip of the water she had thoughtfully poured into a cup earlier. When he studied the cup before setting it on a coaster, she knew something was wrong. She had gotten something wrong.

"Do you want to kill me?" He pointed at his cup. "Cold water on a rainy day?"

Mọ́tárá reached for the jug. "I'm sorry sir."

"You should pay more attention to everything you do," he said.

"I'll get some lukewarm water."

"It's not about that. Sit down, let me talk to you."

Mọ́tárá sat in the dining chair beside her father.

He leaned back in his seat. "You should learn from your sister."

"Yes sir." Of course, St. Wúràọlá, Our Lady of Perpetual Perfection.

"That is one focused young woman. Even when she was your age, focused. And see where she is now. Do you understand what I am saying?"

Mọ́tárá nodded.

"You're so flighty, unfocused. I see that attitude in the way you do things around the house, and of course it was reflected in your results. You need to grow out of it, Mọ́tárá. I want you to grow out of it, or else that attitude will follow you into your future. Imagine you're married and your in-laws are visiting on a rainy day, then without thinking, you serve them cups of cold water. How would that play?"

"And forty-nine." When she began keeping count, Mọ́tárá had not expected to get to fifty within a week, but here she was, just one mention away.

"You said?"

"Thank you sir." On a good day, she could tell Yèyé about her count and use it as a basis for challenging her constant references to marriage as the ultimate motivation for any self-improvement, but with her father, there was no frame for that kind of conversation. Maybe there was for children like Wúràọlá, who had done all he expected her to, but as for Mọ́tárá, she knew she might not feel confident enough to have that sort of discussion with him until she had earned at least one degree.

❖

Wúràọlá came to the house with Kúnlé the next day, wearing a bright blue scarf around her neck. Mọtárá stayed in the living room while they chatted with her parents about the introduction, waiting for a window of time alone with her sister. But Wúràọlá never left Kúnlé's side, not to go upstairs for something she needed to take back to the hospital with her, not even to use the restroom.

Mọtárá studied the scarf all afternoon, noting how large it was, how it hid every inch of Wúràọlá's neck and was not taken off or loosened when they sat at the dining table for lunch. Mọtárá developed a theory before she dug into her Sunday rice. Wúràọlá had to be hiding a giant bruise beneath the soft fabric. Somehow, she could not believe the incident she had witnessed had never happened before. The effrontery of slapping Wúràọlá in her family home, with her family so close by? No, he had to be doing worse when they were alone elsewhere.

As the meal progressed, Wúràọlá seemed too bright and happy, her smile stayed in place even as she chewed, like something painted on. Yet Mọtárá was sure that her sister flinched each time Kúnlé reached for something that was on Wúràọlá's side of the table. Mọtárá had even asked him to pass the salt twice, just so she could observe Wúràọlá and make sure she was not imagining the fleeting movements on her sister's face.

Mọtárá could feel her face heating up as Yèyé talked about the aṣọ-ebí for the introduction. She wanted to scream at her mother as she talked about the merits of coffee-brown gèlè and peach lace. It upset her more than she expected that her mother did not believe her at all. Of course she sometimes lied for fun, but she did not expect Yèyé to be so relaxed a day after hearing that Wúràọlá might be a victim of abuse. Was she that much of a joke to everyone, that Yèyé would not even spend twenty-four hours wondering if she might be telling the truth?

Mọtárá pushed away her empty plate and began with the after-meal comments she'd been taught since she was a child. "Thank you sir, thank you ma."

Yèyé nodded.

"Thank God," her father muttered back.

"Dr. Wúrà, I want you to tell Ọtúnba and Yèyé about what Kúnlé . . . Uncle Kúnlé"—Mọtárá pressed her hands against the tablecloth—"tell them what he did to you."

Wúràǫlá touched her scarf. "I don't understand what you're saying."

"Ǫmǫtárá, if you don't shut up now," Yèyé said, glaring at her from across the table.

Mǫtárá kept her focus on Kúnlé, who continued to spoon rice into his mouth like a thief. "I saw him do it. You need to speak up now."

Wúràǫlá shook her head and looked away.

Ǫtúnba drank some water. "What is this about?"

Mǫtárá swallowed. "Kúnlé slapped Wúràǫlá during Yèyé's birthday."

"She is Dr. Wúrà to you. That is part of your problem. You don't respect your elders. Nítorí Ǫlǫrun, why are you so determined to disgrace us, Mǫtárá?" Yèyé was shouting now.

Ǫtúnba placed his cutlery on a napkin. "Kúnlé did what?"

"She's lying," Yèyé and Wúràǫlá spoke at once.

Mǫtárá stood up. "I'm not lying. Wúrà . . . Dr. Wúrà, you know I'm not. Why are you lying for him? Why are you protecting this, this rubbish guy? He slapped you in this house. Why are you lying?"

"Sit down and stop being hysterical," Wúràǫlá said, pouring water into Kúnlé's cup.

"Jesus Christ! What are you doing? Are you so desperate to get married? What is wrong with you?"

"Kúnlé." Ǫtúnba pushed away his plate. "What is going on?"

"I'm sorry sir. I don't, I don't even understand. It's, er, I went to Yèyé's shop on Friday to have a discussion with her about how Mǫtárá had been rude to me, and I think she might be upset about that. That's really the only explanation I have sir."

Ǫtúnba looked askance at Yèyé, who nodded in support of what Kúnlé had said. "Ǫmǫtárá Mákinwá, sit down right now and stop making a scene."

Mǫtárá sat on the edge of her chair. Her hands trembled. Tears welled up in her eyes. She took a deep breath to steady herself. "Daddy, tell her to remove her scarf."

Wúràǫlá laughed, a harsh barking sound.

"I know she's hiding something with it, tell her to remove it, please. If she has bruises, then you have to believe me."

Ǫtúnba rested his chin on a fist.

"Please."

Ọtúnba nodded. "Okay, Wúràọlá, remove the scarf."

"This is ridiculous," Wúràọlá said. "I'm not hiding anything, it's just a scarf."

"Well then, just remove it," Ọtúnba said.

"I believe you, my dear." Yèyé reached across the table to hold Wúràọlá's hand. "I trust you, but just humour us and take it off."

Mọ́tárá bit her lower lip as her sister untied the knot beneath her chin and removed the scarf.

Everyone leaned forward to examine Wúràọlá's neck. After staring at the column of skin for a few moments, Mọ́tárá stopped fighting her tears and let them fall.

"Would you like to check with a torchlight?" Kúnlé asked.

Mọ́tárá looked at her sister's neck again; the skin was smooth and unscarred.

"Mọ́tárá!" Yèyé sighed. "Shouldn't you be apologising to your sister and Kúnlé?"

Mọ́tárá bit her lip. She was not going to apologise to a man she had seen slap her sister. No way. God forbid bad thing.

"Yèyé, please leave Mọ́tárá, there is no need for all that. It's not a big deal." Kúnlé smiled. "Let's just enjoy the meal."

18

After lunch was over, Yèyé asked to speak with Wúràọlá in private. Wúràọlá began packing up the plates, hoping to delay a conversation with her mother. Her hands trembled, and the bowls she had stacked together clattered as she stood.

"Leave that for Rachel and Mọ́tárá. No, just Mọ́tárá should clean up this afternoon," Yèyé said. "Come, let's go upstairs."

Wúràọlá gave the plates to Mọ́tárá. She sat down again and picked up her scarf, the last birthday gift Nonso had given her, off the floor. It was a large satiny thing she'd pulled out of her wardrobe once she noticed that her neck hurt if she touched it. The skin was tender, probably just shy of bruising when Kúnlé let go the previous night. She had been worried about wincing when her parents hugged her. So far, the scarf had worked as a barrier against the pain their affection could inflict.

"Wúrà." Kúnlé's whisper was both plea and warning. His hand was on her knee, massaging then squeezing until she shook her leg to make him stop.

When he eventually left her flat after the previous night's incident, Wúràọlá had emerged from the bathroom, climbed into bed and fallen asleep right away. He was back at dawn. Although he had his copy of the key with him, he called her to open the door. She did so without thinking, her body slow and heavy from sleep. He told her he had spent the night in his car, too distraught to drive; this time, he wasn't just sorry, he'd realised that he had a problem and he needed her help with it. He needed her. She had struggled to stay awake while he stuttered, voice quivering with exhaustion and fear.

"Óyá, Wúràọlá, óyá, let's go now." Yèyé was on her way out of the dining room.

Wúràolá wrapped the scarf around her neck. If her mother wanted to have a conversation about Mótárá's accusation, she was not sure she could lie or avoid giving a direct answer. Until last night, she was determined not to admit the truth to her mother if Mótárá went ahead with her threats. But now, in spite of all Kúnlé had said that morning as he lay prostrate before her and clung to her ankle, pleading until he began to doze off, Wúràolá was certain that what had happened between them was a significant shift, an escalation that should be met with some different reaction.

"You know, since you people got engaged, Kúnlé's mother has called me every weekend to say hello," Yèyé said as she unlocked her bedroom door.

"We're having dinner with her tonight."

"And Professor, àbí?"

"No, he went to Abuja for a meeting with the party chairman."

"Close that door behind you."

Stepping into Yèyé's room always felt like walking into her lovely embrace. Swaddled in all the layers of smell she associated with her mother—floral notes from her Anaïs Anaïs, the musky scent of her Jōvan powder, the menthol sting from the jar of Robb that lived on her bedside table—Wúràolá felt comforted.

She sat on the bed, expecting her mother to sit beside her and place an arm around her shoulder. It was a pose Yèyé used whenever she wanted to extract a secret.

"The whole world has been telling me I overindulge that Mótárá, but did I listen to anybody?" Yèyé went to her fireproof safe and punched in the combination. "You too, you said it many times, and I blocked my ears. See my life now. My own child is disgracing me in front of an in-law."

Wúràolá pursed her lips to push back her correction. To say "prospective in-law" would be meaningless to her mother. She wasn't sure if Yèyé acted as if the ìdána was done and the vows said because she had been so worried Wúràolá would not even be engaged before she was thirty. She supposed it could also be because Kúnlé was from a family they had known for so long.

"Kúnlé says you think it's okay if I move in with him after the introduction."

"I think it's a good idea."

"Wow, Yèyé, just wow."

"What?" The safe's lock clicked open, and Yèyé brought out a mid-sized jewellery box.

"You're the same woman who threatened to test my virginity with an egg."

"Ehen? I did that?" Yèyé shrugged. "Well, you are no longer a child. Once we do the introduction, that means your parents have approved of the union. You are free. It's kúkú not as if he's not ready to marry you tomorrow if you want. You are free o, move in. I think it's better, sef."

"I really don't think it's a good idea," Wúràọlá said, hoping her mother would ask why she had reservations about living with Kúnlé. But Yèyé sat on the bed, set the jewellery box between them and continued as if she had not been interrupted.

"And I'm sure his mother won't mind either. As long as it is after the introduction. Look at how everything has worked out so well for you, Wúràọlá. Isn't it just wonderful? I won't lie, me, I thought Kúnlé would propose at your induction. When he did not, I was afraid he was waiting for something else, maybe a younger girl, someone in her early twenties, you know how these men are. But look now, some other men would have walked out when Mọ́tárá started saying rubbish. See how calm he was throughout. Everything just fits together so well, you know. His background, family, temperament. It's like a miracle, àbí?"

The miracle was in how Yèyé, who metered moments of joy with a soberness Wúràọlá always attributed to losing both parents in such quick succession, seemed so carefree in her happiness. She seemed happier than she had been when Mọ́tárá was born or Láyí was getting married.

"Àbí?" Yèyé frowned. "Or you think he's very upset about Mọ́tárá's lies?"

This was her window to say Mọ́tárá was not lying. And how would her mother feel then? Yèyé and her sisters liked to brag about how they picked themselves up after their parents died without wasting time on grief. But Wúràọlá knew Yèyé carried the weight of bereavement within her. It was visible in how she sometimes rubbed her injured leg absent-mindedly, staring into a past no one around her could see. It was there in how she'd burst into tears the day a teenage Láyí asked for new stories, complaining that he was tired of hearing the old stories Yèyé recycled for them about her own mother. It was there in how she often handled happiness with nervousness, as though good things could only last for a spell. Wúràolá adjusted her scarf. How could she wrench this rare season of unfettered joy away from her mother?

"Wúràolá?"

"No. No, he's not upset." All she wanted was a way to help Kúnlé so he would stop hitting her. She could figure that out on her own; there was no reason to turn her mother's miracle into something less wonderful than she thought it was. Besides, though last night had felt like an escalation, this morning was a breakthrough. Kúnlé had realised that he had a problem. He was not saying a slap was a mistake anymore, this was now a problem they had to solve. Maybe the fact that he had taken things so far was all that was necessary to shock him into real change.

"What is Mótárá's problem, gan? Just because she is too big to call older people Brother or Sister, àbí? Me that I've told everyone in Mothers' Union about the introduction. I should now go back and tell them that what? No way. That will never be my lot. Orí mi kòó. When I am done with her, ehn, Mótárá will never try this kind of nonsense again."

"Don't punish her, please. I think she has learnt her lesson."

"Forget about that one for now." Yèyé pushed the jewellery box towards Wúràolá until it touched her thigh. "I wanted to give you this after Kúnlé proposed but I forgot because of the birthday and everything. Open it."

Wúràolá opened the latch.

"I want you to have this now that you are getting married."

All the items in the box were wrapped in lavender tissue.

"What we pray for, what I want for you and hope for is that you and Kúnlé will live in health and wealth together for a long, long time. But you never know what can happen. Your father thinks I'm paranoid, but I've always known what I'm saying. Today, everything is fine and fiam." Yèyé snapped her fingers. "Just like that, everything can change. My dear, in this life, ehn, a woman must always have options. This gold is part of your inheritance from me. There are other things you will know about later, but let's begin with this. If all else fails, I hope you will at least have this. Keep it very well, continue to build it over the years."

Wúràọlá went on her knees before her mother. "I'm grateful."

Yèyé ran her hand through Wúràọlá's twists. "I want you to be taken care of in this life, Wúràọlá. It's one of the reasons I'm happy about this family you're marrying into. I'm sure you'll be taken care of there. You should never suffer the way I suffered, Wúràọlá. My children must never suffer like that."

❖

The emergency room pulsed with the screams and groans of patients. An eighteen-seater bus's brakes had failed on the expressway; then it crashed into two saloon cars before coming to a stop. At least twenty-five patients were wheeled or carried into the emergency room within an hour.

It was a week after Tifẹ́'s birthday party. Wúràọlá was on A & E call with Kingsley and Dr. Hassan, a senior medical officer. None of them wore scrubs or ward coats. The nurses on duty did not have their uniforms on either. Things could get intense very quickly in the emergency room, and relatives had been known to attack a doctor or nurse for failing to attend to their loved ones on time. It was important to be able to leave the ward as if you weren't medical personnel.

Kingsley was the one who noticed that passengers from the bus were all dressed in identical ankara fabrics, making it easier to prioritise them, since their injuries were probably more severe. There weren't enough doctors or nurses on ground to cope with the inflow of patients, so some kind of system had to be devised to make sure they attended to the people who needed them most. Wúràọlá asked the road safety officers to put the ten patients who seemed most wounded on the available beds. She did not need to tell them what to do about the others before they began arranging them on the emergency room's floor. On days like this, some patients eventually ended up in the corridors.

Months ago, barely halfway through her first call in the emergency ward, Wúràọlá had run out of the place. She told a nurse that she had to use the restroom but instead went to the back of the ward and vomited until she was light-headed. There had been several RTAs that night, but the gore did not bother her, she wasn't one to panic at the sight of a jutting bone or dislodged eye. It was the chorus of pleading voices that made her stomach churn, all those urgent whispers and screams, the pain-laced cries. *Doctor, nítorí Ọlọ́run, Doctor, please, Doctor, help, Doctor.* What made her nauseous and caused her hands to tremble was the realization that some of those voices would fade into a final silence before any of the doctors on call could get to them. If everyone on the medical team had ten hands and eyes, maybe they could have saved the patients who still had a fighting chance. After she had heaved her dinner into the gutter behind the ward, Wúràọlá rinsed her mouth, splashed her face with water and went back to work.

These days, she could tune out the cries. Most of the time, she tried to work through patients in some sequence. It was always tempting to dash from one patient to someone who was screaming for a doctor. But Wúràọlá did her best to focus on finishing a procedure without wondering if someone she could help was dying because she could not get to them on time.

Kingsley tapped her on the shoulder as she pulled back an unresponsive patient's eyelid. "Please, can you help me suture this guy?"

"Nurse?"

"Everyone's busy." He held up his pen torch. "Let me do this. GCS, right?"

Wúràọlá nodded and stepped back. Kingsley was notorious for how badly his hands shook when he was trying to stich people up. It was terrible when he was under pressure.

The patient had a gash that ran from shoulder to wrist. He stared at the ceiling as Wúràọlá picked up the suture.

Wúràọlá was good at suturing. Her mother believed every good wife should know how to cook, sew and bake. When Wúràọlá was ten, Yèyé taught her how to darn socks and bake queen's cakes, but the cooking lessons were delayed until she returned home from boarding school at the end of secondary school. Of all three skills Yèyé insisted she master in preparation for marriage, sewing was the only one Wúràọlá enjoyed. In medical school, away from home and her mother, she'd refused to darn any clothes and had taken to suturing pads, running through several packs each month and sometimes calming herself by suturing unripe bananas and chicken breasts. Over the past few months, she'd managed a seamless transition to human skin without any of the fears that made Kingsley so anxious about hurting his patients.

Wúràọlá noticed that Kingsley had already pulled the woman's wrapper over her face but was still standing at her bedside as though rooted in place. On a slower night, she would have let him have the minute he obviously needed after losing a patient. Now she ran through the mental queue she'd made earlier and lit on a patient she was sure would not need to be stitched up.

"Kingsley, clerk the guy who's been clutching his stomach."

"Ehn?"

"The one in that Chelsea jersey. He was here before they brought in the RTAs."

"All right."

Done with the suturing, Wúràọlá examined the patient for other wounds, then asked him to get up.

"And go where?"

"Please sit on the floor sir. That way we can move someone who still needs to be treated to the bed."

"Who do you think you are talking to? Me? On the floor? Do you know who I am?"

Wúràọlá took off her gloves. "Please, vacate this bed before I come back here."

"Stupid girl. Nonsense, talking to me as if I'm not old enough to be your father."

Wúràọlá shook her head and walked away. Stupid girl, silly girl, foolish girl—angry men loved to call her *girl,* as if all the while they had been waiting for a reason to ditch her title. She was walking past Kingsley when the man in the Chelsea jersey began to vomit. She jumped out of the line of projectile just in time. Kingsley was not as quick.

"Oh God." Wúràọlá glanced around. There was no one they could send to get a cleaner.

"Fuck." Kingsley's shirt was covered in clumps of vomit and specks of blood.

"Eish Pẹ̀lẹ́." Wúràọlá stepped further away.

"I think I might have some of this vomit in my mouth."

"Go, change, take a shower before you come back." Dr. Hassan waved Kingsley out of the ward. "Send us a cleaner on your way out."

❈

Four days after he was on call with Wúràọlá, Kingsley presented with malaise and some vomiting. He was given the afternoon off to rest. When he showed up in A & E with a cough and chest pain later that evening, the doctor on call suspected Lassa fever and asked that he be transferred to Ifẹ̀ for isolation.

"Do you know when you'll have the Lassa test results?" Wúràọlá asked him when she called to check how he was doing.

"They've taken my sample, but the test can only be done in Lagos. So at least another week after it arrives in Lagos this evening or tomorrow."

"You mean they can't even do it in Ìbàdàn?" She glanced at her wall clock. If she did not leave her flat in ten minutes, she would be late for ward round.

"Someone said there'll be a new lab that can in Akure soonish, but for now, only three labs can do this in the whole country and the closest is in Lagos."

"I'm so sorry." Wúràọlá slid her feet into her green ballet shoes. "How are you feeling?"

"My fever is down, so that's good."

"Temperature?"

"Last check was thirty-six."

"Not so bad." She picked up her handbag. "I have to go now, sorry I can't—"

"I know how it is. Don't worry, I'll be all right."

"I'll call you again later in the day."

"A promise is a debt, golden babe."

She did not remember her promise until much later in the evening when Kúnlé checked her call log while they spooned in bed. Since Tifẹ́'s birthday, Kúnlé had been coming to spend the evenings with her. He cooked or bought dinner for her, cleaned up after her and once hand-washed her pile of dirty underwear while she slept.

"Why did you call Kingsley?"

"He's my friend."

"I said, why did you call him?"

Wúràọlá felt the sudden urge to run into the bathroom and shut the door behind her. Someone's heart was thudding; she was not sure if it was his or hers. Her tongue did not move when she wanted to speak, and although one of his hands was slung across her midriff, she felt as if both were at her throat again.

"Wúrà?"

"He's sick."

"Why are you whispering?"

Wúràọlá cleared her throat. So far, he did not seem upset. "Kingsley has been ill for a few days."

"Why didn't you tell that me earlier?" Kúnlé wrapped his body tighter around her. "Hope he's feeling better now?"

Wúràọlá nodded. She closed her eyes as he tapped out a beat on her belly button. It seemed clear that he was not going to flare up, but she couldn't bring herself to relax. Not even when he began to sing "Òló Mi" to her. During her finals, he would call her and place his phone against his sound system while the song played for exactly a minute. One minute of love, he'd called it. It had been his way of helping her stay calm during such an intense period. He'd also gotten Kay's Chippy to deliver breakfast to her every day. Delivery from campus to the medical students' hostel in Glory Land had probably cost more than the meals themselves, but Kúnlé made sure she got her breakfast anyway. Every single day.

"Do you still like the song?" Kúnlé asked.

Wúràọlá placed her hand over his. "Yes, yes. Keep singing."

So what if he was not perfect? No one was. At least he was doing his best to show her how sorry he was about hurting her. That counted, it had to. Just the previous night, he'd slept over while she was on call, and shortly before three a.m., he'd brought her freshly made coffee and a pack of digestives.

She'd always known he was impressed by the fact that she was a doctor. He led with that detail whenever he was introducing her to people. *Meet my lovely girlfriend, she is a medical student. This is Dr. Wúrà, my amazing girlfriend. This is my brilliant wife to be, Dr. Wúràọlá.* She had met him in the corridor when he brought her coffee the previous night and, as she took the travel mug from him, noticed how he gazed past her into the ward, eyes bright with longing. Kúnlé admired her, yes, but that admiration was tangled up with his disappointments and insecurities. He still wished he could have been the doctor son his parents wanted.

As Kúnlé sang "Òló Mi" to her over and over, she thought of how her parents, especially her father, avoided speaking about or to Láyí now that he was pursuing his own dreams. If her parents, who had two other children, one of whom was already a doctor, acted so wounded by Láyí's decision, what were the Cokers like when they were alone with Kúnlé? Being the sole repository of parental expectations had to be difficult.

Wúràọlá turned to face Kúnlé. "I shouldn't have been snarky about you being a doctor."

Kúnlé raised an eyebrow.

"What I said during my mum's birthday. I know how sensitive you are about that."

"Oh, Wúrà." He kissed her forehead. "I just wish you wouldn't do things that make me so angry. You know how much I love you, right?"

She nodded and let him pull her closer.

"Let's just be happy, please. We've been happy this past week. Everything has been so great between us, right?"

"Yes, you're right."

He tucked her head beneath his chin and enveloped her in an embrace that was a return to some primordial comfort. The safe darkness of a womb, the warmth of her mother's embrace, the relief of being lifted out of a cot the first time she cried out for company.

19

Ẹniọlá's new school, United Apostolic Missionary Grammar School, was one of those the government had taken over from churches long before he became a student there. And according to Mrs. Okon, the friend his father had begged to get him into the school so late in the term, that takeover had ruined most schools. When Mrs. Okon was not complaining about everything that had gone wrong with education in the country, she taught English to the senior secondary classes in United. She was one of the few teachers who always showed up during her period. Two weeks into his time at United, and the chemistry teacher had not shown up to his class even once.

That Monday afternoon, Mrs. Okon griped about how the school's fence had been defaced during the weekend. Although the governorship election was still almost a year away, the fence was plastered with the campaign posters of two men who were contesting the ruling party's nomination. Mrs. Okon hated both men, but she seemed more upset with Honourable Fẹ̀sọ̀jaiyé, an alumnus of the school who had never donated anything, not a single chair.

"Not even one desk, ehn, not even a nail, but one month to primaries and he knows the address of this place."

The students shifted in their chairs, waiting for her to finish her complaints. Ẹniọlá could tell she was close to the end when she picked up the thin cane she wielded when she checked their homework. During morning assembly, the principal often boasted that United's first laboratory prefect was now the federal minister of health. The last time Ẹniọlá's class went into the dilapidated biology laboratory, they were chased out by a black cobra that slithered in through one of the holes in the roof as their teacher dissected a frog. The teacher had not bothered to take them back to the laboratory ever since.

"All of them are foolish, I tell you, wicked people," Mrs. Okon grumbled as she began looking over their work. She moved from desk to desk, pausing to peer at each student's notebook.

Ẹniọlá opened his book in preparation and braced himself as she approached.

"Ẹniọlá, tell me." Mrs. Okon pointed her cane at his notebook. "Why didn't you touch your assignment? You had the whole weekend, and you didn't answer a single question. Why? Young man, why?"

"No time ma. I didn't have time." Ẹniọlá looked at the blank page where his answers should have been. The assignment was a summary exercise he could have done that morning if he cared what Mrs. Okon thought.

"Get up! Get up right now." Mrs. Okon waved her cane in the air.

Ẹniọlá stood and shoved his hands into his pockets.

"Explain yourself, young man."

"I forgot about it." He folded his arms across his chest.

"And you can open your mouth to tell me that you forgot? You forgot your assignment, Ẹniọlá? Did you forget to eat during the weekend?" She pushed her large glasses up her nose with her right thumb. "Did you forget to sleep or drink water?"

He stared at her.

"Ẹniọlá? Ẹniọlá? Is it me you are eyeing like that? Okay, I know what to do with you. Carry your chair, carry it right now."

Ẹniọlá's classmates tittered around him; the boy who sat in front of him stuck out his tongue.

He grasped the grainy back of his wooden chair and began to lift it.

"No, drop the chair." Mrs. Okon grinned. She rapped his desk with her knuckles. "Carry the desk instead. And let me warn you, I'm going to report you to your father if you continue like this, ehn."

On some other day, Ẹniọlá might have obeyed Mrs. Okon and spent the rest of the hour holding his desk aloft. He would have gritted his teeth while his arms trembled. But then she mentioned his father, and he felt like smashing the chair he'd already picked up to pieces.

He dropped the chair and ran out of the classroom. Mrs. Okon followed him.

"Ẹniọlá," she yelled. "Come back here. You are in trouble today, young man. You will see yourself when I catch you. Silly boy, come back here right now."

He could hear her voice behind him as he ran down the corridor and onto the school field, but he did not stop.

Ẹniọlá knew she would not come after him, only the school's principal pursued students around the school until he caught them. Even if Mrs. Okon tried to chase him, he was certain he could outrun her. At least for now. He knew that she would try to sneak in on him during another teacher's period. He had seen her do it before. She usually came through the back door to land a sudden slap on her culprit's back.

He did not mind being punished later if it didn't involve holding furniture aloft. There were over sixty students in a class that had been designed for thirty and Ẹniọlá's school shirt was often stained and sticky with sweat by noon. Any form of exertion would only make it worse. At home, Bùsọ́lá had started calling the sweat marks the map of Nigeria. Let Mrs. Okon report him to his father if she wanted. Whatever happened, he was not going to carry any chair or desk. The only good thing about United was that he did not have a mocking nickname yet; he wasn't going to let her ruin that for him.

Ẹniọlá stopped running when Mrs. Okon's voice faded away. He was moving towards a classroom block that had been abandoned because its roof was lifted off during a storm. United's most troublesome boys, the types his mother warned him not to befriend, had claimed the space as their own. They often spent their breaks there. Some even stayed there all day, but no one dared ask them to return to their classes because they had once beaten up a teacher who did that. Ẹniọlá wandered towards the abandoned classrooms, eager to shelter beyond Mrs. Okon's reach.

The block was quiet as he moved closer to it. There was nobody in the first classroom he entered and the only chair there had no legs. He went into the next room to look for another chair. There were two boys in the room. They sat next to a desk, eating rice from a large plastic bowl. Ẹniọlá recognised one of the boys. Rashidi was an SS1 student who lived on his street, and they'd played football together several times though they never spoke much after the matches.

"You, what are you looking for here?" Rashidi said, dropping his spoon on the desk.

"Chair," Ẹniọlá said, moving closer to the boys and their bowl of rice. "I'm looking for a chair."

The other boy slapped Rashidi's knee and laughed. "See as this boy is looking at our rice with his hungry man eyes."

"Are you hungry, ni?" Rashidi asked, pointing his spoon at Ẹniọlá.

Ẹniọlá nodded, wondering if Rashidi was going to taunt him with the food.

"Why are you asking him?" the other boy said. "How is it our business if he is hungry?"

"Sàámú, he is my boy, he lives on my street. Ṣebí, your name is Ẹniọlá?"

"How is it my business if his name is Ẹniọlá?" Sàámú said.

"Sàámú, I said he is my boy. Come here, jàre, Ẹniọlá. Come and eat."

He'd nodded without thinking he would be invited to eat with the boys, and now that they had welcomed him, he worried that they might be angry if he said he did not want to join them. He was hungry; the only thing holding him back was his mother's warnings about eating the food other children brought to school. When he was much younger, he'd believed her tales about greedy children without questioning them. The boy who became a tuber of yam after eating his classmate's yam porridge, and the girl who reached into her pocket for the biscuits her friend had given her and found two thumbs there instead, were as real to him as Bùsọ́lá. Even when it was clear that those stories had to have been made up, he was still hesitant about eating outside the home. Just because his mother said it was a dangerous thing to do. His mother who had chosen to pay only Bùsọ́lá's school fees. Ẹniọlá dragged a chair across the floor, placed it beside Rashidi and sat down.

Rashidi rummaged through a black polythene bag that lay on the floor and brought out a spoon. Ẹniọlá took it and dug into the rice.

"This your hunger is a serious something, see the way you are devouring the rice." Rashidi laughed. "Slow down, boy. The food is not running away."

When the bowl was empty, Rashidi slapped Ẹniọlá's back. "Seriously, boy, when was the last time you ate?"

"Yesterday night," Ẹniọlá said.

"Before that."

"The night before."

"So you eat once a day?" Rashidi smiled and nodded. "I remember when I used to eat once a day too. Sàámú, do you remember when you used to eat once a day?"

"Thank God for Honourable," Sàámú said, picking his teeth with a fingernail. "He has delivered us from the class of people who eat once a day. May he live forever."

"Yes oh," Rashidi said. "Our Honourable will never die. The god of thunder will strike anybody that wants to kill Honourable."

Rashidi reached into his school shorts and brought out a cigarette. "Do you smoke?"

Ẹniọlá shook his head and pinched his nose as Rashidi lit the cigarette.

"So where are you going to get breakfast and lunch tomorrow?" Rashidi asked.

Ẹniọlá shrugged; he was grateful for the food he had just eaten. The quantity of food available for dinner varied from day to day because his parents were still trying to pay off the landlord. In spite of his mother's pleas, Ẹniọlá now refused to go begging again since none of the money would go towards his school fees. The betrayal he'd felt when he realised that his parents had chosen Bùsọ́lá over him had only intensified over time. Nothing his mother could say could make him budge.

"You don't know how you'll get breakfast tomorrow?" Rashidi shook his head. "You, is it that you have never heard about what Honourable is doing? There's breakfast, lunch and dinner in his house every day. You just need to show up."

Ẹniọlá frowned, he had never heard about what Rashidi was saying. Free food every day? It did not sound possible. "Free food? Honourable gives people free food?"

"Not people, oh, not everybody," Sàámú said.

"Just young men like us. Not everybody." Rashidi puffed on the cigarette. "You are telling us that nobody has ever invited you to come and eat in Honourable's house?"

Ẹniọlá shook his head. He noticed that Sàámú and Rashidi exchanged a look, but he did not think much of it.

Rashidi leaned back and blew smoke rings into the air. "See this life now. There is free food in this town and you are going hungry in a town where you can get free breakfast, free lunch and free dinner."

"And you don't pay any money?" Ẹniọlá asked.

"No o. This food we just ate came from his house and we did not pay one naira for it."

Sàámú stood and stretched. "Honourable is just doing what God has sent him to do. He is doing good things for the young men in the community."

Rashidi patted Ẹniọlá's arm. "You know, if you want lunch, you can go with us to Honourable's house. Sàámú, what did the cook say we will be eating this afternoon?"

Sàámú scratched his head. "Pounded yam, I think it is pounded yam."

"Are you sure you don't pay for the food?" Ẹniọlá asked.

Sàámú and Rashidi laughed.

"Àní, Honourable Fẹ̀sọ̀jaiyé will never die. The food is free, but if you don't want to go with us, there is no problem. Sàámú, lets go."

Rashidi crushed his cigarette with his sandal while Sàámú threw the bowl and cutlery into the black polythene bag.

"Wait," Ẹniọlá said when the boys got to the door. "Wait for me."

Ẹniọlá still did not believe all that Rashidi had said. He followed them only because he was curious.

The boys went behind the classroom block and walked a short distance to the school's fence. Rashidi and Sàámú scaled the fence with swift movements.

"Are you not coming with us again?" Rashidi asked.

Ẹniọlá moved further down along the fence until he got to a place where it was broken down, and then he stepped over the debris to the other side.

❉

Honourable Kọ́lápọ̀ Timothy Fẹ̀sọ̀jaiyé was known by many names. To the university girlfriend who became his first wife, he was Kọ́lá. Before they all died on the day their father was to be buried, his brother and eleven stepsiblings had called him Timo or Brother Timo, depending on whether they were older or younger than him.

During one of the many family meetings before their father's funeral ceremonies, the eldest son had suggested that they all commute together in a hired coaster bus during the celebrations, and though Honourable Fèsòjaiyé would later explain to reporters that he had been opposed to the idea, it took hold. Since everyone else at the meeting was dead by the time he was giving interviews, it was impossible to know if he had actually spoken up against using the coaster bus. Some reporters would also point out that no one could verify that it was the eldest son who suggested this idea. A few even claimed the idea had been Honourable Fèsòjaiyé's.

Of all the children, Honourable Fèsòjaiyé was the only one who was not in the coaster bus when it crashed into a petrol tanker and burst into flames. His first wife, then in her last year as his only wife, was not on board either. The fire spread to other cars in the convoy, such that Fèsòjaiyé also lost several uncles, aunts and cousins on that same day. Fèsòjaiyé and his wife would later claim they hadn't been on the bus because they needed to use the restroom, whereas the other siblings, eager to arrive at their father's graveside, decided to leave.

The only close relatives of Honourable Fèsòjaiyé's father who survived the inferno were his five wives. They had left the church with the hearse long before their children were done greeting the well-wishers who delayed their departure. But four of the five died within a year after the incident. The only one who stayed alive for another decade was Honourable Fèsòjaiyé's mother.

There had always been suspicions that Fèsòjaiyé's mother was able to shape-shift in the middle of the night, fly into trees and hold court while drinking the blood of newborns. Her co-wives claimed that she slept with her legs up on the wall, spreading this detail through the extended family as proof that she was elsewhere while her body lay on the bed. Most people thought these co-wives were lying. It was easy to see how they would be jealous of Fèsòjaiyé's mother, who remained their husband's favourite even though she had just two children. However, when Fèsòjaiyé emerged as the only surviving child of his father and sole inheritor of the estate after all his stepsiblings perished in one afternoon, it was difficult for even his mother's strongest defenders to deny what the co-wives had been saying for decades. And though she had also lost her second son in the crash, the consensus was that Fẹ̀sọ̀jaiyé's mother was not a mere witch but the head of a powerful coven. Surely, she had sacrificed all those people so that her surviving son could become a great man. After the family tragedy, Fẹ̀sọ̀jaiyé's successes were attributed to his mother's powers. When he opened a cocoa-processing plant two years after his father's death, nobody in the extended family showed up for the ceremony because they believed his mother would sacrifice the attendees in some mysterious way so as to expand her son's growing wealth. Family members stopped showing up at the lavish birthday parties he and his wife threw every year. He shared the date with his first wife, Àdùkẹ́, and they had celebrated their birthdays together every year since they met as undergraduates at the University of Ìbàdàn.

A few months after his father's funeral, Fẹ̀sọ̀jaiyé and Àdùkẹ́ were given chieftaincy titles in Àdùkẹ́'s hometown. And so, in the year all his stepsiblings died, Fẹ̀sọ̀jaiyé became Olóyè or Bàbá Olóyè to his friends and associates. Within a few years, he won a seat in the House of Representatives and styled himself as Honourable KTF on the campaign posters for his reelection. By then, Àdùkẹ́, who had become Erelú Àdùkẹ́ after the investiture, was the only one who still called her husband Kọ́lá.

Rashidi and Sàámú told Ẹniọlá all about Honourable Fẹ̀sọ̀jaiyé as they walked to his house for lunch.

"But how do you know these things?" Ẹniọlá asked.

Rashidi shrugged. "Erelú talks to us a lot."

"Don't believe the nonsense people say about Honourable o, that man is a good person," Sàámú said. "People are just jealous."

"His wife talks to you people?" Ẹniọlá studied his companions. Both were almost as tall as he was, but nothing else about them seemed special enough to warrant the confidence of a woman like Erelú Àdùkẹ́.

"Erelú doesn't live with Honourable in Abuja, she stays here to take care of the constituency." Rashidi smiled. "Erelú, relù, she's the mother of all, mama for the boys gangan."

"Erelú, one and only, good woman." Sàámú stabbed a finger in the air. "Till today, she still appreciates us for helping Honourable in the election."

Ẹniọlá wanted to ask more questions, but they were approaching Honourable Fẹ̀sọ̀jaiyé's compound. A small crowd was gathered in front of the gate and a policeman was patting people down before letting them into the compound. Sàámú elbowed a path to the gate. Ẹniọlá followed, worried at first that the policeman would send them back, but the man only nodded at Rashidi as they passed him by. A flexi banner pronouncing Honourable KTF as best choice for governor had been slung over the pedestrian gate, and it grazed Ẹniọlá's head as they passed through.

The house itself was set back from the gate. On the football-field-sized lawn, several people clustered around bowls of food that had been placed before them on the mats that were spread out all over the grounds.

At least a hundred people were already eating when Ẹniọlá and his schoolmates arrived.

Erelú Àdùkẹ́ was supervising the servers herself. Ẹniọlá recognised her without being told who she was. She bore three vertical marks on each cheek as Sàámú had described. Her hair was threaded through with coral beads and her skin shone through the holes in the brown cord lace she paired with shimmery gold slippers.

"Àwọn tèmi," Erelú said when she saw Rashidi and Sàámú.

The boys prostrated before her; then she ushered all three to a corner of the lawn. She chatted with them in the shade of a mango tree while one of her attendants went into the house to get plastic chairs.

"I've never seen this face." Erelú pointed at Ẹniọlá.

Rashidi put a hand on Ẹniọlá's shoulder. "He's from our school."

"Ehen." Erelú grinned. "And your name?"

"It's Ẹniọlá ma."

"What did you say?" Erelú's brow furrowed.

"It's Ẹniọlá ma."

"Hmmmm." Erelú turned to Rashidi. "And he's your friend?"

Rashidi nodded.

"Ẹniọlá, àbí?"

Ẹniọlá nodded, worried that he had somehow offended her by saying his name.

Erelú stepped aside so her attendant could arrange the plastic chairs. "I want Kọ́lá to meet you."

Sàámú gasped.

"Honourable," Rashidi said to Ẹniọlá, as if he might not understand what Erelú meant. "She wants Honourable to meet you. You dey lucky o." A server arrived with a tray of food.

"That name." Erelú adjusted her wrapper and began to walk away. "Make sure you bring him back, ehn."

"We bring many people here that she never allows to meet Honourable o," Sàámú said as they sat down. "And with most people, it takes like weeks before she even says anything about Honourable in front of them."

"Months sef," Rashidi added.

Ẹniọlá watched Erelú Àdùkẹ́ as she made her way across the lawn. She stopped everywhere there was a group of elderly men or women and went down on both knees to greet them. Her face as far as he could see never relaxed, she was constantly smiling. And though she was dressed as if she was about to get into a car and be driven to a fancy party, she did not hesitate to collect plates and trays from the servers when she felt they were too slow. It would take about a week for Ẹniọlá to realise that serving the people who gathered twice a day on her lawn was not an interruption in Erelú's day, a stopover before she went to the places she really needed to be. Her day was all about the people who clustered at her gate for food, and every morning she dressed in her lace, aṣọ-òkè and heeled slippers to hand plates of àmàlà to strangers.

That first afternoon, after he'd finished his àmàlà, Ẹniọlá studied the meat for a while, holding it and turning it over, pressing the tender flesh so that pepper stew oozed onto his fingers, warm and fragrant. His mother would have divided that single piece into at least five before cooking it. For a moment, he considered wrapping the meat in cellophane so he could take it home to Bùsọ́lá. He decided against it and was surprised that he felt no guilt as he chewed the last juicy bite.

❈

Rashidi had a mobile phone. Not one of those torchlight phones with no other feature besides texting. This phone had a camera and could play music. If it was fully charged, Rashidi put Da Grin's *C.E.O* on repeat while the boys played jackpot in the abandoned classroom block. Whenever "Pon Pon Pon" came on, Rashidi rapped along with Da Grin, clutching his cards till they creased as he yelled the refrain. *Pon pon pon pon pon pon*. Repeated gunshots, a car's horn punched over and over, a chant about his place in the world. If Eniolá complained that the sound distracted him from Sàámú's signals, Rashidi shrugged and said the music made him happy. Rashidi's biggest dream was to meet Da Grin in person someday.

For jackpot, Eniolá enjoyed being paired with Sàámú. He was good at gathering his cards quickly and could win without much help from Eniolá. All Eniolá had to do was watch his face for their signal. Rashidi did not have a constant partner for the game. At any point, at least half a dozen boys milled through the abandoned classroom block, and Rashidi was happy to ask whichever boy was interested to partner with him.

Eniolá began skipping class after his first visit to Honourable Fèsòjaiyé's house, and as the week wore on, he skipped more and more periods until all he did before dashing to meet his new friends was attend the morning assembly. They played whot and jackpot, kicked around a partly deflated ball and napped with their heads against a wall.

Every afternoon, they scaled the fence and went to Honourable Fèsòjaiyé's for lunch. Eniolá never joined them for dinner. Though his mother had been lenient with him since he had to change schools, he knew that she would not tolerate it if he showed up at home much later than usual.

Eniolá considered telling his parents about Honourable Fèsòjaiyé but decided he did not want his family coming there to eat meals. The Honourable's house was the only place in his life that was not stained with their betrayal. Even Aunty Caro's shop now felt like part of a plan they'd had all along to nudge him towards tailoring instead of the university. And he had no illusions about that anymore. Maybe ten out of all the students in his class at United would get into university on their first try. He knew he was not part of the ten. Whatever little chance being at Glorious Destiny would have given him was gone now.

On Friday, Erelú told them that Honourable was arriving that evening to spend the weekend in town and would be willing to meet Eniolá on Sunday afternoon. She did not wait for Eniolá to speak before she moved on to another cluster of people. It was a given that if Honourable summoned him, he would be available.

"If he likes you, ehn," Sàámú said, "he will find work for you."

"And plenty money." Rashidi held up his phone.

"Which kind of work?"

Sàámú and Rashidi laughed.

"First you have to meet Honourable." Sàámú paused to bite into his chicken. "If he likes you, then he'll tell you what your job is."

"Like me now, sometimes I follow him to parties when he's in town. I just walk behind him like this." Rashidi stood up, puffed out his chest and stalked around. "Like police escort. Sometimes, Honourable will tell the police escort to stay in the car, then Sàámú and I would be the ones to follow him somewhere. You know that foolish Professor now? The one that has poster in front of the school."

Ẹniọlá nodded.

"We went to one party like this to warn him not to try nonsense but when we were going for the meeting inside the house of the celebrant gangan, Honourable told the escorts to wait under the canopy."

Sàámú hissed, "Professor Rubbish. Honourable is the next governor in this state o, nothing can stop him, lai lai."

By the time Ẹniọlá set out on Sunday, his mother and Bùsọlá were not back from the church where they had gone to beg. In spite of his mother's repeated requests that he apologise for grabbing his father by the collar, Ẹniọlá refused to say anything to the man besides the "hin káàárọ̀, Bàami," he was obligated to say every morning. He saw no reason to change this pattern as he headed out for Honourable Fẹ̀sọ̀jaiyé's house. Probably assuming that Aunty Caro had some orders she had to finish that afternoon, Ẹniọlá's father muttered a goodbye as he shut the door behind him. Ẹniọlá did not respond.

According to his new friends, anyone the Honourable liked enough to put on his list of boys was given an allowance every Sunday. Rashidi and Sàámú had assured him that even if Honourable did not like him, Ẹniọlá would still leave the meeting with five thousand naira in cash. Thank-you-for-coming money, they called it. Ẹniọlá adjusted his T-shirt as he approached Honourable's gate. With five thousand naira, he could go back to Glorious Destiny and pay the required deposit by himself. If Honourable did not like him, though, how would he get the money he would eventually need to pay the balance? He shook his head to dispel the thought. Erelú Àdùké had been warm to him all week, that had to have some impact on what her husband would decide. Maybe she had even put in a good word about how he seemed like a good worker. He did not dwell much on what would be required of him in exchange for the money. Whatever it was could not be terrible. After all, the man fed scores of people every day without asking for anything in return.

Erelú Àdùké was handing out brown envelopes to a group of boys when Eniolá arrived in the compound. He approached the file of about a dozen boys and hung back, close to Rashidi and Sàámú. Everyone in the queue was at least as tall as Eniolá. A few were brawny, with bulging muscles that strained against the seams of their shirts. Together, they were an intimidating crowd.

Once she was done with the group, Erelú beckoned Eniolá and led him to the winding staircase beside the house. She hitched her wrapper up to her knees and took the stairs two at a time. He was breathless when they got to the landing, but after she opened the door, she continued to charge ahead in the unlit corridor, her footsteps clicking ahead of him while his eyes adjusted to the darkness.

Erelú opened a door, and light streamed into the corridor. He followed her into the room. The walls were lined with shelves and each one was bursting with books. Eniolá had never seen so many books in one place.

Honourable was seated behind a large desk, reading from a book, head bowed so his bald spot shone at Eniolá.

"Kólá." Erelú clapped twice.

Honourable looked up and rubbed his eyes with the back of his hand. "He's here?"

"Yes now."

"Thank you, dear." Honourable bowed his head.

Erelú patted Eniolá on the shoulder. "Wait here, he'll be done soon." Eniolá nodded.

Honourable turned a page as the door clicked shut behind Erelú.

Four armchairs were arranged in a circle around an orange rug on one end of the room, while the desk dominated the other. Eniolá squinted at the book spines on the shelf behind Honourable. *Land Law in Nigeria, A History of Customary Land Law in South-West Nigeria, Ten Prayers to*

Destroy Stubborn Enemies, The Bourne Identity, Twenty Prayers Against Satanic Arrows—

"Do you like reading?"

"Sir?" Ẹniọlá snapped to attention. "Yes, yes sir."

Honourable shut the book he'd been reading and studied Ẹniọlá. Ẹniọlá scratched his thigh, worried that there might be a follow-up question. If he were to name titles, what would he say? Mention the copies of *Hearts* and *Better Lover* that Sàámú had been passing on to him? And if Honourable asked him to talk about what he'd read? Lai lai, he could not discuss "Ten Ways to Fuck a Busy Woman" or the escapades of Peter Stringfellow, who according to *Better Lover* had slept with four thousand women. Maybe he could talk about the Bible. He remembered enough stories to give the impression that he'd read it himself.

"You should sit down." Honourable gestured towards one of the armchairs.

"Yes sir." Ẹniọlá took off his shoes before moving towards the seating area. "Thank you sir."

Honourable stood, waited until Ẹniọlá was seated, then settled into the chair opposite his.

"Thank you sir," Ẹniọlá said after several moments passed in silence.

Honourable wrinkled his nose. "You stink."

Ẹniọlá clenched his jaw and said nothing. He stared at his dusty feet while he chewed on all the things he longed to say in response. *So I stink? You are bald and your stomach is bigger than a nine-month-old pregnancy. Your eyes look like a frog's.*

His imagined replies did not take the sting out of the Honourable's words. He bathed twice a day, with soap whenever there was some. His mother always made sure his clothes, though threadbare, were clean before each wear. On Saturdays, she washed everyone's clothes with soda, the round yellow bars peeling back her skin with each soak. She did not allow her children to wash their own clothes because of how harsh the soda soaps were. Her hands, she often said, were ruined already. Ẹniọlá and Bùsọ́lá should keep theirs as long as they could.

"I'll tell my wife to give you a spray before you leave," Honourable said. "Some anti-perspirant. I sweat a lot too, so I understand what's going on with you."

Ẹniọlá looked up. Honourable seemed sincere. He was not mocking him.

Honourable leaned back in his chair and cocked his head to one side. "Stand up, let me see you."

Ẹniọlá stood, pressing his bare feet firmly into the plush rug because he worried that he might sway on his feet. He felt his throat dry up as the older man's gaze swept over his body. Honourable's face was expressionless, as though he were looking not at a human being but an unpainted concrete wall.

"How old are you?" Honourable asked.

"Sixteen sir."

"You're eighteen, do you understand?" Honourable said.

"Yes sir." Ẹniọlá nodded. Maybe Honourable would ask him to register to vote in the next year's election. He had to be eighteen to get a voter's card.

"Tell me the worst thing you've ever done."

"Sir?"

"Out with it. At eighteen, what's the worst thing you've ever done? Stabbed someone? Now, don't lie. Your friends must have told you that is the number one rule here, all liars end up in the fire, they told you that, right?"

Ẹniọlá nodded. They had told him no such thing, but he did not want to get them in trouble.

He cleared his throat. "Last month, I stole a phone from a woman who was sitting in front of me in church."

"Hmmm, were there people beside you?"

"Yes sir."

"How come they didn't see you take the phone?"

"Everyone was praying sir, so their eyes were closed."

"I see. Where was this phone?"

"The phone?"

"When you took it, where was it? Was it in her bag?"

"No sir. She put it beside her on the bench, I just had to reach forward a little."

"So she was careless." Honourable stood up, lifted the folds of his agbádá and settled the dark blue fabric on his shoulders. "You see, if she really valued that phone, it would have been in her bag. She would have protected it. What is that thing they say? A goat can only eat what is left uncared for, àbí? You took your chance, I like that. One must take everything life has offered up. Gobble up every chance and opportunity. And so, what happened after you took this phone? Tell me." Honourable's voice was warm now, his face creased into what might have been the beginnings of a smile.

"I switched off the phone and left the church immediately. I knew she would try to call it once she noticed it was missing, so I didn't want it to ring before I got back home."

"And she might have noticed as soon as the prayers were over, so it's a good thing that you left early. Come with me." Honourable went towards his desk. "And what did you do with the phone?"

"I took out the SIM card as soon as I left the church and broke it." Walking behind Honourable slowly to avoid running into him from behind, Ẹniọlá was pleased that the older man was nodding as though in agreement with the decision to break the SIM card instead of simply throwing it away. "I went to a phone store and changed the casing, then I used the phone for about a week to make sure it was working very well—"

"That's good." Honourable sat behind his desk. "Sit, sit in that one, the black chair, yes. That way you could sell the phone for what it was worth, right? Since you had used it and you knew all the features worked."

"Yes sir."

"Hmmm, when did you sell it?"

"It took like a month to find someone who would buy it." The desk was right beneath an air-conditioner and Ẹniọlá was beginning to feel cold. He clasped his hands together and flexed his palms, worried that rubbing them together would annoy Honourable in some way.

Honourable opened a drawer and brought out a photo. "Your name is Ẹniọlá, right? That was my younger brother's name. Ẹniọlá Theophilus Fẹ̀sọ̀jaiyé. So sharp a boy. But then he died, you've probably heard the story."

"I'm so sorry about that sir."

Honourable sighed. "So why?"

"Sir?"

"Why did it take you so long to find a buyer for the phone?"

"I didn't want to reduce the price." His palms had warmed up, but the warmth did not seem to radiate past his wrists.

"How much was it?"

"I wanted to sell it for fifteen thousand naira." He spoke carefully so his teeth would not chatter; he willed himself to sit still, to hold back the shivers.

"How much did you sell it for eventually?"

"Fourteen thousand five hundred."

Honourable laughed, a surprisingly shrill sound. "That is good."

Encouraged by Honourable's laughter, Ẹniọlá added, "I told the man who bought it I wanted to sell it for twenty thousand naira, so he was very happy when I agreed to sell it for fourteen."

"I like you." Honourable stroked the photo he was holding. "I like you a lot."

Ẹniọlá smiled.

"For now, you'll mostly shadow me at parties. In about two weeks, we'll be distributing rice to market women. I want you there with me. There's no danger in any of this. The market thing, there'll be mostly women who want to collect the free bags of salt and rice. You just have to look formidable. Start doing press-ups now, build some muscles. I might need you for something more." Honourable dropped the photo he'd been holding onto the table. "Something more, let's say, more involved. Our primaries are coming up, and there might be some fighting. Rashidi will train you and, er, I'll make sure you have all the equipment you need for any assignment I give you. When you get downstairs, Àdùkẹ́ will give you a bag. There will be some goodies for your family in that bag. I take care of my boys, Ẹniọlá. Move closer, look at this photo I'm holding. Look very well. Do you have a brother?"

"No sir, but I have a younger sister." Ẹniọlá leaned forward. The photo was old and stained, a black-and-white shot of a little boy decked out in aṣọ-òkè.

"What's your sister's name?"

"Bùṣọ́lá sir."

"Olubùṣọ́lá, right? Imagine if something happened to her." Honourable shook his head. "Forget I said that. That's my brother in the photo, my blood. But he's dead now. Ẹniọlá Theophilus Fẹ̀sọ̀jaiyé. You people share the same name, so you are already special to me. Don't worry about anything during your assignments. Not even police. Nobody can do you nothing."

"Thank you sir." Ẹniọlá prostrated.

"Ẹniọlá." Honourable placed his elbows on the table. "I don't tell people my brother's name anyhow. Let this detail stay between us, you hear?"

"Yes sir."

"Okay, now you can go. Just look for Àdùkẹ́ when you get downstairs. She'll be waiting with your bag."

The bag was larger and heavier than he'd expected. It contained small bags of rice, beans and gaàrí, a jar of vegetable oil and several bottles of the anti-perspirant he had been promised. There was a brown envelope beneath the jar of oil, and once he was out of Erelú's sight he counted the notes inside it. Ten five-hundred-naira notes. He decided to keep the money for himself. As for the food items, he did not mind sharing that with the parents who had betrayed him. He would have to find a way to get his mother to accept the largesse without telling her the whole truth. As he approached the house, he felt confident that he could tell her a convincing lie. After all, the story that had so delighted Honourable was made up. His family had not even been to Mass in years, and he had never tried to steal in his life.

20

I t's been years since I kept a journal, and since yesterday, I've been wishing I still had a proper one. This to-do notebook will have to suffice for now. Kingsley died.

I have written this out, hoping that reading my own words will help me believe them, because this must be a mistake. But Grace says it is true, she's confirmed.

Kingsley died.

It's been a day since Grace called to tell me this happened.

Kingsley died. His organs have shut down. There is no heartbeat. He is not breathing. He is dead dead. Circulatory collapse. Respiratory failure. Brain death. Thinking about it this way does not help. There is no iteration of this fact that is acceptable.

Kingsley died.

I thought writing it out would make this comprehensible, but even these words do not seem real. I cannot imagine him dead.

His phone is off. He will switch it on very soon and pick up my call. Any moment now, he will be breathing "golden babe" down the line. He will ask how my wedding planning is going, and though I shouldn't, I will pause for a few moments before telling him it is going very well. I will pause because even without love, desire is alluring. And then in that too-bright voice he uses when he is lying, he will say how thrilled he is for me. Any moment now.

Dead? Since yesterday morning, I've been unable to dredge up any memory of him even sleeping or supine. In my mind, Kingsley is alive, vital, in constant motion. Kingsley is introducing himself to me in part one while we sit through one of those interminable orientation lectures in amphitheatre. My name is Kingsley, he says, but you can call me King.

Tifẹ has changed her BlackBerry status to a photo of Kingsley. When I *called her earlier, she was crying so hard I could not understand what she was saying.*

Kingsley is reading with his feet in a bowl of cold water. On his bed, I drift in and out of sleep with a textbook on my chest. We both have an end-of-posting coming up, but whenever I open my eyes, I do not look at my textbook. My eyes are drawn instead to Kingsley's bare, hirsute chest. I want so much to press my face against all that hair.

Grace just sent a text about a candlelight procession tomorrow. The dress code is black on black. She is organizing this procession, but she wants me to speak because I am closer to Kingsley.

It's Kingsley's birthday and he's having a photo session at Klicks Studio with a group of friends. I notice Tifẹ́ whisper something to Grace when Kingsley and I are being photographed together. She thinks I should never have broken things off with Kingsley. She wants me to be in love with him, and from her grin, I can tell she thinks that this has happened. I smile as the flash goes off again and wish Tifẹ́ knew how, for so long, I wanted to be in love with Kingsley. It wasn't for want of desire that the pleasures of his embrace never bloomed into some more transcendent form of affection.

In the corridor outside my apartment, some other house officers have clustered to discuss Kingsley. Someone cries softly as he talks about how generous Kingsley is to patients. Then, a voice rages about how long it took to even get a test result, how bad it was that Kingsley could not even be isolated in our hospital unit because we did not have the facilities, how terrible it was that after hematemesis set in and a strong suspicion of Lassa fever was established by his doctors, the hospital had no Ribavirin in stock. No Ribavirin in the hospital for Kingsley, who had stocked the paediatric ward with antibiotics after he lost a patient during the night because there was not one bag of intravenous antibiotics available in the ward.

It's Kingsley's birthday. All our friends have dispersed, but I've waited with Kingsley to collect the images on a flash drive. We're standing behind the photo studio when I tell him I'm in love with Kúnlé. And though I've suspected that he thinks our continued friendship means we will be a couple again someday, I'm still surprised by the stricken look on his face. He looks away, training his gaze on the yellow balustrades along the walkway to the sports complex. When he turns to me again, that pained look is hidden behind a wide smile. I'm so thrilled for you, he says.

The group in my corridor has moved further down and I can no longer make out their words. I have a headache. Kúnlé should be here soon but I do not want to talk to him about Kingsley. Not today.

Kingsley is standing in the emergency room with vomit all over him from the patient I told him to prioritise. Oh my God. How can he be dead? I always thought we would have more time.

PART IV

Every Day Is for the Thief

What if everything that is to happen has already happened,
and only the consequences are playing themselves out?
—*Every Day Is for the Thief* by Teju Cole

21

Ẹniọlá's worry about what his mother would say concerning the food-stuff he'd gotten from Honourable's house had been for nothing. He arrived home long before she did and spent the evening thinking about explanations that could help him evade a truth he suspected would upset his parents. He was not bothered about giving his father any explanations; he only worried about what his mother might think. After all, if the man had done what he should in the last few years, the family would not need the things Honourable had given. His mother, though, she always tried. Even if her efforts did not amount to enough money to pay his fees and Bùsọ́lá's, she had tried. When his mother returned home, it was late in the night. She nodded weakly and smiled when he showed her the foodstuff. As she counted out seven cups of rice, ten cups of gaàrí and five of beans, he waited for her to insist that she would not eat any of the items until he explained their origin. She did not. Instead, she hugged him until his arms felt numb.

The following day, Ẹniọlá got up from the mattress while his parents snored and Bùsọ́lá drooled in her sleep. He sang as he went into the courtyard, feeling lighter than a chick's feather, sure some weight he'd long carried had melted off him during the night. He hummed and tapped a foot to the tune while he brushed his teeth, not with salt sprinkled on a toothbrush whose bristles had long flattened against his teeth but with actual toothpaste and a new brush. What made him break into a dance as he went back into the corridor was the thought that his mother and sister would also feel the chill of menthol when they brushed later that morning.

The first thing he'd done after he left Honourable Fẹ̀sọ̀jaiyé's house the previous day was to buy a tube of toothpaste and new toothbrushes for everyone. While he selected the brushes, picking blue for himself, cream for his mother and green for Bùsọ́lá, his hand hovered for so long over the fourth one that the vendor asked if he wanted three instead of four. In the end he'd picked a black one, not bothering with choosing one in his father's favourite colour as he had done for everyone else.

Bùsọ́lá was stretching and yawning when he returned to the room.

"Ahn, ahn. Is that a new toothbrush?" she asked.

"Why are they still sleeping?" He pointed his chin in their parents' direction.

"Maybe it's because she came home late last night and he . . ." Bùsọ́lá shrugged as if their father's actions were beyond explanation or reason.

Ẹniọlá took his bath and dressed up for school in a hurry. When he tucked the envelope Honourable had given him into his breast pocket and rushed out of the house, his parents were still asleep. The sun was not visible, but one half of the sky above him was speckled with orange clouds that announced it was ascendant. He walked slowly and came to a halt at almost every opportunity. He paused to kick a deflated ball back to a little boy who had thrown it from a front yard into the street, then stopped to scratch a sudden itch behind his ear until he was satisfied, and spent minutes plucking flowers from the hibiscus bush in front of his school. He'd had nothing before his meeting with Honourable, but now? Even time belonged to him. The world around him seemed clearer and brighter, as though a film of dust he hadn't known was there had been wiped away during the night. He hummed as he went and was at intervals overwhelmed with the urge to break into a dance. Not some foot-tapping sway but a real dance like galala. All morning he expected this feeling to dissipate, but it persisted as he walked to Glorious Destiny around noon, branching off as Rashidi and Sàámú headed to Honourable's house for lunch.

When the other boys asked about his destination, Ẹniọlá lied that he had to do something in Aunty Caro's shop. He did not want to reveal that he was returning to his old school to ask if they would take him back. He could not bear the mockery if his attempt did not work out. It was not difficult for him to imagine being nicknamed Glorious Destiny. Going from one stupid nickname to another was not a risk he wanted to take. Before he met his new friends, the only good thing about changing schools had been that no one in his class knew he had been nicknamed Unity where he was coming from.

Ẹniọlá considered stopping by in the house to change into his Glorious Destiny uniform but decided against it. United's brown shorts and yellow shirt would have to do for his meeting with Mr. Bísádé.

Rashidi had assured him there would be another envelope at the end of that week, just three thousand naira this time, because that was what Honourable gave his boys every Friday. Ẹniọlá figured that in a month he would have paid off his school fees. After that was done, he planned to keep saving his own money for the next term's school fees. No, he would not buy a phone yet. It did not matter how many times he wondered how Maria would respond if he showed up in Aunty Caro's shop with a blue XpressMusic in his hand.

Classes were on when he got to Glorious Destiny, so he could go straight to Mr. Bísádé without interacting with anyone. Mr. Bísádé counted the money twice and warned him that he would not be able to write exams if he had not completed payment by then.

For the first time since he started secondary school, Ẹniọlá was not worried about whether he would be able to write his exams. The feeling he had considered strange earlier settled into him and he finally recognised it as the lightness of being that came with freedom. Freedom from the worry and fear that stalked him, because he never knew if his parents would be able to afford something he needed.

Ẹniọlá had no intention of attending classes at Glorious Destiny that day or for the rest of the week. He planned to return halfway through the next week, after he had collected another naira-lined envelope from Honourable. With that, he would sew a set of school uniforms that had no holes. He would do that during his time at Aunty Caro's place. She'd let him use the machines for as long as he wanted once he was done with any assigned tasks. There would be money left over to buy a new pair of sandals. The sandals would have to be rubber, though, not the pair of Kitos he really wanted.

Once he returned to United, Ẹniọlá told Rashidi and Sàámú that he would be going back to Glorious Destiny at some point during the next week. There was a pocket of silence before both boys shrugged as though they had been expecting this all along and it did not matter whether he stayed or left. Ẹniọlá bit his tongue to keep from saying he would miss them.

While Rashidi fiddled with the XpressMusic, Sàámú informed Ẹniọlá that Honourable had moved his market visit forward. The boys would now be needed that Thursday.

"Àbí, Glorious Destiny students are too important?" Rashidi asked without looking up from the phone.

"What?" Ẹniọlá said.

"You are too important to be one of us now."

"Rashidi has started again." Sàámú tapped the desk in front of him. "Stop stuffing words in Ẹniọlá's mouth. He's just going back so he can prepare for the school cert, he's still one of us. Àbí?"

Ẹniọlá nodded. "I just want to prepare better for the school certificate. Don't worry, I will still be coming to Honourable's house in the afternoon. The school doesn't have a compound or anything. I can leave very easily."

Rashidi exchanged a look with Sàámú before training his gaze on Ẹniọlá's face. Seated opposite the other two, Ẹniọlá felt as though he was being examined for some hidden flaw—a loose thread tucked in the hem of a finished dress, threatening to undo the seam.

"I mean it, Rashidi, you'll see me there almost every day. Where will I get money for my school fees or the exam if I don't come?"

"Okay." Rashidi turned to Sàámú and nodded.

"Holy Michael said we should give you." Sàámú reached into his knapsack and placed a black nylon bag on the desk.

Ẹniọlá smiled before he could stop himself. Holy Michael was a towering man who sometimes followed Erelú around like a bodyguard. He only spoke to the boys when he wanted to pass on a message from Erelú or Honourable himself. Ẹniọlá picked up the nylon and looked inside.

Rashidi laughed. "See the way he's opening teeth. This one thinks it is money."

"It's a knife," Sàámú said.

It was the smallest knife Ẹniọlá had ever held. The hilt was brown with two silver dots, and the blade disappeared into a black sheath. When he placed it in his palm, the tip did not extend beyond his middle finger.

"What is it for?" he asked.

"Swimming," Sàámú said. "What else would it be for? It's for your training, you need to learn to protect yourself."

"From what?"

Rashidi laughed. "Your voice is shaking, Ẹniọlá. Don't worry, it's just to scare anyone that wants to try nonsense."

The next day, Holy Michael gathered all the boys together before they'd even had lunch. He took them behind the house and made them move closer to each other until he was sure none would be visible to the crowd that was spread out on Honourable's front lawn. Ẹniọlá tried to count the boys who crushed him from all sides but was distracted half-way through at some point between thirty and thirty-five. Most of the other boys were much older. A few who seemed like men had beards that covered most of their faces. Rashidi and Sàámú were far from him, but he could see they were grinning at and greeting the boys around them.

Around Ẹniọlá, there were backslaps and hellos, arguments and concerned questions about aging parents, introductions and reunions. All conversations ceased once Holy Michael began talking. He spoke in a low, husky voice that demanded full attention, counting off the things he wanted them to note on his left hand. Honourable would start the distribution at ten, but they were all expected to arrive by nine-thirty. Five people had to join the police on the podium with Honourable. Four would man the podium's edges, while the others fanned out into the crowd. Their job was to remain invisible as the distribution was happening. They were only to approach the podium if they saw that anyone was trying to attack Honourable.

As Thursday approached, Sàámú taught Ẹniọlá to make himself seem even taller, showed him how to arch his back so his shoulders appeared wider. Spread out, spread out, he would bark, demanding to know whether Ẹniọlá was really doing press-ups in the mornings as he had instructed.

Rashidi showed him how to walk with the sheathed knife on his person, one hand in his right pocket, always cupping the hilt so he could pull it out as soon as was necessary. He reassured Ẹniọlá that all he would need to do with the knife he'd been given was wave it around or stab the air before him. They were only going to distribute food and gifts to traders in the market after all, and it was unlikely that anything would go wrong. He began walking around with the knife in his pocket as Sàámú had suggested, to get used to it and prepare himself for Thursday. The hilt pushed against his hip bone, forcing him to walk sideways if he wanted to avoid sudden jolts of pain.

On Thursday morning, he met Rashidi and Sàámú in front of United. They spent some time arguing about whether they should join the morning assembly, but Sàámú was the only one arguing for it. Ẹniọlá had observed how interested Sàámú was in the rituals of schooling. His school uniform was always clean and ironed, shirt sleeves stiff with starch. Though he skipped the few classes where teachers showed up, Sàámú owned textbooks and occasionally flipped through them when he did not think Ẹniọlá was paying attention.

Rashidi began flagging down taxis once they talked Sàámú out of his desire to line up and sing anthems.

"Taxi, kẹ́? I'm not ready to waste money like that o," Sàámú said.

Sàámú was saving up money to get his own apartment so that all his younger brothers and sister could move in with him. He lived with an uncle who had taken him in after his parents died in an accident when he was ten. Now well over eighteen, he had seen his siblings only once since all four of them were distributed across the country amongst relatives. Last year, his aunt in Abuja had seared his sister's neck with an iron because she broke a china set.

"Rashidi, stop, let's walk, jàre. My rent money must be complete this year."

Rashidi slapped the back of Sàámú's head. "I will take care of you, and you too, Ẹniọlá. I will pay for everybody."

Ẹniọlá expected him to pay the fare for three of the six people who would board the taxi. Four in the back and two in front, shoulders, arms or sleeves hanging out of all the windows. Instead Rashidi insisted that they wait until an empty one came by, and they could all sit comfortably, in the way the vehicles had been designed. Rashidi beside the driver, Ẹniọlá and Sàámú in the back. When the driver tried to pick up another passenger, Rashidi slipped him enough money to cover the fare for six people.

The taxi rattled as it went along. It had to be restarted several times during the trip. There was no key or ignition, just two wires that the driver rubbed together until the engine hiccupped and the car lurched ahead.

They managed to arrive at the stop closest to the market just in time. Ojúde Ọwá was right opposite the stop, part of a complex that included the city hall and bordered Ọwá's Palace and the market. By the time they got out of the taxi, Ẹniọlá's heart was going so fast, he was surprised he could not hear it slamming against his rib cage. He was not afraid. What he felt was excitement. Trembling with anticipation as they walked towards Ojúde Ọwá, he slipped his hand in his pocket and gripped the knife. In only a few days, he had gone from walking sideways to feeling calmed when he rubbed the knife's leather sheath.

A platform had been set up in Ojúde Ọwá, next to the wall that bordered the market. Speakers blared Salawa Abeni. A lorry was parked by the small gate that led to the market. Holy Michael stood by the lorry, yelling at the driver who was trying to open it up. When he spotted the boys, he glared at them.

"Is it now that you are supposed to arrive?" Holy Michael yelled. "Did you crawl here on your bare buttocks?"

"No sir," Ẹniọlá said. "We took a taxi."

A jab in his rib from Rashidi or Sàámú, he couldn't tell which, told Ẹniọlá he had made a mistake.

"You took a taxi, àbí? A taxi? Answer me, you with the big mouth, are you deaf?"

"Y-Yes sir." Although he did not dare look away from the man who was advancing on him, he could sense that Rashidi and Sàámú were no longer standing by him.

"So why are you just getting here? Why?"

"We're not late sir, we are here on time—" He moved his head just in time as Holy Michael's fist lunged towards his face, and he felt nothing of the intended blow except the man's knuckle grazing his ear. He ducked as another punch flew towards his face, jumped so a kick grazed his trousers, then dashed away when Holy Michael tried to grab him by the shoulder. He stopped running when he heard applause.

Holy Michael continued clapping while Ẹniọlá tried to catch his breath.

"Come, come." Holy Michael spread his arms wide as though to give

Ẹniọlá a hug. "Don't fear, come near now, what's your name again, new boy?"

"Ẹniọlá sir."

"Me, I like the way you dodged and dodged, ehn. It is people like you that we need here. You are natural, ehn. You know what else I like?" Holy Michael gripped Ẹniọlá's shoulder. "Your hand never left your pocket, ehn, you were always ready to pull out your knife. Very good, very, very good."

Holy Michael squeezed Ẹniọlá's shoulder before walking away, shouting instructions at everyone within earshot as he went. Honourable's boys kept trooping in through the main gate that opened into Ojúde Ọwá. A few came in through the pedestrian gate that led into the market. Holy Michael called the boys by name, voice booming as he assigned them to various tasks. Several to man each entrance into the space, some to hang a banner behind the platform and others to go into the market with megaphones and fliers.

Ẹniọlá and his friends joined a group that would offload the lorry. Rashidi and Sàámú were to pile bags of rice in a corner while Ẹniọlá and other boys were to arrange kegs of vegetable oil in another. There should have been fabric in the lorry, yards of Ankara embossed with Honourable's face. Someone had forgotten to put them in the vehicle before it left Ìbàdàn that morning. Now Holy Michael yelled at the driver when he realised there would be no fabric to give the women who were expected to join the rally. This time, the exchange ended in Holy Michael slamming the man's forehead against the side of the lorry.

"God saved you earlier, that would have been your head," Rashidi whispered into Ẹniọlá's ear as they watched the driver dab blood from his face.

"You boys have never seen a human being before? You've never seen blood before? Why has everybody stopped what they are doing? Did you come here to watch television?" The veins in Holy Michael's neck rippled as he yelled.

The boys returned to their tasks with fear-induced fervour.

Once offloaded, the rice had to be portioned from large sacks into little black nylon bags. Ẹniọlá and some other boy emptied the kegs of oil into large basins while another two funnelled the liquid into transparent nylons. A group of new arrivals tied up the nylons of rice and oil with double knots before placing one of each in a cloth bag. The cloth bags came in several bright colours, and all bore photos of Honourable's face.

When Honourable arrived around noon, flanked by Erelú and four policemen, the offloading and organizing was done. A small crowd had gathered in front of the platform, and Ẹniọlá was standing behind it, watching as Rashidi and Sàámú danced to the makossa song that had just come on.

Holy Michael shoved a pair of sunglasses into Ẹniọlá's hand and pushed him towards Rashidi. "Óyá, óyá," he said before dashing off towards Honourable.

Ẹniọlá was confused at first, but Rashidi knew what Holy Michael meant. He grabbed Ẹniọlá's hand and pushed ahead of him through the crowd until they climbed the platform. They were the first on it as Honourable and his entourage had stopped to speak with an old woman in the crowd.

"Put on the specs," Rashidi shouted over the music.

Sunglasses on, Ẹniọlá reached into his pocket and touched the hilt of his knife. He was not afraid. He felt protected by the weight of wood in his palm, thrilled by the knowledge that everyone would be looking up to the space he now occupied. It had to be special that the first time he was joining a rally, Holy Michael asked him to stand on the platform with Rashidi and two boys he knew had been part of Honourable's campaign nearly four years ago. He was the only new boy trusted with one corner of the platform the candidate would stand on. It was something special. Rashidi had spoken with pride all week about how he was one of those who was often asked to stand with Honourable, a space he was not allowed to occupy until the sixth rally he'd attended. Sàámú had never been chosen for the role, not even once. Rashidi directed Ẹniọlá to one of the front corners on the platform and told him he must watch the crowd for signs of trouble when Honourable was speaking.

Honourable was sweating by the time he climbed the platform with his entourage. He wiped his face with a handkerchief, then waved it above his head, triggering a round of cheers from the crowd below.

Policemen fanned out into a semicircle behind Honourable and Erelú. The song on the speakers faded to silence. Ẹniọlá tightened his hold on the knife in his pocket. While someone from the party made sure the microphone was working, Erelú dug a powder compact out of her handbag, turned her back on the crowd and powdered her forehead.

Once Honourable took the microphone, Ẹniọlá moved closer to the platform's edge and scanned the upturned faces in the crowd. There were groups of sneering young men, several girls whose ware-laden trays had been set down beside them, a few children in tattered uniforms. Although Holy Michael must have told them to spread out in the crowd, Ẹniọlá could easily pick out the hundred or so women who had been bussed in from different parts of the state. Almost all were dressed in the pink campaign ankara that bore Honourable's face.

Most of the market women whose votes Honourable wanted to secure before he was even his party's candidate for governor would not show up. Few would leave their stores or stalls to spend hours standing in the sun. Some might send apprentices or assistants, and those whose stalls lined the walls of Ojúde Ọwá could probably overhear the rally.

Erelú, Holy Michael and a select group of boys would go from shop to stall in the market after the rally was done. They would spend the rest of the day handing out rice and vegetable oil. Later in the evening, Honourable would meet with heads of market associations in their homes. Sàámú had explained all this earlier in the week. He had been there the last time Honourable ran a campaign and he could remember how plans unfolded in the early days.

For now, Honourable went on about the difference his constituency projects—a borehole Ẹniọlá knew had stopped working months ago, an uncompleted classroom block, the freshly tarred stretch of road that led to Honourable's house—had made in the lives of those who were listening to him.

People chatted amongst themselves while first Honourable and then Erelú thanked them for the votes that sent him to Abuja as a representative. Only a few people seemed to be paying attention when Honourable complained about the limits on what he could accomplish as a legislator. When someone from the party took over the microphone to ask the crowd if they thought Honourable could serve them better as state governor, only the women in the campaign ankara screamed yes. No one else seemed all that interested in what Erelú or the other party representatives had to say. People kept glancing at the corner where the bags of rice and oil had been piled on top of each other.

Holy Michael came to the platform just as the last speaker, a man who slurred his words and swayed as if he was drunk, rounded off his story about how Honourable was fighting for a university to be established in the town. The point of his story seemed to be that Honourable was good at getting federal allocations into the town. Ẹniọlá wondered if the man would collapse in a drunken heap before he finished speaking.

The policemen led Honourable and Erelú off the platform, clearing a path for them as they made their way to the pile of items that would be distributed.

Holy Michael beckoned Ẹniọlá and Rashidi to himself.

"Sunday. Not this one o, the one after this," Holy Michael said. "We have a special assignment that night, direct order from Honourable. Rashidi, you remember that foolish professor? The one that wants to be governor?"

"Yes now. We went to that his friend's wife's birthday party to see him."

"That's why I like Rashidi. His brain cells are complete. He remembers things like this." Holy Michael snapped a finger in Ẹniọlá's face. "The professor and that his Ọtúnba friend, ehn? Honourable wants the two of them to know that the lion is the cat's senior father."

"I've wanted to ask you since," Rashidi said. "Nobody should be talking to Honourable the way they were talking that day, nobody."

"Yes! Àní, your brain cells are complete. Honourable wants us to use that Ọtúnba to send a warning to the stupid professor. We have information that Ọtúnba is one of the major people funding the professor's campaign. So we go for him first. If Professor doesn't hear word after that, we move closer to home with our warning. That's how Honourable likes to do his thing, we warn people first. So the two of you need to be there that Sunday night. We'll leave from Honourable's house."

Ẹniọlá nodded. He could get away at night if he wanted to; all he had to do was leave from Aunty Caro's shop instead of going home first. He could deal with his parents and their anger whenever he made it back home.

"Okay, Holy Michael. I will tell Sàámú," Rashidi said.

"No, I mean you and Ẹniọlá."

"This one? Ah, Holy Michael, this one? He's not ready o." Rashidi shook his head. "Rárá, not for special assignment."

"I like him, and I want him there."

"He's just a baby, Holy Michael."

"What's that, Rashidi? I'm not a child," Ẹniọlá said. Ehen, what if he was the youngest person in the conversation? That did not mean Rashidi should insult him in front of Honourable's right-hand man.

"Shut up, there," Rashidi said.

Holy Michael gripped Ẹniọlá's shoulder. "Do you want ten thousand naira?"

"Sir?"

"Is there any problem in your life that ten thousand naira will solve?"

Ẹniọlá nodded, too excited to speak without stuttering. Was this why Rashidi did not want him involved? So that Sàámú would be the one to get the extra money?

Holy Michael threw his hands in the air. "You see? He's ready."

"Sàámú, ńkọ́?"

"No, Rashidi. Don't annoy me. I said just you and Ẹniọlá. Do you understand?"

"Yes sir."

Rashidi waited until Holy Michael was out of earshot before turning on Ẹniọlá. "Are you insane?"

"What did I do now?" Ẹniọlá backed away from Rashidi's swinging arms.

"Have you gone crazy? Who brought you here? Is it not me and Sàámú? You? Special assignment, báwo? See his mouth like, *I am not a baby.* If I say you are an infant, Ẹniọlá, you are an infant nìyẹn."

"I know Sàámú is the one that was first your friend, but me too I need ten thousand naira now."

"You think this is about money? Do you know what you will have to do for that money? Ah, Ẹniọlá, you think it is this child's play we just did here? You think you will just have to stand like a statue?"

"What is it?" Ẹniọlá asked. He could tell now that Rashidi was more alarmed than angry, and the worry that lined his friend's brow was getting to him.

"I didn't even think Holy Michael would like you, talk less of special assignment."

"Tell me, what will I have to do?" Ẹniọlá was aware that his hand had left his pocket while Rashidi's had not. Further proof that he was not ready and in a moment like this would forget that he had to be on guard at all times.

"When we asked you to join us at Honourable's for lunch, I didn't know now. I did not know Holy Michael will just choose you so fast. Ọgbẹ́ni, you are not ready."

"Tell me now, Rashidi, just tell me."

"Are the two of you going to sleep on this thing?" Sàámú was standing on the last rung of the steps that led up to the platform.

"Aren't you joining the people that are distributing—"

"Holy Michael said I can go home," Sàámú said. "Has he released you and Ẹniọlá?"

"Sàámú, wahala has come now o, serious problem." Rashidi went towards Sàámú.

Ẹniọlá trailed the two as they left the platform. Rashidi explained the exchange with Holy Michael to Sàámú, who stopped walking and turned to Ẹniọlá.

"I did not ask Holy Michael to include me or anything. It was his decision. Sorry." Ẹniọlá could not resist the urge to apologise, Sàámú probably needed the extra cash more than he did. Even if his father was useless, he still had his mother. Sàámú had only himself.

Sàámú pointed at Ẹniọlá, squinting as though trying to see an ant clearly. "You mean he is going and I'm not?"

"That's what Holy Michael wants," Rashidi said.

"Are you serious?"

"Why would I joke about this? I don't know what to do, this one will be scared. He's just a baby. And there will be trouble, I just know."

Sàámú closed the distance between him and Ẹniọlá with one long stride. "You, you're going to collect the ten thousand naira, ehn?"

"I tried to get Holy Michael to change his mind, but you know how he is." Rashidi coughed and dropped his voice to a whisper. "What if we are asked to do what we did the last time, can this Ẹniọlá even cope with that? No. He's not ready, this one doesn't have the heart for special assignment, he's not like us."

"But he has the heart for collecting money."

Ẹniọlá could tell that Sàámú was jealous. It was there in the way he spat out his words, in the sneer that pulled at the corners of his lips, in the force with which he shoved Ẹniọlá. It was there in how he tried to do it again when Ẹniọlá staggered backwards but did not fall.

Rashidi grabbed Sàámú's arms and held him still.

"Go home," Rashidi said to Ẹniọlá. "I said go! We'll see you later."

❈

Ẹniọlá could hear voices as he approached his family's room. Thank God, a woman's voice and not the landlord's. He opened the door and stiffened when he realised the voice he'd heard belonged to that teacher from United who tried to order Ẹniọlá around in school just because she'd once been his father's colleague. Ẹniọlá stepped into the room to find her sitting on the edge of the bed, hands folded on her knees as though to keep from touching anything in the room.

"Good afternoon." Ẹniọlá mumbled the words in Mrs. Okon's direction as he dropped his bag on the mattress. His father was beside Mrs. Okon, looking weary, as if exhausted by the effort it had taken to sit up in bed.

"Is that how you speak to your teachers now, Ẹniọlá?" His mother was standing by the food cupboard, filling a cup with water.

"Good afternoon ma." He glared at Mrs. Okon, knowing already that she had come here to complain about him to his parents.

Mrs. Okon pursed her lips and turned to his father. "I'm so disappointed in him. He's not like you at all. No, not at all. Given what I knew of you when we used to work together, I wasn't expecting your son to associate with hooligans, but that's what has happened."

"Ẹ̀niọlá?" His mother gave the cup of water to Mrs. Okon. "What do you have to say?"

Ẹ̀niọlá sat on the mattress beside Bùṣọ́lá, who was either reading or pretending to.

"I can't even remember the last time I saw him in my class," Mrs. Okon said.

"Did someone nail your ears shut? Ẹ̀niọlá, I said—"

"My friends are not hooligans. They are good people."

"Good people?" Mrs. Okon laughed. "Those boys are hoodlums. I've been watching you. Is Sàámú not one of the boys you are following up and down? He has been in that school for at least eight years. For eight good years he has been repeating class after class, is that who you want to be like?"

Ẹ̀niọlá watched his mother place her clasped hands on her head like someone befallen by great tragedy.

"Sàámú is not a hooligan, he's an orphan, and what do you know? About anything? Why should I be sitting in that class? How many teachers show up to teach us in a day? You are just one of the few that do." Ẹ̀niọlá knew he was shouting when Bùṣọ́lá shut her book.

"See your son? See how he's talking to me?" Mrs. Okon stood.

Ẹ̀niọlá's father rubbed his palms together in apology, but it was his mother who spoke. "We are sorry, Mrs. Okon, we are so sorry."

"I've done my best for you people," Mrs. Okon said. "I will leave now."

"Thank you ma." Ẹ̀niọlá's mother spread out her hands. "Please don't be offended, he's just . . . I don't even understand what is going on with him. We will talk to him."

Ẹ̀niọlá's father stood when Mrs. Okon got up and followed her to the door. When the door shut behind them, Ẹ̀niọlá leapt to his feet and went towards the food cupboard.

"What is this boy doing? Cover my pot, jàre. Who told you to serve food? Is that the next thing after all we just heard?"

"I have to eat before going to Aunty Caro's place."

"You are not eating anything in this house until you explain yourself. Bùṣọ́lá, you start sorting the beans we are going to have for dinner. Óyá, Ẹ̀niọlá, start talking."

Ẹ̀niọlá took off his school shirt and put on a T-shirt. He needed to get out of the house, to think some more about his fight with Sàámú. Was it even a fight?

"Me, I don't have anything I want to say."

"Why have you been skipping classes?"

Ẹ̀níọlá shrugged. "I'm not going to that stupid school again."

His mother sighed. "Are you still angry about the school fees? I'm so sorry, Ẹ̀níọlá. But you see, you can manage—" She paused while his father came back into the room, breathing as though he'd run all the way back from wherever it was where he'd parted ways with Mrs. Okon. "Your father and I are sorry about it, but there is nothing we can do right now. We can't afford—"

"Yes, I know, you couldn't afford my school fees, but you could afford Bùsọ́lá's own."

"Ẹ̀níọlá, that is no excuse. That is no reason for you to fall in with hooligans. No reason at all in this world. Mrs. Okon told me she thinks they work for politicians, those are the worst people you could possibly associate with on this earth."

Ẹ̀níọlá stared at his father, trying to understand what seemed so strange about him in that moment. The man wasn't just speaking, he was shouting and waving his hands in the air. Soon he began pacing, combining voice and motion with a fervour Ẹ̀níọlá no longer associated with him.

"Do you know what could happen to you in that kind of company? Do you know those boys could be criminals?" he shouted. "Let's forget that for a moment, are you planning to repeat the class in United?"

"I'm leaving United," Ẹ̀níọlá said.

"No child of mine is dropping out of school."

It was something the father Ẹ̀níọlá had known as a little boy would say. In the past few years, his father would just turn and face the wall. That was it then, the strange thing Ẹ̀níọlá was trying to figure out about his father. The man was moving, talking and showing emotion in one go. For the first time in a while, he did not look like someone preparing for death; he seemed alive again.

"I'm going back to Glorious Destiny," Ẹ̀níọlá said. "I've paid my school fees myself."

"You have what?" Ẹ̀níọlá's father placed a hand on his shoulder.

Ẹ̀níọlá shrugged off the hand and stepped back. "I've paid half of it."

His father glanced at everyone else in the room as though expecting to hear an explanation from them. When he turned back to Ẹniọlá, his face was creased with something like rage. "Where did you get the money?"

"Honourable Fẹ̀sọ̀jaiyé." Ẹniọlá took off his socks and school sandals.

"The politician? My God, Mrs. Okon is right."

Ẹniọlá slid his feet into his slippers. He would go to Aunty Caro's in his school shorts. "Sàámú introduced me to him."

"The same Sàámú that has been repeating for almost a decade introduced you to a politician? Fẹ̀sọ̀jaiyé? Why is an Honourable giving you money? Are you one of his thugs now?"

"I'm going to Aunty Caro's place. Please let me pass." Ẹniọlá trained his gaze at a spot beside his father's ear.

"Oh, you now think you can talk to your father anyhow in this house, àbí?"

"What did I say?" Ẹniọlá glanced at his mother. "I just asked him to let me pass. Is that a crime?"

"You've not answered his question. Are you a thug now?"

"Why didn't you ask me this when I gave you the foodstuff, ehn? You didn't ask, but let me tell you now, the foodstuff I brought home? It's from Honourable. What are you going to do about that now? Are you going to vomit the food?"

"Ìyá Ẹniọlá, I'm disappointed in you too." Ẹniọlá's father turned to his mother. "Your son brought food into this house, and you didn't ask him how he got it? When did that start? You know there is no legitimate way for him to have gotten foodstuff, and you took it from him."

"You? You are disappointed in me? When was the last time you dropped one naira for food in this house?" Ẹniọlá's mother's voice barely rose above a whisper. "Tell me, when?"

The room was quiet. In all the years since Ẹniọlá's father had lost his job, his mother had never accused him of failing the family. At least, it had never happened when Ẹniọlá was present. There had been times when he wanted his mother to say something like this, worse things, sure her cutting words might push him out of whatever it was he had sunk into after he was sacked. Now that it was happening, he wished he could be elsewhere. Why had it taken both of them so long to become the parents he needed?

"You're disappointed? Answer me now. When was the last time you gave me one naira—no, one kobo—for our upkeep in this house?"

"Abọ́sẹ̀dé," Ẹniọlá's father said. "Abọ́sẹ̀dé, please."

It was strange to hear his father call her anything other than Ìyá Ẹniọlá, to watch them stare at each other across the room as tears spilled down his father's cheeks. He felt as if he had walked in on them as they undressed, witnessed something he was not meant to see. Ẹniọlá headed towards the door. This time, his father stepped aside and let him go.

In Aunty Caro's shop, Ẹniọlá had to clear his throat twice before he could greet anyone. His day had gone well until Sàámú became angry with him. Since then, everything that had happened made him want to cry.

He did not chat with anyone after he sat at his station. Not even Maria, who kept trying to catch his eye. Instead, he focused on the dress he had been working on the previous day, worried that he might burst into tears if he opened his mouth. When he was done with the dress, he picked up the patchwork blouse he had started making for Bùsọ́lá. Aunty Caro had showed him how to lay the scraps of fabric on top of one another so there would be no gaps. Once he was finished with his assigned tasks for the day, he was free to work on the blouse.

Yèyé came in after the sun had set. The girls had already left, and Ẹniọlá was the only one who had waited behind to help Aunty Caro put away half-sewn fabric.

He prostrated when Yèyé came in. She was accompanied by a younger woman who was carrying a cloth bag.

"Thanks again for the other day ma," Ẹniọlá said to Yèyé.

Aunty Caro gestured to Ẹniọlá while she exchanged pleasantries with the women. He followed her unspoken instructions and cleared room on the cloth-laden sofa for the women to sit on.

"Ìyàwó, yawò," Aunty Caro greeted the younger woman. "Congratulations o, Dr. Wúrà."

"Thank you ma."

Yèyé grinned. "Ìyàwó nìyẹn. Hope the clothes are all ready?"

"Yes ma. Ẹniọlá, check that table for that cream bag, I put Yèyé's things in it this afternoon."

"My own is just ìró and bùbá, but I want Wúràọlá to try her dress now in case it will need adjustment."

Aunty Caro stood up. "Should we go to my sitting room so she can change there?"

"That will be good." Yèyé cupped a knee with one hand and stretched out the other to her daughter, who gripped it and pulled her up. "It's been a long day for me, ehn. I've been going up and down to prepare for this introduction."

"Well done ma." Aunty Caro glanced towards Ẹniọlá. "Bring the bag to us once you find it."

In the corridor, the women continued to talk about all the arrangements that had to be made before the introduction on Saturday. Then their voices faded into murmurs as they went into Aunty Caro's living room, and Ẹniọlá could no longer follow the conversation.

He found the bag tucked beneath the sewing machine Maria was using but did not immediately go across the corridor. He continued tidying up, taking extra care and sweeping up the useless bits of fabric he usually left for one of the girls to take care of the next morning. It was dark out already, but he was not ready to go home. And once he had given Aunty Caro the bag, what was left but to go there?

"Ẹniọlá! Have you not found the bag yet?" Aunty Caro shouted.

Yèyé was speaking when he stepped into Aunty Caro's living room. "Help me to beg Wúràọlá o, tell her that she should be on top of everything. This dress, I've been asking her to come and pick it up since Monday and try it on."

"I just haven't had the time to come here."

Yèyé scoffed at her daughter. "No time, no time. But she still had time to travel to Ifẹ̀ yesterday."

Dr. Wúrà shook her head. "I went for my friend's burial."

"What?" Yèyé said. "Which friend?"

"The bag ma," Ẹniọlá said, unsure if he was to give it to Aunty Caro or one of the other women.

❀

"Wúràọlá, which friend?" Yèyé shifted forward to the edge of her chair.

Wúràọlá turned to Ẹniọlá and stretched out her hand. "Thank you, give it to me."

"You didn't tell me anything about one of your friends dying."

Wúràolá took the cloth bag from Ẹniọlá and set it on her lap. She lifted her mother's shimmery ìró and bùbá to reveal the dress she was to wear for the introduction ceremony on Saturday. Only Friday stood between her and the ceremony where her relatives and Kúnlé's would be formally introduced to each other. Aunties, uncles and an assortment of cousins and friends bearing witness as her parents and Kúnlé's gave blessings to set them firmly, almost irrevocably, on the road to matrimony. She held up the dress. Peach and coffee-brown fabric, because Yèyé thought it would make Wúràolá's skin look gorgeous, *just so gorgeous.* The fabric had been lined from bust to knee with coffee-brown satin so her arms and legs would be visible through the dainty lace.

"Do you like it?" Aunty Caro asked.

Wúràolá nodded without considering the question. All day, her mother's breathless concern about the dress had seemed vulgar to her. Kingsley was dead. How was she supposed to care so much about a few yards of lace and satin?

During Kingsley's burial, Tifẹ́ had shocked everyone by wailing with such abandon, Wúràolá worried she might fling herself across the coffin. Her own eyes were dry throughout and after, but for days she had to ask people to repeat what they were saying to her. Even then, a single repetition was not always sufficient to pull her back into the present, away from the way Kingsley flipped his tie over a shoulder as he strode towards his car after postings or the exact shade of the wallet he had used for as long as she knew him. An orange billfold that reminded her of a bank's logo. She'd always wanted to ask him if it was given to him by the bank as a souvenir but never got round to doing so. She obsessed over this detail after the funeral was over. Had he picked that loud orange from a shelf for himself? Was it a gift from someone he loved? Something inherited from an uncle he respected? She wanted desperately to uncover something new about Kingsley. Some fresh discovery that might stave off the realisation his consciousness would now be confined to a receding past.

"Wúràolá, it is you I am talking to." Yèyé leaned forward. "Which one of your friends?"

"Kingsley." Wúràolá traced a pattern on the dress. In the right light it could look like orange. "You don't know him."

"Good night, Aunty Caro."

Wúràolá looked up. The boy who had brought the bag was back again to say goodbye.

"Don't come so late tomorrow," Aunty Caro said.

Wúràolá began to unbutton her shirt once the boy shut the door behind him.

"Come here. Let me help with your skirt."

She stood with her back to her mother.

"No, pull it over your head," Yèyé said, before Wúràolá could step out of the skirt.

Aunty Caro and Yèyé helped her into the dress. Fussing and adjusting, they pushed her arms into the sleeves and pulled the dress down until its short train swept the floor.

"You've lost weight," Yèyé said, circling Wúràolá's wrist with a thumb and an index finger. "Does Kúnlé like that?"

Wúràolá ignored the question. She walked a few paces with the dress's hem bunched up in her hands.

"Should I take in the waist?" Aunty Caro asked.

"No, don't worry ma. It's okay."

"Wúràolá, let them adjust it now, so it can fit perfectly."

Wúràolá shook out the dress and noted how it floated down to the floor. Would it be better if it were fitted? She didn't care. It was too difficult and bizarre, this attempt to manufacture interest in a dress when her friend was dead.

"No," she said, standing before Aunty Caro and pointing at her zipper. "This is all right, thanks."

When they were in the back seat of Yèyé's car, her mother reached across the bag of clothes between them to squeeze Wúràolá's shoulder.

"I'm sorry about your friend."

The firm squeeze brought her close to tears for the first time since the burial. Perhaps because the tenderness was so unexpected. In her last year of primary school, her class teacher was a grandmother who kept a jar of Eclairs on her desk and gave sweets and hugs to students who got perfect scores in their class work. Before their second term was over, she suffered a heart attack while she was teaching and died before she could be taken to the hospital.

It was the closest Wúràolá had ever come to death. For days she would weep when she was asked to come have dinner. Her mother became impatient with her tears after a couple of days and spent the better part of an hour warning Wúràolá about being too soft. If she was crying over someone she saw only in school, what would she do when someone she loved died? Yèyé's phrasing of a possibility as certainty had only upset Wúràolá more. She bawled until her father, who was already done with dinner, came back into the room to see what was wrong.

It was her father who held her while her sobs subsided into occasional hiccups. Then he told her about àkúdàáyà. How people who had died in one city could show up in another to continue their time on earth. Not everyone got to be one, but what if her class teacher did? He invited her to imagine that her teacher was still somewhere on earth, settling into a new life, having an adventure. She had fallen asleep while her father was still speaking, weary from all her wailing.

"Wúràolá, you must wipe your tears and think about the things you have to do before Saturday," Yèyé said now as the car came to a stop in the hospital car park. "Life doesn't stop because you are sad."

"Thanks for the ride," Wúràolá said, glad she had insisted on going back to her place to spend the night. "I'll see you tomorrow evening."

❦

The introduction ceremony had been scheduled for noon, to give family members who were coming in from other states enough time to arrive. After she'd greeted her parents at dawn, Wúràolá returned to her room and covered her head with the duvet. She'd texted with Kúnlé until way past midnight and wanted to get more sleep before her day began.

"Get up, get up." Mótárá was shaking her awake with more force than was necessary.

"Why are you here?"

"Yèyé asked me to be with you while you get ready for the thing." Mótárá pulled the duvet away. "Since your friends won't be here."

Wúràolá rolled onto her stomach. Neither Grace nor Tifé had been able to get out of their weekend calls.

"Get up, the photographer and makeup artist will be here soon. Come on, Yèyé is going to blame me if you are not ready by the time the thing is supposed to start."

Wúràolá sat up as Mótárá proceeded to switch on all the lights in the room, even the two fluorescent tubes that were not in use anymore. Mótárá had taken to calling both the introduction ceremony and the marriage that was to follow *the thing* or *this nonsense thing,* as though naming the ceremonies would be a capitulation.

"Mótárá, you should get to know Kúnlé. He's—"

"Yeah. I know, he's a nice guy, there's more to him than what I've seen. He's sweet and loving and kind. He's a saint except he has not been martyred. Oh yeah, I know. Kúnlé is motherfucking Father Teresa."

"Don't swear."

"Don't marry an asshole."

"This is just the introduction."

"Introduction, and then what?" Mótárá laughed. "What follows that?"

"I'm sure he'll be like a brother to you. If you really get to know him, you'll see—"

"I already have a brother. So . . . I'm good."

"Has Láyí arrived?"

"Yèyé spoke to him before I came here, he's already on his way. Will you get out of bed, please?"

Wúràolá put on a customised satin robe after she showered. *Intromímò* was stitched across the back, *Dr. Wúràolá* over the breast pocket. It was a gift from Grace and Tifé.

"There's just one more thing I have to say about this nonsense thing."

"Okay." Wúràolá sat in front of her dressing mirror.

"If you marry this guy and become Wúràolá Coker, your initials will be W. C. Guess what you'll be full of?"

"Mótárá, you're not helping, you're just trying to hurt me now. That's what you want to do?"

"If it'll bring you to your senses."

"Actually, I would be Wúràolá Elizabeth Àbèké Coker."

Mótárá refused to speak to Wúràolá after this exchange, but did as she was told without comment, fetching: the make-up artist and the photographer from the living room, two apples and an orange from the kitchen, the day's jewellery from Yèyé's room.

The photographer took a few shots of Wúràọlá's face. Then he focused his attention on the outfit she would wear, opening the curtains so he could photograph the dress, gèlè, heels and jewellery in the best light possible.

Wúràọlá watched in the mirror as the makeup artist, who introduced herself as Praise, began to shave her bushy eyebrows into an arc. She shut her eyes as bits of hair fell on her cheeks.

"Is this fine?" Praise asked.

"Yes," Wúràọlá said without looking in the mirror.

Wúràọlá's phone vibrated in her robe's left pocket. A text. Maybe a congratulatory note from a friend or someone in the family. Probably a *Good morning, lovely,* from Kúnlé. Today's text would be longer. After an attempt to articulate how much he loved her—*more than life itself, to the moon and back, forever and then some more*—there would be something about how momentous the day was for their relationship. His sentiments were no less affecting because he often repeated the same phrases. He cared and he was consistent, that was what counted. He'd even started including random quotes to lift her spirits since Kingsley died. The day before, he'd added one from someone who claimed that gratitude for air and water would cause light to flood one's path. Wúràọlá did not even understand what on earth that was supposed to mean, but she was grateful that he cared for her in this way. Mọ́tárá could mock all she wanted, Wúràọlá saw more in Kúnlé than her sister could surmise from an encounter that did not last five minutes. Wúràọlá cupped her phone but did not remove it from her pocket. Better to save the rush of pleasure that would come from reading the text until later.

"Do your friends know Kúnlé?"

Wúràọlá could see Mọ́tárá in the mirror. She was perched on the edge of the bed, her face fixed in a grimace. "You are done sulking."

"I mean, do they know who he *really* is? Have you told them—"

"Shut it, Mọ́tárá, we have company."

Mọ́tárá stood. "You have my number if you need something. Me, I'm going."

As Wúràọlá turned to watch her sister flounce out of the room, she felt a sharp pain above her eye. The blade had nicked her skin.

"I'm so sorry," Praise said, dabbing blood from Wúràọlá's brow with a wipe. "The problem was when you moved and the blade . . . I didn't know you were going to turn."

"It's fine," Wúràọlá said. The cut was small, and the blood only trickled, soon it would stop. No one besides her sister had seen Kúnlé hit her. Why would she volunteer information about any of the incidents to a friend? She already knew how they would react. Tifẹ́'s face would twist with rage while she cursed Kúnlé. Grace might be calmer, but disgust and disappointment would lurk behind her even expression when it became clear that Wúràọlá did not want to leave Kúnlé.

And how would she explain herself to them? These women whose opinion of her mattered so much that imagining their disappointment drenched her in shame. Tifẹ́ and Grace. Professor Ezenna, who had supervised her community health project and told her she had a brilliant future in epidemiology. Mrs. Hamid, the assistant principal in her secondary school whose argument that Wúràọlá's grades qualified her to give the valedictory speech, instead of the senior boy, buoyed her through the first years of medical school. And of course, Mọ́tárá. Wúràọlá channelled her thoughts to the reasons she might give to her friends. She did it to steel herself in preparation for some future in which they knew the truth. To stave off the worries her sister's questions had stirred; the latent fear that she might be making the worst mistake of her life.

One—she loved him. Not in the way she had once loved Nonso, with an aching tenderness she did not understand until he could no longer be hers. The depth of her affection for Kúnlé was clear to her once they became lovers. Wúràọlá loved him utterly and possessively. She wanted to marry him because then he would belong to her. She was claiming what she wanted. That smile, that body, that charm, all hers.

"Look up." Praise said. She was working on Wúràọlá's eyes, tracing a line towards her lateral canthus.

Wúràọlá blinked and looked up at Praise.

"No. Up, up. The ceiling, focus on the ceiling."

Two—Kúnlé loved her. He did. She had never doubted his affection, except when— But even those moments. What if they were a manifestation of his intense feelings? Of how his affection tethered on the edge of obsession? Aunty Bíọ́lá had once told Wúràọlá that it was better to marry someone who loved you more than you loved them. Now, how to determine the quotient of love. If verbal or physical expressions were a unit of measurement, Kúnlé loved her with his whole being then? Even the parts he tried so hard to suppress.

"Can you look in the mirror?" Praise said. "Do you like what you see? So far."

So far, her eyes had been shadowed and lined. They seemed more clearly defined as a result, the pupils bigger and wider than they really were. Praise was good at her job. Wúràọlá's eyes were nice enough but had never been remarkable, they now seemed exceptional.

"I like it."

"Okay." Praise brought out a small tube and pressed out a blob of orangey liquid.

"Aren't you done with the foundation?"

"Yes. I need some concealer for your shoulder, there is this discolouration. Your dress is lace, àbí? It might show. Is it a birthmark?"

The mark was fading. In a week or two, it would blend into her skin but under all this light, it was visible to someone who was not even looking for it. Kúnlé checked her body for discolouration now. He pretended he was just caressing her, but she knew he was studying her skin, hoping her bruises had faded. When he found any, he pressed his face into her flesh right there. Sometimes, that was the beginning of their most tender lovemaking. His fingers dancing across her skin, featherlight as though she was made of porcelain and he did not want to break her. And that was reason number three. The sex was not simply good, it was polyvalent, constantly changing in register, always pulsing with the possibility of surprise.

"Can you please smile for the camera? I want him to get a good 'after' shot for me," Praise said. "Can you smile more, make your smile wider? That's great."

Wúràọlá studied her face in the mirror as the makeup artist began to pack up her products. "This is very nice, Praise, thank you."

"I'm glad we finished before ten. It is better this way, ehn. I don't like to be in a rush." Praise placed her makeup box on the floor beside the dressing table. "Should we tie the gèlè now or wait until closer to twelve when we do the touch-up?"

"Not now, maybe like eleven-thirty."

"Can I wait in the sitting room? This one upstairs."

"Yes, the two of you can stay there. If anyone asks tell them I gave you permission."

Wúràolá reached for her phone after the makeup artist and photographer were gone. Kúnlé had texted her. Other people had too, and she read those messages first, saving his for last.

Grace had sent two words: *Congratulations, Wúràolá*. Tifé managed to say more: *Congrats babe so glad for you TTYL*. Each one of her aunts had sent long texts, mostly prayers that Wúràolá skimmed over before going to the next one. Her in-laws—she already thought of Kúnlé's parents that way—had sent a thoughtfully crafted message from his mother's phone that was signed *B & C Coker*.

Reason number four—they fit seamlessly into each other's families. She understood his family. It was like hers, only smaller.

"Can I come in?" Two soft knocks. "Wúràolá."

"Yes sir."

Wúràolá pushed back from the dressing table. Her father stepped into the room. He was already dressed in the àlàárì he'd worn when he married her mother. Yèyé had no use for such sentimentality, she was wearing wine to match his outfit but in brand-new lace and damask gèlè.

"It still fits!"

"And your mother said I'm too old to wear it." He spread his arms and turned round. "Is it tight around the belly?"

"You look amazing."

He wiggled his brows. "Make sure you tell your mother that."

"Don't worry, she'll notice once she's done running after the caterers."

"I stopped by to get my hug before going downstairs." He held his arms wide open.

"My makeup will stain your—"

"Come on now."

She let him envelope her in the folds of his agbádá. He began to sing a song he'd taught her as a kid, one he often returned to when he wanted to hype her. *Tẹ̀rù bá ń bà yín ẹ wí o,* he called. *Ẹ̀rù ò b'ọmọ Mákinwá,* Wúràọlá responded.

He pulled back. "Celebration-of-life drinks on my balcony after all the drama is over?"

"Yes, please."

"We'll have scotch." He winked. "I'll even let you finish yours this time."

Wúràọlá grinned. Aged eleven or twelve, she had taken two of her mother's gold bracelets to school without her permission and lost both by the time she returned home for the holidays. Hoping that a show of contrition would satisfy her mother, she'd stupidly ignored Láyí's advice that she lie about taking the jewellery in the first place. After all, what were two bracelets out of the dozens Yèyé owned? As it turned out, her brother was right. Wúràọlá ended up on her knees in her mother's bedroom, arm outstretched as Yèyé struck her left palm with a pankere. The punishment Yèyé had decided on was four strokes of the cane, but halfway through, Wúràọlá pushed her mother back onto her bed and ran.

Once she escaped, she had no real direction. She kept racing down the corridor until she was in front of her father's study. She went in because she knew her livid mother would emerge into the corridor at any moment, still brandishing the pankere, ready to double the allotted strokes because of Wúràọlá's defiance. Her father was sorting through his copies of *Tell Magazine* when she barged into the study. Too terrified to do anything but babble, she'd dashed through the room to its balcony. She stood on the furthest end of the balcony, barely breathing when Yèyé came into the room to ask if her father had seen her. Not only did he lie, he also claimed he might have heard footsteps rushing downstairs.

When Yèyé was gone, he'd come to her in the balcony, giggling to himself and bearing two glasses of scotch. One was to help her stop trembling, but he allowed her just one sip. She only told her father about the bracelets, certain he would also become upset with her if he knew she'd pushed her mother. In spite of her father's reassurances, Wúràọlá was convinced Yèyé would invent new punishments just for her that day. When she began whining that she was not ready to die, he'd laughed for a while before helping her hatch her ultimate escape from Yèyé's punishment. He let her hide in the study until Yèyé's wrath had given way to worry. Then he snuck her out of the side staircase so she could reenter the house into the arms of a relieved mother who never mentioned the bracelets again.

That evening, when she went to his study to say thank you, her father closed the file he was looking at and invited her out onto the balcony for another round of drinks. This time he gave her a glass of orange juice. *I see she didn't kill you dead, so, celebration-of-life drinks,* he'd said as they clinked glasses. They continued to celebrate subsequent moments of triumph this way, switching to wine for both of them after she turned twenty.

"I don't want scotch," Wúràọlá said now. "I deserve champagne today."

Her father smiled at her and that was reason number five. He was smiling the way he had during her matriculation into the university and at her induction into the medical profession. Those iterations of his smile were predated by an earlier one she only remembered from a photo that was taken on her first birthday. In it, she is walking away from the cake table towards her father. He is at the edge of the frame and her back is to the camera, her face is not visible, but his smile is. This proud smile. How could she call off the introduction now and ruin that?

"See you downstairs." Her father hugged her once more and left.

And there it was. Five reasons for all the women she was disappointing by putting on her new dress, slipping her feet into the shoes Yèyé had bought for her, turning her head this way and that as Praise tied her gèlè, going ahead as planned. Heedlessly? No, no, only regardless. This was her decision and she'd identified five things that mattered to her. That was enough. It had to be for now.

Doubt still slithered around in her as she went downstairs to join the ceremony. Then she was under the canopy and the alága was singing for her.

Tẹ̀rù bá ń bà yín ẹ wí o, ẹ̀rù ò b'ọmọ Mákinwá.

A man stood before her, hitting his curved drumstick against a talking drum. Her family was singing along, hastening the rhythm until the refrain became a chant, an anthem that dispelled doubt and fear until she was jubilant. Yes, she was a Mákinwá. No, she was not fearful.

After that, the ceremony passed in a blur of several songs and endless prayers. Aunty Bíólá did not let go of the microphone for almost half an hour. Her opening prayer meandered through family history, to complaints about divorces before settling on blessings for the intending couple.

When the alága called on Wúràolá to introduce her fiancé to her family, she picked him out of a crowd without pretending she did not know where he was seated on his family's side of the canopy. Her feet hurt already. She could not perform the drama of searching for a man who was right before her. Standing between both families, she faced hers and held up Kúnlé's hand like he was a trophy she'd won for her relatives. She reeled out all his names, segueing into all the terms of endearment the alága insisted she add to this moment of introduction. As she handed over the microphone, Kúnlé prostrated before he was even instructed to do so. Yèyé's grin was dazzling as she caught Wúràolá's eye and nodded approval.

After her family had blessed the proposed union, Wúràolá and Kúnlé were ushered to the love seat that had been prepared for them.

"God, this is amazing," Kúnlé kept saying while each relative stood to introduce themselves.

Wúràolá leaned into him and let his excitement blaze into her until she too was euphoric.

22

Wúràọlá moved in with Kúnlé the day after their introduction, but they called it a test run. She would stay for a week and then return to the hospital, which worked well with his schedule since he was planning to travel with his father to Abuja during the following week.

At first, she barely saw him because she was on call Monday and Tuesday. But from Wednesday until the weekend, she wasn't on call because she swapped with a colleague.

Kúnlé volunteered to drop her off and pick her up from work during that window, and she gladly agreed. Riding shotgun meant she could eat the breakfast he fixed for her on their way to the hospital. He graduated from margarine-slathered slices of bread to a pack of dundun and egg sauce by the end of the week.

He brought her cold drinks in the evenings and relaxed her seat all the way back before she got into the car. She spent most of the drives to his place in a somnolent state, slurping her La Casera through a straw while he told her about his day. Sometimes, he sang along to the Styl Plus album that played in the background during their rides, and she laughed at how off-key he was. He'd laugh along, his face crinkling with delight.

The mirth replenished her. Their laughter made everything between them wondrous and luminous, caused their affection to blaze with a radiance that obliterated any memory of pain. She stopped wincing or startling when he reached for her, and they were calling that week their pre-honeymoon by Friday.

Wúràọlá went to church with Kúnlé's parents on Sunday. He stayed home to spend that morning packing for his trip to Abuja. He picked out an outfit he liked for her, a floor-length boubou that she paired with a turban, six-inch heels and a clutch. She sat with his parents during the service, and because she was next to his mother, Wúràọlá made sure she stayed awake throughout the sermon.

When they got back from church, Wúràọlá went into the main house with the Cokers. Kúnlé was waiting there. He embraced her as they walked into the living room, cupping her face for a moment before greeting his parents.

Sunday lunch with the Cokers was coconut rice with peppered turkey. When Wúràọlá began to cough after tasting the turkey, Kúnlé rubbed her back and lifted his glass of water to her lips. His mother brought her fried fish after Wúràọlá's second attempt to eat the turkey proved she couldn't tolerate that much pepper.

They went upstairs to the family room after lunch to decide which movie to watch together. As Kúnlé's father sorted through the CDs, Wúràọlá noticed the jacket of *Owó Blow: The Revolt* and mentioned that she had never seen it.

"Just this one or all three?" Kúnlé's mother asked.

"I've not seen any of them."

"You don't mean it," Kúnlé's father said. "Let's watch it, àbí? Good."

"It's one of our favourite movies in this house." Kúnlé's mother dropped her voice to a conspiratorial whisper. "Kúnlé has had a crush on Bímbọ́ Akíntọ́lá since we watched it."

Kúnlé rolled his eyes and kissed Wúràọlá's forehead. She studied his profile as the movie began. They were never this affectionate in front of his parents, but all afternoon, he'd been touching her every chance he got. And now a kiss? He raised an eyebrow and smiled when he caught her staring. She turned her gaze to the television. Well, they'd had their introduction after all, maybe it was time to feel less self-conscious about displaying affection in front of his parents.

Wúràọlá and Kúnlé left for his apartment after nightfall. They took a small cooler of spaghetti and corned beef stew with them at his mother's insistence. He was holding her hand when they left the main house, but he let go as they crossed the lawn to his place.

He seemed distracted as she warmed up the corned beef stew, mumbling to himself when she asked about how ready he was for the trip to Abuja.

"Are you all right?" she asked as they sat down to eat.

"Why wouldn't I be?"

"You could just say you're all right," Wúràọlá said.

They didn't speak to each other until they were halfway through the meal. Then he began to quiz her about Kingsley.

"Why are you asking me these questions?" she asked, after she'd explained why it had been important for her to attend Kingsley's funeral.

"I just want to know if you still think about him."

"All the time. When we sang 'Abide with Me' in church today, I remembered how we sang it just before his body was committed to the ground."

"Do you still think about fucking him?"

Wúràọlá dropped her fork. "What kind of question is that?"

"You've not answered it."

"Why are you doing this?"

"Answer the question."

Wúràọlá dropped her plate and went into the bedroom. Even though his footfalls were muted because he was wearing socks, she knew he was following her. She sat on the bed and watched him pace.

"You need to calm down, Kúnlé. You've been so supportive since he died. What is all this now?"

" 'My eyes are drawn instead to Kingsley's bare, hirsute chest. I want so much to press my face against all that hair.' "

"What?"

" 'It wasn't for want of desire that the pleasures of his embrace never bloomed into some more transcendent form of affection.' "

Wúràọlá's breath caught as she recognised her words. Kúnlé was quoting the journal she'd written right after Kingsley died. She'd left her handbag on the bed when she transferred her wallet and phone into her clutch before church. "You went through my bag?"

Kúnlé made air quotes. " 'I always thought we would have more time.' "

He kept talking, but she could not hear him. She scooted back on the bed till her back was against the wall, wondering if she could run out of the room before he caught up with her. His bathroom was not an option, since it had no lock. Soon there was no escape. As his rage amplified, Kúnlé paced in front of the bedroom door.

He was shouting now. "Time for what? For what?"

Wúràọlá flattened her back against the wall and braced her body.

"Come to think of it, sex has been so great in the last few days. Were you thinking about him all this time?"

"Look, I never loved Kingsley." Her words came out in a trembling, hoarse whisper.

" 'I will pause because even without love, desire is alluring.' "

"Did you memorise the whole thing? See, I was just working through all the guilt and regret I felt at that time. It had nothing to do with you or us."

He sat beside her on the bed and for a few moments she thought they could get out of the argument. Then he began to speak.

"Do you know what it was like for me to read that while you're in church? Do you know how much you have hurt me?" He ran his hand through her hair and grabbed a fistful. "What will I find on your phone if I check it?"

"Kúnlé, you need to calm down."

He leaned into her, brought his lips close as though he was about to kiss her, then pulled at her hair with such force she couldn't breathe for a moment.

"Please," she begged. "I'm sorry."

"My God, so it's true, you've never apologised for anything so quickly. I'm right about you and Kingsley."

"No, no, no, no, no, please, no."

He relaxed his hold. She looked at him, pleading with her eyes. She realised that he was not as angry as he had sounded. This terrified her. He wasn't merely losing his temper. What was happening in that moment was not accidental, and whatever was to follow was premeditated. He had thought about this all day and decided that he would punish her.

"Kúnlé. Please."

He pulled her off the bed by her hair, then dragged her across the room by it once, twice, thrice—she lost count when he began to kick her. She was sure then that he was going to kill her. Not that he might, but that as he went through her notebooks while she was in church, he had hatched a plan that ended with her dead at some point during the night. She tried to kick him, but he was moving too quickly for her. So she shut her eyes and screamed until she felt her own eardrums tingle. The main house was not too far away, his parents could hear her now, someone would come and make him stop.

Wúràọlá screamed until her voice was gone and she couldn't even whimper. No one came.

23

As he drove them to the special assignment in a fourteen-seater HiAce, Holy Michael sang along to *Opelope Anointing*. A sullen man sat beside him in the bus's front seat. Ẹniọlá recognised the man as one of Honourable's police escorts, even though, like Holy Michael, he was wearing a black T-shirt and blue jeans. Instead of the rusty-looking gun he sometimes slung across his shoulder when he was in uniform, the policeman had a handgun on his knee.

Ẹniọlá sat behind them with Lápàdé, one of the other boys he'd seen around Honourable's house. Lápàdé also had a gun, which he held barrel down between his legs. Ẹniọlá did not have a gun. Neither did Silas, the fourth boy on the trip. Silas and Ẹniọlá had been given machetes instead. Rashidi, who also had a gun, sat in the last row with Silas.

Before they left Honourable's compound that night, Holy Michael had explained all that would happen, for what felt like the hundredth time. Once he was done, Rashidi had asked Ẹniọlá if he was afraid, but before he could answer, Lápàdé was pushing past them to jump on the bus.

Now Rashidi whispered into Ẹniọlá's ear from the back seat, "No fear?"

Ẹniọlá shrugged. That afternoon, his sister had asked for money to get her hair done. He'd laughed at first, because he thought she was joking. Bùsọ́lá wore her hair in a low cut, and it had never occurred to him that she was interested in weaving or threading it. She seemed to care only about those storybooks she was always borrowing from her classmates. But when she'd pulled at her ear and looked away, he realised that his laughter had hurt her. He gave her two one-hundred-naira notes from the envelope he got from Honourable's house the previous Friday. It didn't bother him too much that he was reducing the amount he could add to his school fees at Glorious Destiny on Monday. He was simply happy he could give his sister something she had obviously longed for and couldn't have otherwise.

His mother had also started asking him for money. Insignificant sums. Five naira for matches, twenty naira for salt. She did not revisit the question of how he got his money. Meanwhile, his father seemed to have retrieved the voice he swallowed years ago. Every day now, he had something to say to Ẹniọlá about Honourable Fẹ̀sọ̀jaiyé.

Ẹniọlá pressed his forehead against the window. So what if he was carrying a machete? Holy Michael had not asked him to hurt anyone with it, he was just going to scare people a little. If he could help his mother and sister, could whatever made it possible be as wrong as his father claimed?

The bus stopped in front of a black gate, and everyone pulled on the cloth mask they'd been given earlier. Ẹniọlá was still adjusting his to make sure he could see through the eyeholes when Lápàdé went to knock on the gate. The first step proceeded as Holy Michael had drilled into them all week. A knock. Light enough to be made by a windblown thing knocking against the gate. Then another and another until the security guard got tired of asking if anyone was there and opened the gate to remove whatever was making the annoying sound.

When the security guard opened the pedestrian gate, Lápàdé grabbed him and pointed the gun at his head. Holy Michael switched off the headlamps before he drove into the compound. He waited for the guard to shut the gate. After Lápàdé and the guard boarded the bus, Holy Michael sped across the lawn toward the duplex that stood in the middle of the large compound.

The bus came to a stop again, and this time everyone except the policeman got down. Holy Michael pressed his gun between the guard's shoulder blades and pushed him ahead of the group towards the house.

At the front door, Holy Michael knocked. The gateman answered when a young female voice asked who was there. The woman who opened the door dropped to her knees as soon as she saw the group.

"Evening sir, evening, good evening. Please, I don't have money, I'm just the house girl. Please, God bless you, good evening, God bless you."

"Shut up," Holy Michael said.

The woman seemed unable to stop speaking even after she crawled away from the door to let them in. "I'm just the house girl. Please, God bless you, good evening, God bless you."

"I said you should keep shut."

"Yes sir, I agree sir, thank you sir."

Holy Michael nodded at Rashidi. "Shut her up."

Rashidi stepped closer to the woman and pointed the gun between her eyes. He did not shoot. He just held the gun in place until she stopped talking.

Ẹniọlá noticed the photos as they moved further into the sitting room. He paused to study them, peering at the middle-aged woman who had caught his eye. Yes, it was Yèyé, there was no mistaking it. She was there in almost every one of the framed family photos that adorned the walls. Yèyé surrounded by what he imagined was her family, Yèyé alone, Yèyé and the man who must be her husband. The man Honourable was going to use to teach his rival a lesson. Ẹniọlá felt dizzy. He did not want to be part of this anymore. These were not faceless people he could not care less about, this was Yèyé. She had been kind to him. What sort of person would he be if he followed through with what was required of him tonight?

"Ẹniọlá?"

Holy Michael had been trying to tell him something.

"Sir."

"Did you come here to look at photos? I said let's go."

He followed Holy Michael up the stairs. The first room they searched was empty. When they opened the second door, Yèyé was coming out of the bathroom, her dress still hiked halfway up her hips. She finished adjusting it before kneeling before them as Holy Michael commanded.

"Where is your husband?"

"Don't worry, I will cooperate, don't worry." Yèyé kept her head bowed.

Holy Michael nodded to Ẹniọlá.

Ẹniọlá ran into the bathroom, slashing the air before him with his machete as he went. "It's empty," he reported to Holy Michael.

"My brothers, we are all children of the same God, so you're my broth-ers." Yèyé's words came fast and loud. "Take the gold. If you open that drawer, there is a lot of gold there, just take the gold, please."

"I said, where is your husband?"

"Italian gold mà ni. It is not—"

Holy Michael slapped the next word back into Yèyé's throat. "Stand up, stand up now, or I will blow your head off."

Ẹniọlá winced, pushing away memories of Yèyé's kindness. Thinking about that now would only get him into trouble with Holy Michael.

Yèyé gripped her knee and shook her head. "You need to help me, my leg, I can't . . . not by myself."

Holy Michael nodded in Ẹniọlá's direction. "Help her."

Ẹniọlá stretched his hands out to Yèyé. Whose fingers trembled? Hers or his?

Yèyé kept her head down and did not look up as they pushed her out of the room into the corridor.

"Where is he?" Holy Michael twisted the doorknob of the next door they came to; it did not yield.

"No o, he's not there, he's not there, please. That room is empty. Let's be going, I will take you to him now, he should be in his study."

"Move." Holy Michael kicked Yèyé in the shin.

At the end of the corridor, Yèyé knocked on a door.

"Mọ́tárá?"

"No, it's me."

"Ìyá Láyí?"

"Yes." Yèyé twisted the doorknob.

"Give me a minute, I'll open it."

Yèyé held her head while they waited.

An older man opened the door.

"Ọ̀túnba Mákinwá?" Holy Michael gave the man two quick slaps. "Honourable sent me to greet you."

"He has BP, he has BP," Yèyé said. "Stop, please, he has high BP."

"He knows he has high blood pressure." Holy Michael kicked Ọ̀túnba's kneecap. "And he is struggling with his seniors in life."

"Please, please. There is gold, I have gold, take the gold." Yèyé looked up at her husband. "Do you have money in the house?"

Ọ̀túnba bent over, groaning as he gripped his knee.

"What is going on?"

Ẹniọlá glanced in the direction the voice had come from and saw a girl about his age.

"Mo dáràn," Yèyé screamed. "Go back into your room and lock the door, Mọ́tárá."

Holy Michael fired a shot in the girl's direction. Ẹniọlá froze as the bullet whizzed past her and lodged in a pillar. "Don't move unless you want to die."

"Mo gbé." Yèyé clasped her arms over her head. "Anything you want, please, don't touch . . . Please, anything."

Holy Michael silenced her with a slap. "You said there was nobody in that room. Why are you lying? You want to die? You want your child to die?"

Yèyé shook her head, eyes bulging as she held a palm over her lips.

"Is there anybody else in this house?" Holy Michael asked. "Answer me!"

"Just our maid. Nobody else sir, no one."

"You're lying again."

"I swear on my father's grave, my mother's grave."

"Move," Holy Michael barked.

Holy Michael pushed Ọ̀túnba down the corridor, poking his gun into the folds of the older man's neck. Ẹniọlá followed with Yèyé. He rested his machete on her shoulder and turned the cutting edge towards her jaw.

The girl Yèyé had called Mọ́tárá was already sobbing when they got to her. Still, Holy Michael slapped her before commanding her to move.

Downstairs, they ushered everyone outside and asked all of them to kneel on the lawn.

Lápàdé brought kegs of petrol out of the bus. Rashidi grabbed one and began to douse all the cars in the compound. Silas took two and went back into the house. He was going to soak the furniture in the living room.

Ẹniọlá was supposed to prepare Ọ̀túnba for departure. He was meant to blindfold the man, stuff a rag in his mouth and bind his wrists together.

"Are you an idiot?" Holy Michael asked. "How many years will it take for you to tie a blindfold?"

"I will finish soon." Ẹniọlá had already fetched the blindfold from the bus, but he'd forgotten the rag and ropes. Now he could not even move without his knees knocking together, and the blindfold kept slipping from his hands. Why had he thought he could do this? He wanted to be anywhere else but here right now. He wanted to run across the lawn and out of the compound, going away and away until he was home. That was impossible, because the gate was locked and Holy Michael had the keys. Besides, he understood things a little better now—Holy Michael would shoot him if he ran. He was sure of it.

The policeman emerged from behind the duplex. He led the domestic staff who lived in the boys' quarters towards the front lawn.

"Ọ̀gá, help me finish what this stupid idiot is doing," Holy Michael said. "Stupid idiot, get the phones."

Glad to have a task that did not involve gagging someone, Ẹniọlá began with the security guard. Before he was done removing the man's SIM card, the others were dropping their phones on the grass without being asked.

Holy Michael spoke to Yèyé as she fished her phone from her pocket. "We heard that your daughter celebrated her introduction."

"Y-Y-Yes," Yèyé said.

"Honourable Fẹ̀sọ̀jaiyé asked us to congratulate you."

Yèyé's jaw slackened as she finally realised that this was not an armed robbery.

After the house and cars were on fire, the policeman dragged Ọ̀túnba onto the bus. Ẹniọlá was still breaking SIM cards after all the others had boarded. His hands shook too much for him to do an effective job. His chest hurt and his temples ached; it was all because of the muffled sobs around him, the crackling fire, how he was now a criminal. A kidnapper. All week, Holy Michael had said nothing about taking Ọ̀túnba with them. Wasn't the plan just to terrify the family? Tie Ọ̀túnba up and deliver a message from Honourable?

Yèyé had looked up. She was staring at him, studying his face as though trying to confirm something to herself. Maybe his mask was rubbish. Yèyé could still see his eyes, nose and lips. Yèyé's eyes widened. Oh God, she had recognised him. She knew it was him. Why else would she be glaring at him?

"Do you want to sleep there?" Holy Michael had started the bus. "Come here, jàre, you can break the SIM cards as we are going."

Ọtúnba had been pushed into a seat beside Lápàdé on the second row. Ẹniọlá got in and sat by the door. Beside him, Ọtúnba was groaning, still trying to speak in spite of how he'd been gagged.

"Man yìí, Mákinwá, àbí, what's your name? Keep shut there."

Ọtúnba's groans grew louder. As they drove out of the compound, Holy Michael turned back, and with a swift motion that made Ẹniọlá jump, he slammed the butt of his gun against Ọtúnba's head.

The man's head lolled to the side, and he was quiet.

"These people don't hear word," Holy Michael said, and began to fiddle with the vehicle's CD player. Soon he was singing along with Dunni Olanrewaju. *Yóò ṣagolo lọ́jà* . . .

Ẹniọlá worried that Ọtúnba had fainted or died, but the man was only still for a while. When Ọtúnba lifted his head, Ẹniọlá saw that blood was trickling down his face.

The ache in Ẹniọlá's temple began to spread. He felt like throwing up. He did not know what was next, where they were headed, what was to happen, what might be expected of him. He had doused someone's house in petrol. And not just anyone, the home of a woman who had once been kind to him. He had also participated in kidnapping her husband.

Something in the way Holy Michael had swung the gun towards Ọtúnba earlier terrified Ẹniọlá. It was as if he could just as easily have shot the man. Were they still going to shoot Ọtúnba? Would they shoot to kill? The ache had spread from his temple to every inch of his skull. He had to get away. He looked out of the window and recognised nothing of what he saw. The buildings they passed by were unfamiliar.

Beside him, Ọtúnba began grunting.

"Hear word now," the policeman shouted. "Àní, shut up."

"Maybe he wants water," Ẹniọlá said.

"To drown in, àbí?" Holy Michael said. "Shut up there."

Ọtúnba was quiet for a while; then he began grunting again, and this time he pointed his bound fists towards his mouth. Ẹniọlá threw the SIM cards he was holding on the floor and leaned closer to Ọtúnba. It was impossible to make out what the man was trying to say.

In front, Holy Michael gave the policeman a look. "Abeg, deal with this fool. We've warned him enough."

Ẹniọlá reached for his knife. He only meant to brandish it. Say he could not be part of a murder and maybe explain that this man's wife was a kind woman, but when the policeman shoved his gun towards Chief's face, Ẹniọlá's voice was trapped in his throat. His hand kept moving. Swiftly, just as Rashidi had taught him, Ẹniọlá slashed the policeman's forearm.

The policeman screamed in agony and dropped his gun.

"What is happening? What now?" Holy Michael shouted. "Why are you shouting?"

"Ẹniọlá cut ọga police," Lápàdé said.

"What? Ẹniọlá? Ayé ẹ ti bàjẹ́ lónì." Holy Michael shut off the music and looked at the policeman. "Hold it well to stop the blood. I can't stop now, but we'll soon get there. Be a man, ehn, stop crying, bear it like a man."

Ẹniọlá glanced outside. He could not recognise the street, but what were his options? He opened the door and jumped. He fell facedown, scrambled up immediately and began to run. Was someone calling him? Did the footfalls behind him belong to Holy Michael or one of the people he wove past as he ran? He did not dare look back, the only way to go was forward. First, off the main road into an untarred side street, zigzagging through its length because he'd heard somewhere that it was the best way to avoid gunshots, stumbling in the darkness because there were no streetlamps. When the untarred road ended, he turned into a footpath. He ran until his sides ached, and he had to stop so he could breathe. If anyone had followed him, they would have caught him by then. He leaned against the side of a building. His cheeks were wet. From tears or sweat, he did not know. It could be both.

The street he'd passed by was not busy, but there were still people outside. It could not be midnight yet. Most streets had rules about people going around after midnight, some had guards who enforced that too. He began walking as fast as he could with the pain in his sides. If he followed the pathway into a street he recognised, he could be home before midnight.

❧

Bùsọ́lá was waiting for him outside when he got home.

"Where have you been? Everybody is worried about you." Without pausing for a reply, she bent her head so he could see her hair had been threaded. "I did it. It was only àjànkólokòlo they could thread for me, but I like it so much. Thank you, thank you."

She hugged him, then pulled back to give him a smile before they went inside.

His mother swept her gaze over him as he walked in. "Why are you so dirty?"

"Where did you go?" His father was pacing the floor. "It's those politicians you were following, àbí?"

"It's too late to start that one." His mother's voice was sharp. "We'll talk about it tomorrow."

Ẹniọlá wanted to take a bath, but first, he needed to rest for a few minutes. He would go to Honourable's house the next day and beg Holy Michael. He would plead and prostrate, he would roll on the floor if he had to. Sàámú was right, he was not ready for special assignments. He lay on the mattress and let his eyes drift shut. He kept his feet on the floor. Soon he would get up to take his bath, soon.

He woke to a loud banging. Electricity had gone out at some point, and it took a minute for his eyes to get used to the darkness. The banging was on their door. His parents were rousing themselves as the noise continued.

"Who? Who is it?" his mother shouted. "In the middle of the night, who is that?"

"Maybe it's Bàbá Landlord." The whispered words were his father's.

Beside Ẹniọlá, Bùsọ́lá mumbled to herself and sat up.

His father was getting off the bed when the flimsy lock broke and the door swung open.

Ẹniọlá was blinded for a while by the swinging torchlights. His father was panting, *Jésù, Jésù, Jésù*, his mother was whimpering, and he could feel Bùsọ́lá shift closer to the wall as though trying to melt into it. He was the last to register what was happening because the torchlights were trained on his face. But then he recognised Sàámú's voice.

"I told you this was the coward's house," Sàámú said.

"Ẹniọlá." Holy Michael's voice was low and calm. "When you are not insane, why would you run when we had not finished our task. You want to tell police, àbí? You want to report? Reporter, ni ẹ àbí?"

Ẹniọlá tried to speak—all he could do was gasp.

"You need warning. Serious warning." Holy Michael swung the torchlight towards the bed. "And, you, his parents, you need to warn him very well. Just in case he forgets, this is his first warning. Warning number one is for him. Until the day he makes his home in the grave, he must never snitch to anybody about what he saw this evening. If he does, we will not kill him o, that is too easy. But he will get another warning from us if he dares it."

"Are you hearing well?" Sàámú waved a gun in the air.

"Warning number two is for everybody that will be left in this house after we are gone. What we are about to do must never be reported to anybody. Don't say you are going to police o. I'm telling you now, you will never see your daughter again if you do."

Sàámú grabbed Bùsọ́lá's arm and pulled her off the mattress.

"What is happening? Ẹniọlá?" Bùsọ́lá's voice was still heavy with sleep. "What is happening? Ẹniọlá? Ẹniọlá?"

Ẹniọlá tried to stand up. Holy Michael kicked him back onto the mattress. "Look at my face. If I see you in Honourable's house ever again, what I will do to you, ehn, it will be worse than being buried alive. Idiot. Now everybody listen to me very well. We are going to leave now, and you will not move until you hear us zoom off. Understood?"

"If you move pẹ́rẹ́n." Sàámú pointed his gun at Bùsọ́lá's head.

"Nod twice if you understand." Holy Michael smiled. "Good, very good."

No one spoke after the men left with Bùsọ́lá. Ẹniọlá's parents crept towards the window to listen for the sound of a vehicle leaving. Ẹniọlá wanted to get up, but he could not. He was trembling so hard his teeth chattered.

Suddenly, his parents ran out of the house. Of all the words they were screaming into the night, Ẹniọlá could make out only his father's plea: *Take me, take me instead, please take me instead.*

24

Wúràọlá did not check or tend to her bruises. Not even when Kúnlé placed Savlon and a pack of cotton wool beside her.

"I'll make tea," he said. "Black or ginger?"

Neither of them had slept after he stopped hitting her. He'd helped her up from the floor, to the bed, and she'd stayed there since then, doing little besides blinking and breathing. Kúnlé sat on the floor with his knees tucked beneath his chin.

"Ginger tea? I'll make ginger tea."

She cupped her breasts when he left the room. For what felt like an hour, he'd clawed at them while he barked, *Did Kingsley suck them? Did it feel good?*

Kúnlé returned with two steaming mugs. "My dad wants us to leave by seven a.m., so we need to start getting ready soon."

"We?"

"Yeah, we'll drop you off at the hospital before heading out. He said it's fine."

"I didn't ask for a ride."

"I'm just looking out for you. I don't think you should drive in your state. You can take your car to work tomorrow, but no, not today." Kúnlé sat on the bed. "Is there anything you'd like to say to me?"

Wúràọlá glanced at him. She had scratched his face while he clawed at her breasts, but his skin seemed smooth now, unhurt. Her cheeks and forehead felt raw, but she could not bear to study her face in a mirror just yet. There was a stabbing pain below her breasts each time she took a breath, but she didn't think any rib was broken.

"I mean about last night."

Wúràọlá turned away from him.

"Say it, I know there's something on your mind. Come on. You're giving me the silent treatment now?" Kúnlé set the mugs down on the bedside table. "We'll have to talk when I get back from Abuja. You need to be more mature. This kind of behaviour must stop. You can't be giving me the silent treatment when we're living together already. That's just so childish, Wúràọlá."

What annoyed her was how, after he'd used her body to mop his floor tiles, he was still confident that she would not want to delay moving in with him. Wúràọlá felt a sadness that bordered on despair. Was this who she was now? A woman he could take for granted even when he'd behaved abominably to her?

"You can keep quiet if you want, but I'll say what's on my own mind." Kúnlé pulled off his T-shirt. "I want to go through your phone when I get back—no, I'm going to. And from now on, I want to be able to go through it at any time. It's the only way I can trust you again after . . . after the things I read yesterday. I'm giving you a chance now to clean up your act while I'm away. Delete anything you want but know that you can't be writing rubbish to or about anybody once I'm back next week, okay? Do you have something to say to that?"

She was going to leave him. That was what she had to say. It was easy to predict how he might respond if she broke up with him now. He would plead with her and argue; then he would smash her head against the wall. He had not gone that far yet, but she knew now that he could. She was going to break up with him before he did.

"You won't talk?" Kúnlé sighed and stalked to the bathroom. "We need to start getting ready."

She was leaving him. All the complications that could arise from her decision lapped at the edges of her mind, but she focused on this one thought. She was going to leave him. There was no joy in it, no sense of liberation; there was no sorrow either. There was only a nothingness for which she was grateful, a numbness she hoped would stay in her for as long as possible.

She would break up with him. That was it, she did not need to contemplate the reasons to give herself or anyone else. She would do it because she could: she would have a meat pie for lunch, she would wear a purple blouse to work, she would tie her hair back before going into the wards, she would leave Kúnlé.

❈

Hi, by this weekend I will have informed my parents that I'm not going to marry you. I suggest you pass this news to your parents too.

Wúràọlá sent the text when she got to work; then she blocked Kúnlé's number.

Throughout her morning round, her phone vibrated until she reached into her pocket and switched it off. When she put it on again just before noon, there were several messages from a number she did not recognise. All said she should call back immediately.

"Kúnlé, I don't want to talk—"

"Why did you switch off your phone?" Yèyé said from the other end of the line.

Wúràọlá smiled at a colleague who passed by her in the corridor. "This is not your number."

"You need to come home right away."

"I'm at work ma."

"I mean *now* now."

"I can come this evening."

"Wúràọlá."

"What is going on?" She was impatient to get back to the consulting room.

"Your father was kidnapped last night."

"You said?"

"I've been trying to call you since we got new phones. Láyí is already here."

"How did . . . When did . . ." Wúràọlá felt faint. "What do you mean?"

"This is not something to be discussed on the phone. Come home."

Wúràọlá chartered a taxi and paid the driver to take her home directly. Her mind darted in all directions. It could not be a joke, no. Her mother did not believe in practical jokes. Yèyé was too conscious of the possibility of tragedy to consider joking about disasters. Wúràolá wondered if there was some mistake and her father had only travelled and was unreachable. Maybe he would be home by the time she got there. She tried to call her mother while she was en route, but the calls went unanswered. She fired off texts to the number Yèyé had called her from.

> Have you informed the police?
> Have you heard from him?
> Is there a ransom request?

There was no response. As they turned into the street that led home, she dialled her father's number, and a voice informed her that the number was switched off.

Two strange men at the gate made Wúràolá call Yèyé before letting her into the compound. She began to run when she saw the house but had to slow to a walk because it hurt too much to move her bruised body.

The walls of the ground floor were blackened beyond recognition. Only the metal bars of the burglary-proof windows remained where there had once been glass and curtains. There was no need to knock, because there was no door anymore. Everything that had been wood was now ashes. Though all the walls were still standing, they were blackened, and the floor was littered with glass and incinerated furniture. Wúràolá pulled her blouse over her nose and picked her way through the wreckage to the staircase. Everyone except her father was in the living room upstairs. Láyí was out in the balcony, shouting at someone on the phone. Mótárá was asleep with her head on their mother's knee, a posture she had resisted even as a child. Yes, their father was missing. Whatever caused Mótárá to offer herself for mothering had to be something that awful.

Wúràolá sat beside her mother and placed a hand on Mótárá's head. "What happened?"

"How are you?" Yèyé said, as though it was a normal day, and they were not sitting in a room with broken windows. "Is your face swollen? What happened to your face?"

"It's nothing." She had worn a turtleneck blouse to hide the bruises on her neck and arms and trousers to cover the cuts on her leg. There was little she could do about her face.

"Nothing, kẹ̀, with all these bumps on your skin."

"I'm reacting to something I ate yesterday." She would come to the real reason later, not right now.

"It's bad o." Yèyé peered at Wúràọlá's face. "Hope you've taken drugs?"

"Leave my face for now. I said, what happened? You said he was kidnapped?"

Yèyé sniffled and blinked. "I think it is connected to your in-laws, because the only name they gave us was Fẹ̀sọ̀jaiyé, the one that wants to contest the primaries with Kúnlé's father. They said he was the one who sent them."

Wúràọlá nodded. It was not the right time to mention that the Cokers would no longer be her in-laws now.

"The first person I called after we bought new SIMs and, um, and . . . and everything was your father-in-law. He was already on his way to catch his flight in Lagos. He's going to, to, um—"

"Abuja."

"Ehen. Láyí has a friend who knows the Honourable's wife, and he has called that one to help us talk to them and, um"—Yèyé took a shuddering breath—"Láyí's friend said that Fẹ̀sọ̀jaiyé's wife says they don't know anything about this, that the kidnappers must have been lying or I didn't hear the name well."

"We need to think about ransom." Láyí had come in from the balcony. "Just in case the kidnappers ask for something, how much cash can we raise quickly? Say, within twenty-four hours."

"Twenty million," Yèyé said.

"I mean on our own, without him. We can't access his account, right? Or are you a co-signatory?"

"I'm not talking about your father's money." Yèyé pointed at the centre table. "Wúràọlá, bring my phone, I need to talk to Aunty Bíọ́lá. The land in, um, the land in Ẹ̀pẹ́ and the one we sold last year in . . . um. Bring that phone."

After she had spoken to Aunty Bíọ́lá, Yèyé was calmer. She assigned tasks to everyone. Láyí was sent to the police station to file an official report. Yèyé had already called everyone she knew who had a friend or relative in the police force, someone who could make sure there would be an actual investigation. Now she had to inform relatives and close family friends about what had happened. Wúràọlá and Mọ́tárá were to sweep up the glass in the family room and check for damage in the other rooms upstairs.

Mọ́tárá was still sleeping, so Wúràọlá began cleaning alone. She started out in the living room. Everything smelled like smoke, the windows and sliding doors were all shattered, cracked or broken, but nothing in the room was burnt. The fire had been put out before the flames climbed up.

On the phone, Yèyé told relatives that she was sure her husband would be back home in no time. Yèyé's reassurances sounded wise, like insight drawn from her life experiences. Perhaps somewhere in a past that preceded her children or even her marriage, Yèyé had seen something like this unfold. Had watched as a kidnapped man returned home mostly unharmed, full of stories that would delight party guests for decades to come. Wúràọlá felt steadied by her mother's calm conviction. All afternoon it helped her to squelch the panic that welled up in her from time to time to constrict her throat or blind her with tears.

Wúràọlá swept the glass into a corner. Going downstairs to dispose of the broken pieces was out of the question. She could not bear to look at the charred remains again. Elsewhere on the top floor, only bathroom windows seemed to have been affected. She was sweeping shards off Yèyé's bathroom floor when Mọ́tárá joined her.

Wúràọlá opened the text she had sent to Kúnlé and gave the phone to her sister. "I did it, I did it this morning."

Telling someone else made the breakup real. It was over, she was not going to marry Kúnlé Coker, he was never going to hurt her again. The nothingness she'd felt in the morning was giving way to relief. Maybe telling Mọ́tárá would also help her squash the temptation to call Kúnlé and talk through the kidnapping with him. He was the first person she would have reached out to on a day like this, and it felt strange that she could not.

Mọ́tárá's face lit up as she read the text. "You mean it? For real?"

Wúràọlá's back and stomach hurt when Mọ́tárá hugged her, but she bore it without complaining.

"At least there's some good news today," Mọ́tárá said, pulling away.

"You told me to do this earlier. Maybe none of this would have happened to Daddy if I had listened to you."

"He's been close friends with Professor Coker since like before I was born? No, come on, this is not your fault."

Wúràọlá began weeping when Mọ́tárá held her again. Every bruise Kúnlé had left on her, visible and invisible, ached with an intensity that transformed relief into regret. No matter what Mọ́tárá said, how could she not consider the possibility that if she'd listened earlier this would not have happened? She sobbed into her sister's shoulder until she was dizzy; then they went to lay together in their mother's bed.

Kúnlé's mother came to visit that evening, bearing coolers of food and cartons of bottled water.

There was no awkwardness in the way she hugged Wúràọlá to herself. "Don't worry, my dear. Kúnlé told me you said you will need the week off? Understandable, very understandable. So I've explained everything to your head of department and you don't need to go in until all of this is sorted out. Pẹ̀lẹ́, dear. And I brought your car, our gateman helped me to drive it here."

"Thank you ma." Wúràọlá stepped out of the woman's embrace and settled into a chair beside Mọ́tárá. It wasn't her business if Kúnlé lied to his parents.

Kúnlé's mother offered repeated apologies to Yèyé and Láyí. Her husband was already speaking to everyone he knew in Abuja to make sure the Honourable would pay for what had happened. "In the meantime, you should all come stay with us. We have enough room in the house for everyone."

Yèyé shook her head.

"That won't be necessary ma, I've already paid for a hotel."

"But—"

"My in-law, my wonderful in-law." Yèyé smiled. "Don't worry. It's so thoughtful of you, but it's not necessary."

"I've booked the hotel for a week," Láyí said.

"Such good people," Yèyé said to her children after Kúnlé's mother left. She did not seem to notice that only Láyí nodded in agreement.

"We need to start packing for the hotel." Láyí glanced at his wristwatch. "Can we try to leave within the hour?"

"Which hotel?" Yèyé asked. "Were you serious just now?"

"We can't sleep here," Láyí said.

"Kílódé? Nobody can chase me from my home." Yèyé frowned at Láyí. "The person who will chase me from this place has not been born. Even his mother has not been born yet. My husband is going to come here, and when he returns, you want him to meet an empty house?"

"But everything smells like smoke," Wúràọlá said, realizing that a brittle layer was hidden beneath all her mother's optimism about the kidnapping.

"As long as there is a roof over this house, this is where we stay. I don't want to hear another word about sleeping elsewhere. What nonsense."

No one suggested hotels again.

By Wednesday morning, Kúnlé was texting apologies to Wúràọlá from another number. She was too distracted to block him or to respond. Policemen had come to question Yèyé, Mọ́tárá and everyone in the boys' quarters. Láyí was sitting in on the interrogation, so Wúràọlá was alone in her room when the texts began coming in, one every fifteen minutes. She did not care if he wasn't able to eat or focus because of how sorry he was; her mind was preoccupied with her father. Were his abductors making sure he took his medication? Was he afraid? Was he getting enough sleep? When would she see him again?

Kúnlé's apologies turned to insults by noon. She was a coward, an idiot, a fucking whore. She had to face him and say they were over. It did not count if she wouldn't face him. She responded with one sentence—*you know my dad is missing right*—before blocking that number.

When he began texting curses from another number within an hour, Wúràọlá left her phone on her bed and went into the family room.

The policemen were gone. Yèyé was alone in the room. Mọ́tárá and Láyí were chatting on the balcony. Láyí beckoned her to them.

"We need to talk about Daddy," Láyí said, glancing back at the living room where Yèyé was moving throw pillows around as though life on earth depended on the right arrangement.

Teenaged Wúràọlá and Láyí had switched to calling their parents Ọ̀túnba and Yèyé. But since Monday, their missing father had become Daddy again.

"I think we need to start looking at the morgues," Láyí said.

Wúràọlá blinked at her brother. "What do you mean?"

"I think he might be right." Mótárá's eyes were red and swollen. She'd been crying.

"I can't believe you people are saying this."

"We have to start considering . . ." Láyí took a deep breath. "Could you just speak to someone in your hospital? Since you work there, it might be easier for you to ask. . . ."

Wúràolá walked away from her siblings. She went back into the family room, towards her mother's certainty that her father would return before the end of the week.

❊

On Friday morning, after a night spent arguing with her siblings, Wúràolá spoke to a registrar in pathology while they listened in to make sure she did what they had agreed on.

She asked to be put in touch with someone in the morgue who could let her know if any corpse that resembled her father was brought in. Later that day, an attendant reached out and ask her to send a photo of her father.

A text came in while she was in church.

I've been trying to call you. We have a body that resembles the photo. Please come and check.

It was Sunday, and Yèyé had insisted that everyone attend service together that morning. No one had the heart to argue with her.

Wúràolá slipped out the back door without telling anyone where she was going. The service had just started. She would probably be back before it ended. Looking at a body and saying it was not her father's felt like something that would make her worry less and assure her that he was still out there somewhere, about to return. Láyí had driven the whole family to church in his car. She took a taxi instead of asking him for his keys.

She arrived at the hospital with no sense of trepidation. The mortuary attendant seemed puzzled when she greeted him with a smile. He asked if she needed a moment before going into the morgue, but she shrugged off the suggestion.

There were five embalming tables in the room. The first two were occupied. She trailed the attendant past the body of a girl who could not have been older than thirteen to the last table in the room.

It was her father. She studied the body, desperate for signs that it wasn't his but could find none. He was there in the hair he dyed black so he could look younger, in the dimple that divided his chin into two halves, in the vertical scar that cut through his left brow to graze his eyelid. She counted the toes on his right foot. There were six. It was her father.

"Don't look for what is not there," the attendant said. "Usually, when it is your relative, you will recognise them immediately. People change in death, but once you look at the face, you will know. You don't have to be looking at his leg before you recognise him—he's not your father."

"Really?" Wúràolá turned away from her father's body. Already, she regretted not taking the moment he'd suggested outside. She wished she had enjoyed another minute in a world where her father was not dead. Now all she had was one in which she was the only person who knew; she was not ready to let that go.

"Yes, you will know once you look at the face, unless it's damaged, shá o. But this man, they didn't damage his face," the attendant said. "Well, thank God, àbí? We'll call you if there's another corpse, but by God's mercy, your own father will be found alive very soon."

Wúràolá stopped by the other body on her way out of the morgue. Even though she was not going to claim him yet, she wanted to be in the same room with her father for a little longer. "Who is the girl?"

"We don't know o, but she and that man, their corpses were found in the same bush. Maybe they are related."

The girl's face was swollen, but her hairdo remained intact, its black threads gleaming against her scalp. Unbidden, a refrain from Wúràolá's childhood came to her, that taunt for girls who returned to school with this hairstyle: Àjànkólokòlo eléṣinṣin lórí.

"Aren't you ready to leave?" the attendant asked. "We'll call you or text if there is anything."

Wúràolá realised she'd been standing on the same spot for a while. "Thank you. Sir."

Outside, she wandered in the parking lot, weaving through the gaps between cars, knocking her knees on bumpers and stubbing her toes against tires because her eyes kept clouding over.

Once, she thought her father was standing by the hospital gate, beckoning her. She knew immediately that she was mistaken. It was just a security guard who was about his height. Yet she let the possibility linger and thought about the àkúdàáyàs he'd talked about when her schoolteacher died. The idea steadied her for a while. That her father, having died in this iteration of his life, had woken up in another one in which he was a security guard who retained his gait, height and age. But then she remembered all the caveats. Àkúdàáyàs reappeared in distant cities from the one they had once lived in, because in their new life, they must not have contact with anyone they had known before they died.

Wúràolá's phone rang.

"Where are you?" Mótárá sounded happier than she had all week. "We're about to leave the church."

What was it her mother had said the other day? This was not a matter to be discussed on the phone. "I'm . . . I'm—I will meet you people at home."

"Ehen? Okay, there's news o. Professor Coker is back from Abuja, he just spoke to us now. He said his guys have a lead on where those people are keeping Daddy. They're planning to do a rescue by tomorrow. He thinks Daddy will be home in a few days." Mótárá's voice was bright with hope.

Wúràolá cut the call and began walking towards the hospital gate. It was time to go home.

She flagged an empty cab and got in. It had barely moved before it stopped again to pick up more passengers, but she did not mind. If she chartered the cab, her trip home would be faster. She was not in a hurry. Let Mótárá and everyone else stay enveloped in hope for the extra ten or fifteen minutes.

A boy opened the cab's back door and got in. His legs pressed against Wúràolá's because there wasn't enough room to fit his long limbs. The boy was followed by a middle-aged man who was probably his father. As he scooted closer to Wúràolá to make room for the middle-aged man, the boy's elbow hit a bruise on her arm and she groaned.

❈

"I'm sorry," Ẹniọlá said. He wrapped his arms around his body, making himself smaller to avoid bumping into the woman beside him again. The woman said something in response, but he didn't look at her. He could only see his sister, could only think of her.

Ẹniọlá had spent hours apologizing to his parents, trying to explain that he would not have returned home if he knew anyone in his family would be in danger. His father had cursed him every day since Bùsọ́lá was taken; more than once he'd raised his fist to strike Ẹniọlá but so far had never let it land. Ẹniọlá welcomed the curses as deserved punishment. His mother still hadn't responded to any of his apologies. Anytime he told her that he was sorry about Bùsọ́lá, she looked elsewhere. To the door of their room, off into the street, towards the ceiling or the skies, her brows arched in almost constant expectation that Bùsọ́lá would return, appear, even descend.

❈

When she was a child, Ọtúnba would sometimes ask Wúràolá to sit beside him when he noticed she was in a bad mood. Most times, he did not even ask what she was upset about; he would just put his hand on her shoulder until of her own accord she lay her head on his lap. Then he would rock her to sleep. Wúràolá felt her phone vibrate. Láyí was calling her. She pressed the power button until the phone went off. He had been right to insist they check the morgues. Did that mean he would be better prepared to handle the news? Should she tell him first? Was it best to inform everyone at the same time? Now Mọ́tárá might finally spill the tears she'd been close to shedding in the last few days. Wúràolá looked out the window. What she had seen was real, but it did not feel true just yet. It would when she told Yèyé, she was sure of it.

❈

Until this afternoon, Ẹniọlá and his parents had obeyed Holy Michael's warnings. They had told no one about what happened. Not even the land-lord or their neighbours. Ẹniọlá did not go to the Honourable's house. He did not go anywhere. Not to Glorious Destiny or United. He sat by his mother all day and fetched her things she did not ask for: water, food, a hand fan when the room was too hot. He watched the door with her while his father hovered around in the room, asking Ẹniọlá questions about Holy Michael and Sàámú. More alert and involved than he'd been for years, he surprised Ẹniọlá by thinking through the options available and eliminating courses of action that might endanger Bùsọ́lá. Meanwhile, his mother was a deflated version of herself. It felt as though his parents had traded places.

Ẹniọlá glanced at his father. Something in his eyes made Ẹniọlá won-der if he might start cursing him again right here in the cab. He looked away from his father to the woman beside him. She was glaring at him, unblinking. He recognised her after a minute. There was a fading bruise on her cheek that wasn't there the last time he saw her. But it was her. Yèyé's daughter, the doctor. She would not stop glaring at him. Yèyé must have recognised him somehow that night, this was why her daughter was staring at him. Any moment now she would grab him and drag him to a police station.

"I did not know that it was your family, please," Ẹniọlá said, spilling the words over each other.

The woman said nothing.

Ẹniọlá clasped his hands together as if in prayer. "I'm so sorry."

"What?"

"They came for my sister too, please, I'm sorry."

"Do I know you?"

He realised then that she was merely staring in his direction. Her eyes were unfocused, flitting now to his father before coming back to him. She had not recognised him. He turned his face so he was looking away from her and she could see only the back of his head.

❈

Wúràọlá's body ached. The injuries Kúnlé had punched into her skin felt newly flayed. She wished someone would hold her head and rock her the way Ọ̀túnba used to when she was a child. She should have chartered the cab when she could. Her eyes welled up. She needed to be with her family right away. She wanted to lay her head on her father's knees and be rocked to sleep.

❊

This afternoon, his father asked him to lead the way to Sàámú's house. When his mother objected, Ẹniọlá's father argued that Holy Michael had only warned them against going to the Honourable, he'd said nothing about visiting Sàámú's place.

Ẹniọlá had never been to Sàámú's house, but he knew how to get there. They would only have to walk a few minutes from the cab's final stop. Past a bank and the central mosque, into the street where Sàámú lived with his uncle.

There Ẹniọlá would make his plea in the uncle's presence so that any resistance in Sàámú would be overcome by the threat of his uncle's wrath. Ẹniọlá was ready to stay prostrate for however long it took for Sàámú to relent. He could not cover the distance between that moment and his reunion with his sister, but he knew, he just knew that once Sàámú accepted his plea, a reunion would happen. It might take a few days or even a week, but Holy Michael would release Bùsọ́lá. Back home again, Bùsọ́lá would be upset with him at first. There was no escaping the weeks of insults she'd launch with words she knew he did not understand. Eventually, she'd smile at him with mischief in her eyes, and he would know forgiveness was near.

The cab came to a stop, but none of its passengers moved. Ẹniọlá wanted to sit for a while before they continued the journey to Sàámú's place. To his right, his father muttered what he assumed were prayers under his breath. To his left, Yèyé's daughter was weeping. He fought the urge to apologise again by looking away. It was better to think about the future that might be within his reach soon. Bùsọ́lá insulting him, smiling with mischief and then, on some glorious day, hugging him as she had the last time. Ẹniọlá shut his eyes and focused on this image: his sister looking at him, her smile laced with gratitude, her eyes full of love.

Foreman

When a buffalo walks over a hard-rock outcrop,
We do not see his footprints.
When a heavy rain falls over a hard-rock outcrop,
We do not see the footprints of the rain.
  —*Kinsman and Foreman* by T. M. Aluko

Caro glanced at her wall clock. If she left early, she could get to Yèyé's house and come back in time to finish some of the dresses she was working on. She'd heard a partial broadcast of Ọtúnba Mákinwá's one-year remembrance service on the radio a few weeks ago and decided she owed Yèyé a second condolence visit. She was taking a gift with her, an orange adire dress. After a year of wearing black, Caro hoped Yèyé was ready for something bright.

She folded the adire dress and tucked it in a paper bag. Once Ẹniọlá arrived, she could set out and leave the shop in his care. He resumed work before any of the other apprentices now, sometimes arriving before she even opened her front door. She was grateful for his dedication but was sorry that he seemed convinced that he would never return to school. This boy who just over a year ago would do his assignments in her living room no longer seemed to care about moving forward with his education. The few times she'd brought it up with him, he'd insisted he did not deserve school. She still did not understand what he meant by that. People said his sister was the smarter one. Did school remind him too much of her? Caro hoped he would change his mind soon.

She saw the posters when she stepped into her front yard to wait for Ẹniọlá. They had been pasted on her wall at some point during the night. She'd chased away some boys who had tried to plaster her wall with leaflets a few weeks before the governorship elections were held. Those very boys had probably returned during the night to deface her wall with the new governor's thank-you-for-voting-me-in posters. Caro began to tear them off but decided to wait for Ẹniọlá to arrive. He was tall enough to reach the posters without standing on a stool. Besides, these days, he was eager for extra work beyond his tailoring tasks. She suspected that he kept his body moving and moving so whatever thoughts plagued his mind would not be able to catch up. Who wouldn't need to? All this time and his sister was still missing.

Ẹniọlá prostrated flat on the floor when he arrived and stayed there for almost a full minute, as though he did not want to stand up again. He had always been a respectful boy, but recently she wondered at how his demonstrations of honour were so drawn out they seemed like an apology. Someday soon, she would discuss this with him. They stood together in front of the thank-you posters while she told him to take them off without damaging her wall.

Caro realised he was weeping when she heard a whimper. She stepped closer to him, put an arm around his shoulders and squeezed. He leaned into her but kept staring at the new governor's grinning face as his sobs grew louder and louder. Caro held him tighter. She couldn't leave for Yèyé's place just yet. She had to wait until Ẹniọlá was calm. It was the first time she was seeing him like this. She wiped his damp face with her sleeve. He'd been a muted version of himself over the past year, but not once had he broken down while he was in her shop. Ẹniọlá paused to draw a breath, and Caro heard rain hammering down on roofs in the distance. Elsewhere, a storm had been unleashed, and its clouds were already darkening her front yard; soon enough it would be here. She might have to wait until later in the day to see Yèyé.

Acknowledgments

I'm grateful to: Clare Alexander, for her unstinting support and encouragement. Kathy Robbins, for continued faith in my work. Everyone at Aitken Alexander, Canongate, Knopf and Ouida.

Thank you to my extraordinary editors, Jenny Jackson and Ellah Wakatama, who have made this book better. Special thanks to Tiara Sharma, Melissa Yoon and Rali Chorbadzhiyska for their help.

I'm grateful to: Jamie Byng, Jenny Fry and Lọlá Shónẹ́yìn, who have supported my work over the years. Professor Chima Anyadike, Dr. Bisi Anyadike, Suzanne Ushie and Dr. Joanna Lipper, for their continued generosity and kindness. Trezza Azzopardi, Richard Beard, Andrew Cowan and Jean McNeil, for early guidance when I began working on this as their student. Kọ́lá Túbọ̀sún, for helping with diacritics.

Ox-Bow School of Art, MacDowell Colony, Saari Residence, 9mobile Nigeria and the University of East Anglia provided fellowships that made continued devotion to this novel possible. I am grateful.

My life is possible because of my family. Thank you: Professor Fámúrewà, for your endless love and immeasurable sacrifice. Dr. JọláaJésù, for your companionship and sustaining laughter. The OmoNoahbi clan—the three Fábìyís, the Ògúnlùsìs, the Ẹ̀sans, the Adébáyọ̀s and the Adéyẹmís—for steadfast support. The Idumas—Mummy Sarah, Rev. Emeka, Neme, Enyi and Amara—for a place in your hearts.

Dear Daddy, I hope I've made you proud.

My beloved husband Emmanuel, I am blessed by your tender light. Thank you for love that abides, now as always.